SAVAGE ILLUSION

"I've never felt so alive," Jolena said. "I feel wicked. What came over me?"

Spotted Eagle drew her against him. "You are not wicked. What you did was done out of love. I will cherish these moments. So should you."

She leaned her cheek against his chest. "Oh, how I want to. It was pure heaven, being with you. I've never felt so free, yet so possessed. How can that be?"

"Loving fiercely is a combination of the two. Let that frighten you not. I welcome being possessed by you. I will never be lonely again."

"I feel so many things," Jolena said, clinging to him, loving him so. "But most of all, I feel an intense happiness. Hold me, Spotted Eagle. I never want to leave you."

He cradled her, his eyes closed to the past, thinking only of the future and this woman who had awakened him again to loving....

I see you in my mind,
Touch you in my dreams,
Your voice keeps calling to me,
A spirit that's wild and free.

I feel your breath caress my neck,
As I turn to you to say,
I will love you for forever,
Only to find, you've gone away.

Were you ever really there?
What is this thought that torments me so?
And I am caught between two worlds,
As if I lived another life long ago.

I feel your strength in the wind,
Sense your gaze through the sun,
Hear your voice speak to me in the streams,
You keep saying, "This love has only begun."

I lie in sleepless nights,
Staring out at the dark sky,
Then I feel a breeze blowing,
And I know you are at my side.

I can almost see your eyes,
As they stare at me in the night.
I can just about feel your arms,
They are warm, and hold me tight.

"Come back to me," you whisper,
As I feel my heart start to race.
I will somehow, my love.
I'll find you somewhere, some place.

I'll not stop until I'm home,
Back with my People, and my heart.
I will never stop searching till I find you.
And when I do, I know we'll never again be apart.

—Sheila Bilbrey

SAVAGE
Illusion

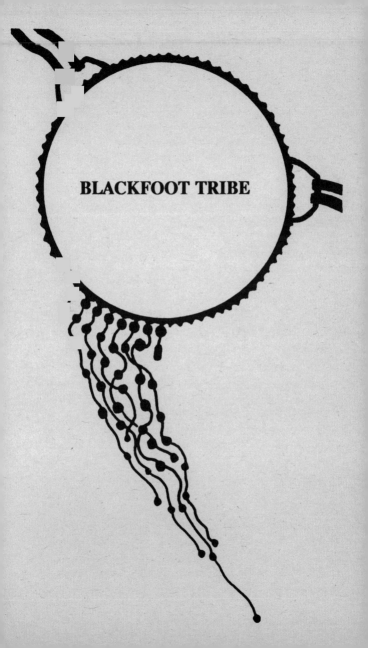

BLACKFOOT TRIBE

Chapter One

The Montana Territory—1852

The bull train, consisting of four eight-yoke teams, drawing twelve covered wagons, moved slowly through the wind-blown tall buffalo grass, following the Yellowstone River that ran snake-like through the Montana Territory.

It was August, a perfect time of the year for traveling. To the west rose the dark Rockies, their sharp peaks standing out sharply against the pale blue sky. Northward were the three buttes of the Sweetgrass Hills. Eastward dimly loomed the Bear Paws; South, across the Yellowstone River, the pine-clad Highwood Mountains were in plain sight.

On all sides buffalo and antelope grazed quietly on the healthy, spring-fed grass.

Sitting in the lead wagon, in the shade of the canvas that had been stretched over the seat to protect the new mother and child from the hot rays of the sun, were Bryce Edmonds and his wife Charlotte.

Charlotte gazed lovingly down at her two-week-old son, adoring him, yet regretting that he had not been born in more civilized surroundings, with a real doctor to look after her, a real bed on which to be comfortable, and with food readily available. As it was, the expedition's food supply had dwindled, and everything was now being rationed until they reached the Missouri River, where they could board a steamboat and return to the comforts of their palatial home in Saint Louis.

When Charlotte had offered to join these lepidopterists, led by her husband, she had not even thought of becoming pregnant on the long, tiring journey.

It had just happened.

"Are you too disappointed, dear?" Charlotte asked, gazing lovingly at Bryce, her husband of six years, whose blond hair had bleached almost white beneath the hot Montana sun.

But the sun had not changed his handsomeness. Even now, sitting so close to him on the rugged seat of the wagon, she wanted to reach out and touch his face or run her fingers through his thick hair. She loved him more each day, as though each was their first kiss, their first caress.

When a fly started buzzing around the face

of her son, her thoughts were averted to things other than romancing her beloved husband. She shooed the fly away from her child, whose tiny lips were contentedly suckling at her breast.

Her Kirk.

Her adorable Kirk.

She had fought off mosquitoes, ticks, and flies until she was weary from it all.

Bryce cast Charlotte an easy smile.

"Am I disappointed over having not found the *euphaedra*?" he said, referring to the rare Venezuelan butterfly they had been hunting. "Naw, can't say that I am."

His gaze shifted, enjoying the sight of his son nursing from his mother's milk-filled breast. It was a sight that would linger in his memory until the day he died. It was so wonderful to finally have a child.

After five years of trying, he and his wife had almost given up on ever having children. Then, suddenly, as though someone had touched Charlotte's womb with a magic wand, she was pregnant. That the child had been born in the midst of such hardship seemed almost a miracle. Indeed, it was a miracle that any of them were alive.

There were Indians everywhere: the Cree, the Crow, the Blackfoot. For some reason, this wagon train had been spared any raids, as though God were there with them every inch of the journey, watching over them.

"I *would* have been terribly disappointed over not finding the rare butterfly," he continued, nodding. "But that little surprise package you're holding in your arms makes all the difference in the world in my attitude. I couldn't be happier, darling. First the prettiest woman in Saint Louis accepts my proposal of marriage, then I am appointed curator at the science museum, and then, by God, to top it off, I now have a son. Who could complain, darling? Who?"

"But you so looked forward to finding the *euphaedra*," Charlotte said, easing Kirk's lips from her breast as his eyes closed in a contented sleep. She wrapped him in a lightweight blanket and cradled him in her left arm as she began rebuttoning her dress. "If you had caught it, you could have completed your collection. Then you could settle down and write that book that you have spoken of so often to me—a book explaining your ventures and all the butterflies that you have captured in detail, as well as the life history of each. How nice it would have been, darling, if . . ."

Bryce returned his eyes to the trail, so that Charlotte would not see the disappointment that lay shadowed in their depths. He had sworn that the expedition's failure was not troubling him, yet in truth, it was eating away at his gut.

"There'll be another time, another place," he said. "Right now all I'm concentrating on is getting you and Kirk out of Indian territory and to the safety of a steamboat. It shouldn't be much longer now, darling. We may even reach the Missouri by sundown tonight."

The thought that this dreadful journey was soon

to be behind her excited Charlotte.

Something up ahead, lying on the ground just beyond the shade of some tall bushes, drew Charlotte's attention. She leaned her head forward, then gasped when she saw that it was not an animal, but a lifeless hand.

Charlotte paled at the thought of coming across someone that had been murdered, even perhaps scalped by the Indians. It would be their luck, she thought to herself, to just barely get within sight of the steamboat and the Indians come down upon them with a vengeance.

"Bryce—up ahead, do you see?" Charlotte said, pointing. They were close enough now for her to see that this was not the hand of a white person.

It was copper in color!

It was an Indian's!

A panic seized Charlotte's insides, fearing this might be a trap.

"By God, it's a hand," Bryce said, drawing rein and stopping the slow-traveling bulls.

Charlotte grabbed for Bryce's arm. "Be careful," she whispered, her eyes wild. "It could be a trap. We could be attacked by Indians any minute now."

Bryce reached a gentle hand to her flushed cheek. "Now, now," he said, as though he were soothing a child. "Let's not let our imagination run away with us."

He drew his hand away from her and leaned out so that he could see the other wagons that had come to a dead halt behind his, his traveling

15

companions already off their wagons and heading hurriedly toward him.

Bryce gave Charlotte another quick glance. "You don't leave this wagon unless it's at my side, do you hear?" he said sternly. He reached back inside his wagon and grabbed a small, pearl-handled pistol. "If I don't get back to you, and you and our child become threatened by a redskin—by God, woman, shoot to kill."

Charlotte flinched at the sight of the firearm, having never liked them. But having no choice, she took the pistol and held it tightly within her grip as she watched Bryce leave the wagon, warily approaching the dead person. His pistol was drawn, and the other men were armed with rifles.

Bryce crept slowly toward the hand, and when he saw that there was no one there, ready to pounce on him, he swung his pistol back into its holster and hurried onward.

When he separated the lower branches of the bushes and got a closer look, he was stunned at what he discovered.

"It's an Indian woman and a child—I'd say no more than a few hours old," one of his companions said, mirroring Bryce's very thoughts. "And, Bryce, the woman is dead."

Bryce knelt down beside the woman and closed her eyes, then gently picked the child up into his arms. It was apparent that the mother had at least managed to cut the umbilical cord, but she had surely died before she had a chance to cleanse the child, or perhaps even feed it.

The dark eyes of the baby looked up at Bryce

trustingly. Then the child began to cry softly—a cry of hunger. . . .

Without further thought, Bryce carried the tiny thing to the wagon.

"Oh, my lord, it's a baby," Charlotte said, gasping.

"The mother is dead," Bryce said sadly, holding the baby out so that Charlotte could see the infant better. "The child is a girl. Isn't she just too beautiful, Charlotte?"

"Oh, yes. So *very*," Charlotte said softly, the baby's cries tearing at her insides. "But the poor thing. Surely she's hungry." She glanced down at Kirk, then at her milk-filled breasts, so heavy she knew that she had more than enough milk for two children.

She turned a smiling face to her husband. "Let me feed her," she murmured. She reached a hand out to Bryce. "Please, darling? If not, she may die."

"For sure she would," he said. "But let me give her a quick washing. I'll bring her to you then."

The others had come to their wagon and were watching. Bryce took the child to the back of his wagon. Taking warm water from a canteen, he bathed the baby, then took her to Charlotte, handing the child up to her after she had placed Kirk comfortably across her lap.

Giving Charlotte the needed privacy, the men walked away and stood in a group, discussing the find.

Charlotte opened her dress to the tiny baby girl. Tears came to her eyes when the child began suckling from her breast. She gazed with wonder at the child's beautiful copper skin and tiny toes and fingers. It came to her that the child was now motherless and that perhaps Kirk could have an instant sister. She was not sure if she could have any more children. It had taken so long to finally have her adorable Kirk. . . .

Bryce still stood beside the wagon, watching the baby nursing. "I don't know what to do," he said, his voice drawn. "If we try and find the village from which this woman came, we might somehow be accused of the woman's death. I don't think I want to trade my scalp for the chances of trying to find this woman's people."

"And the child?" Charlotte said, her heart pounding at the prospect of getting to keep the child as her very own.

"We've got to keep her, Charlotte," Bryce said, giving her an easy stare. "Would you mind? It's your breasts that would be feeding her."

Tears came to Charlotte's eyes as she gazed down at the tiny bundle of joy that still so hungrily fed from her breast. "Do I mind?" she said, slowly shifting her gaze to her husband. "Darling, I couldn't leave her behind, not after having held and fed her. She'll be our daughter. Kirk will be raised with a sister. We will give her the name that we had picked out should we have a daughter instead of a son."

"Jolena?" Bryce said, reaching a hand to touch the soft thigh of the girl child.

"Yes, Jolena," Charlotte said in a sigh, as she again watched the child with adoration. "It's such a lovely name to fit such a beautiful little girl."

"Then it's settled," Bryce said firmly with a nod of the head. "She's ours from now on."

He turned and looked toward the bushes beneath which lay the lovely Indian woman. He had not taken much time to look at her, being too worried over the child's welfare. But in one glance he had seen her exquisite loveliness and knew that some Indian warrior would mourn deeply over such a loss. If Jolena took her looks from her mother, this new daughter of his would one day be just as exquisite!

"I can't bury her," Bryce said quickly. "I must leave her out in the open for her people to find her. Her soul would not rest if she was not given a proper Indian burial ceremony and placed with her people's dead. We have no choice but to leave her like that, instead of hiding her in a grave in the ground."

"How soon do you think she will be found?" Charlotte asked, worrying about animals feeding on her.

Bryce kneaded his brow thoughtfully as he looked into the distance. "It is said that the Indian women go far enough away to have their child so that it takes three days' travel on foot to get there," he said. "On horseback, the way the warrior husband will travel when he comes looking for her, it will take only one day. So he should be here I'd say at least by tonight."

"That means that we most certainly must be aboard that riverboat before he arrives," Charlotte said, her voice wary. "Can we truly, darling? Can we make it?"

"I'll see to it," Bryce said, climbing aboard his wagon. He leaned out and shouted for everyone else to be on their way, then turned to Charlotte with heavy eyes. "I hate like hell depriving a man a look at his newborn child, but once he finds his wife dead, he will become enraged enough to kill anything and anyone in his path. We have no choice but to take his child and raise her as our own."

"She will be given many more opportunities than she would have had among Indians," Charlotte murmured, taking the child from her breast. She reached behind her and grabbed a soft blanket to wrap the baby in.

Then she positioned a child in the crook of each of her arms, a contented smile on her lovely face.

"One thing we must prepare ourselves for," Bryce warned. "When she gets old enough to mingle with the other children in Saint Louis, she will be pointed out as different, even as perhaps peculiar in her coloring. She might be tormented by the white children, even called a savage."

Charlotte paled at the thought. "We will make up the difference in *our* attitude toward her," she said determinedly. "We will teach her to ignore those who would belittle themselves by being prejudicial in their judgments and viewpoints."

Bryce smiled at Charlotte and nodded his approval of that which she had so strongly declared in defense of this child that was theirs by only moments.

Chapter Two

A semicircle of cone-shaped tepees dotted the green of the plain. A stream, tree-fringed, fresh from the distant mountains, flowed by the camp pitched upon a tableland where he the enemy, red or white, could pass by unseen.

Men hunted. The Blackfoot women were busy drying meat and tanning robes and cow hides.

The smell of roasting meat and the sound of children at play filled the afternoon air.

Spotted Eagle, who had only recently earned his new name by having fasted far from his people for four days and nights, paced before his parents' tepee. He found the games of the children much too childlike this day. He had other things on his mind which were more important to him. He knew that today Sweet Dove should have returned to her people, proudly carrying her newborn child within her arms. When Brown Elk, her husband, had begun to worry over her absence—the required days a Blackfoot maiden should be gone to give birth to her child having passed—he had left with many warriors to search for her.

"She is dead," Spotted Eagle whispered to himself, his long flowing hair around his shoulders as he made another troubled turn to pace again. "I know she is dead."

He lifted his eyes to the sky. "I am only a boy of ten winters, but I will mourn such a death as though she were my own woman," he prayed. "Never have I looked upon such a face of beauty. Never has any woman besides my mother been so caring, so understanding. Oh, hear me now, Sun, the supreme chief of the Blackfoot. Let Sweet Dove enter the camp soon with her child held close to her bosom. Oh, powerful one, please hear my prayers."

The sound of hooves entering the far side of the village, making a sound like distant thunder against the bare, packed earth, caused Spotted Eagle's heartbeat to quicken. He wanted to run and meet the warriors, to see if they had found Sweet Dove alive and well.

But it was as though his black moccasins were fastened to the ground, for he could not move, fearing the worst.

And he was only a boy with an infatuation for an older woman!

Many would call him foolish if he showed his

feelings for Sweet Dove. He had guarded them well, even while running, playing, and hunting with the other young braves of his village.

Dressed in only a breechclout and his prized black moccasins, with a beaded headband holding his waist-length, raven-black hair in place, Spotted Eagle stood with his hands doubled into tight fists at his sides. His heart throbbed so hard that it felt as though someone were inside him, beating drums.

With worried, dark eyes, he watched the solemn procession of horsemen. Then everything within him cried out with despair when he saw the travois being dragged behind the last horse, on which lay a body covered with a bear pelt.

Spotted Eagle's gaze shifted jerkily upward, and he could hardly contain the cries within his heart when he saw that the warrior whose horse was dragging the travois was Brown Elk. He then knew that the one beneath that covering of fur was the beloved Sweet Dove.

As Brown Elk stopped his horse and dismounted, the people of the village crowded around him and the travois, waiting for him to uncover his wife's body. When she was finally in full view, and everyone saw that it was in truth the adorable Sweet Dove, whose sharing gentleness had touched everyone in the village during her lifetime of only eighteen winters, wails burst forth into the air.

Fighting back tears and trying to muster the courage to push his way through the people to get his own look at Sweet Dove, Spotted Eagle swallowed hard and walked stiffly toward the assemblage of wailing Blackfoot, finally managing to squeeze through them.

He soon found himself standing over Sweet Dove's body. The sight almost caused his knees to buckle beneath him.

She was so quiet.

She was so dead!

And the sight of the blood on the skirt of her dress made him stifle a sob beneath his breath, knowing that childbirth had caused the bright red stain.

A sudden thought came to him. He looked desperately up and down the full length of the travois, panic seizing him when he did not see the child anywhere.

"The child?" he blurted, looking up into the woeful eyes of Brown Elk. "I . . . see no child."

Seeing Spotted Eagle as a mere boy, who should not be showing such an interest in an older woman, especially Brown Elk's very own woman, Brown Elk looked away from Spotted Eagle, flatly ignoring him.

Spotted Eagle's mother came to her son's side. "*No-ko-i*, my son, this is not a place for young braves," she said, taking his hand.

When she tried to move him away from the travois, Spotted Eagle defied his dear mother for the first time in his life, refusing to budge.

He had not taken a long enough, final look at Sweet Dove before she was prepared for burial.

No one, not even his mother, could deny him that!

And still, there was the wonder of the child. "Mother, please tell me," he pleaded, his eyes dark and wide as he gazed up at her. "Where is the child?"

His chieftain father came to. Spotted Eagle's side and laid a heavy hand on his shoulder. "*No-ko-i*, my son, the child was gone," Chief Gray Bear said sadly. "Someone took the child before Brown Elk and our warriors found Sweet Dove. They have searched far and wide. The child is nowhere. They searched even as far as the river. There were many wagon, hoof, and footprints there, but no people. Those people were surely many miles away by then, down the river. Those who boarded the large white river raft might have seen the child—might have even taken the child from her mother."

The thought of white people having a child borne of a Blackfoot woman, especially Sweet Dove, caused an intense pain to circle Spotted Eagle's heart.

He could not envision a white woman caring for the child that was meant to feed from Sweet Dove's breast!

And no one would ever know now whether the child was a boy or girl.

Wanting to flee to the hills to say his private prayers for Sweet Dove, Spotted Eagle spoke no more, only gazed sadly down at the woman whose hand had been soft in his and whose voice had spoken to his heart as though he were her brave, and she his woman.

She had never known the depth of his feelings.

Only now she might, when his prayers lifted high into the heavens, where she would be starting her long journey to the land of the hereafter. He would speak to her, as well as to the fires of the sun.

She would hear!

He knew that she would hear!

And she would protect their secret well until one day he joined her in death in the Sand Hills, the ghost place of the Blackfoot.

His eyes heavy, his muscles tight, he gazed with a longing now denied him at this woman whose death had touched him so deeply. Even in death she radiated a natural beauty, with her hair blacker than charcoal, her eyes browner than the bark of the tallest fir tree.

Spotted Eagle's heart bled when, for the last time ever, he was able to look at her exquisite facial features, so perfect that surely there could be no one that could compare to her.

Not able to contain his feelings much longer, Spotted Eagle turned and pushed his way through the wailing people and ran from the village. His heart pounded, and tears flooded his eyes as he sought to find that highest peak, hoping to one day find the child borne of the woman of his childhood dreams.

Blinded by tears, he ran onward until finally he was high above the forest, his village in the distance hidden to him by the thick covering of trees that reached up to this bluff on which he now sat on bended knee.

Spotted Eagle became conscious of a drumming—the double beat of Indian tom-toms, so far away that it was like the throb of the pulse in his ear. The drums were vibrating and speaking to the spirits.

The wailing of his Blackfoot people reached Spotted Eagle's heart with a renewed despair.

He lifted his eyes to the heavens and began pleading with the fires of the sun to give him strength to accept this horrible thing that had happened to his people, the death of someone so cherished, someone that everyone would sorely miss.

"Pity me now, oh Sun!" he cried. "Help me, Oh Great Above, Medicine Power!"

There was a strange silence, and then Spotted Eagle's eyes widened and his heartbeat momentarily wavered in its beats when he heard something that seemed unreal, yet wonderful!

"*A-wah-heh*—take courage, my son!"

Those words, the strength of the voice, startled Spotted Eagle. He looked quickly around and saw no one, then looked slowly up at the sky again, smiling. He knew that Old Man, the chief god of the Blackfoot, their creator *Napi*, had heard his heart's sadness, his prayer, and had spoken to him. The Sun and Old Man knew his feelings, even though perhaps it had been wrong to love a woman twice his age.

He smiled as tears rushed from his eyes, knowing now that, yes, they understood.

They would lift the burden of sadness from his heart, for he must look to the future. They, as well as he, knew that he would one day be chief of his people. To learn the ways of a powerful chief, one must prepare oneself for it.

And a part of that preparation was learning how to accept death. . . .

As the tom-tom droned song upon song, Spotted Eagle lifted his thoughts to the heaven again. "Oh, hear now, Sun! *Wo-ka-hit*, listen to my pleas. Help lift my burdens. Send them away from me, like an eagle in flight. *Hai-yah*, my heart cries out to you to let me accept my loss. Send my words into the heart of Sweet Dove as she walks the road of the hereafter. Touch her heart with a song that will stay with her until I, too, become one of the stars in the sky, twinkling down upon those I have been forced to leave behind."

He prayed until night fell like a black cloak around him. He peered into the depths of the stars, watching the aurora as the death dance of the spirits began. He searched slowly for that special star, that which twinkled the brightest, and when he found it, he knew that Sweet Dove was there, looking down upon him with a smile, understanding a child's heart and a child's despair.

There was no wind.

Then suddenly a sound came across the valley below him and up the hill like the noise of thunder, as a great owl came flying toward Spotted Eagle, its wide wings just barely missing his face.

A shiver soared through Spotted Eagle. The owl was warning him that it was time to leave his sorrows behind.

28

With a lifted chin, a proud stance, and dried eyes, he began descending from this place of private prayers and knew that one day, he *would* see Sweet Dove again.

And he now felt more man than child.

Chapter Three

Eighteen Years Later
Saint Louis, Missouri—1870

The tepees were colorfully designed with paintings depicting the sun, lightning, and the various seasons of the year. The village seemed deserted as Jolena crept through it after having become separated from her companions in Blackfoot country.

Scarcely breathing, she tiptoed through the village. The smell of meat cooking somewhere close by came to her, but food was the last thing on her mind. She was terrified to be alone in the deserted Blackfoot village, wondering where everyone was. She expected them to pounce on her from all directions at any moment now. Even though Jolena's own skin was of a copper coloring and her hair was jet black, proving her Indian heritage, she was dressed as a white woman dresses, and she knew not a word of the Blackfoot language should she come face to face with one.

How would she explain her dilemma?

Would they even care?

Suddenly she stopped with a start and gasped when a Blackfoot warrior came from one of the tepees and blocked her way. She soon discovered that she was not so stunned by his sudden presence as she was by the warrior's utter handsomeness, and when he reached a hand out and very gently touched her face, all of Jolena's fears melted away. . . .

Jolena's bedroom windows were swathed with sheer, lacy curtains, gentling the first beams of sunlight to reach her pillow, awakening her. Her dark eyes flickered open. Her pulse was racing; she still felt the same melting sensations that she had just experienced in the dream. So many nights now she had dreamed the same dream of the same handsome warrior—only this dream was different.

He had actually touched her!

Placing her hand on the same cheek that he had touched in her dream, she closed her eyes and allowed herself to imagine that her hand was his and, going even further, imagined that she was feeling his lips against hers. . . .

Knowing that she must stop these fantasies, Jolena wrenched her eyes open and dropped her hand from her face. Instead of the handsome Indian, now the center of her attention was the sudden excitement filling her with the remembrance of what lay ahead of her, beginning today.

As she plumped the pillows more comfortably beneath her head and ran her hands along her satin coverlet, she gazed toward the window and watched the sun etch its patterns through the lace, knowing that this would be the last morning in her bedroom for many months, perhaps even as long as a year.

That she would actually travel clear to the wilderness of the Montana Territory seemed hard to believe. She had fought hard to convince her father to allow her to travel with the party of lepidopterists who were searching for the *euphaedra*, the rare butterfly that had once again migrated far from the jungles of Venezuela. So long ago her father had followed the same lead and had not found the butterfly. It seemed that the only thing he had discovered and taken back to Saint Louis with him was a daughter. . . .

Slipping out of her four-poster bed, her bare feet sinking into a thick carpet, Jolena could not help beaming, caught up again in the tale that her mother and father had shared with her after she had been taunted once too often by her playmates for being an Indian.

Her floor-length sheer nightgown streaming along behind her, Jolena went to a full-length mirror and gazed intensely at herself. She ran her fingers over her face, studying her smooth, copper skin, high cheekbones, and dark brown eyes.

Then she ran her fingers through her waist-length hair that was blacker than charcoal. When she had just been six years old, she had begun to realize the difference between herself and the other girls with whom she attended school.

It had been a rude awakening when some had mocked her for being an Indian, even calling her a "savage."

She had quickly learned that having a different color of skin made a difference.

She had asked her parents to explain about her "difference"—why wasn't her skin like theirs if she was their daughter?

She had listened raptly when they had told her about having found her lying with her dead Indian mother on the trail while they had been searching for the rare butterfly. They had fallen instantly in love with her, had taken her in, and had raised her as their own.

She had been told that they did not know her Indian tribe, nor did they know who her true father was.

Ever since then, she had wondered about her true heritage—her true people.

Yet she had held her head high and had accepted what life had handed her. Her adoptive parents had always treated her wonderfully and she was as close to her adoptive brother, Kirk, as any sister could be to an older brother—well, he was only a few months older.

Kirk was postponing his further college studies

to accompany her on this journey to the Montana Territory, hoping to succeed at what their father had failed at all those years ago—to find the rare butterfly that had been sighted there.

A shiver raced up and down Jolena's spine when she thought about the Indians of the Montana Territory. The Blackfoot were among those tribes, and her dreams had always been about the Blackfoot. She had known this by the color of moccasins the handsome Indian always wore.

Black.

In her studies of the Indians of that region, she had learned that the Blackfoot Indians always wore black moccasins.

It gave her a strange sort of thrill to know that she would soon be mingling among the Indians of the Montana Territory. The guides for this expedition were, in fact, supposed to be Indians . . . perhaps one of the guides might be as handsome as the warrior in her dreams!

And perhaps she might even discover her true heritage. Yet she doubted she would. She was now eighteen years old. Her Indian mother had died long ago, and her Indian father had probably forgotten the child that had been born the day he had lost his wife.

And the Montana Territory was a wide and spacious land.

It did not seem at all possible, or logical, to Jolena that her true heritage would be revealed to her all that easily, if ever at all.

Sighing, Jolena hugged her nightgown around

her and went to the window. Outside, she could see willowy branches of purple spirea drooping over the white picket fence separating the front lawn from the street. Daisies flourished inside the fence, and redbud, dogwood, and azaleas spangled the landscape with their pastel glory. If her window were open, she knew that the air would be thick with the scent of flowers.

Saint Louis was a lovely city, a city that had been good to her.

But it was June, the beginning of summer, the season that stirred the side of Jolena's personality that yearned for adventure.

She was going to bid Saint Louis a fond farewell, looking forward to the land that awaited her—and perhaps her precious discoveries!

Eager to get her day on its way, Jolena hurriedly dressed in a floor-length demure gray dress. It was void of any frills or fanciness of any sort for this, her first day of travel on the steamboat *Yellowstone* up the Missouri River.

After she was dressed and her long, black hair was spilling down her back, she went to her desk and began sorting through papers and books, deciding which ones to take that would be the most valuable in her search for the rare butterfly.

Choosing one and then another, she soon had more than one valise stuffed with journals and books. Smiling, she grabbed them up into her arms and left her bedroom.

Her arms too full even to see her feet, Jolena made her way slowly down the steep staircase.

"That's a sure-fire way to break your neck, sis," Kirk said, coming quickly up the stairs to rescue her. He took her heaviest books and tucked them beneath his own arms. "Lord, Jolena, are you taking your whole library with you? You know it's only going to make the journey more cumbersome for you. I don't see that as wise."

Jolena did not have time to comment before a loud, commanding voice spoke from the foot of the stairs.

"I think this whole foolishness about going after that elusive butterfly isn't wise," Bryce Edmonds said firmly. "I'd hoped you'd reconsider, but by the looks of those trunks by the door and those stuffed valises, I see that I was foolish to think that you might decide against this venture at the last minute."

Jolena gave her brother a nervous grin as he glanced at her, then smiled more gently at her father. She was always saddened to see how he was wasting away with a strange sort of paralysis, now confined to a wheelchair for the rest of his life. There was only a trace of his former handsomeness in his smile and eyes. His hair was gray and thinning. His face was all lines and shadow. His shoulders were bent and lean.

She could hardly bear to look at his legs as they rested limply in the wheelchair. They were mere bones, his muscles having atrophied almost to nothing.

She scarcely remembered how he had once looked, except that when she looked at her brother, she knew that she was seeing the mirror-image of their father with his boyish freckles, blond hair, and a face that made girls take a second look at him.

She could envision her beautiful mother having been enamored by her young husband all of those years ago, and it saddened her that her mother was no longer there to share life with her husband and children. Charlotte had died trying to give birth to a second child.

Jolena thought that if her mother were still there to look after her father, he would not have that lonely, haunted look in his eyes as often as he did now.

She felt guilty for being so eager to leave him. Without her and Kirk there to keep him company, what might his days and evenings be like? Though there were many servants at his beck and call in this great mansion perched on a high cliff that overlooked the Mississippi River, they might not be enough.

But nothing was going to stop Jolena from going to the Montana Territory.

She was being drawn there for more than one reason.

She raced on down the stairs and gave her father a warm hug and a kiss on his cheek. "Please be happy for me," she whispered to him. "I so badly want to go. Say that you understand?"

Bryce placed his bony fingers to Jolena's shoulders and leaned her away from him, his eyes meeting hers as he gripped her shoulders. "Daughter, I don't think I've ever been able to talk you out of anything," he said thickly. "You've been willful and adventurous for as long as you've been able to walk and talk. As for going to search for that damnable butterfly—I understand. I was driven to search wide and far for it myself. But damn it, Jolena, Montana Territory is so far away. Anything can happen."

"Yes, I know," Jolena said, easing from his grasp. She took her valises and set them on top of her trunks, then turned and faced her father again as he wheeled his wheelchair around to meet her sad stare. "But I do so badly want to go, father."

"And I do give you my permission and blessing," Bryce said, hanging on to how she called him father today—for next week, even next year, she might be saying that to someone else. If she should manage to somehow discover her true heritage and find her true father, he would lose everything that was most precious.

His daughter—his beloved daughter!

He wasn't sure if he could bear it.

"Now let's not talk anymore about it," he quickly added. "Breakfast is waiting in the dining room. Let's go and eat our fill. Especially you two young'uns. Who's to say what sort of food you're going to get on that steamboat?"

Kirk laid the rest of Jolena's valises aside and went to his father's chair and took over pushing it for him. He gave Jolena a nervous stare as she walked on ahead of the wheelchair, a bounce in her steps this morning that seemed different.

And he knew why.

Though she had not spoken about it, he knew

that she was anxious to see if she could find which tribe of Indians was her own, and to see if she could even find her true father. Although she was not going to just out-and-out search for these things of her past, he knew that it would be at the back of her mind day in and out, and that somehow she just might come upon the answers by chance.

He feared this clean to the core of himself, for he knew what this would do to their father. It would devastate him, perhaps even kill him from the heartache of losing her to another. Losing her to a man by exchanged marriage vows was one thing. Losing her to a man whom she would be calling "father" was another.

Kirk had tried his damndest to talk Jolena out of going on this expedition with the other lepidopterists, despite having become one herself at the age of sixteen because of their father's teachings.

But she had vowed to her father that she would find the elusive, rare butterfly and bring it home to him for his collection.

No matter how hard their father had denied wanting to have the butterfly, no matter if deep within his heart he wished now that he had not taught her the skills of his science—doing so mainly to fill the void in his life that his paralysis had caused—Jolena would not be convinced that this rare butterfly was not still as important to him as it had been those many years ago when he had also traveled far to search for it.

Jolena could feel the strain between herself and her father and brother. She knew she was the cause, yet she would not allow anything to ruin this wonderfully exciting day for her. As each moment passed, her excitement built in leaps and bounds.

She walked smoothly on down the long corridor, where doors opened on each side of her into a home enchanted by the play of the light from the chandelier in each room.

Jolena moved into the dining room with eager steps. The walls were mellow with flickering light from the great stone fireplace along the far wall, the furniture and glass and memorabilia in the spacious room glinting in sunshine as it poured through the row of windows opposite the fireplace.

She stepped up to the table and stood behind her chair. She waited to sit down after Kirk arrived and positioned their father's wheelchair at the head of the table.

Placing her hands behind her, anxiously clasping and unclasping them, she gazed around her, knowing that when she became homesick, she would remember this room best of all. It wasn't only a dining room. There were also comfortably plush chairs and a sofa that sat in a wide circle before the fireplace. The room was painted a glossy burgundy, making it a cool retreat at luncheon and a warm haven at night as the family nestled around the fire.

French doors opened to a wide and spacious balcony that hung out over the high cliff that overlooked the winding, muddy water of the Mississippi.

On a foggy day, the sound of foghorns wafted upward, mysterious and beautiful.

Today, Jolena would be a part of the mystery, her heart thrilling anew at the thought of traveling so far on the steamboat, her destination one of intrigue and expectations that she could not deny made her heart begin thumping, as though drums inside her were beating out a steady rhythm.

Drums.

Indians.

The thought of finally finding at least a part of her heritage by being near Indians caused her to feel a strange sort of headiness.

If only . . .

Her thoughts were interrupted by her father's voice. "Go and lay more wood on the fire, Kirk," he said, sounding shallow as he held his emotions deeply guarded within him, those same emotions that were there in his eyes every time Jolena looked at him.

He now sat at the table and was spreading a napkin across his lap. Torn with emotions herself—emotions that battled inside her over this decision she had made to leave the life she had always known to step into the unknown—Jolena silently pulled her chair out from the table and sat down. She gingerly spread her napkin across her lap as Kirk laid two more split walnut chunks against the backlog of the fireplace.

Avoiding her father's steady stare, which made Jolena feel guilty again for leaving him, she watched Kirk as he came to the table. She felt blessed to have such a brother. He was a highly intelligent young man, who was setting aside his future for her, to be her escort. Today he was ever so handsome in his blue corduroy trousers and white linen shirt.

The one thing that was distracting and somewhat threatening was the holstered pearl-handled pistol belted at his waist. It had been a gift from their father, for Kirk to carry with him during the journey to and from the Montana Territory.

It gave Jolena a dried-throat feeling to believe that her brother would ever have need of the pistol, yet she knew that the chances were greater than not that he would be forced to use it.

There were reports of Indian attacks and massacres in the Montana Territory.

Not even realizing that she had picked up her fork and was toying with her platter of scrambled eggs, her father was a sudden, loud reminder.

"Stop playing with your food and eat, damn it," Bryce said, frowning at Jolena, practicing his duties as a father for as long as he was allowed to.

Jolena smiled weakly over at him and nodded. "Yes, father," she murmured. "I . . . I was just lost in thought. Within the next hour I shall be boarding the steamer. I can't help but be excited."

Bryce gave her another lingering, unnerving stare, then swallowed hard and looked down at his untouched eggs. He so feared losing Jolena once she entered the land of her ancestors. If she came face to face with her true father and

42

people, she might want to stay with them and become one of them—one *with* them.

Bryce slowly shifted his eyes to Kirk. He had taken his son aside more than once and had begged him to keep Jolena from the truth of who her true tribe of people were, at all cost.

But he understood too well that Kirk was the less willful of his two children.

If Jolena set her mind on something, nothing on God's earth would change it. Not even her devoted brother.

He threw his fork down and slapped at his legs angrily. "Damn these legs," he said, his voice breaking with emotion. It was his place to watch after his daughter and he was no longer able. "Damn them all to hell and back."

Tears came to Jolena's eyes as she witnessed her father's frustration. She felt utterly helpless and for a brief instant thought she should change her plans.

Then the dream of the handsome Blackfoot warrior came to her again in her mind's eye and she knew that nothing—not even a grieving, sad father—could sway her decision from seeking out her destiny.

Chapter Four

Three Months Later—
The Montana Territory

Montana. A wilderness of steep, wooded slopes and flowery mountain meadows, where streams tumbled over the waterfalls and blue lakes lay in peaceful valleys.

The leaves of the cottonwoods rustled and whispered in the wind, seemingly answering the soft sounds of the brook as its crystal-clear water rippled and splashed over the rocks.

The glow of the moon reached down from the velvety black sky of night, caressing the grassy mound upon which lay a fresh spray of wild flowers, the daisies with their gold and brown faces the most prominent of them all.

Spotted Eagle rested on his haunches beside

the grave, something like a silent bidding that
he did not understand having drawn him to
Sweet Dove's burial spot. He had been there
this time since the sun had begun its descent
behind the distant mountains, praying and
offering his gift of flowers to a woman who
was long gone from him, yet who still remained
within his thoughts and heart as vividly as when
he had looked upon her lovely face as a youth
enamored with an older woman.

When she died, a part of him had gone to the
grave with her.

And because of his infatuation, even still at
his age of twenty-eight, he had not yet found a
woman who compared with Sweet Dove, and
so his blankets were only warmed at night by
his loneliness.

"Spotted Eagle, *ok-yi*, come. *Wo-ka-hit*, listen,
my friend. If we are to make Fort Chance by
morning, we must leave now," Two Ridges said,
chancing disturbing his friend's private moment.

Two Ridges did not understand his friend's feelings for Sweet Dove, for he himself enjoyed the
company of women his own age, having at sixteen taken many beautiful maidens to his blankets
with him, enjoying the sensual moments shared
with them. Although he knew that Spotted Eagle
was not practicing celibacy, he still had not chosen a particular woman to sweeten his dwelling.

Two Ridges planned to make a choice soon, so
that he would look older and more virile in the
eyes of his more mature, special friend. Now it
sometimes seemed to him that he was only an

annoyance to Spotted Eagle.

Two Ridges felt his friend's annoyance even now, as Spotted Eagle turned angry eyes up at him for having disturbed his silent vigil at the grave site.

Yet Two Ridges did not allow this anger to reach inside him and make him lower his eyes in shame, for he knew that he was right to remind Spotted Eagle that time was quickly passing—time that should be spent in their saddles instead of beside the grave of a woman whose heart and soul had belonged to another man.

Spotted Eagle gazed up at Two Ridges. He had long ago welcomed this youth as a friend, at first amused by the young lad's way of shadowing him from the time he could walk. The bond of friendship had strengthened through the years and had matured into something special. Spotted Eagle could not help but admire Two Ridges' ability to shoot, ride, and hunt.

He smiled to himself, even admiring his young friend's prowess with women. Spotted Eagle at times thought that he might learn from his friend's behavior with women, yet still could not allow himself to be that free with his heart and feelings.

He was one day to be a powerful chief.

He must present himself as a man of great pride and restraint!

Spotted Eagle took a last, lingering look at the grave, leaned a hand upon the grass still warmed by the sun, then turned his eyes up at Two Ridges. "You are right," he said, rising to his full height, which was not much over his friend's height, Two Ridges standing at least six feet without moccasins. "We must leave for Fort Chance. It is an interesting time for us, would you not agree? Who of our people have ever seen—how do you say the word—lep-i-dop-ter-ist? I have to wonder if these white people will be as strange looking as the title they bear?"

Spotted Eagle chuckled as he swung an arm around Two Ridges' shoulder and then walked together toward their grazing horses.

"My heart is happy that you chose this Indian to join you in being a guide this time, to help protect the white people from the Cree renegades while they search for the rare butterfly that you, my friend, spotted in this area," Two Ridges said, casting Spotted Eagle a quick glance. He admired, yet envied more, this man who would be chief after the passing of his chieftain father. "I will learn much from you during this trip. Already you have taught me much that makes me look good to the women."

"There will come a time when you will find life as good without women as with them," Spotted Eagle said, offering a soft, amused laugh to his friend. "When you find that special woman and join hands with her, then perhaps you can find other purposes in life. She will tend to your nightly needs, and during the daytime hours you will not be as busy shifting your eyes from woman to woman, hungering for each of them. You will become a man whose wife is envied for the feats you will perform as a proud warrior of our people."

"Yes, soon I will choose that perfect woman to warm my bed at night and sweeten my tepee with her smile," Two Ridges said, nodding. "I have been thinking that Moon Flower might be the right one." He shifted his gaze once again his friend's way. "You, also, must find that certain woman. Is it not important that you soon bring a son into your life, to teach him all that you have taught this boy who is fast growing into ways of a man? To have a son, you must first have a *nit-o-ke-man*—a wife."

"You need not tell me the ways of the world and what is required of me to make sons," Spotted Eagle said, his voice no longer light and carefree, but annoyed at the impertinence of this young man at his side. "In time, a woman will fill my arms and warm my blankets. Until now, none has interested me."

"Except for my father's first wife," Two Ridges dared to say, giving his friend a guarded glance after he said it.

"Watch your words with me," Spotted Eagle snapped back. He paused, then added, "I was a mere boy then, yet I felt, I am sure, the feelings of a man for your father's first wife. But I rightfully and respectfully kept those feelings to myself. Still, I feel them and mourn her I believe even more than your father has ever mourned her."

"My father did mourn Sweet Dove and married soon after her death because he could not bear the loneliness and pain of his first wife's absence,"

Two Ridges said in defense of his father, Brown Elk. "And should he not have married my mother then, you would not have a best friend to shadow your every move now. Would that not sadden you?"

"It would not be something that would make me sad, because you would not have entered my thoughts had you not been born," Spotted Eagle said matter-of-factly.

"That is so," Two Ridges said thoughtfully. Then he cast a big smile toward Spotted Eagle. "You are glad that Father remarried and had a son, are you not?"

"Yes, it makes my heart happy," Spotted Eagle said. Speaking of Brown Elk having a son catapulted his mind back eighteen years, when Brown Elk had also had another child born to him—a child that had been stolen from its dead mother and never seen or heard from again.

Spotted Eagle had wondered often about that child, whether or not it was a boy or girl, for that child would be a half-brother or -sister to Two Ridges.

Spotted Eagle had wondered if Two Ridges had ever been told of the child. It was not a question he had ever tested by asking.

It was for Brown Elk to make such confessions to a son!

Having reached their horses, Spotted Eagle stroked the mane of his mount—a black stallion, a very fast horse with a white spot on its side— then swung himself into his saddle.

Two Ridges followed his lead, soon sitting tall

and square-shouldered on his strawberry roan.

"Let us be on our way!" Spotted Eagle shouted, sinking his moccasined heels into the muscled flanks of his horse. The fringes of his buckskin shirt and breeches blew and fluttered in the wind as he rode off at a fast gallop into the moonlight-drenched night, his friend close beside him.

When Fort Chance came into sight at the break of dawn, it was not the fort and the tall fence surrounding it that drew their attention. It was the sight of a huge paddle-wheeler moving down the Missouri River, its tall smokestacks blackened with smoke, many people lining the rails on the top deck, waiting for the boat to stop and deliver them to the Montana Territory.

Two Ridges drew a tight rein and stopped. He forked an eyebrow and gestured toward the steamboat with a wide swing of his arm. "Is not that a strange floating canoe?" he marveled. "It is so large! It carries many people in its bowels!"

Spotted Eagle drew rein beside his friend, yet offered no conversation. His insides were tight with more thoughts of Sweet Dove. It had been said that perhaps her child had been taken by those who rode the large river vessel those many years ago.

He tried not to be angered by this possibility.

Long ago his father had made peace with the white people. He had dug a hole in the

50

ground and in it the Blackfoot had placed their anger and covered it up, so that there was no more war. His father still being chief, dealings were peaceful with the white people. The rival Indian tribes of this region were now more their enemy than anyone else.

The friendship of his Blackfoot people toward the whites had been fostered by decades of commerce with beaver hunters who roamed their mountain homeland. Spotted Eagle himself had chosen to walk the white man's road in peace, having felt that it was important to win favor with those who seemed destined to inherit the future.

Many Blackfoot warriors had even gone as far as saving many emigrants' lives by guiding and protecting them against the hostile Indians of the territory, as Spotted Eagle, in the capacity of a guide, had agreed to protect these people arriving on the river vessel from the Cree.

This would be easily done, for Spotted Eagle now spoke the English language well, from having become so closely associated with those at the fort and at the many trading posts in the area.

Feeling that enough time had been spent watching the large river vessel, Spotted Eagle sank his heels into the flanks of his horse and thundered onward toward the fort, Two Ridges soon beside him.

"There are many beautiful white women," Two Ridges said, smiling devilishly at Spotted Eagle.

"Your business is scouting, not women-watching," Spotted Eagle said, giving his friend another annoyed glance. Two Ridges' love for women would one day get him in a barrel of trouble.

Silence fell between them as they grew closer and closer to the river boat that was inching its way closer to land for docking.

Jolena leaned her full weight against the rail as she combed her fingers through her wind-tousled hair, absorbing everything as the steamboat moved closer to shore.

The air was clear, the sunshine burning.

A spotted eagle soaring majestically overhead sent shivers down her spine because of its loveliness.

She had witnessed many marvels of nature on this long and tiring three-month journey from Saint Louis, a distance of two thousand miles. From Saint Louis they had passed one continuous prairie, with the exception of a few of the luxuriant forests along the banks of the river and the streams falling into it. There she had seen deer, antelope, bison, and various types of birds whose magnificent colors had stolen her breath away.

Now and then she had gasped when she saw a butterfly sweeping overhead, soon blown by the incessant wind away from her.

This had always reminded her of why she was taking this trek to the Montana Territory, yet deep down inside herself, where her dreams and desires were formed, she knew that the true reason was to follow the calling of her dreams.

She could not help but hope to find her destiny.

Soon the riverboat was docked and its large walking plank swung around and positioned securely onto the rocky beach that was only a few feet from the towering palisade that protected Fort Chance, a very substantial fort three hundred feet square which housed an American Fur Company post.

Very quickly, almost before she could catch her breath, Jolena was catapulted into the hubbub of unloading from the riverboat, the several other scientists in her party scrambling to get to shore with her and leave their "sea legs" behind them.

Jolena, her arms piled high with valises stuffed with her research materials and journals, clumsily made her way through the throng of people.

Their horses left behind inside the fort walls, Spotted Eagle and Two Ridges stood a few feet from the riverbank, curiously watching the people unload the boat. Spotted Eagle's attention was drawn to one lady in particular, whose waist-length, flowing black hair made his eyebrows lift, thinking that such hair did not seem appropriate for a white woman. Sweet Dove's hair had been as long and as black—blacker than charcoal. He did not see how a white woman could have the hair of a Blackfoot woman!

He continued watching her, his eyes narrowing when a white man stepped to her side and began relieving her of her burden. He thought this man must be her brother, for he looked too young to be anyone's husband.

Yet this young man had hair the color of wheat, nothing like the woman's.

Spotted Eagle's interest peaking, something compelled him to continue watching the woman until finally her face was revealed to him and he saw that she was not a white woman at all, but had the coloring and features of an Indian.

And that was not all!

A choking sensation grabbed at his insides, and he stood in leather-faced silence, struck numb by the resemblance between this woman and Sweet Dove!

Memories rushed over him, remembering anew when he was a boy obsessed with an older woman.

It was as though he was a young boy again, taken by the same lovely face—Sweet Dove's!

It was strange to see such an Indian woman mingling with the white people, dressed like them, as though one *of* them!

He could not help but continue to stare at her, his heart pounding in his ears as the excitement built within him.

This woman radiated such a natural, enchanting beauty. There was a look of keen intelligence in her dark eyes. Her face was expressive of strong passions lying just beneath the surface.

Again he could not help but make the comparison with Sweet Dove—her eyes browner than the bark of the tallest fir trees, her long and flowing hair down her slim back blacker than charcoal, her exquisite, perfect facial features on a copper skin such as his own.

His palms were sweaty. His throat was dry, as he came to the only possible conclusion.

This must be the long-lost child of his beloved Sweet Dove!

It had to be!

Her every feature spoke to him of Sweet Dove!

Sighing with relief that the burden had been removed from her aching arms, Jolena smiled up at Kirk. "Thank you so much for rescuing me," she said, laughing softly. "I'm not sure I could have moved another inch. I surely would have dropped the valises for everyone else to trip over."

"I've come on this expedition to look after you, sis," Kirk said, "and by damn, I will. Just let some man look at you crosswise and he'll have me to answer to."

Jolena glanced down at his holstered pistol, hoping that didn't give him too much confidence. He was not a man of action. He had been a man of books too long to be able to change into someone who was that skilled in guns to speak out when perhaps he should be listening.

She feared for her brother more than for herself in this strange, even forbidding land.

As she was walking at a fast clip toward the fort, trying to keep up with Kirk, Jolena's footsteps faltered. She felt almost certain she was being watched. She could feel the heat of someone's eyes branding her.

Pausing for a moment as Kirk kept walking ahead of her, Jolena slowly turned around. Growing pale, her eyes widened and her knees grew weak when her searching gaze stopped on the Indian warrior who was staring back at her from the darkest eyes imaginable.

She covered her mouth with a hand, gasping. The more she stared back at him, the more she was aware that this was not just any Indian.

This was the Blackfoot warrior of her midnight dreams!

This Indian was as tall and straight. His features were as regular, his eyes midnight dark, large, and well set. His nose was moderate in size, straight and thin, his chest splendidly developed. His long black hair hung free of braids and ornaments. His cheeks were well-pronounced, and he was wearing a neat suit of buckskin with fringes on the sleeves, across the shoulders, and down his trouser legs.

The front of his shirt was decorated beautifully with the embroidery of porcupine quills, matching the band at his head that held his hair in place.

Jolena's heart raced, now understanding why some called the noble Indians knights of the prairie, mountains and forests. Never would she find anyone else as handsome and as intriguing as this Indian.

She blinked her eyes and swallowed hard.

How could she have possibly dreamed of this man whom she had never seen before?

As in her dream, this warrior was wearing a necklace of distinction. Could he be the son of a powerful chief?

Jolena was stunned and uneasy by the way he was staring at her, as though he was seeing a ghost!

Her head reeled with the feeling that she too was seeing a ghost—a fantasy that had frequented her midnight dreams. She was glad when Kirk stopped and turned, discovering that she was no longer walking with him, and came back to her, whisking her away with him with just the command in his eyes.

"Why were you looking at that Indian like that?" Kirk said accusingly, leaning close to Jolena so that no one else would hear. "It's playing a dangerous game, Jolena, allowing yourself to get caught up in make-believe about Indians."

Jolena scarcely heard what Kirk was saying and scarcely noticed that he was actually scolding her. "Kirk, do you know if that Indian is Blackfoot?" she asked, again giving the handsome warrior a look across her shoulder, her heart throbbing again when she discovered that he was still watching her.

"Never you mind about that," Kirk said, his voice drawn. "I suspect you'll find out soon enough, though. If I'm right, he's one of the Indian guides that will be traveling with our expedition."

When Kirk turned his eyes back to the Indian,

Jolena followed his gaze and then felt somewhat faint at a new discovery! This Indian was wearing black moccasins! He *was* Blackfoot! The man of her dreams! How could this be? How?

When she felt another set of eyes on her, Jolena shifted her gaze and stared back at the slighter, younger Indian who was standing next to the handsome one. A shiver ran through her when he continued to stare at her, a strange sort of glint in his eyes.

"Kirk, is that other Indian one of the guides, also?" she asked, wrenching her eyes around.

"I'm sure of it," Kirk said, then pursed his lips tightly together, realizing exactly why he was needed in defense of his sister.

Her skin coloring. Her dark hair and eyes. All of those things were drawing too much attention her way from the Indians. They were surely seeing that she was most certainly not of the white community, except in her dress and relationships.

If they knew that she was of this region, therein lay the true danger!

Two Ridges could not keep his eyes from watching Jolena as she walked hurriedly toward the entrance of the fort. He had been quickly taken by her loveliness and knew that Spotted Eagle was as taken as he.

And why wouldn't he be?

This woman with the skin of an Indian and the clothes of white people was a woman of mystery!

Two Ridges would know more of her, soon! Forgotten was the young maiden of his village whom he'd been courting. Moon Flower could not compare to this mysterious beauty.

Suddenly his mind was made up.

He would take this woman as his wife before Spotted Eagle had the chance.

And he most definitely would not let Spotted Eagle know of his sudden infatuation with the copper princess. The danger in that was that friends could easily become enemies over a woman. And Two Ridges meant to have this woman, no matter the cost.

Chapter Five

As Kirk and Jolena walked through the wide, opened gate of the fort, a heavy-set man with a loud, throaty voice came lumbering toward them. "Welcome to Fort Chance," Ralph McMillan said as he stopped and extended a hand toward Kirk, than laughed and dropped his hand to his side when he realized that Kirk was too burdened for greetings. "Here. Let my clerks, Steven and John, give you a hand."

"Gladly," Kirk said, laughing softly as the two young men dressed in suits of black fustian with brass buttons began taking the valises from him. "Thank you. Your assistance is greatly appreciated."

Now that Kirk's hands were free, Ralph McMillan extended his hand once again toward him. "One of your scientific friends, who arrived at the fort from the riverboat before you, pointed you out as the main reason this voyage has been made to Montana Territory," he said, shaking Kirk's hand eagerly as he looked from Kirk to Jolena, then back again at Kirk. "Your father was here many years ago. I heard about his attempts to find the elusive butterfly. You've come to capture it to take back to him for his collection, I assume?"

"And for his memoirs," Jolena interjected softly, her gaze taking in this short, compact man with bowed legs, whose age appeared to be perhaps forty. He was dressed well in a suit of blue broadcloth with brass buttons, and his long brown hair was neatly combed and hanging down to his shoulders. She had been told that he was a kind-hearted and high-minded Scotsman, in charge of all of the fur company business in this region, clear to the Rocky Mountains.

"He is presently writing a book," she quickly added. "I would like the ending to say that he has the *Euphaedra* among his collection. My brother and I hope to make this possible. Our father is not well. A strange sort of paralysis has claimed not only his dignity, but also the use of his legs, or he would be on this journey instead of his children."

Ralph dropped his hands to his sides, then clasped them behind him. "That is a fine thing you do for your father," he said, his eyes roaming over Jolena, realizing that she was, indeed, Indian instead of white, yet, he was too polite to question her or her brother about it.

Ralph's gaze was drawn to Spotted Eagle and Two Ridges as they strolled toward the wide gate of the fort, then raised a hand and shouted at them. "*Ok-yi*, come!" he said. "I will introduce you to those who are in charge of the expedition!"

Jolena's eyebrows rose, wondering who he was addressing, then her insides trembled knowing that it must be the handsome Indian, for he and his companion were the only two Indians present today at the fort.

Her pulse racing, her cheeks hot with an excited, anxious flush, she turned and found herself looking squarely up into the most beautiful eyes she had ever seen, which quickly mesmerized her, as the handsome Indian stopped only an arm's length from her.

"Let me make introductions," Ralph said, stepping in front of Jolena, momentarily blocking her view of the Indian, then moving to the Indian's side, placing a fond arm around his shoulders. "This, my friends, is one of the most skilled guides of the region. You are in the proud company of Spotted Eagle, whose father is Chief Gray Bear. His companion is Two Ridges, the son of Brown Elk. They will guide you through the wilderness and also protect you from the marauding Cree."

Ralph turned to Spotted Eagle and Two Ridges. "My special friends, may I introduce you to Jolena and Kirk Edmonds, who make their residence in Saint Louis, Missouri," he said, gesturing toward Jolena and Kirk. "They are on a mission of the heart," he explained. "They have come to search for and find the elusive butterfly that you, Spotted Eagle, have spotted. They wish to take their knowledge of it and specimens back to their ailing father."

Spotted Eagle had not taken his eyes off Jolena, unnerving her. It was as though he was looking deeply within her soul, perhaps trying to pull from within her the answers to the questions that his eyes were asking.

She had to wonder why. Did she resemble someone he knew?

Or was it because he was instantly attracted to her, as she was to him?

If he only knew that she had met him before, in her midnight dreams, then he would have cause to stare at her!

She could not wrench her own eyes away, having loved him before ever having met him face to face!

This was confusing to her, these feelings for a man who was, in truth, a complete stranger to her.

And he was not just any man. He was an Indian.

In Saint Louis she had seen few Indians. They had mostly kept to the riverfront, where they traded with people of the city. She had never ventured there herself, her father having forbidden it.

"You come to this land for your father's benefit?" Spotted Eagle said, finally breaking the silence between them, which had begun to be strained. "His name is—?"

"Bryce," Jolena said, her voice slight and filled with awe. "Bryce Edmonds."

"He is Indian in coloring?" Spotted Eagle could not help but ask. "He is Indian, yet has taken on a white man's name, the same as you?"

Kirk's eyes widened and he swallowed hard, not liking where this conversation was leading. "*Our* father is quite white, thank you," he said stiffly. He placed a hand to Jolena's elbow and whisked her away, walking her briskly away from the questions and introductions.

"That damn Indian is asking too many questions," Kirk growled. "He's been hired to lead, not to interfere in our private lives."

Jolena tugged at Kirk's hand, trying to get free. "Let me go, Kirk," she said, anger brimming in her eyes as she glared at him. "What you did was most impolite. He was just making conversation."

"He saw your skin coloring," Kirk grumbled, flashing an angry look back at her. "And it wasn't just polite conversation that caused him to say what he did. Jolena, you *are* Indian, through and through. He saw it. He wants to make it his business to know why, and I won't allow it."

Jolena ceased struggling with her brother, knowing that although she was the more willful of the two, he was the stronger.

Throwing a glance over her shoulder, she gazed at Spotted Eagle—this Indian whose name, as well as his handsomeness, intrigued her.

She did not know how, but Spotted Eagle was one and the same as the Indian in her dreams!

She did not see how that could be so, yet it was. No one could say that all Indians looked alike, for the slighter Indian companion of Spotted Eagle's looked nothing like the man in her dream. In her eyes, he was not handsome at all.

He, too, had looked at her strangely, but she had defined this as an interest in her. She knew lust in the eyes of a man when she saw it, and this man lusted after her. He seemed ready even at this moment to throw her to the ground and cover her with his body. He frightened her, and she knew to keep an eye on him, especially if she was left alone for any length of time with him.

"Kirk," Jolena blurted, finally yanking herself out of her brother's grip. "I hope that today isn't a sample of how guarded you are going to be of my every move and new acquaintance. You made me look helpless in front of everyone. You know better than that, so please think before you act next time."

"It doesn't take much thinking to know when you need your brother to look after your welfare, especially when an Indian warrior is becoming too inquisitive about you," Kirk said, giving Jolena a frown. "I promised father I would . . ."

His words broke off as a guarded look came into his eyes, then he looked away from Jolena, silent.

"You promised father you would keep me from finding out about my heritage, didn't you?" she snapped back. "Is he . . . are you . . . so threatened by the truth that you will do anything to keep me from even talking to an Indian? Kirk, that won't work and you know it. If I want to talk, for instance, to Spotted Eagle, I will, and I will not allow you to humiliate me, *nor* him, ever again."

"Didn't you see the way he was looking at you, sis?" Kirk said urgently. "He was looking at you as though he wanted to possess you, or perhaps already did. And I saw the way you were looking at him. Damn it, sis, don't get infatuated with an Indian just because your skin is the same color as his. I—I don't want you deciding to stay behind when it is time to return to Saint Louis."

Knowing that Kirk's worries were well-founded, and that even she saw the dangers in allowing her feelings for Spotted Eagle to grow, Jolena did not offer him a response. In truth, she did not know what to say. She could not deny even to her brother that she was intrigued by the Blackfoot warrior, for she was not skilled in telling lies.

Instead, she escaped further conversation with him by gazing around her, taking in the scene around them. The site of the fort had been well selected, on a beautiful prairie on the banks near the junction of the Missouri and Yellowstone rivers. Jolena's father had told her that since this was the principal headquarters of the fur companies of this region, a vast stock of goods was kept on hand. At certain times of the year, the numerous traders from the distant outposts concentrated here with the profits from their season's trade and outfitted themselves with a fresh supply of goods to trade with the Indians.

This post was also the general rendezvous of a great number of Indian tribes, who were continually concentrating there for the purpose of trade.

It appeared that those who lived within the walls of the fort lived in a comfortable style. Jolena could count some eight or ten log houses and stores and knew that forty or fifty soldiers were stationed there. She was amazed at the number of horses in the corral at the far end of the courtyard, not far from the long row of barracks. There had to be at least one hundred horses inside the fence!

"Here now, let me take you to my private dwelling," Ralph said, suddenly nudging his way between Jolena and Kirk. "You can get comfortable with a cup of hot tea before everyone else arrives for supper. Your trunks and personal belongings are being seen to. Tomorrow they will be loaded into the covered wagons that should be arriving from another outpost. These wagons will take you where you need to go. Spotted Eagle knows the avenue of travel that will take you around the worst, impassable terrain."

The name Spotted Eagle made Jolena's heart leap. She looked guiltily at Kirk and saw that his reaction to the name was much different from her own. In his blue eyes she could see a trace of guarded anger.

Steve guided her and Kirk toward the largest and most handsome of the log cabins. She followed him inside, finding a huge stone fireplace where a soft fire burned in the massive grate;

plush, deeply cushioned chairs were positioned before the fireplace.

As she looked slowly around the room, she found signs that only a man lived there and concluded that Ralph was not married, or perhaps was widowed. All the furniture was manly and crude, and lined along the far wall were his trophies—stuffed heads of deer and every other kind of wild animal to be found in this untamed Montana Territory region.

Jolena turned quickly when a Mexican woman came into the room, wiping her hands on an apron. Her graying hair was worn in a tight bun atop her head, and her eyes were wide and smiling as she gazed from Kirk to Jolena.

"We have visitors, *sí*, Mister Ralph?" Maria Estefan said, still smiling her approval. "And isn't she the pretty one?" she said, looking Jolena slowly up and down. "Indian? Which tribe?"

Jolena had been returning the woman's smile until she had referred to her as an Indian, going as far as asking her tribe.

There was a strained silence.

Ralph quickly interceded. "Maria, this is Jolena and Kirk Edmonds from Saint Louis," he said, gesturing toward them. "They have come to search for a rare butterfly. They will be leaving on the expedition tomorrow. Don't you think you should show them the supper you've prepared for them and their associates?"

Maria squinted curiously up at Jolena from her extremely short height, but said no more as she guided them into the dining room, which was set for the evening meal. The long oak table seemed to groan under the luxuries of the country—buffalo meat and tongues, beavers' tails and marrow fat. A bottle of Madeira and an excellent port sat glistening in the light of several candles in the center of the table, and piles of bread and cheese looked tempting midst the other delicacies.

"Does it meet with your approval?" Ralph said, moving to the table and running his hand along its smooth, highly polished top.

"I wasn't even aware of being hungry until I saw this," Jolena said, laughing softly.

One by one the rest of the scientists and their assistants filed into the room. Jolena sat down beside Kirk and welcomed a cup of tea as Maria then filled a long-stemmed glass with wine. She smiled her thanks, yet was remembering the woman's question—which tribe was she from?

It ate at her insides, the not knowing.

Now, more than ever before, she had to find out her true heritage . . . her true father . . . her true people.

Somehow, some way—she would.

Her thoughts switched quickly to the handsome warrior. Perhaps he could help her discover the truths that until now were kept from her?

She tingled from head to toe to think that she had a true reason to become closer to Spotted Eagle.

Still in awe of this woman who was Indian, yet was dressed in white clothing, Spotted Eagle only went through the motions of making camp just inside the fort's walls. Everything he did he did mechanically, without thought. He could not conceive how this woman could be anyone but the daughter of Sweet Dove and Brown Elk. No one could look so like someone without being related!

He glanced at Two Ridges as he was spreading his pelts for the night close beside the fire. He found it impossible to share with Two Ridges his suspicion that Jolena was Two Ridges' half-sister.

Looking away from Two Ridges, again occupying himself with his own chores of preparing his pelts for the night, he decided that knowing who Jolena surely was would be his secret, to be savored until the time came that Jolena would be taken to meet her true people. Then Two Ridges would know.

Only then.

Spotted Eagle did not want to share Jolena with Two Ridges for any reason as yet. It was going to be difficult enough to find ways to get her away from her white brother, this man seemingly obsessed with her.

In time, this would change, he thought, smiling to himself.

The only man who would possess and be obsessed with her would be Spotted Eagle!

He took a piece of dried meat and back fat from the buckskin pouch that he had brought from his horse, sat down by the fire, and began eating slowly, his thoughts still on this woman who so resembled the woman of his past. It was bringing back many memories that made a slow ache around his heart.

Two Ridges looked guardedly over at Spotted Eagle. When he thought that his friend might be too lost in thought to notice his absence, he moved stealthily away from the campsite. He had noticed the arrival of another Blackfoot friend of another Blackfoot village making temporary camp outside the fort walls to trade his pelts on the morrow.

White Mole did anything for payment, even if it was telling a lie to add horses to his corral back at his village.

For two horses, White Mole would do most anything.

Even lying to Spotted Eagle, a most revered Blackfoot warrior!

But Two Ridges saw no other way to get the copper princess all to himself. He wanted her badly enough to try anything to have her, even if, in the end, he lost Spotted Eagle's friendship.

Hurrying anxiously, he came upon White Mole's campsite. He embraced his short, squat friend, whose eyes were strangely disfigured by a white mole above each of them. "My friend, it is good to see you again," Two Ridges said, stepping away from his friend. "Would you share a smoke with your Blackfoot neighbor?"

"*Kyi-ok-yi*, come. It will be good to share my pipe with Two Ridges," White Mole said, kneeling to reach inside his buckskin travel bag for his long-stemmed pipe.

Two Ridges sat down on White Mole's blanket as White Mole settled down beside him, stamping Indian tobacco into the bowl of the pipe. After the pipe was lit by a burning twig, they took turns drawing from the stem, then laid it aside and talked.

"You have come to White Mole for more than smoke?" White Mole asked.

"That is so," Two Ridges said stiffly, his legs crossed, his hands on each of his knees.

"You tell White Mole why," the smaller Indian said, leaning his face closer to Two Ridges.

"First I want to say that I will pay you two horses if you do as I ask," Two Ridges said, watching White Mole's thick lips form a slow smile.

"Two horses will be fine payment," White Mole said, nodding. "Tell me what to do. It is the same as done."

Two Ridges looked over his shoulder to see if Spotted Eagle had noticed where he had gone, glad to see that a row of bushes hid him from his friend's view.

He then leaned closer to White Mole. "I must say this quickly, then return to my campsite before my friend finds me with you," he said softly.

White Mole strained his neck, looking around the bushes. "You are with Spotted Eagle, I see," he said.

"Yes, as I usually am," Two Ridges said, then leaned closer again to White Mole. "My friend, there are many white people who will be leaving the fort in covered wagons tomorrow. Follow them a full day and night, then go into their camp and give this false message to Spotted Eagle— that another brave has come to you and told you to relay a message to Spotted Eagle that he must return home, that his father is ailing. By the time Spotted Eagle discovers the deceit, Two Ridges will have a chance to draw the one called Jolena into loving him. You will not be accused of the deception, because you will say a brave whose name is not known to you has told you."

"*Hai-yah!* You are deceiving your favored friend?" White Mole said, his voice filled with wonder.

"For a beautiful woman, would you not do the same?" Two Ridges said, smiling devilishly at White Mole. It was important to Two Ridges to have something to cause envy in Spotted Eagle! As he saw it, it was not fair that Spotted Eagle received so much adoration from their Blackfoot people, especially the elders, and Two Ridges so little. Two Ridges had a strong drive to change that.

White Mole returned the smile. "I will make hasty trade of my pelts at early sunrise then wait hidden for the white people to leave on wagons and will follow."

He placed a hand on Two Ridges' shoulder. "You pay me well with best horses for such a deceit?" he said, his eyes dancing.

"The best," Two Ridges said, nodding.

"*Kyi.* The deed is the same as done," White Mole said, chuckling.

Two Ridges rose quickly to his feet and made a wide circle so that, should Spotted Eagle turn and see his return to the campsite, he would not see where he had been.

But Two Ridges found quickly enough that he had nothing to fear. He reached his camp without even a sidewise glance from Spotted Eagle. Spotted Eagle was as though in a trance, his mind surely locked on the beauty of the woman of mystery, Two Ridges' copper princess!

This made Two Ridges even more determined in his private pursuit of this woman that had stolen the hearts of two friends!

Chapter Six

Comfortably full from the large meal and feeling sparkling clean from a bath, Jolena stared from the window of the bedroom that she had been assigned for the night. She hugged herself when a shiver raced across her flesh, the small dot of a campfire against the falling dusk making her think of Spotted Eagle. He was out there, making camp just inside the walls of the fort.

She could not make him out in the darkening shawl of evening, yet knew that it must be his campfire she could see flickering softly in the night in the courtyard of the fort.

Something akin to a silent bidding seemed to be calling her there, to discover why there had been an instant attraction between herself and the Blackfoot warrior. The thought of being with him day and night in the coming weeks made the pit of her stomach take on a strange churning. To imagine how it might be to be held by him, to be kissed by him, made her heart thud wildly.

And, oh, what answers might he be able to tell her about her heritage?

Could she be Blackfoot?

Could her true father be somewhere near for her to go to, to confess to him that she was his long-lost daughter?

Would she love him instantly as daughters should love fathers? Or would she feel too awkward for such a love between herself and a father she had never known?

The only father she had ever loved and embraced awaited her return in Saint Louis.

Oh, Lord, she could not let him down by loving another father perhaps even more than he!

"Sis?"

Kirk's voice drew Jolena from her thoughts. She swung around, smiling almost guiltily at Kirk, for if he had been able to read her thoughts, he would have been stunned. He would put her quickly in her place for thinking about another father, when in truth there was only one man whom she should ever call by such a name.

"Sis, I've come to have a talk with you," Kirk said, moving into the room.

He closed the door behind him and walked across the room and took Jolena's hand. He led her down onto a sofa before a blazing fire in the fireplace.

Lamplight from a lone kerosene lamp flickered soft light around the room and onto Jolena's face, making it take on an even more lovely, copper sheen. Kirk gazed at her and thought how beautiful she was in her fully-gathered cotton dress; then he frowned when his eyes shifted to the low-swept bodice of her dress, thinking that it revealed too much of the deep cleavage between her well-rounded breasts.

She already had enough men leering at her.

Yet he did not condemn her for her choice of dresses. No one else would see her tonight but himself, and tomorrow she would be wearing a plain travel skirt and blouse, hiding the inviting traits of her figure from the boisterous wagoners and . . . and the Blackfoot guide.

"You came to have a talk," Jolena said stiffly. "What about?" She feared that she already knew the answer to her question and even felt foolish asking it. He was going to talk about Spotted Eagle again. He was going to warn her once again about being too friendly to Indians. She could almost speak his exact words as they breathed across his narrow lips.

"Jolena," Kirk said, turning toward her, now holding both of her hands. "We need to set things straight about a few things—about how you are to behave in the presence of the Indian that has shown an attraction to you. Jolena, you are Indian. Not only are you Indian, you are beautiful. That is a lethal combination when it comes to being around an Indian warrior who may not yet have chosen a woman as his lifetime companion. Jolena, always keep father clear in your mind. He could not bear to lose you—especially to Indians. He has feared this all of his life. You can't make his fears real!"

Her thoughts scrambled, her loyalties toward her white father already threatened within her heart, Jolena turned her eyes away from Kirk.

She swallowed hard, feeling guilty for not being able to keep her thoughts from straying to the Blackfoot warrior.

She closed her eyes and set her jaw tightly, knowing that the battle within her was just beginning. She was wondering now if she could survive it.

How could she live between two worlds?

Until now, there had only been one, the other having been locked within the deepest recesses of her heart and soul. Coming to the Montana Territory and seeing the man of her midnight dreams had changed things the instant she had stepped on the soil of her ancestors . . . and she could not help but let things unfurl as they would and live with the decisions that she would finally make.

She was still young, with so much of her life still stretched out before her. She would choose the path that would make her the happiest and hope that she did not cause too much hurt to those she sorely loved in the process.

"Jolena, for God's sake, say something," Kirk said, placing a firm hand to her shoulder, causing her to turn her eyes quickly back to him. "Your silence is frightening me."

He searched her dark eyes for answers that she was not saying aloud to him, fear stabbing him when he saw something there that he had never seen before. At this moment, his sister seemed a stranger to him. It was as though he was looking into the eyes of an Indian instead of his precious sister's.

For too long, it seemed, he had played a game within his heart that made him forget that she was Indian instead of white. Now the reality was coming to him in leaps and bounds, and it hurt.

It hurt to think that she might be changing right before his eyes into the exact thing that he had always dreaded.

He had placed his own future aside temporarily just to prevent this from happening. But he now realized that nothing or no one could change what was true—that she was Indian and she would be feeling it, deeply within her soul, now that she was in the land of her ancestors.

He cursed himself for ever allowing her to come to the place.

But he knew deep down inside himself that she would have come alone, had he not come as her escort. She was too willful and determined once her mind was made up about something.

He also knew for certain now that finding the rare butterfly came second to her true reasons for having come to the Montana Territory.

"Kirk—dear, sweet Kirk," Jolena finally said, placing a hand to his cheek as he dropped his hand from her shoulder. "Please don't worry about me, and please don't preach to me. Although you are my older brother, please remember it is only by a few weeks. I am old enough to take care of myself, and most certainly to make my own choices in life. The Indian? Yes, I must admit I noticed his attraction to me. Please don't be threatened by that. I am sure he was intrigued to see an Indian woman who wears white woman's clothes. It's not surprising that he should wonder about an Indian woman who lives among the white people as though one of them."

"But don't you see, Jolena, you *are* one of us," Kirk pleaded. "Although you have the skin coloring of an Indian, you are in all other ways white. Please don't forget that and don't allow yourself to fantasize over finding your true people. It could inflict many hurts."

"Kirk, if your skin was copper and you had only Indian blood flowing through your veins, wouldn't you also want to know the truth of your heritage?" Jolena said, trying to reason with Kirk, yet thinking that she was truly wasting her time.

He had his mind set—as did she!

She would search for her true heritage, no matter what Kirk said. She was driven to find the answers now that she had the opportunity!

"I would hope that I would be grateful for the life that had been handed me," Kirk said bitterly. He rose from the sofa and began pacing back and forth in front of the fireplace, his hands clasped tightly behind him.

Jolena moved slowly to her feet. She placed a hand to Kirk's arm and stopped him. She gazed into his eyes with a pleading in hers. "Kirk, no one could ever be as grateful as I am for what my white father and mother did for me," she said solemnly, but was interrupted before she could finish.

Kirk yanked himself away from her, flinging a hand wildly in the air. "Did you just hear yourself?" he shouted. "Did you hear how you called father your 'white' father? Lord, Jolena, you've never said that before. He is your father in every way. How can you forget that?"

Tired of this arguing and being made to feel ashamed for her natural feelings, Jolena's eyes suddenly glittered mutinously. "Kirk, please leave," she said, her voice and jaw tight. "I would like to stop discussing these things before we say something we might regret. Just leave it be, Kirk. Do you hear? Leave it be."

"Jolena, I will say this one more time," Kirk said stubbornly. "Don't be friends with Indians. They can't be trusted."

The venom in her brother's voice made Jolena leap to the defense of Indians. She leaned into his face. "*I* am Indian, aren't I?" she said, her eyes flaring angrily. "Can't I be trusted?"

When Kirk did not respond and still stood his ground, refusing to budge, Jolena sighed heavily and walked in a huff past him.

Her fingers were trembling as she yanked the door open and began running down the narrow corridor lighted by candles flickering in wall sconces. With Kirk close on her heels, she ran on outside and across the courtyard, angry, frustrated tears blinding her from where she was actually going as Kirk began shouting at her to stop.

"Jolena!" Kirk shouted. "Yes, you are Indian, but it's not the same for you. You were raised in a civilized manner. Indians are raised as heathens!"

His words tore at Jolena's heart. Almost blinded with rage, she sobbed furiously and kept on running, then stopped suddenly when she collided with someone.

Raising her eyes, she swallowed hard and her heart raced when she found herself looking squarely up at the handsome Blackfoot warrior.

And when his hands went to her shoulder to steady her from falling from the jolt of the collision, the melting she experienced deeply within her was so sweet that she feared it.

Kirk's warnings kept flashing on and off within her mind, yet they seemed to be growing dimmer the longer she stood in awestruck silence facing Spotted Eagle.

Spotted Eagle gazed down at her when he saw her eyes all swollen and red from crying; he wanted to draw her into his tight embrace to protect her from her brother's scalding words, which Spotted Eagle had overheard.

But he did not dare cause any more turmoil between a brother and sister and quickly released her as Kirk came in a breathless rush to her side.

Staring at the Indian, Kirk reached out for Jolena and placed an arm possessively around her waist. He fought to keep his voice steady as he began ushering her back toward the fort. "Come now, sis," he said softly. "We must get you back to your room. It is best that you get to bed soon, for we will be leaving before sunrise on the morrow."

Jolena moved in a half-stumble alongside Kirk, stunned by her true feelings for Spotted Eagle. It would be hard to hide them, especially from Kirk. "Yes, I imagine you are right," she murmured. "Suddenly I am so tired."

"And must I remind you again of the true reason we are in the Montana Territory?" Kirk persisted, thinking that perhaps if he hammered it into her brain, she might finally believe it to be so. "The butterfly, Jolena. The rare butterfly. *Only* the rare butterfly."

Jolena turned soft, dark eyes to her brother. "Kirk, you can say that all you want," she murmured. "But I feel that I am here for a better purpose. I even feel as though I belong here. My dreams have drawn me here, Kirk."

"Hogwash," Kirk exclaimed loudly.

He stopped and drew her into his gentle embrace. "I'm so sorry for battling with you about so many things," he said softly. "And I admit that I was a bit rash in my remarks about the Indians. I apologize."

"I understand why you did it, and I accept your apology," Jolena said.

Over Kirk's shoulder she was watching Spotted Eagle as he moved to his haunches beside his campfire. Just the sight of him caused her heart to race. She was filled with anticipation for the coming days, when she would come to know Spotted Eagle better.

She closed her eyes, envisioning him holding and kissing her, wishing it to be true, soon. . . .

Spotted Eagle stared into the flames of the fire, yet did not see it. He was still too caught up in feelings for this woman who had suddenly entered his life like wildfire rushing through his blood to see anything but her image everywhere he looked!

It was not like him to allow a woman to rule his every thought.

Until today he had allowed but one woman to enter his heart, and she was long gone from him.

He had put the importance of learning everything that he would need when he was called to rule his people, as their powerful chief, above all else. He had listened well to his father's instructions about the requirements of being chief.

His father was not a well man, having mourned the death of Spotted Eagle's mother for too long now, so that he had begun ailing himself, and Spotted Eagle feared that it was more from a broken heart than anything else physical. This also had made Spotted Eagle shy away from allowing another woman inside his heart. He did not want to ever feel the same pain again that he and his father had felt over the loss of a woman.

There were many things in life to enjoy besides women!

Yet Spotted Eagle could not grasp exactly what, now that he had met the woman called Jolena.

"She has drawn you inside yourself, has she not?" Two Ridges said, suddenly breaking Spotted Eagle's train of thought. "She is this special to you?"

"The woman who has arrived with the white people on the large river canoe?" Spotted Eagle said, looking guardedly back at Two Ridges. "She is nothing to me. Nothing."

"Then your thoughts are on the travel ahead?" Two Ridges said, grinning smugly, knowing that his friend was not speaking the full truth to him. Yet he did not want to pursue further conversation about it when he had his own hidden thoughts and desires regarding the copper princess. "You think perhaps of having to fight off Cree renegades, especially the one called Long Nose, while protecting these people who know little of the dangers the Cree impose upon them?"

"Long Nose will dare not pursue a confrontation with the white people when he sees who guides them through the wilderness," Spotted Eagle said. "He understands that he will incur the wrath of this Blackfoot, whose warriors number three times those of the Cree. He learned long ago not to interfere in Spotted Eagle's life. My father taught me well the art of warring when it is required against those whose heart is dark."

"That is so," Two Ridges said, nodding. "You are respected far and wide. It is with the same admiration that this friend respects you and will humbly ride with you while guiding the white people on their search for the rare butterfly.

"The white woman," Two Ridges dared to say, having realized that his friend did not want to speak about her to him. "She is most beautiful, is she not? And it was strange how you acted as though you had seen her before."

Spotted Eagle's shoulders tensed as he looked away from Two Ridges, gazing toward the large cabin where he knew that Jolena was perhaps even now undressing for bed. Ah, but if he were only there, to touch her, to kiss her, to tell her that she had always been his.

Two Ridges stared at Spotted Eagle, hurt that he was ignoring him again. He set his lips tightly together and narrowed his eyes, feeling that this friend would one day show his annoyance one time too often.

Two Ridges looked away from Spotted Eagle, who was again glaring into the fire. He was beginning to sorely resent this behavior of his friend!

He would show him.

Chapter Seven

The bright sunrise and scurrying clouds were accompanied by a brisk wind. Several covered wagons pulled by mules were lumbering along this land that was a wilderness of wooded slopes, flowing mountains, and meadows. Streams tumbled over waterfalls. Blue lakes lay in peaceful valleys. Wild sage, balsam root, and wild larkspur spotted the land with their brilliant colors.

Spotted Eagle rode straight in his Indian saddle ahead of the wagons, Two Ridges faithfully at his side. Spotted Eagle shifted his eyes heavenward, feeling the effects of the Sun God shining brightly overhead as his buckskin clothes clung damply to him like a second skin.

Then Spotted Eagle took a look over his shoulder at Jolena as she wiped perspiration from her brow with a lacy handkerchief. Her brother handled the reins of their wagon, while experienced wagoners were at the controls of the other land vessels.

He frowned, recalling the bold, boisterousness of the wagoners, having seen them tease and flirt with Jolena more than once when the convoy stopped to allow their mules to drink from the streams and to give the men and women of this expedition time to eat and drink and to find private moments behind the tallest bushes before boarding their wagons again.

Not only had Spotted Eagle found the attention of the wagnoners to Jolena annoying, but he had watched Kirk's reaction, which was near the exploding point.

Spotted Eagle moved his eyes from Jolena and returned to watching for anything that might signal that the Cree were near. He smiled at the idea of Kirk trying to defend his sister against the large and bulky wagoners. It was obvious to Spotted Eagle that Kirk was not a man of muscle and would not be able to fight off his offenders if ever he tried. It would be up to Spotted Eagle to prove to Jolena who was the strongest of those who fought, hopefully causing her admiration to blossom into something more than what it might be now.

Spotted Eagle nudged the flanks of his stallion with his heels and rode off in a stronger lope, wanting to find a campsite quickly for this first night out from Fort Chance.

Jolena was uneasy on the hard wooden seat

beside her brother. It was not altogether the heat that troubled her, but something else, as though she had just felt a silent bidding from someone.

Her heart raced, looking ahead at Spotted Eagle. Only moments ago he had given her a quick glance, but it had been long enough for her to see that same inquisitive look as before, as though he saw her as someone he had known in his past. She would never forget the first time he had looked at her, when he had reacted as though he had seen a ghost.

Whose, she wondered?

Who could she look like that he knew?

This gave her cause to hope that it had something to do with her true Indian family. If she resembled one of them, then perhaps she was not all that far, indeed, from the truth of her heritage!

Squirming again to get more comfortable on the seat, the sun pouring its heat down upon her, Jolena tried to focus her thoughts elsewhere, to pass the time until they stopped to make camp.

She was anxious for tonight.

She wanted to find a way to be with Spotted Eagle, alone, to try to make her midnight dreams and daytime fantasies come true.

After Kirk was asleep, she would go to Spotted Eagle. He was surely the reason she was feeling this silent, strange sort of bidding. She felt that it could come from no other than he whose heart was crying out to her.

Jolena gave Kirk a steady stare. He was stonily silent, his jaw tight, after having had another confrontation with the brash wagoners the last time they had stopped to stretch their legs and to eat. She wanted to reach over and pat his knee and thank him for coming to her rescue, but she held her hand at bay. She did not want to encourage these confrontations and bouts of chivalry over a sister. She knew what his reaction would be if he ever caught her talking with Spotted Eagle. If he knew the deep feelings that she already had for Spotted Eagle, he would explode into a rage that no one would want to witness—especially Jolena!

She turned her eyes and thoughts away from her brother, now watching around her again for butterflies, but disappointed anew. Even though it was a warm and sunny day and flowers dotted the land, all the butterflies had been elusive today. She hadn't spotted any, especially the *euphaedra,* with its turquoise, black and orange coloring, and a streak of pink on its wings.

But what was lovely to look at was this glorious country where nature had reared great mountains and spread out broad prairies. Along the western horizon, the Rocky Mountains lifted their peaks above the clouds. Here and there lay minor ranges, black with pine forests. In the distance they were mere gray silhouettes against a sky of blue.

Between these mountain ranges everywhere lay the great prairie, the silver gray of the wormwood lending a dreariness to the landscape. At intervals the land was marked with green, winding river valleys, and it was gashed everywhere with deep ravines, their sides painted in strange colors of red and gray and brown. Their perpendicular walls were crowned with fantastic columns and figures of stone or clay, carved out by the winds and the rains of ages.

Here and there, rising out of the plain, were sharp ridges and square-topped buttes with vertical sides. They were sometimes bare, and sometimes dotted with pines—short, sturdy trees whose gnarled trunks and thick, knotted branches had been twisted into curious forms by the winds which blew unceasingly through gorges and coulees.

An occasional herd of buffalo or antelope was sighted, and along the wooded river valleys and on the pine-clad slopes of the mountains, elk, deer, and wild sheep fed in great numbers.

The scorching breath of early summer stirred the tall, weaving stems of the buffalo grass. Jolena had been told that there were all kinds of roots and berries growing in abundance in this land of sky, sun, prairie, and mountains—wild carrots, wild turnips, sweet-root, bitter-root, bull berries, cherries, and plums among them.

Thinking of this wilderness food made her gaze up at Spotted Eagle again, thinking that surely the women of his village were kept busy searching for these different foodstuffs.

She closed her eyes, momentarily envisioning herself among such women, dressed as they were in soft doeskins, with perhaps a touch of blood-root on her cheeks to liven up her color for the man she loved, for the man she would take her basket of berries and roots home to. He would enjoy the fruits of her labor, then take her to his bed and pay her in the way husbands everywhere showed their gratitude to their wives.

Feeling the slowing of the covered wagon in the way the seat swayed and shook beneath her, Jolena's eyes flew open. She looked questioningly over at Kirk as he drew a tight rein when Spotted Eagle came riding toward their wagon, which was the first in the expedition.

Spotted Eagle drew a tight rein beside the wagon on Kirk's side, and when he talked, it was to Kirk; yet his eyes were on Jolena all the while, sending a sensual thrill through her heart.

Jolena clasped her trembling fingers to the seat and smiled nervously back at Spotted Eagle, his nearness filling her insides with something strangely sweet and foreign to her. Each time their eyes met, she knew that he was speaking to her without words.

And she knew that he could tell by her response to his eyes that she was answering him in kind.

Soon they would be able to speak aloud to one another, and she wondered what he would say to her first, and how she might respond to him without revealing her heartfelt feelings for him.

"We will camp here for the night," Spotted Eagle was saying to Kirk. "There is water for drinking. There are many cottonwood trees. They give us shade for setting up camp. Also horses and mules like to eat the bark of these trees. It is good for them. The grass here is young and healthy also for the animals."

Kirk glanced from Jolena to Spotted Eagle, another warning shooting through him when he saw again how her sister and this guide were attracted to one another. He hoped that Jolena's attraction was only because of her heritage and her burning questions about it.

He hoped that the Indian warrior's questions were only because he could not understand why a woman with copper skin was called Kirk's sister, or why she mingled with the white people, as though one of them.

Hopefully, once Spotted Eagle's curiosity was abated, he would place his thoughts on other matters.

Kirk silently prayed to himself that this would be soon, for he feared these feelings that might grow between Jolena and Spotted Eagle.

"Whatever you say, Spotted Eagle," Kirk said, nodding. "If you think this is a safe place, then who's to argue about it?"

Kirk gazed around him at the seclusion of this valley in which they would be making their first camp away from civilization. He could not deny that part of him that was afraid. Yet he had to continue looking brave in Jolena's eyes, especially in front of Spotted Eagle.

Kirk did not want the Indian to take over as his sister's protector!

Everyone left their wagons and worked together gathering wood for a fire, and just as flames were leaping around heavy logs, the afternoon was fading into shifting shadows. A haze of heat settled over the valley as the sun set into a purple cradle of clouds on the horizon.

Spotted Eagle and Two Ridges made a silent kill with their bows and arrows, and soon meat was dripping its tantalizing juices into the flames of the campfire.

Billy, one of the wagoners, the most burly and outspoken of them all, with a thick sprouting of whiskers on his craggy face, lifted a coffee pot from the hot coals at the edge of the fire. After he poured himself a cup, he held the coffee pot toward Jolena, where she sat silently beside her brother, nibbling on a small portion of the roasted meat.

"Hey, pretty thing, are you hungerin' for somethin' to drink, or someone to cozy up with?" Billy asked, his pale blue eyes raking over Jolena. "If I covered you with my body, you'd sure as hell not need a blanket."

The other wagoners chuckled as they peered at Jolena, their eyes revealing that their thoughts were anything but decent.

"Well?" Billy persisted. "How's about it? Cat got your tongue? Or do you think you're too good for ol' Billy? Let me tell you, pretty thing, there's more fire in this here man than ten other men combined. I'll show you just what lovin' is all about."

Jolena's face grew hot with an angry blush, and her heart pounded with embarrassment. She gasped and grew cold inside when Kirk slammed his coffee cup down on the ground, splashing it empty, and rose to his full height over the wagoner.

"You've been hired to drive the wagons, not insult my sister," Kirk said, doubling his hands into tight fists at his sides. "You apologize or . . ."

Billy tossed the coffee pot and his cup to the ground and pushed himself up to his full height, towering over Kirk at six-feet and four-inches. He leaned his craggy face down into Kirk's clean-shaven face. "Do you want to say all of that again?" he dared. "I ain't one to apologize, especially to a squirt like you. I'd quickly make mincemeat outta you. Want to give it a try?"

"I ask for no fight, just for you to leave my sister alone," Kirk said, swallowing hard as he gazed up into eyes of fire, and onto shoulders twice the size of his. "Now let's just forget about all of this and resume our supper. We've many more days to have to be around one another. Let us make the best of it."

Billy would not let up. Leering, he leaned even closer to Kirk's face. "That's fine with me," he snarled. "I don't see what the fuss is about anyhow. She ain't no sister of yours. She's nothin' more than an Indian squaw dressed in white woman's clothes. Why, as I sees it, she ain't nothin' but a redskin savage."

Gasps wafted through the scientists who had been watching with bated breath.

Jolena stiffened when she saw a quick anger leap not only into her brother's eyes, but also

Spotted Eagle's. Spotted Eagle looked as though he was ready to pounce on the wagoner, yet Kirk beat him to it.

Jolena took a quick step back and covered a scream behind her hand when Kirk hit the wagoner in the chin with a doubled fist, knocking Billy off balance. When Billy stumbled backward and fell to the ground, Kirk was quickly atop him, hitting him again and again.

Then when Kirk started to rise away from Billy, thinking that he had gotten the best of him, Billy grabbed a knife from his waistband and started to raise it for a death plunge in Kirk's back.

But Spotted Eagle saw the danger. He ran to the wagoner and kicked the knife from his hand, then helped Kirk up and away from him.

Kirk stepped aside as Spotted Eagle reached down and grabbed Billy's shirt just beneath the chin and bunched it up between his fingers. Yanking on the shirt, he soon had Billy on his feet again, blood streaming from both his nose and mouth.

"I think you do not listen well," Spotted Eagle said in a low, threatening grumble as he stood eye to eye with Billy. "You were told to mind your business. That is good advice. Soon we will be entering Cree territory and all hands and guns will be needed if the Cree decide to attack."

Billy reached a hand up and wiped the salty blood away from his lips, then stumbled backward when Spotted Eagle released his hold on him.

Spotted Eagle followed Billy's retreat. "And

white man, I believe you forgot to apologize to the woman," he said, his teeth clenched. "She is no squaw. She is no savage. Let me hear you tell her that she is neither."

Billy growled something down deep inside his throat, then turned to Jolena. "Sorry, ma'am," he said, then slouched back to the fire and sat down, his shoulders slumped.

As everyone resumed eating the evening meal, Jolena was hardly able to keep her eyes off Spotted Eagle, who had turned away from her too soon for her to thank him for what he had done in her defense.

She glanced at Kirk, thinking that it was perhaps best that she hadn't thanked Spotted Eagle for anything. She could tell that his pride had already been injured, in that he had been outdone by the Blackfoot guide.

The rest of the evening meal was completed in silence. Everyone then retreated to their own bedrolls or small tents. Jolena watched Kirk crawl into his tiny cubicle of a tent, and she soon heard her brother's familiar snores.

She smiled to herself, glad that some things had not changed. In the own privacy of her small tent, where blankets were spread warm across the ground, she made her entries in her journals, then laid them aside and stretched out on the blankets. She closed her eyes and pretended that she was back home in her room and that she had not yet been faced with problems of identities and whether or not it was meant for her to be a part of the white world—or the red.

The sound of movement outside caused her eyes to blink quickly open. She scarcely breathed, wondering who was stirring around outside, when only moments ago it seemed that everyone was asleep for the night.

Too curious not to see who it was, Jolena threw her blankets aside and crawled to the tiny opening of her tent. Her breath seemed suddenly lodged in her throat and her heart skipped a beat as she watched Spotted Eagle leave the campsite carrying a large bow, a quiver of arrows at his back. With an anxious heartbeat, she watched Spotted Eagle until he became hidden in the shadows of night.

Without further thought, she scrambled from her tent and began following him.

Chapter Eight

Cicadas vibrated their wings and made loud buzzing sounds on all sides of Jolena as she crept along beneath the trees, the cicadas' song drowning out the rustling of the cottonwood leaves overhead as a brisk wind blew through them.

Fear made Jolena's throat dry, for she had yet to see Spotted Eagle. She was even beginning to think that she should turn back, to return to the safety of the camp.

Then the spill of the moon's light revealed Spotted Eagle's muscled body through a break in the trees, where he was sitting beside the river, seemingly in deep thought.

Jolena's pulse began to race, wondering if Spotted Eagle could possibly be thinking about her. Could he have wished her there?

She felt foolish for allowing her fantasies to continue causing her to believe the impossible. Just because she had experienced strange, sensual dreams about an Indian, she could not keep allowing herself to believe that this Blackfoot warrior was, indeed, the man of her dreams. That was not possible, and she must stop thinking that it was!

Yet she could not help walking toward the Blackfoot, her heart pounding harder with each step she took closer to him. She knew that she should not be acting like a loose woman, actually seeking out the company of a man—and not *any* man, a handsome Indian warrior!

But nothing less than a bolt of lightning striking her dead would prevent her from going to Spotted Eagle, to talk and to . . .

Jolena's face flooded with color as she stopped her thoughts, feeling shameful for once again allowing herself to think such things about Spotted Eagle. She must gain control of her thoughts and her desires, for he was now only a heartbeat away as she stepped out into the spill of the moonlight. Not far away, where the horses were reined upstream, they whinnied softly.

She jumped when Spotted Eagle sprang suddenly to his feet, an arrow already drawn from its quiver as he turned quickly on a heel, his lips parting and his eyes widening when he found Jolena standing there frozen, it seemed, to the ground as she gazed with startled eyes up at him.

Spotted Eagle easily slipped his arrow back

into its quiver and bent and laid the large bow on the ground beside him, his eyes never leaving Jolena. His heart thundered wildly against his ribs, finding her even more intriguingly beautiful beneath the play of the moonlight. He gazed at the magnificent lines of her body as the wind pressed her skirt and blouse tightly against it, then watched the wind pushing the dark cloud of her hair back from the finely cut lines of her face. He desired her as he had never desired any other woman, except when he was a boy with the desires of a man for a woman twice his age.

He was that boy again, desiring a woman no less than then, and perhaps even more. He had to fight back speaking Sweet Dove's name, for surely the Gods had sent her back to him, to love with a man's heart and a man's body.

Jolena could feel his eyes on her, as though he were branding her as his, and blushed beneath the close scrutiny. Yet she did not look away from him with lowered eyes. She held her chin high and squared her shoulders even more, which made the magnificent swell of her breasts even more pronounced.

"I did not mean to disturb your moments alone," Jolena finally said, her words seeming to come in a mad rush—as mad as the beat of her heart over being this close to Spotted Eagle and to be silently admired by him. "If you want me to, I can turn back and return to the camp."

Spotted Eagle said nothing for a moment, then drew himself out of his reverie and reached a hand out to Jolena. "No, do not return to the camp unescorted," he said, giving her a scolding look as he frowned. "You were foolish to come this far alone." He reached out a hand to her. "But now that you are here, *ok-yi*, come. Sit beside me. The night is warm. The moon and stars speak gently from the sky to me. Enjoy them with me."

"Thank you. I would love to," Jolena said, her knees weak at the thought of taking his hand.

When she reached her hand to his and his flesh met hers as he circled his fingers around hers and drew her on toward him, Jolena's breath was sucked away and drawn deep down inside her, causing her to sway from lightheadedness. She swallowed hard and steadied herself, then moved toward him.

Her knees trembled as he helped her down onto the warm grass beside him, regretting it when he released her hand.

Jolena could not keep her eyes off his uncovered chest. She had never seen such muscles, and he was bare of hair, unlike her white brother and father, whose chests were covered with featherings of golden hair.

Beneath the light of the moon, the sleekness of Spotted Eagle's copper skin was very tempting. Yet she was not daring enough to place a hand there, to feel how it might resemble her own when, at age six, she had stood in front of a mirror and had run a hand over her body, wondering why it was different in coloring than her playmates'.

She had then discovered how smooth and soft

her copper skin was and took pride from that time on that it was of that color and texture.

"You followed Spotted Eagle to river," he said, yet not looking at her. "That was foolish. Many creatures stalk at night."

Jolena felt awkward, knowing that to reveal the truth to him was to open her soul and heart to him. Instead, she said something else, hoping that might satisfy him, at least for the moment. "I could not go to sleep," she said softly. "I, too, followed the path of the moon to the river." Then she told a lie that she thought was needed. "I had no idea you were here. Again, I'm sorry if I've become a bother to you. Just say the word and I'll leave."

Spotted Eagle quickly looked her way. "You will leave when I leave," he said. "My weapons will protect you."

Jolena was surprised that he was being so talkative with her. All day, in the presence of everyone else, he had been grave, silent, and reserved.

She was glad that he was more open with her. She so badly wanted to question him about what there was about her that was familiar to him, and then tell him about her dreams and what they might have foretold.

She also wanted to prod him for answers to her questions about the Indians in this area, about whether or not he knew of a father whose child had been lost to him eighteen years ago.

But now that she was here, the opportunity staring her in the face, she could not find the words to ask him anything. If he was from her tribe, then she would want to be taken to his village to meet her true people.

Perhaps even her true father.

Then she might never want to return to Saint Louis, to the man who had raised her with much love and warmth. She felt a keen devotion to Bryce Edmonds.

"Whenever you wish to return to the camp, I would be grateful for whatever protection you lend me as I accompany you there," Jolena said, nervously drawing her legs up before her and circling her arms around them to hold her skirt in place.

Spotted Eagle gazed at her, smiled, and nodded. As their eyes locked in an unspoken understanding, he was reminded of the many questions that he wanted to ask her, yet at the same time he saw no need to ask her why she had been raised as white, for he believed he already knew the answer. He would wait for the perfect time to tell her.

When he knew that her heart belonged solely to him, then he would tell her. . . .

"You like stars and I like butterflies," Jolena said, laughing awkwardly as she wrenched her eyes from his, feeling the danger in his hypnotic stare. She could feel herself being pulled deeper and deeper into the mystique of this man, her very soul crying out to be held by him.

She wanted to experience everything with him. She wanted to share her deepest feelings and emotions with him, if he would allow it.

For now, she must make small talk only.

She must move slowly into this true knowing of him and his people. She did not want to regret later something that she might do now because of the sensual lethargy that she was experiencing at his nearness.

She wanted it to be totally right when she moved into his arms and allowed him to teach her the true meaning of being a woman. . . .

"You seek a special butterfly," Spotted Eagle said softly. "I have seen it. Soon I hope you will also see its loveliness."

He was glad to be drawn into small talk, knowing that this would delay what he so badly wanted to do. He had waited a lifetime for her, and it was hard not to hold her and tell her that she was already everything to him without even that first kiss.

In time, he thought to himself.

In time, the moment would be right for him to draw her into his arms, to kiss . . . to hold . . . and to claim her totally as his.

For now, he would just enjoy being with her, absorbing her every move, her every word, her every smile.

All of these things pleasured him more than he would have imagined a woman could affect him ever again.

But she was not just any woman. She was the mirror image of Sweet Dove.

She was Sweet Dove's daughter.

"I hope you are right," Jolena said, giving him a sweet smile, then turning her eyes away from him again when she felt him looking at her as though she were something precious. "And I do thank you for notifying those at the fort that you sighted the *euphaedra*. I enjoy watching and studying the interesting life cycle of butterflies. It was my father's deepest desire long ago to find the rare, elusive butterfly. I hope to fulfill his dream by taking it home to him for his collection."

"Collection?" Spotted Eagle said, drawing Jolena's eyes back to him by the guarded way he had said the word. "How do you mean ... collection? Ralph spoke of this at the fort. I did not understand then. I do not understand now. I thought you were coming only to study the butterfly, to take your knowledge back to the white people who learn and teach about such things as that."

Jolena nodded. "I *will* take my knowledge of this butterfly back with me, but I will also take a specimen," she explained. "My father must see the butterfly to fully appreciate its loveliness. One cannot tell someone something is lovely and express it in a way that this person can see it as the one who sees it firsthand. If I find the rare butterfly and catch it, I will be taking it to my ailing father. That is my purpose for being here."

"Ailing?" Spotted Eagle said, raising an eyebrow. "Your white father is not well?"

Jolena's pulse began to race as she noted his reference to her white father. Obviously, he was aware that her true father was someone other than Bryce Edmonds.

She looked away from Spotted Eagle, thinking

this would be the wrong time to delve into those questions that she so badly wanted answered.

Later.

Later when they were drawn together with more ease and understanding.

"My father is not well at all," she murmured, tears burning the corners of her eyes as she saw her father in her mind's eye. "His legs are paralyzed. He is also weakening generally. I fear terribly for him. I must find the rare butterfly before . . . before . . ."

She could not help the deep sob that leapt from her throat at the thought of her father dying before she could see him again.

Embarrassed for allowing her emotions to get so out of hand so quickly in the presence of this man whose face had so often filled her midnight dreams, she stumbled to her feet.

"I must return to my tent," she said, wiping the salty tears from her lips. "I've stayed much too long as it is."

She started to run away but was stopped abruptly by a firm grip on her wrist. Her knees weakened, and her heart seemed to stand still for a moment. She turned slowly around and gazed up into Spotted Eagle's dark eyes as they stood facing each other in the moonlight, her heart now racing out of control.

"Why did you stop me?" Jolena asked, breathless from the tumultuous emotions swimming through her.

"Did I not tell you that I would escort you back to the camp?"

Jolena smiled softly up at him. "I guess I forgot," she murmured. She glanced down at his fingers still circled around her wrist, then up into his midnight-dark eyes again. "You can unhand me now. I don't need any further reminding."

Spotted Eagle's heart throbbed and his eyes raked over her as he still held her by the wrist and drew her slowly toward him.

"Stay with me tonight by the river," he said, the words rushing across his lips without even any conscious forethought. "You are lovely, so very lovely. Let me hold you. Let me kiss you."

Stunned and thrilled at the same moment by his sudden decision to bring more into their relationship than mere talk of butterflies and stars, Jolena felt dizzied from the passion his suggestion evoked within her. She folded without hesitation into his arms. They kissed dazedly, his arms nudging her closer.

A noise from somewhere close by drew them quickly apart. When a black panther appeared at the edge of the clearing, its green eyes glinting in the moonlight, Jolena became frightened and darted off in the opposite direction.

The panther bounded after Jolena, as Spotted Eagle stood numb at the sight. . . .

Chapter Nine

Her knees too weak to run any longer, Jolena turned around and stared with a throbbing heart at the panther, which also stopped, crouching, its eyes glaring at her. Too frightened to look past the panther to see what Spotted Eagle was doing, Jolena stood frozen on the spot, her screams seemingly frozen in the depths of her throat.

As the panther began slinking toward Jolena on its belly and four paws, Spotted Eagle acted swiftly. He notched an arrow onto his bow, and just as the panther's great mouth opened with a roar and it leapt suddenly at Jolena, Spotted Eagle sent an arrow flying through the air.

Jolena felt faint as she watched the panther leap toward her, then gasped when a whistling arrow pierced the sleek fur of the cat's back.

She covered her mouth with her hands and stood wild-eyed as she watched the panther fall to the ground on its side, howling in rage, then spring to its feet and leap at her again.

Spotted Eagle had already notched his arrow on his bow a second time and this time made a more accurate aim, sending his arrow into the heart of the animal.

A momentary feeling of unreality swam through Jolena's dizzied head, as though the whole thing had never happened.

Then she seemed to come out of her frozen reverie when she saw Spotted Eagle throw his bow aside and begin running toward her.

Feeling so much more than simple gratitude for Spotted Eagle, Jolena began running toward him. When she reached him, she flung herself into his embrace, clinging to him with all of her might, sobbing.

Her nightmarish experience fled from her mind, and her wonderful dreams came to life as their lips met and they were suddenly kissing passionately, reveling in feelings long denied them.

Spotted Eagle's lips trembled into Jolena's as he felt her body soften in his arms, her lips warm and sensual against his. In his heart she had always been his, but tonight it was all too real—the way he held her, the kiss, the shared passion.

Soon Spotted Eagle had swept her up into his arms and was carrying her away from the death scene. When they reached a place of moonlight and shadows, far from the camp and the dead animal, he placed Jolena on her feet.

Again he drew her into his embrace and kissed her, the air seeming to quiver with the intensity of their feelings for one another.

Jolena gasped with a dizzying pleasure when Spotted Eagle slid his hands under her blouse and felt the warm weight of her breasts. Her insides melted as he caressed her breasts, hardly even aware that he was leaning over her, gently laying her on the ground.

The grass now a soft cushion beneath her, Jolena closed her eyes and enjoyed and accepted the feel of one of Spotted Eagle's warm hands as he crept it beneath her skirt. She trembled as he slid his fingers slowly upward, setting small fires everywhere his flesh touched hers.

He kissed her gasp of surprise away when he lowered her undergarment, then slipped completely away from her and tossed it aside. She lay perfectly still, scarcely breathing, filled with the wonder of these rapturous feelings that were overwhelming her as once again his fingers crept up her leg, then cupped the soft, downy patch of hair at the juncture of her thighs.

Jolena's heart raced, and she trembled with an acute pleasure when his fingers began skillfully caressing the center of her passion. Jolena had never been aware that this part of her anatomy could give her such pleasure. In her midnight dreams of this handsome Indian, she had felt strangely hot and wet where he was now touching and caressing her, but never had she explored these feelings with her own fingers. When she had awakened, the heat and the wetness had been gone, only a part of her sensual dreams and fantasies.

But now the wonderful feelings were building into something sweet, almost unimaginable in the keen pleasure they roused.

Her breath came in short gasps, and then she lurched and opened her eyes wildly when one of his fingers was suddenly thrust inside her, causing her a momentary, brief sense of pain, where she had only moments ago been feeling such pleasure.

Spotted Eagle drew his lips away, yet he did not offer to withdraw his finger.

"You are a virgin," Spotted Eagle whispered. "Do you still wish to be? Or does your heart cry out to know the feelings of a woman?"

Her heart was throbbing so that Jolena could hardly think. The longer his finger remained where her heart seemed to be centered, moving softly within her, awakening new desires throughout her, she did not know what to say or how to react to the delicious lethargy he was causing within her heart and mind.

Spotted Eagle seemed to understand her silence. She was new to this world of sensuality, and not to disappoint her, he crushed her lips with a fiery kiss, his full hand now caressing her love mound which had grown moist against his palm.

Having hungered for her so long, Spotted

Eagle was finding it hard to control his own wild desires.

But he could not rush this fierce hunger that was eating away at him, spreading, spreading . . .

He wanted Jolena to feel every aspect of the ecstasy that he was feeding her. And by the way she was returning his kiss and was clinging to him, he knew that she wished for more of the same.

Close to the height of euphoria that he was seeking, yet finding it dangerous to bring it to the surface with Jolena too soon, Spotted Eagle leaned away from her. Without further words or questions as to whether or not she wished for the same as he—for he already knew the answers by the way she responded to his foreplay—he placed his fingers at the hem of her blouse and slowly lifted it away from her and over her head.

As the moonlight shimmered along the soft and smooth contours of her body, his eyes traced the shape of her firm young breasts. He could not help himself. He leaned down over her and enfolded one of her breasts between his hands and flicked his tongue over its nipple.

His insides quavered; he had never touched or tasted anything as soft and sweet.

He moved his hands to her other breast and did the same there, aware that she was enjoying this by the way she moaned sweetly, then reached a hand to the back of his head and twined her fingers through his hair.

Jolena felt as though she were floating, and all doubts of whether she should allow all of this to happen were washed away as though on moonbeams soaring through space. She closed her eyes and tossed her head slowly back and forth, thrilled that he loved her so much already, as she had known that she loved him just as quickly.

They were becoming as one.

Whether or not it should be happening, she knew that all of their tomorrows were now linked, forever and ever.

She smiled secretly at this thought and relaxed, the anticipation of what else was to transpire tonight between them before the lovemaking was complete causing a headiness to claim her.

So caught up in her feelings was she that Jolena seemed hardly aware of when Spotted Eagle had fully unclothed her and was unclothed himself. As he stood over her to toss his final piece of clothing aside, she gazed up at him, admiring his wide shoulders, muscled chest, and the lean lines of his torso.

Her pulse raced as her gaze lowered and she saw the magnificence of his manhood. Although a part of her feared it, since he was so well proportioned, she reached her arms out to him, sighing as he came to her, wrapping her in the warmth of his body.

Spotted Eagle's eyes swept over her face with a silent, urgent message; then he held it within

his hands and kissed her with a fierce, possess-
ive heat.

Jolena gave herself up to the rapture. When
one of his hands slipped down and covered a
breast, rolling her nipple with his fingers, soft
moans repeatedly surfaced from inside her.

She kissed him with quavering lips and clung
to him, her pulse racing maddeningly as she
felt his throbbing manhood as it began probing
at the center of her desire.

As though practiced, yet truly from instinct
instilled in a woman from the time Eve lured
Adam into her arms in the garden of Eden, she
spread her legs, opening herself more widely to
him, an open invitation for him to do what he
pleased, and what she now hungered for.

When he thrust himself deeply inside her,
Jolena whimpered against his lips with pain.
But the pain was soon replaced with something
wonderfully sweet and sensual. She drew a ragged breath as a raging hunger swept through
her.

Spotted Eagle slipped his mouth down from
her lips and showered her breasts with feathery
kisses. His heart hammered wildly within his
chest, his body growing more feverish as the
pleasure mounted.

His hands moved down her body until they
were cupping her buttocks in a sensual ecstasy of their own. He forced her hips in at his,
crushing her against him, her buttocks smooth
and as soft as cotton as she strained into him.

Their naked flesh was fused. It was flesh

against flesh in gentle pressure.

Again he kissed her. He touched his tongue to hers, aflame with longing. Desire washed over him.

Then he paused and leaned only a fraction away from her. He reached his hands to her hair and smoothed it away from her face. He gazed into her eyes, feeling as though he were looking into her soul, and he experienced something that he had never felt before with other women. It was as though this woman was an extension of himself, as though they were of one heartbeat, even of one soul.

"I love you," Spotted Eagle said softly, sending soft butterfly kisses across Jolena's parted lips. "I shall always love you."

He paused, looked into her eyes again, then said, "I have always loved you."

Jolena was startled by this confession, knowing that she could say the same words to him, and they would be true. Somehow, they had been soul mates even before they met eye to eye, and had loved, cheek to cheek.

She placed a gentle hand to his face. "I have also always loved you," she whispered, then shuddered with pleasure when he swept her fully into his arms again and gave her an all-consuming kiss.

Lost forever to this man, she kissed him back passionately, locking her legs around him as he rose over her and plunged himself deeply inside her. She strained her body upward, meeting his eager thrusts, feeling his heartbeat against her own as he held her within his powerful arms.

And then he released her and crawled on his knees around her, soon placing himself in a position that gave her access to him in a way that made her heart seem to stop and her throat grow dry, understanding his silent bidding as he moved himself closer to her mouth.

Wanting to reciprocate in this sort of loving, since he had already unselfishly pleasured her so wonderfully, she first ran her fingers up and down his throbbing shaft, then touched the tip of his hardness with her tongue, his sensual moan revealing to her just how much he enjoyed this way of being loved.

Getting herself in a comfortable position, she cupped him within her hand and led him to her lips once again. She swept her tongue around him, over and over again, then took him into her mouth. She could feel his body stiffen, then quaver with pleasure.

But soon he urged her away from him and led her to another new way of lovemaking. He urged her to her knees and soon entered her from behind, magnificently filling her where she so unmercifully throbbed for completion.

She closed her eyes and held her head back, awaiting that moment of release, knowing that it was near.

Her whole body seemed an extension of her heart, throbbing . . . throbbing . . . throbbing. . . .

And then once again they reached that higher plateau of pleasure that rocked and shook them, as though the earth was shaking beneath them.

Exhausted, they fell apart and lay beside one another on the grass.

"I've never felt as alive," Jolena said, sighing as she gazed lovingly at Spotted Eagle. "Yet what we did, making love in those strange ways? I cannot think it was proper. What came over me? Why did I allow it?"

Spotted Eagle placed his hand at her waist and drew her against him, her breasts crushing into his chest. "What you did was proper," he told her, "because it was done out of love. I will cherish these moments. So should you."

She leaned her cheek against his chest. "Oh, how I want to," she murmured. "It was pure heaven, Spotted Eagle, being with you. I've never felt so free, yet so possessed. How could that be?"

"Loving fiercely is a combination of the two," Spotted Eagle explained. "When you love, your emotions run free, yet your body becomes possessed by the one who loves you. Let that not frighten you. I welcome being possessed by you. You fill the void left in my life many years ago. I will never be lonely again, not while I have you."

"I feel so many things," Jolena said, clinging to him, loving him so. "But most of all, I feel an intense happiness. Hold me, Spotted Eagle. Hold me tightly. I never want to leave you. Never."

He cradled her close, his eyes closed to the

past, thinking now only of the future and this woman who had awakened him again to loving.

Two Ridges awakened and found Spotted Eagle gone. He scurried from his blankets and went to Jolena's tent. He sucked in a wild breath when he found it empty.

Almost tripping over his feet, he turned and looked in all directions, wondering which would lead him to Spotted Eagle and Jolena. He wanted to get there before they could make love.

He wanted to be the first with her.

He wanted her never to have cause to think about another man, especially not Spotted Eagle.

An expert tracker, he peered at the tall grass, the moon's glow revealing which route had been taken by his friend and his copper princess.

His eyes continuing to follow the trail of crushed grass, he traveled a far distance, then gasped when he found the body of the panther, two arrows piercing its side.

He knelt close to the panther and examined the arrows.

"Spotted Eagle's," he hissed.

His jaw tight and his heart thundering, he again followed the trail, stopping with a start when just up ahead, in a clearing, he saw two nude figures intertwined on the ground.

His throat went immediately dry and his

heart seemed to tumble to his feet, knowing who the lovers were without taking another step.

"I am too late," Two Ridges whispered angrily to himself. "But I still will not give her up. She will be mine. Soon. It cannot bc any other way. Even if friends become fast enemies, this woman will be my wife!"

When Spotted Eagle wove his fingers through Jolena's dark hair and drew her lips to his again and kissed her, Two Ridges bitterly turned his eyes away, his hands circled into tight fists at his sides.

"You will be sorry," he said, his voice level and filled with venom.

Chapter Ten

Jolena was deliriously, deliciously in love for the first time in her life. Yet she felt bashfully awkward in the presence of Spotted Eagle now that she had given herself to him. Whenever he looked at her from his powerful stallion as he rode beside her and Kirk's wagon, a sensual thrill attacked her insides.

She could not help but feel somewhat ashamed for what her heart had led her to do beneath the mystical spill of the moonlight. Yet deep down, where her desires and wants were molded, she knew that she would allow it again. She was even eager for her next tryst with the man she loved. Just thinking about it made her warm all over.

Jolena avoided her brother's occasional questioning glances, thinking that surely he saw the difference in his sister today by the way her eyes shone and her lips curved into a smile filled with secret, wondrous thoughts.

As now, as she sat straight-backed on the uncomfortable wooden seat of the covered wagon, she could feel two sets of eyes on her from each side of her. Without even looking at her brother and at the man she loved, she knew that their eyes were filled with a keen possession.

Not allowing herself to even conjure up the possibility of her brother and lover clashing over who possessed whom, Jolena smiled softly and kept her eyes straight ahead. The wind whipped her long black hair back from her shoulders, and her clean, fresh blouse, which she had put on after her brief bath in the river this morning, clung to her breasts as the wind pressed against the cotton fabric.

As the wagons began traveling on a path that had been cut out of a towering forest, the wind was silenced. Everything in the forest was still in the moist heat of mid-morning, as if every leaf of every tree was breathing slowly in the moist air, tasting its fragrance.

Thin shafts of sunlight fell in criss-cross patterns between the gently rising tree-trunks. Some trees were gigantic. Some were small. Some were round and smooth, others gnarled and coarse, some rotting and ready to drop.

It was living so intensely, this forest, that Jolena felt as though she dared not breathe loudly or give signs of her animal restlessness.

All around her, saplings, shrubs, flowers, and grasses rushed to close the hole that had been torn in the fabric of the forest roof. Slender growths stretched upward. The soil burst with irrepressible vegetation, and masses of parasitic foliage were entwined with the glorious blossoms of creepers, laced and bound and interwoven with interminable tangles of vines.

The air hummed with flying creatures, with birds as bright as butterflies, startling Jolena into thinking that finally she was going to find the elusive, rare butterfly.

She watched more intensely for any signs of butterflies as the sunlight streamed through many tints of green overhead onto the black masses of moldering wood and leaves beneath the trees.

But still there were no signs of butterflies, and when this stretch of forest was left behind and they were traveling over a more rocky terrain, where neither trees nor grass grew, Jolena settled down, sighing resolutely, now worrying more about the sun that was beating down upon her, scorching her as if a heated iron were being held only inches away from her flesh. She fanned herself with one of her hands, while with the other she gripped the seat of the wagon, the journey having become slow and rough as the wheels of the wagon rolled and bumped over the rocks.

Out of the corner of her eye, Jolena saw Spotted Eagle dismount, then begin traveling on foot, his horse's reins held limply in his fingers as his steed fell back away from him at a much slower gait.

Jolena shifted her gaze and watched Spotted Eagle as he walked tall and proud beside the wagon, so close she could reach out and touch him if she wished to.

But she dared not touch him, for it might start a chain reaction of feelings tumbling through her—feelings she could not act on until privacy was once again granted to her and her handsome warrior lover.

She smiled to herself, finding it hard to believe that her life had changed so drastically since she left Saint Louis. She had hoped for many things as she traveled up the long stretch of the Missouri, but never had she imagined that she would find love, and that she would be taught the true meaning of being a woman while locked within her lover's powerful embrace.

Her midnight dream had come true, she thought. Now if only the other thing that she had prayed upon the stars for each night would happen—then she would feel fulfilled. She would be whole. As long as she never knew her true father and people, she was only half a person.

It was not fair, having been cheated of a lifetime of being with her people and being loved by her true father.

But now she had hopes that even this would soon change. If she could find the courage to ask Spotted Eagle the important questions that were burning within her heart, perhaps then she would not have to search any further for answers!

As Spotted Eagle walked quietly beside the wagon where his woman was so close he could reach out and touch her if he so desired, he was lost in memories of the moments he had spent alone with her. Soon he would tell her many things that would thrill her heart. He was proud that he would be the one to put back together the pieces of her life that had been wrenched apart all those years ago when the white people had taken her from her beloved mother. Once he revealed this truth to Jolena, she would be Blackfoot instead of living the pretense of being white.

His heart leapt when, up ahead, a fox emerged from the forest. When the fox crossed Spotted Eagle's path from left to right, Spotted Eagle smiled, knowing that meant good luck.

At this moment in his life, he felt blessed, for of late everything good had been happening for him and the Blackfoot of his village.

The only thing that worried him was his father's failing health. He was suffering a slow descent into a strange, debilitating illness which would quickly take from him the ability to think or remember where he was or who he was.

These episodes had begun to be more frequent, giving his father cause to tell Spotted Eagle that soon he would be chief instead of Chief Gray Bear.

Spotted Eagle was saddened over his father's need to give up his title of chief because of the reason it was going to have to be done, yet he knew that it would be necessary if his father's mind ceased to function as a leader's mind must.

Spotted Eagle was ready to lead his people.

He had been an astute student of his father's teachings!

Something sparkling beneath the beating rays of the sun in his path drew Spotted Eagle's eyes. He smiled broadly when he recognized what the object was. It was an *I-nis-kim*—a buffalo stone. This was the Blackfoot's strongest medicine. It gave its possessor great power with the buffalo. One who found the stone was regarded as very fortunate.

"Twice in one day I have received good signs," he whispered to himself, stopping to bend and pluck the buffalo stone from the rocky terrain.

Smiling, circling the stone in one of his hands, Spotted Eagle continued on his way, then stopped and gazed guardedly at an approaching horseman. When he recognized the man in the Indian saddle as White Mole, a warrior of Spotted Eagle's neighboring village of Blackfoot, he relaxed his shoulders and awaited his arrival.

White Mole drew tight rein beside Spotted Eagle. He gave Two Ridges, who sat on his horse only a few feet back from Spotted Eagle, a quick, knowing glance.

"What brings you here?" Spotted Eagle said, drawing White Mole's full attention to him. "Do you wish to join the expedition? If so, you are welcome."

"No," White Mole said. "I have come for other reasons."

"Tell me then the true reason," Spotted Eagle said, stiffening as White Mole did not offer a smile, only frowning as if his news was anything but good.

"It is your father," White Mole said, not meeting Spotted Eagle's gaze. "He is ailing. He has asked for you. He wishes you to come to him quickly."

"Father?" Spotted Eagle said, fear rising inside him that perhaps his father was more ill than he had thought. "How do you know this?"

"While journeying toward Fort Chance, I came upon a warrior from your village," White Mole said, the lie slipping easily across his lips since it was being paid for with two horses. "This warrior whose name I do not know asked if I would bring the message to you. I saw that he was eager to return to your village, so I said that I would do this deed for you, as a friendly gesture from my village to yours."

"That is most kind," Spotted Eagle said, reaching a hand to White Mole and tightly clasping his hand as it was extended to him. "Somehow I will return the favor."

White Mole smiled smugly, slipped his hand from Spotted Eagle's, gave Two Ridges another quick glance, then wheeled his horse around and rode quickly away.

Spotted Eagle was torn, not wanting to leave

Jolena's safety in the hands of anyone but himself, yet knowing that his first loyalties were to his father. He slowly opened his fingers and stared down at the buffalo rock, having only moments ago felt that much luck was his today, especially after having also seen the fox.

Two Ridges rode up and dismounted. He placed a hand on Spotted Eagle's shoulder. "What news did White Mole bring?" he said, pretending concern. "It is in your eyes that something has pained you."

"*Ni-nah-ah,* my father," Spotted Eagle said, his jaw tight. "I must go to my father. You are now in charge. Keep a sharp eye out for the Cree or any other renegades that might be stalking the expedition."

"It is done, my friend," Two Ridges said, dropping his hand down to his side. His insides glowed warm with glee as he watched Spotted Eagle glance at the copper princess, not realizing that when he returned, she would no longer belong to him!

His ploy was working, Two Ridges gloated to himself. Tonight he would finally have his lusts satisfied beneath the moonlight, as Spotted Eagle had the previous night. Just thinking how soft her skin must feel all over was setting small fires inside Two Ridges' loins.

Spotted Eagle's eyes lingered on Jolena, then he turned his eyes back to the rock. Without further thought, he went with proud shoulders to Jolena.

"I did not hear what the warrior said to you,

but the news seems to have disturbed you," Jolena said, before he had a chance to say anything to her. "What is it? What's happened?"

She had watched with intense interest as the strange warrior relayed a message to Spotted Eagle that had sent quick alarm and concern into his dark eyes.

"I must leave you," Spotted Eagle said, his voice drawn. He paused and looked at Kirk, his spine stiffening when he saw that that bit of news made Kirk smile. It took every bit of Spotted Eagle's will power not to lash out at the brother of his woman and tell him that he could feel as smug as he wanted now, but Spotted Eagle would return. He would never allow himself to stay far from his woman—not after waiting a lifetime for her!

Jolena was jarred by the news. "You must leave?" she gasped, her eyes widening. "But why? Where are you going?"

"My father is ailing," Spotted Eagle explained. "He beckons me to his bedside. This devoted son responds quickly to his request. I leave now, but as soon as I see that everything is being done for my father, allowing me to leave him again, I shall return and be your humble guide."

"Two Ridges will do just fine in that capacity," Kirk quickly interjected. "So don't worry about how long you are gone. In fact, Spotted Eagle, I'm sure we'll get along just fine without you. I haven't seen any signs of the Cree." He frowned. "Nor of butterflies. I'm beginning to wonder if you invented the story, perhaps to win approval from Ralph McMillen when you reported it."

Jolena's heart skipped a beat, and she stared wide-eyed at her brother, who had just insulted Spotted Eagle. This wasn't like her Kirk. In Saint Louis, he had been a kind and gentle young man who never made an enemy.

But it seemed that the minute he had looked into Spotted Eagle's midnight-dark eyes, he had gone on the defensive, just watching and waiting for Spotted Eagle to say or do something that he could pounce on with insulting remarks.

She turned wondering eyes to Spotted Eagle, fearing his reaction, yet proud of him for ignoring the insult as nothing important.

Yet perhaps that was not intentional. The rock that he was holding in his hand, and seemingly studying as he looked intensely down at it, seemed to have drawn his mind away from Kirk—and perhaps even from Jolena.

She stared at the rock, seeing nothing special about it, except that it was sleek and brown and picked up the rays of the sun, reflecting a soft light back at her. She was so distracted by all of this that she did not even see a monarch butterfly drifting past overhead.

Suddenly Spotted Eagle thrust the rock toward Jolena, causing her to flinch with the quickness of his motion.

"Keep this for me," he said, thrusting the buffalo stone into her hand. "It will bring me back to you."

Curious, Jolena wondered what the value of the rock was. She started to ask, but just as she opened her mouth with the question, Spotted

Eagle was already walking away from her.

In one leap he was in his saddle. He coiled his reins around his fingers and paused to take one last look at Jolena, then turned his eyes ahead and rode away, stirring rocks and clouds of dust into the air and blocking Jolena's further view of him for a moment.

Two Ridges walked his horse to Jolena's wagon. She was studying the stone again, as though mesmerized by it. "Do you wish to know the importance of such a stone?" he asked, ignoring Kirk's icy stare.

"Yes, please," Jolena said.

"It is called *I-nis-kim*," Two Ridges said softly. "It is a buffalo stone. It is strong in medicine. It gives its possessor great power with buffalo. The person who succeeds in obtaining an *I-nis-kim* is regarded as very fortunate. It has been said that sometimes a man who is riding along on the prairie will hear a peculiar faint chirp such as a little bird might utter. The sound is made by a buffalo rock. He stops and searches on the ground for the rock, and if he cannot find it, he marks the place and very likely returns next day to look again. If it is found, there is great rejoicing."

"It is so small to be so important," Jolena said, turning the rock from side to side as she studied it again.

"The size does not matter," Two Ridges said, reaching over to stroke the rock with his fingertips. "It is said that if an *I-nis-kim* is placed in a buckskin pouch and left undisturbed for a long time, it will have young ones. Two small stones similar in shape to the original one will be found in the pouch."

Jolena smiled at the pretty story, careful not to look as though she was poking fun at the lovely Blackfoot myth. "Why is it called a buffalo rock?" she asked softly.

"The one who has found the rock takes it and puts it in his lodge close to the fire, where he can look at it and pray over it and make medicine," Two Ridges said, squaring his shoulders proudly at the opportunity to be the one to teach his copper princess the ways of his people. "The next day this warrior will find many buffalo!"

"I must return it to Spotted Eagle then," Jolena said, looking into the distance, no longer able to even see dust sprayed up from the ground behind Spotted Eagle's horse. "When he returns, I will be sure that he has it for his next buffalo hunt."

"Isn't that enough talk of rocks and such nonsense as that?" Kirk said suddenly, drawing Jolena's eyes quickly to him. "We're here looking for butterflies, not damn rocks. Two Ridges, you are in charge now. Let's get on our way."

Two Ridges glared at Kirk, then stamped away and quickly mounted his horse.

Once again they made a slow trek over the jutting rocks, breathing in dust. Jolena clung to the buffalo rock with all of her might, feeling as though it was her only link now to the man she loved.

Chapter Eleven

The day had been long for Jolena, the hours seeming to drag by since Spotted Eagle's departure. The sky was now in bloom with the splash of the setting sun, the campfire crackling and popping as the greenest of the wood stacked among the circle of rocks became awash with flames.

Jolena sat on a blanket close to the fire. She was trying to join in with the laughing and joking as the other members of the expedition sat around sipping coffee from tin cups. But her thoughts kept wandering to Spotted Eagle. If his father's health was bad enough to draw him back to his village, then it might be bad enough to cause Spotted Eagle to stay there to look after him.

Because she missed Spotted Eagle so much,

the excitement of the search for the rare butter-fly had waned.

Jolena sat her empty cup on the ground and drew her knees to her chest, encircling her legs with her arms. She felt strangely empty, and she knew that was not only because Spotted Eagle wasn't there. It was also because she had not learned anything about her heritage yet. She was angry at herself for not having come right out and asked Spotted Eagle when she had been given the chance.

Sighing heavily, she stretched her legs out before her and placed one of her hands inside her skirt pocket. Her fingers circled the buffalo rock. Bringing it out, she gazed down at it as she turned it around within the palm of her right hand, wondering if she would ever have the chance to give it back to Spotted Eagle so that his next buffalo hunt would be blessed by the rock.

Strange, how everything that had transpired between them now seemed only an illusion . . . a savage illusion.

"Are you all right, sis?" Kirk asked, scooting closer to her. "You've barely said a word since we made camp." He glanced down at the rock in her hand, then moved his eyes slowly up again, giving her an angry stare. "What're you doing with that thing? Throw it away. It's a useless rock."

Jolena slipped it back inside her pocket. "To you it's useless," she said somberly, eluding his steady stare. "But to the Blackfoot, and now to *me*, it has much meaning."

"Like what?" Kirk asked, sarcasm thick in his words.

"The *I-nis-kim* is strong medicine to the Blackfoot," Two Ridges said as he knelt down on his haunches on Jolena's other side. He gazed around Jolena at Kirk. "So it is not wise to make mockery of it."

"I wasn't mocking it," Kirk said irritably. "In fact, if you want to know, I don't care a damn about it." He gave Two Ridges a look of annoyance. "Can my sister and I have a little privacy here? Or do you feel you have the right to interfere in anyone's conversation just because you are the only guide left to take us through this godawful land?"

Two Ridges glared at Kirk, then jumped to his feet and stamped away. He squatted down onto his haunches in the thickening shadows of dusk and watched Kirk until Kirk left to find refuge behind bushes to relieve himself before retiring for the night in his tent.

Two Ridges saw this as his chance to make his first advances to Jolena. He jumped to his feet and took a few steps, then stopped and stared as Jolena quickly went to her tent after seeing him walking toward her.

Knowing that she was purposely evading him, Two Ridges doubled his hands into tight fists at his sides. Looking slowly around him and noting how close everyone else's tent had been pitched to Jolena's, he knew that this night he would not approach her with his skills of drawing a woman into wanting him. He would have to wait another full night and day before the opportunity would arise again.

And that would be the last chance he would get, for Spotted Eagle would have had time by then to reach his village and return to the expedition after discovering that his father's health was no worse than the last time he had seen him.

Disappointment lay heavily on his heart. Two Ridges had thought endlessly of Jolena the whole day, his images of being with her building at each beat of his heart. He had believed that his desires would be quenched tonight while holding her in his arms and making love to her.

Grumbling to himself, Two Ridges turned and marched away from the camp.

Hoping to find escape from her loneliness and despair, Jolena settled herself down on a blanket, stretching out on her right side as she drew another blanket atop her. Clutching the buffalo rock, Jolena sighed and drifted off into a restless sleep.

Suddenly her sleep was filled with images. It was the same dream that had visited her most nights in Saint Louis. She was dressed in a soft fringed doeskin dress, beaded moccasins, and a headband about her head to hold her long and flowing dark hair in place as the wind blew briskly around her.

On each side of her were colorfully painted tepees, yet outside the dwellings she saw no people until suddenly before her was the handsome warrior whom she now knew as Spotted Eagle!

Her insides melted as he approached her, for never had she seen such a handsome, proud man, and as his eyes locked with hers, she could feel him silently bidding her to come to him.

Following this bidding, Jolena began walking slowly toward him, then broke into a mad run. Yet she never seemed to get closer.

The faster she ran, the more distant he became.

She reached her hands out to him, crying his name as she tossed, turned, and sweated in her sleep.

Then, finally, she reached him.

Sobbing with joy, she flung herself into his arms, and when his lips bore down upon hers, tears flowed from her eyes from the thankful bliss of the moment.

A strange sound drew Jolena quickly away from Spotted Eagle. She stepped aside and turned to see what was making the strange swishing noise.

Wild-eyed, she realized that it was an arrow!

Her heart sank as she turned and watched this arrow pierce her lover's heart!

A scream lodged in her throat, awakening her in a cold sweat. Her pulse racing, Jolena sat up quickly and stared wild-eyed around her.

Oh, Lord, the dream had seemed so real!

She placed her fingertips to her mouth, still feeling Spotted Eagle's lips warming hers.

She put her hands over her ears and closed her eyes, still able to hear the eerie sound of the arrow as it whizzed through the air.

She groaned and moved her head back and forth, trying not to remember how it had sounded when the arrow had pierced her lover's body.

"Jolena?" Kirk said, from outside her tent. "Sis? Are you all right? Moments ago it sounded as though you were choking. Tell me. Are you all right?"

Trying to compose herself so that her voice would have its natural sound, Jolena swallowed over and over again and willed her heart to stop its pounding. Then she crawled to the tent entrance and drew the flap aside.

"I'm fine," she murmured. "I . . . I just had a nightmare, that's all."

"It must've been some nightmare," Kirk said, frowning at her, seeing the perspiration-dampness of her hair as it clung to her brow.

Then he reached a hand inside and touched her cool, clammy cheek. "Are you going to be all right?" he asked with brotherly affection.

"Yes, I'll be fine," Jolena said, then leaned out and gave him a soft kiss on his cheek. "Sorry I awakened you."

"You didn't awaken me," Kirk said, taking her hand. "So far this expedition has been nothing but trouble. I'll be glad when it's over and we can return to some sort of natural life back in Saint Louis."

Jolena gave him a wistful stare, thinking that

nothing would ever be the same again—not since she had arrived at her homeland, and had experienced how it felt to be totally, mindlessly in love.

"Jolena?" Kirk said, leaning closer. "You are going to return with me to Saint Louis, aren't you? You aren't going to allow your heart to be swayed into staying to search out your Indian heritage? If that happens, I'll curse the day I agreed to accompany you on this expedition."

"Kirk, don't blame yourself for anything that might happen," Jolena said softly. "Don't you know, dear brother, that sooner or later I would have come to the Montana Territory anyhow, to find answers to questions that have plagued me since I realized there was a difference between me and my white playmates? I must find answers, Kirk."

Kirk gazed at her silently for a moment longer, then placed his arms around her shoulders and drew her against him. He stroked her long, dark hair, understanding the yearnings in her heart.

He knew that if it were he, it would be no different.

The mountains in the distance were shrouded beneath the purple cloak of night. The moon was dappling the land that stretched out before Spotted Eagle with a silver sheen as he rode hard toward his village, feeling no less torn now than when he had cast that last look upon the woman he loved.

He wished he were two persons so that he could be in two places at once—with his woman and with his father.

Until he made Jolena totally his with a commitment of marriage, he had to accept these times when he would be separated from her.

In his mind's eye he was acting out their sensual moments together, and how it had felt to cradle her close while they had made passionate love.

His body craved to be with her now as then.

He wished to taste her lips.

He wished to feel the magnificent softness of her breasts again within the palm of his hands.

He quavered at the thought of flicking his tongue over one of her nipples, feeling how this would make Jolena moan with pleasure.

Sweat beading his brow, these thoughts were the last thing that he should be thinking about at such a grievous time, when his father might be spending his last moments on earth. Spotted Eagle forced himself only to concern himself about his father.

He frowned and his jaw tightened as he remembered exactly what White Mole had said, trying to determine whether or not Spotted Eagle, the son of the powerful Blackfoot chief, Chief Gray Bear, might have overreacted to the news brought to him.

It was strange that it was White Mole who delivered the message to him. Strange that it was not . . .

A sudden realization stopped him in mid-thought, as though a bolt of lightning had struck him. If his father was ailing, no warrior from his village would send the message by way of someone *not* of his village, Spotted Eagle thought, suddenly drawing his horse to a halt. If his father was truly ailing, a warrior of his village would have searched until he found him, to give him the message firsthand. Depending on others was not the way of his people. The Blackfoot of his village were a close-knit people whose hearts beat in the same rhythm.

Something was not right about this message that had been brought to him.

Especially the messenger.

All that he could come up with was that his deep concern for his father had prevented him from thinking clearly. He knew that his father did not have many days left on this earth. Perhaps one more winter, surely no more than two. He even felt guilty for leaving the village for any length of time, fearing his father might need his decision on this or that.

Yet if Spotted Eagle stayed behind because of this, he knew that it would take his father's self-esteem away, especially if his father guessed why his son would not leave him for more than a sunrise at a time. His taking on the duties of a guide had given his father more time to feel important and needed.

Spotted Eagle's eyes narrowed, realizing that someone had duped him, yet wondering who—and why?

What did anyone gain by his absence from the

wagon train of butterfly-seekers?

His breath caught in his throat when he came up with an answer to his questions that seemed logical.

"Jolena's brother," Spotted Eagle hissed, his heart pounding angrily at the thought of her brother being this deceitful.

Before the wagon train left Fort Chance, Kirk must have sought out White Mole and paid him many horses to do this trickery. Spotted Eagle remembered how easily White Mole had lied.

He felt a desperate need to get back to Jolena. He would show her brother that no ploy his white man's mind might conjure up would keep Jolena and Spotted Eagle apart!

He gazed down at his horse. He was a powerful stallion that could endure hard travel, but Spotted Eagle did not want to push his horse to the limits of its endurance.

Spotted Eagle gave the river at his right side a lingering stare, then slapped his stallion's rump and gently nudged it with his heels, easing his mount into the shallow river.

After his horse had drunk his fill and seemed rested enough, Spotted Eagle turned his stallion around, left the river in a great splash, and rode in a hard gallop across land that he had just traveled. He knew that by the time the sun hung directly overhead in the sky tomorrow, he would be gazing into his woman's eyes again.

Words would not be needed between them.

In their eyes would be the excitement of being together again.

Chapter Twelve

In the slight breeze of the day came the scent
of blossoms and a hum of bees. After a clear
blue sky all morning, during which the crisp-
ness of the air was sapped away, the clear calls
of birds faded to a deadness in the droning,
sticky air. Noon found the forest in which the
expedition was traveling shimmering with a
layer of hot haze above the dark-green canopy
of trees.

But it was a day that Jolena had been waiting for.

It was a day of butterflies!

They seemed everywhere—all colors, all
sizes, all kinds flitting everywhere!

A thrilling excitement filled Jolena as she ran
through the forest with her butterfly net, Kirk
following her with jars that were equipped with

cotton soaked with alcohol which would quickly numb, then kill the butterflies before they were able to destroy their wings by flapping them against the insides of the jars.

To Jolena it was good to think about something else besides Spotted Eagle and her quest to find her true people. Presently, all that she could think about was collecting butterflies to take back to her father in Saint Louis, hoping that among these hundreds of butterflies that she was seeing today would be that one which was the most elusive of all.

"Slow down, sis," Kirk shouted as Jolena ran around, swinging her net in the air as she spotted another specimen of butterfly that she had not yet caught. "You've got the rest of the afternoon."

"Perhaps not," Jolena said, breathless. "They will probably disappear as quickly as they appeared."

Casting all thoughts aside now except for catching the butterflies to take back to Saint Louis, not only for her father, but for others to see and study and record in their journals, Jolena continued her hunt. As she worked, her long skirt sometimes threatened to trip her. Her white, long-sleeved blouse became spotted and soiled with dirt and stains from scraping against trees and from the humid moisture dripping from the leaves overhead. Her long hair bounced on her shoulders, her face was flushed with a mixture of heat and excitement, and beads of sweat pearled on her copper brow.

"Oh, look and see, Kirk," Jolena said, her eyes wide as she spotted a group of "painted lady" or thistle butterflies. "Follow me. I must catch at least one of them!"

Orange, yellow, and black-spotted, the painted lady butterflies were flying in groups of hundreds. They were known to travel more widely than most insects. Many spent the winters in Mexico, flying northward during the spring and summer.

After Jolena had one painted lady secured in a jar, she walked briskly along beneath the canopy of trees, her eyes darting around. The sunlight filtering through the trees overhead gave sharp definition and intense blackness to the shadows of the thickest, impenetrable part of the forest. She shuddered as she thought of the panther that had threatened her the other night.

She gasped when she discovered another butterfly that she knew would thrill her father. The *colotis etrida*, whose small, golden-tipped wings changed form according to the season. She could tell that this was the summer butterfly because of its stronger, blacker markings, which later would disappear entirely.

After securing one specimen, she continued the search and soon also had a jezebel butterfly housed in a jar. The day wore on and finally, exhausted from her labors, Jolena returned to the wagon. The calves of her legs and the small of her back were aching. She was soaked with perspiration, and the mist which had accompanied the setting sun was like a cool sponge on her face.

"I hope Two Ridges finds a place for a campsite soon," Kirk grumbled. "I've never seen you as driven as you were today. Lord, sis, I can imagine how tired you are. It seems that every bone in my body is aching."

"That's because of your lack of exercise," Jolena said, wiping her hands across her face, smoothing the fine mist from it. "You spend too much time with your books. You need to be outdoors. Father has spoiled you, Kirk, by hiring someone to do everything, instead of allowing you to do some of the work yourself."

"You are just as spoiled," Kirk said, his voice drawn.

"Perhaps so," Jolena said, shrugging. "But at least I take time to go for long walks. I love the forest that fringes our property in Saint Louis. Always when I've walked through it, I have felt so free, so at peace with myself. Sometimes I feel connected with the forest, as though I was meant to live there, instead of in a large mansion."

She said no more, for Kirk's heavy sigh told her that he wanted to hear no more conversation about her Indian heritage.

Her thoughts returned to Spotted Eagle. With him, surely she would be able to talk about anything, any time.

She frowned as she gazed into the darkening shadows of the forest. Soon night would cover everything with its cloak of darkness, and she could not help but be worried about Spotted Eagle and wonder where he might be, and if he was on his way back from his village.

Her gaze shifted. She stared at Two Ridges' back as he rode a few yards ahead of her wagon. A desolate feeling overcame her, wishing the back she was looking at was Spotted Eagle's.

Oh, when would he return? What if he did not return at all? What if she never ever saw him again?

If he did not return by the time the lepidopterists were finished with their search for the rare butterfly and were ready to board the riverboat back to Saint Louis, what then?

Would she be able to actually board the riverboat without seeing Spotted Eagle again?

She doubted it.

They rode on for a while longer, then Two Ridges drew a tight rein and stopped his horse. "We will make camp here," he said, turning his gaze to Jolena, then shifting it to Kirk.

Kirk nodded. He let his reins go slack, then jumped from the wagon. Before he could get around to help Jolena, she had already left the wagon, stretching and yawning. He gave her a lingering, silent stare, marveling at her endurance, then went to the back of the wagon and began unloading their equipment for the night.

Jolena yawned one more time. Then she stopped and listened, hearing a strange roaring and hissing through the trees. It sounded like water dropping by stages into a deep chasm.

Her sense of adventure and curiosity sent her walking through the forest until she came to a clearing that led upward. Lifting the hem of her skirt, she climbed higher and higher, then stopped when she came to a high point on a cliff from where she could see not only the waterfall a short distance away, but the river down below her as it flattened out and made a wide sweep around a bald granite hill before fingering out across the valley.

The water down below was smooth and glassy, and the broken river stretched into the distance like dull streams of silver.

The sunset was lighting the eastern hills, sending long sunbeams through the mist into the valley below.

Captured by the loveliness of the waterfall, Jolena gazed at it, sighing. Although the sun was fast lowering in the sky, the waterfall was still lit and it shimmered with myriad colors. The waterfall's spume rose far into the sky like a cloud of smoke from a forest fire, then descended to the earth as mist, keeping the vegetation at the top of the chasm dripping wet.

The sunset shining on the waterfall made rainbows, multiple and immense and so brilliant they seemed palpable. They moved with the light, fading and emerging and forming again at different angles and in different sizes, so that sometimes one could actually see where they began and ended.

Standing on the cliff, soaking up the beautiful tranquil setting, Jolena grew tense with excitement when a butterfly flew just past her nose.

"Lord, it's a *nymphalid*," she gasped. The *nymphalid* was steeped in Indian lore, and perhaps almost as rare as the *euphaedra*.

She continued to watch the butterfly as it seemed to change colors before her very eyes, a defense mechanism to protect the creature from predators such as herself.

The butterfly seemed to be teasing her as it brushed past her nose, then flew down as if it was going to land on her hand. Her heart racing, she looked desperately around her, suddenly realizing that her net and jars were back at the camp.

The butterfly landed on her arm, and Jolena held her breath as she watched it furl and unfurl its antennae, as though tasting her to see if she were a copper flower.

Jolena started moving one of her hands guardedly toward the butterfly. Just as she was about to place her fingers on either side of the butterfly's wings, the butterfly took flight again. Yet still it remained close at hand, teasingly brushing against Jolena's face or hair.

"I *have* to have it," Jolena whispered to herself.

Moving away from the edge of the cliff, her eyes never leaving the butterfly, Jolena's heart pounded as for a moment it seemed to be following her. As Jolena moved backward, so did the butterfly flutter forward.

Then the butterfly suddenly soared widely around in a half circle and moved back to hover over the very edge of the cliff. "Just you stay right there," Jolena whispered. "Don't move. Please, please don't move. Be there when I get back with my net."

In her excitement and haste to get back to the camp, Jolena almost tumbled down the steep embankment. After steadying herself, she moved with sure footing on down the hill, then broke into a mad rush through the forest. When she reached the campsite, where a fire had already been started, she went to her wagon and reached inside, quickly finding her net.

"The jar, Kirk!" she cried. "Get the jar and follow me!"

"Jolena, stop," Kirk shouted, not making any move to do as she said. "I'm not going anywhere. Nor should you. It will be dark soon."

Jolena turned on a heel and gave Kirk a frustrated stare. "Kirk, I've found a *nymphalid*," she cried. "Now come with me. I may be too late. It's probably already gone!"

Sighing, his shoulders slouched, Kirk grabbed the jar with its soaked cotton from the back of the wagon and began running after Jolena.

Two Ridges had been watching Jolena for some time. When he caught sight of the butterfly she was chasing into the forest, he frowned. He knew the lore of that butterfly. It was a butterfly shunned by the Blackfoot and all other tribes of Indians!

It meant bad luck to anyone who looked upon it!

He broke into a mad run. He had to stop Jolena. She should not be near the butterfly, much less catch it to carry with her for the rest of this expedition.

If she did, everyone would be in jeopardy!

Winded, yet too filled with excitement to stop, Jolena rushed back up the steep hill, then sucked in a wild breath of relief when she got to the cliff and saw that the butterfly was still circling around at the very edge, as though it had waited for her.

Clutching the handle of her butterfly net, Jolena inched closer to the edge of the cliff. "I can't believe it," she said, giving Kirk a quick glance over her shoulder as he lagged far behind her. "Kirk, it's still here. Can you believe it? It's as though it waited for me."

"Don't get too close to the edge of the damn cliff," Kirk warned, wiping perspiration from his brow. "Watch it, now, Jolena. Don't go any closer!"

Jolena did not hear anything but the thunderous roar of the waterfall and the cry inside her to catch this butterfly for her father. She inched her way along the land now, but when she got to the edge of the cliff, where below her rapids were swirling, she stopped.

But the butterfly seemed to be teasing her again when it flew only a few inches away from where she could reach it.

Fearlessly, she leaned out, swinging her net in a desperate attempt to catch the butterfly, then screamed as she lost her footing and tumbled over the side of the cliff.

Kirk stopped in mid-step, his eyes wild. "Jolena," he whispered, his throat so suddenly dry he could scarcely breathe. "Jolena . . ."

Chapter Thirteen

Spotted Eagle had just arrived at the campsite when he saw Two Ridges enter the forest. When Spotted Eagle dismounted and discovered that neither Jolena nor Kirk were among those busying themselves around the fire he concluded that perhaps Two Ridges was following Jolena and her brother to protect them while they explored.

Spotted Eagle recalled the cliff nearby and his heart skipped a beat. Quickly securing his reins, he glanced toward the forest again, where he had last seen Two Ridges.

Then, without saying anything to anybody, he broke into a hard run. He felt slightly relieved when he finally reached the slope of land that would lead him up to the cliff. Jolena was nowhere in sight.

Nor was her brother, or Two Ridges. Perhaps they had gone another way.

Suddenly an eagle rose into the air with a snake which soon dropped from its claws and escaped. Spotted Eagle felt that was a bad omen. The lowering sun, too, was painted with sun dogs—a sure warning that danger was near!

Then a mind-shattering scream suddenly pierced the air, startling Spotted Eagle.

His insides grew cold when he heard Kirk shouting Jolena's name.

"*Hai-yah!*" Spotted Eagle cried in despair, knowing what had happened.

His woman!

Just as he had feared, she *was* in danger!

She might even now be dead, for he had heard but only her one scream and the shout of her brother.

Now everything was too quiet!

Almost blinded with fear, Spotted Eagle raced up the hill. When he reached the summit, his eyes shifted from Kirk to Two Ridges, who were standing, motionless, their eyes wide as they peered over the sides of the cliff.

Spotted Eagle's heart seemed to plummet to his feet, afraid now to look over the cliff, fearing that he would see nothing but the crash of the waterfall and the whirlpools below. If his woman had fallen into the river, she would not survive the fall, much less the powerful surges of the water.

His jaw tight, his throat dry, Spotted Eagle rushed to the edge of the cliff, roughly edging himself between Two Ridges and Kirk. When he gazed downward, silently praying to the fires of the sun that his woman had somehow lived through the fall, he gasped at what he saw.

"*Wo-ka-hit*, listen to my pleas," he prayed desperately to the fires of the sun. "Do not let my woman die."

He looked quickly up at the sky, from which he thought he heard a voice say, "*A-wah-heh*—take courage, my son." Then he fell to his knees and gazed wild-eyed down at his woman, who was only moments away from death's door.

"Jolena?" he said as he stared disbelievingly down at her where she clung desperately to a huge, mangled root of a tree that had grown out of the rock at the sides of the cliff.

"Save me," Jolena whispered. "Oh, Lord, Spotted Eagle, I can't . . . last much longer. My fingers. I . . . feel them weakening!"

Spotted Eagle flattened his stomach against the rock beneath him and scooted out as far as he could over the ledge without placing himself in danger of toppling over. He had to give his body enough leverage so that it could tolerate Jolena's weight, as well as his own, once he grabbed her hands to pull her up to safety.

He knew that he should ask the assistance of Two Ridges and Kirk, but they had already proved their cowardice too often to be able to depend on them for anything.

They had just stood there watching when they could have been working together to save her!

But now was not the time to condemn.

Now was not the time to confront Kirk with his suspicion that he was the one who had paid White Mole to come to Spotted Eagle with lies about an ailing father!

It was the time to save his woman's life.

If she slipped away from him to her death, he felt as though he just might follow her.

Without her, he would be only half a man!

"Grab my hands, one at a time!" Spotted Eagle shouted, scooting out a little farther, as far as he possibly could, and reaching his hands out for Jolena.

"One . . . at . . . a . . . time, Jolena," he cautioned again.

Her heart pounding and dizzy from fear, Jolena took a deep breath, then quickly reached one hand up, relief rushing through her when Spotted Eagle grabbed her around the wrist.

Then just as quickly, she reached her other hand out to him and a grateful sob lodged in her throat as she smiled through tearful eyes up at him.

"I am going to pull you up slowly," Spotted Eagle said throatily.

Spotted Eagle's heart was filled with gratitude that Old Man, the chief god of the Blackfoot, had heard his silent pleas and had answered them. He now knew, beyond a shadow of a doubt, that it was his and Jolena's destiny to be together, to share life as though one soul and one heartbeat.

Today was proof enough to him that they were meant for one another, for otherwise, she would have not been given back to him, as though a gift from the gods!

Jolena scarcely breathed as Spotted Eagle slowly drew her up the side of the cliff. She could hear the roar of the waterfall on one side of her, almost deafening, and the crash of the water below, where she would have surely fallen to her death.

Tears rushed from her eyes again as she gazed up at Spotted Eagle who had risked his life to save hers. She wanted to be held in the protective cocoon of his arms, never to part from him again!

She wanted to find ways to thank him, for she would always be in his debt.

"Soon you will be safe," Spotted Eagle said, as he worked hard at keeping hold of her. Although she was slight in build, his shoulder and arm muscles were straining as he struggled to pull her up in this awkward way.

Jolena saw that she was almost able to reach up with her knees, to help place herself on solid land. She leaned against the side of the cliff, the sharp edges of the rocks piercing her blouse and cutting into her breasts as she was pulled up to safety. Her knees gave her that last boost she needed as she pushed herself up and fell down limply beside Spotted Eagle.

He drew her fiercely into his arms and held her close, his face burrowed in the depths of her black hair. "My woman," he whispered, easing her away from the edge of the cliff as he held her tightly within his aching arms. "You are safe now, my woman."

Jolena sobbed as she clung to him. "If not for you, I would have died," she cried, her tears soaking his buckskin shirt as she pressed her cheek hard against his chest. "Thank you. My darling, thank you."

So glad to have his woman safe in his arms, Spotted Eagle was speechless. He held on to her, yet looked past her shoulder at Two Ridges and Kirk, glowering at them because of their cowardice. He could understand the white man's failure to save his woman, for he was too lacking in muscle to have dragged her up to safety.

But Two Ridges? He was a noble Blackfoot whose bravery and courage had never faltered, especially when a woman's life was at stake!

As Spotted Eagle's eyes locked with Two Ridges, he saw something more than shame. It was as though Two Ridges was hiding a seething anger within his eyes, and this puzzled Spotted Eagle.

Spotted Eagle was the one who had cause to be angry at his brother Blackfoot! Two Ridges should be bending his head in shame, not defying his friend with a steady, angry stare, his jaw tight, his lips pursed tightly together.

Not understanding his friend's strange attitude, Spotted Eagle wrenched his eyes away, instead focusing his full attention on his woman. Placing his hands on each side of her face, he lifted her gaze to his.

"Let us return to the camp," he said. He glanced down at her torn clothes, wincing when he saw the bloodstains on her skirt.

His gaze moved slowly upward, stopping where her blouse was torn, partially exposing her breasts. He sucked in a wild gulp of air when he discovered blood oozing from a wound on one of her breasts, the blood spreading along the white fabric of her blouse.

Without further thought, and ignoring Kirk's angry stare, Spotted Eagle whisked Jolena quickly up into his arms and began carrying her down the side of the hill. He held her near, his fingers gripping her as gently as possible as she leaned against him, her cheek pressed against his chest.

"I love you," Jolena said, twining her arm around his neck, pulling herself up so that she could brush a soft kiss across his lips. "I shall always cherish you."

"No more than I, you," Spotted Eagle said, gazing down at her with heavy eyelids. "Should you have died . . ."

Jolena placed a finger softly to his lips, silencing his further words. "Darling, I didn't," she murmured. "But only because of you. I don't understand why Kirk and Two Ridges . . ."

Spotted Eagle was the one this time to place finger to lips. He sealed hers with his finger, not wanting her to waste her breath worrying about things that should have been.

This was now. She was alive. She was safely with him. They were in love.

He did not want to take the time and effort to cast blame.

He would now be there, always, for her.

If ever he were called to his village for true reasons, he would take her with him!

No one would get the chance to trick him again!

This time such foolishness had almost cost his woman her life. If he had ventured on to his village, Jolena would most certainly have died!

The thought made an ache circle his heart, so he cast the thought aside and centered all of his attention on making Jolena comfortable after her terrifying experience of only moments ago.

When they arrived at the camp and everyone circled around Jolena and Spotted Eagle with frenzied questions after seeing Jolena's condition, Spotted Eagle answered their questions quickly, then pitched Jolena's tent and they sought refuge within, alone, away from everyone and everything but themselves as night fell in its purple and black shadows over the land.

"Remove your blouse and skirt," Spotted Eagle said as he wrung out a cloth in a basin of water that sat on the floor of the tent. "Let me bathe your wounds while you tell me how you happened to fall over the cliff."

Feeling no bashfulness in Spotted Eagle's presence, Jolena did not hesitate as her fingers went to the buttons of her blouse.

"I know I was foolish," Jolena said, unbuttoning her blouse, cringing then as she eased it off, the dried blood painfully adhering her blouse to her sensitive breasts. "But it is so strange. There was this butterfly. It seemed to be teasing me. It lured me onward until . . . until I lost my footing."

159

She laid her blouse aside and quickly slipped off her skirt, and as the large campfire outside cast its golden dancing light along the inside walls, Jolena gasped, shocked to see just how scratched up her legs were. Blood was dried in streaks up and down her thighs, and she winced as Spotted Eagle began dabbing the blood away with the damp cloth.

"A butterfly lured you into danger?" Spotted Eagle said, giving Jolena a shadowed glance. "You know butterflies well. What was the name of this particular one?"

"I am sure that you know it well," Jolena said, tightening her leg muscles as Spotted Eagle continued cleansing her of the dried blood. "It is called the *nymphalid,* and it is a butterfly steeped in Indian lore."

When Jolena described the butterfly's destinctive markings, Spotted Eagle stared at her with a guarded look. "You call this butterfly *nymphalid?*" he said, his voice drawn. "That is the butterfly that lured you to danger?"

Jolena's spine stiffened, hearing the caution in his voice, frightening her. "Yes, I am certain it was that butterfly," she murmured. "I have studied about it. I would not be mistaken."

Spotted Eagle stared at her a moment longer, then wrung his cloth out and leaned closer to her, now softly dabbing the blood from one of her breasts. He ached to cup the breast and kiss its nipple, but instead he simply continued cleansing her wound.

"If you studied the butterfly of Indian lore well

enough, you would know that it is a butterfly that Indians shun," Spotted Eagle said in a scolding fashion. "In your studies, you would have learned that the *nymphalid* causes bad luck. It makes people afraid. When it flies out of its pupa, it drops a red liquid like blood from the air. It is a sign of death."

"Yes, in my studies I learned these things," Jolena said softly. "But I don't take things like that seriously. Darling, surely you know myth from fact. The myth that the *nymphalid* causes bad luck, or is a sign of death, is only that. A *myth*. I can't allow myself to think that the butterfly caused me to plunge over the edge of the cliff."

As she tried to convince Spotted Eagle, Jolena began to remember how the butterfly had seemed to tease her, not once but over and over again.

A chill rode up and down her spine, as she thought that perhaps *she* was wrong and that Spotted Eagle was right to fear the *nymphalid*.

"You will ignore the beckoning of the *nymphalid* should it try to lure you again into danger?" Spotted Eagle said as he dropped his cloth into the basin of water, then clutched his fingers gently to Jolena's shoulders.

"Yes, I will," she said, then flung herself into his arms, forgetting the soreness of the scratches on her breasts. His fingers now on them, softly kneading, creating fires within her, meant more to her than anything else at this moment.

As he crushed his mouth to her lips and kissed her wildly, almost savagely in the way he moved

161

his mouth over hers, Jolena cried out against his lips and wrapped him within her arms and pulled him down over her.

Frantically, almost desperately, she tried to shove his breeches down across his hips. His need rising for her, Spotted Eagle helped her, kicking them to the side.

Then his hand cupped her mound at the juncture of her thighs, thrusting a hungry finger inside her.

Jolena closed her eyes and sighed as he pleasured her in this simple way, then sucked in a wild breath of rapture when she felt something much better as he plunged his thick shaft deeply within her, magnificently filling her.

Spotted Eagle braced himself above her with his arms, his hands catching Jolena's and holding them slightly above her head as he started his rhythmic strokes within her. He kissed her eyes, her nose, and then her mouth, pressing his tongue through her trembling lips.

Jolena shuddered sensually when their tongues touched and danced against the other, in time, it seemed, with Spotted Eagle's continued strokes, his hips moving, hers rising, meeting him.

Spotted Eagle paused momentarily. He leaned up away from her and gazed with an intense longing into her eyes. "Am I hurting you?" he questioned softly. "Are your wounds too severe for my body to be against them?"

"They are mere scratches," Jolena whispered, leaning up, flicking her tongue across his lips. "What you are giving me is ecstasy."

He responded to her as she thrust her pelvis toward him, resuming the strokes that made his whole world seem to be suddenly spinning around him as the passion built like heated strikes of white lightning through him. He held his head back and groaned as she clamped her legs around his waist, drawing him more tightly and deeply into her. He pressed down against her, his hips thrusting hard.

Jolena writhed pleasurably beneath him, scarcely aware of her own soft whimpering sounds as Spotted Eagle's lips closed over a nipple, sucking, biting, licking.

Jolena splayed her fingers across his tight buttocks, hearing him moan as her fingers tightened around him, her fingernails sinking in, mixing pain with pleasure.

Suddenly Spotted Eagle placed his hands at Jolena's waist and rolled with her until he had her sitting astride him, her eyes filled with wanton pleasure as he entered her and began bucking wildly up into her.

Heated waves of pleasure spread over Jolena. She held her head back, her hair billowing luxuriously across her shoulders. As Spotted Eagle's hands cupped and kneaded her breasts, her shoulders swayed in the incredible beauty of her passion, feeling herself drawing near to that joyous bliss of release.

When Spotted Eagle made another deep plunge inside her, and then made many more quickly repeated thrusts as he groaned and held on to her breasts, she relaxed and closed her eyes as the flood of pleasure swept raggedly through them both as he cried out his fulfillment. . . .

Her heart pounding so hard it made her dizzy, Jolena slipped away from Spotted Eagle and lay down at his side. Taking several ragged breaths, she laid her hand over that part of him that still seemed alive as it throbbed against her flesh. Circling her fingers around him, she slowly moved them, his gasp of pleasure proving that he wanted it.

Soon he spilled his seed into her hand, then drew her against him once again, holding her tight. "My woman," he whispered huskily. "My beautiful, beautiful woman. Oh, how you make me alive when for so long I did not even know that I was dead."

Jolena knew that this was the perfect time to question him about so many things, but she did not want to ruin the intimacy of the moment with questions. There would be a more perfect time and place for such conversation. At this moment, she just wanted to cherish being with Spotted Eagle—and being alive.

She would not allow herself to remember that her brother had been too cowardly to save her.

Chapter Fourteen

Traveling in the back of the wagon instead of on the seat beside Kirk, Jolena spread her journals around her, her fingers gingerly pinning first one specimen of butterfly onto a board, then another.

She stopped, and with a magnifying glass studied one of the most colorful and beautiful butterflies she had ever seen. Its wings were covered with overlapping scales, thousands of these tiny scales giving the insect its brilliant colors.

Jolena was scarcely aware of the thunder that was rumbling outside the wagon, muffled somewhat by the trees of the forest. Only moments ago, she had been sitting outside beside her brother, admiring the brilliant orange flowers staring out boldly from vines on the sides of the trees, their scent trapped in the steady air. She had been in awe of a colorful lizard as it basked on a rock in the ribbons of sun that broke through the thick foliage overhead.

She was not even aware of the struggling efforts of those who were leading the teams of mules through the thick forest in an effort to enable everyone to continue traveling along the narrow path that had been cut through the forest by earlier travelers, instead of being forced to travel on the mules or on foot.

Jolena busied her fingers to get together the collection of butterflies for her father, while her mind was busy elsewhere.

"Spotted Eagle," she whispered, thrilling at the mere sound of his name as it breathed across her lips.

She had never thought that being in love could make one feel so much more alive. It was as though all of her feelings were intensified now that she had fallen in love. She felt as though her very heart was singing!

A lurid flash of lightning close by outside the wagon and an ensuing crash of thunder caused Jolena's fingers to slip so that the pin she was readying to stick into the board pricked her finger instead.

"Ouch!" she whispered harshly, wincing even more as blood began trickling down her finger.

Reaching for a clean, dry piece of cotton, she placed it over the tiny wound.

She then jumped with alarm when lightning flashed again, sending its lurid light through the canvas of the wagon, followed by an even louder crash of thunder.

As a small child, Jolena had always covered her head with a blanket if it stormed in the middle of the night while she was alone in her bedroom. Now she crawled to the front of the wagon and gazed upward, gasping. Black, billowing clouds were visible through the break in the trees overhead. She grabbed for Kirk's arm when lightning flooded the forest with another series of blue-white flashes, thunder booming only seconds later.

Kirk gave Jolena a frown over his shoulder. "We're in for one bad storm," he shouted over the loud thrashing of the leaves overhead as the wind suddenly began whipping through the trees. "It's going to hit us head on. There's no way to get away from it."

"Is there anything I can do?" Jolena asked, glancing around her as the canvas cover of the wagon began to strain against the bolts that were keeping it in place.

"Go to the back and tie down the cover as tightly as you can," Kirk shouted. "Close the front opening also, or everything we own might get blown away or soaked. Then all we can do is sit tight and ride this one out."

Jolena nodded.

She crawled to the back of the wagon and tied the canvas down as tightly as possible. She went from bolt to bolt, testing them, glad to find that they were all tight and snug.

Then she stared at her journals and the delicate specimens of butterflies spread out on the wagon floor. To make sure they were not harmed, she covered them with sheets of canvas that they had brought along just for this purpose.

When she felt that everything was secured as well as possible, she turned and stared at Kirk again, then at the empty seat beside him, wondering if she wanted to ride out the storm at his side or within the canvas walls of the wagon.

Fearing being alone during the storm, she chose to sit outside with her brother. She rushed to the seat and sat down, then turned and drew the canvas together behind them and tied it securely in place.

She clung nervously to the seat, her eyes darting around, trying to find Spotted Eagle. He was usually there, close to her wagon. But this time he was missing. He was probably going from wagon to wagon, checking to see if everything was readied for the storm.

Two Ridges was still there, riding a little behind her wagon. A strange coldness seemed to seize her when she found him staring at her, his eyes shadowed as everything became dull and gray with the approach of the storm.

She could not put her finger on what troubled her about Two Ridges. It was not only that he had been too cowardly to save her from the fall over the cliff. She had felt the same way before her accident. There seemed to be something about him that tugged at her soul, as though perhaps she had known him in another time, another life.

It was not the same feeling that she had about Spotted Eagle. Somehow *he* had appeared in her dreams, becoming real to her before she'd met him.

She had known nothing of Two Ridges until she first laid eyes on him. Yet since that first eye contact, something had been there, troubling her and seemingly haunting him as well.

Fear gripped her as another menacing bolt of lightning lit the trees with its silver light, followed by a fast roll of thunder. She gripped the seat with her fingers as the menacing black clouds raced overhead with enormous speed, pushed by tremendous winds that were curling the tree tops.

Then the rain began falling in torrents, the wind lashing the rain against Jolena's face. She screamed as the trees began swaying jerkily, threatening to hurl down their branches.

"Get inside the wagon!" Kirk shouted, wiping water from his face with the back of one hand, while with his other he tried to keep the wagon steady as the mules reared and brayed.

Spotted Eagle was suddenly there on his magnificent stallion, grabbing the reins from Kirk, steadying the horses. "Get inside out of the rain!" he shouted at Jolena.

The rain had blown her hair and plastered it against her wet face. She gathered it in her fingers and parted it, yet the rain was coming down in such blinding sheets that she still could not see Spotted Eagle clearly.

She nodded and turned to untie the leather thongs that held the front canvas of the wagon in place, but stopped and stared up at the sky as the storm abruptly stopped. It was as though someone had waved a magic wand in the air, ordering the sky to clear.

Jolena turned back around, and as she combed her fingers through her drenched hair, she gazed slowly about her. As the sun broke through, the colors of everything seemed brighter, the air was fresher, and the birds sang cheerfully.

The leaves of the trees were coated with a film of water, and as the air grew slowly warmer, white vapor formed in the tree tops, drifting idly upward to the clouds. The forest looked as if a thousand campfires were smoldering below the trees.

Jolena started to step down from the wagon, then stopped and screamed when her gaze fell upon something that had been uncovered at the side of the path by the hard, pelting rain.

Spotted Eagle slid quickly from his saddle and rushed to see what was causing Jolena's alarm. He stopped and his jaw tightened as he gazed down into a grave, from which the dirt had been washed away slowly through the years.

His eyes wide with curiosity, Kirk leaned around Jolena trying to see, angry to find that his view was being blocked by Spotted Eagle. "What was it, sis?" he asked, gazing over at her.

"I'm not sure," Jolena said, a shiver racing up and down her spine as she returned his studious stare. "It . . . it looked like a baby."

"Baby?" Kirk gasped, paling.

Kirk continued sitting there as Jolena stepped down from the wagon and went to Spotted Eagle's side. She covered her mouth with a hand as she stared down at the tiny remains of the body in the grave. It was lying curled up as if it were still in the womb. Its blanket, which seemed to have been made of turkey feathers, was rotted.

Spotted Eagle knelt down upon one knee and began shoveling mud back onto the tiny thing. "It is Pueblo," he said solemnly. "Turkeys were in many ways sacred to them. To bury a child wrapped in turkey feathers was to give it wings to the land of the hereafter."

Seeing the buried infant catapulted Spotted Eagle back into time to the day when he heard about Sweet Dove's death and the fate of her newly born child. He was grateful for the white people who had found the child and cared for her as though she were their own. But for them, that child might have seen the same end as this child lying in this shallow grave.

Perhaps she would still have been alive when her father found the body of his wife, yet the chances were the child would have died by then. Without nourishment, and lying exposed beneath the beating rays of the sun to any four-legged animal that might pass by, the child's chances of surviving would have been slim.

"How lonely the baby looked," Jolena murmured, having been saddened deeply by the sight of the infant. "It must have broken the mother's heart to have to bury her child so alone. I could not bear it if a child of mine died."

"This child has been dead for many years," Spotted Eagle said, shoveling the last pile of mud onto the grave. "Her mother is surely now dead, also. Perhaps her grave is also nearby. We shall never know."

Wiping his dirty hands on the thick leaves of bushes, he turned to Jolena, not caring that Kirk was near enough to hear him.

"We will have many healthy children," he assured her, ignoring Kirk's loud gasp and not seeing Two Ridge's glower as he sat on his horse just behind the wagon. "And there will be no graves necessary for our children. Nor for their mother. I shall stay at your side while you are birthing. Never would I send you away from our village to give birth to your child alone."

Jolena's eyes widened with horror. "Are you saying that some Indian women leave their villages to ... to have their children?" she asked, shocked at the thought. "Why would their husbands allow it?"

"It is not for me to say the wrongs or rights of another man's customs," Spotted Eagle said, rising to his full height and placing a gentle hand on Jolena's cheek. "But for us, when the time comes, we want only what is safe for you and the child. Never will I allow anything to harm you."

Aware that more than one set of eyes were on her and Spotted Eagle, Jolena could feel her cheeks becoming hot with a blush. She flatly ignored Two Ridges' steady gaze, but she gave Kirk a sideways glance. Her eyes wavered when she saw her brother's irritation with Spotted Eagle for having spoken so openly about children.

Jolena quickly changed the subject. "I'm cold," she said, hugging herself with her arms. "I'd best change into dry clothes." She looked Spotted Eagle up and down. His buckskin clothes were so wet they looked as though they might be his second skin, embarrassing her when she lowered her gaze to that part of his anatomy where he was so very well equipped.

Smiling awkwardly, she shifted her gaze quickly back up again, yet discovering that she had not lifted her gaze upward fast enough. There was a quiet amusement in the depths of Spotted Eagle's eyes.

Before she had the chance to turn around and climb into the wagon, she felt Spotted Eagle's eyes on her, also rediscovering her body with their heat as they roved over her, where her wet skirt and blouse clung sensually to her curves and the generous mounds of her breasts. It was as though everywhere he touched with his eyes he lit small flames, causing a gentle passion to rise within her.

Knowing the dangers in this, since they were the center of attention now that everyone had returned to their wagons and were waiting for

Spotted Eagle's command to continue on with the journey, Jolena turned her back quickly to Spotted Eagle and began to climb aboard the wagon.

But her breath seemed to lock in her throat when Spotted Eagle's hands were suddenly there at her waist, helping her.

She wanted to cry out to him that this was not the time for him to touch her anywhere!

She felt as though she was ready to melt right on the spot, and she feared that her feelings were too vivid in her eyes and in the way she was so rapidly breathing.

One more quick look over at Kirk told Jolena that he was perhaps at the end of the limit of what he would allow between her and the handsome warrior. She was afraid that they soon would come to blows, and that was the last thing she wanted—trouble between the man she had grown up with and the man that she loved, with whom she wanted to spend the rest of her life!

Chapter Fifteen

The afternoon was ending. Dull and red, the sun was lowering in the sky. The campfire blazed low, and the aroma of coffee wafted through the air. The expedition had stopped earlier than usual to make camp for the night because everyone needed to dry out their belongings that had gotten wet during the torrential rains and winds of the storm.

Jolena had crept away from the others, seeking privacy enough to take a bath in the river, although she feared being alone enough to have sneaked Kirk's pistol out of his holster after Kirk had removed it while he was changing into something drier and more comfortable for the long hours of night that lay ahead of them. She didn't expect that he would miss the pistol until tomorrow, when he dressed for travel again.

And she didn't expect him to miss her. She had set up her tent and closed its flap, making a pretense of already having retired for the night.

She knew the dangers of setting out on her own in this untamed land, yet deep down inside herself she realized that there was someone who had not missed her escape from the campsite.

Spotted Eagle.

She even suspected that he was following her.

She smiled to herself, pretending not to hear his moccasins stepping on a twig, creating a crackling sound that broke the silence.

The river sparkled through a break in the trees up just ahead of her, and Jolena hurried her pace, a towel thrown over her left arm and a bar of soap in the front right pocket of her skirt. The pistol was heavy in her left hand and she now felt foolish for having brought it. She had known that Spotted Eagle would follow her. She had made sure that he had seen her path of escape from the campsite.

Her smile faltered as she thought of Two Ridges. She had looked for him, too, before leaving the campsite, but he had been nowhere in sight. Somehow, she just could not find it in herself to trust him.

A strange foreboding filled her. All the while she had been confident that Spotted Eagle was following her. Could it have been, instead, Two

Ridges? Spotted Eagle could have had other reasons for entering the forest behind her. Perhaps he hadn't even seen her.

Fearing this possibility, Jolena stopped short and swung around, her eyes searching the deepening shadows behind her, praying that the man she loved would be there—not Two Ridges!

As she waited for the person who was following her to show his face, her pulse raced. Her forefinger sought out the trigger on the pistol. The longer she had to wait, the more nervous she became.

She found herself slowly lifting the pistol, holding it up as a man might do, taking steady aim. She pulled back the lock with a flick of her thumb, her knees weak.

When Spotted Eagle finally came into sight, Jolena sighed with relief and slowly lowered the firearm.

Spotted Eagle eyed the pistol warily, then shot his gaze up, locking his eyes with Jolena's. "And who did you think was following you besides Spotted Eagle?" he asked. "I have never seen you carry a firearm before."

"That is because I found that I was not only foolish, but trusted too easily," Jolena said, her heart hammering within her chest as Spotted Eagle came closer.

She wondered if this strong desire for him would ever lessen. Just looking at him dizzied her.

Spotted Eagle stepped up to her and reached

slowly for the pistol, then gingerly took it out of her hand. "It is good that you are learning to be cautious," he said, nodding. "But still you did not answer me about who you thought was following you. You were ready to shoot whoever it was. Tell me. Who has made you feel threatened?"

Jolena felt awkward, knowing that her fear of Two Ridges was thus far unfounded. Except for eyeing her in that strange way, he had not actually given her cause to be afraid of him.

Not wanting to cast blame until she had just cause, Jolena cast her eyes downward. "At first I thought it was you," she said, slowly moving her eyes upward again. "But when you did not make yourself known to me, I began to worry. That's why I decided to ready my gun, in case I was being stalked by someone who might harm me."

Spotted Eagle gazed down at her with frowning eyes for a moment longer, feeling that she was not being altogether truthful with him. Then he shrugged. There was no reason for her to evade the truth. There was no one near in this forest except those of the expedition. He did not see any of them as a threat to her. If so, Jolena's white father would not have chanced allowing such a person to accompany his daughter on such a journey.

"Say something," Jolena said, smiling weakly up at him. "Did I do something so terribly wrong?"

Spotted Eagle placed a hand on her cheek,

his doubts melting away as he smiled slowly down at her. "No," he said tenderly. "You did everything right. It was wise to carry a firearm while you were away from the others. I cannot condemn you for thinking ahead to what might happen while you are taking a bath in the river."

"How did you know what I was planning to do?" Jolena asked, laughing softly. "Are you not only handsome and intriguing, but also a mind reader?"

He nodded down at the towel. "That is how I read your mind," he said, chuckling low. His gaze shifted. "And I do not believe my sense of smell fails me. Is that not also a bar of perfumed soap in your skirt?"

Jolena glanced down at the bulge in her pocket. "You are right on all counts," she said, lifting smiling eyes up at Spotted Eagle again. "But now that you are here, I don't have the need for the pistol. You will keep watch for me while I bathe, won't you?"

"Spotted Eagle has his own reasons for coming to the river," he said, reaching one of his hands to her hair and letting it drift through his spread fingers. "This warrior needs a bath, also. Do you think the river is large enough for both of us?"

"I think so," Jolena giggled. "But who will stand guard if we are both swimming and bathing?"

"Old Man, the chief god of the Blackfoot, looks out for the Blackfoot warrior, and now his woman, always," Spotted Eagle said, leaning down and laying the pistol on the grass on the river embankment. "*Ok-yi*, come. *A-wah-heh*, take courage. Enter the water with me. Let me rub the perfumed soap all over you. Let my fingers awaken you again to feelings of a woman."

Seeing the heat of his desire for her in the depths of his eyes, Jolena felt her fingers trembling as she began unbuttoning her blouse.

As Spotted Eagle began undressing, Jolena's eyes followed his fingers, watching as each new inch of flesh was revealed to her feasting eyes. Her pulse raced as he tossed his shirt to the ground.

She finally stepped out of the last of her garments, then kicked her shoes aside and stood feasting her eyes on the sight of him—his muscles, his tight, firm buttocks, his flat belly that led to that valley between his hips where his passion for her was evident in the way his manhood stood out from his body ready, thick, its purple tip shedding a tiny droplet of white, creamy liquid that he nonchalantly swept away between his thumb and his forefinger.

This simple, yet sensual act caused Jolena to sway somewhat and swallow hard, having grown wet herself where the center of her desire throbbed with want of him inside her.

Then she felt his eyes on her and stood as still as a statue might, allowing him to touch her everywhere with his dark eyes, enjoying it as though it were his fingers or his tongue pleasuring her.

Spotted Eagle stood with his legs spread wide,

feeling the heat of his manhood as it throbbed unmercifully with need of being cradled within her, taking comfort from her warmth and tightness as he took his rhythmic strokes within her. He gazed at length into her eyes, feeling as though he was reaching clean into her soul, discovering again her true thoughts and love for him.

He swept his eyes slowly downward to where the swell of her breasts gave way in a smooth descent to her flat, firm belly and the triangle of soft, feathering black hair that gave him much pleasure.

Hardly able to stand any further waiting, Spotted Eagle went to her and nestled her breasts within his hands, finding them again so warm and oh, so supple.

Bending, he flicked his tongue over one and then the other, hearing her gasp of pleasure kindling his own fires.

Waiting not even to kiss her, he swept her up into his arms and began walking her into the river, her head against his chest, one arm twined around his neck. He could hear her uneven, anxious breathing, which matched his own.

And then he was startled as she lurched and leaned away from him, peering wide-eyed up at him. "The soap," she murmured. "It's still in the pocket of my skirt."

"Now do you truly believe that soap is necessary?" Spotted Eagle said, not hesitating even one moment as he continued walking into deeper water. "My woman, when have you ever truly needed soap? I have never been near you when you have not smelled like wild roses of the forest. Even now, if I kiss your breast, it will taste no less like a rose than after you cover your body with the false aromas of soap."

He shifted his arms and hands, bringing her next to him again, relishing the touch of her flesh against his, especially where her breast rested against his chest. "And, my woman, when you become a part of my village, living as the Blackfoot women live, rarely will you have soap that is scented for bathing," he said. "Will you be able to accept a life that does not allow such pampering as that? Will you accept that which your Blackfoot husband would supply you? As my wife, there would not be too many ways to spoil you, except that I would offer my loving to you both day and night and even sometimes in between, should time and circumstance allow. Would that be enough?"

Jolena's breath was stolen and her eyes were wide with wonder as he continued talking about how it would be were she his wife, when he had not actually asked her to marry him!

Perhaps this was the way it was done by the Indians.

It did not matter how, or even *if*, a proposal was ever offered her. The fact that he was speaking to her as though it were assumed that she would be his wife amazed her, yet she knew deeply within herself, where her hopes and desires were formed, that she did not have to be asked!

She wanted to be his wife, now and forevermore.

She wanted the dreams that she had of him so often to cease being a savage illusion, but instead be very, very real.

At this moment in her life, her loyalty to the only father she had ever known was dimming within her heart. She knew now that if she had to choose whether to return to be a devoted daughter to Bryce Edmonds, or stay in the Montana Territory and be a dutiful wife to Spotted Eagle, there would be no quarrel within her.

Spotted Eagle was her destiny, mapped out from the beginning of time, even before she had snuggled in the womb of her mother, taking breath and life from her.

It had been God's plan to bring her and Spotted Eagle together, and she would let no man or thing stop this bonding.

Not even Bryce Edmonds, whose life now seemed centered on a daughter whom he had perhaps feared losing from the very day he had taken her from the arms of her dead mother.

Spotted Eagle stopped where the water was just brushing against Jolena's breasts. He eased her to her feet, onto the pebbled floor of the river, then encircled her within his arms and drew her close. He gazed down at her intensely.

"You have not answered my questions," he said, his voice drawn. "Are they too much of a challenge? Were they untimely spoken? Had they been asked later, after you have been able to test the strength of your love for me, would you then have given me a quick response?"

Jolena reached her hands to his hair and

stroked it away from his brow, then placed her hands on each side of his face. "My darling, I need no more time to know the strength of my love for you," she murmured. "The reason you did not get quick answers was because you stunned me with what you were saying—not so much with the questions as the way you talked so matter-of-factly of how it will be when we are married."

"My lodge is good, my parfleches are never empty," Spotted Eagle said softly, yet with much meaning and emotion. "There are always plenty of tanned robes and soft furs for winters in my lodge. These will be yours."

She traced his lips with her fingertips, then leaned up and softly kissed him. "I love you so much," she then whispered against his lips. "I'm so happy that you want me to be your wife. I want to be with you, my handsome warrior, forever. When you talk of all tomorrows, please always include me, for I want to be there even when we are old and feeble. I want to grow old with you, my darling. I want to feel the joy of being a grandparent with you."

She gazed through a haze of joyous tears up at him. "Make love to me, darling," she murmured. "Oh, how I want you."

Spotted Eagle framed her face between his hands and kissed her passionately, trembling with pleasure as her hands sought out that part of him that had become delicately tender in its waiting for such caresses.

When her fingers began moving on him, the

water warm and caressing in itself, a keen euphoria began claiming him. Slipping his hands down her body, finding the soft curves of her buttocks, he splayed his fingers against her and lifted her up, soon thrusting his thick shaft within her.

Jolena reached around and sank her fingers into the flesh of his buttocks, urging him more deeply into her as she gave him a gentle shove. Then she twined her arms around his neck and placed her legs around his waist, locking her legs together at her ankles.

She closed her eyes as the ecstasy began swimming through her.

Spotted Eagle groaned as he felt the pleasure rising ... rising ... spreading ... spreading, this time much more quickly than the others. He thrust himself over and over again inside her, the heat scorching his insides, his desire a sharp, hot pain in his loins.

As the final rays of a magnificent sunset flamed across the sky, rapture welled up inside Spotted Eagle and Jolena, filling them, spilling over, drenching them with warmth and deep feelings of fulfillment.

Afterwards, Jolena clung to Spotted Eagle, her cheek on his shoulder. She caught her breath, daring not to breathe, afraid that if she did, she would discover that this was just another illusion, one that she would awaken from with empty longings.

She was soon aware that this was no illusion. She sighed leisurely and tremors cascaded down her back when Spotted Eagle began stroking her legs, his fingers moving slowly upward, the sureness of his caress lighting her with desire again.

When his fingers teased circles around her belly, up to her breasts, just missing the nipples each time so that they strained with added anticipation, Jolena felt as though she might melt right into the water.

The air heavy with the inevitability of added pleasure, Spotted Eagle took Jolena from the river and lay her down on a soft bed of moss. She closed her eyes and bit her lower lip to keep from crying out with rapture when he began making his way down her body with his lips and tongue, awakening anew her every secret place with fresh desire.

When he began caressing her tender mound of pleasure with his tongue, she sucked in a wild breath and closed her eyes. The feelings were so wonderfully sweet, she felt as though she might be floating high in the sky, a bird with wide-spread wings, soaring higher and higher and higher. . . .

Then Spotted Eagle moved over her and filled her once again with his thick shaft. He held her hands above her head as he kissed her, his body thrusting maddeningly fast within her.

Surges of warmth flooded Jolena's body once again and she knew that Spotted Eagle was finding as keen a pleasure as she by the way he groaned and continued plunging himself into her, continuing at this speed until his seed splashed against the walls of her womanhood.

Jolena lay perfectly still when Spotted Eagle rolled away from her.

"I've never been so content," Jolena finally said, her eyes still closed, feeling at peace with herself and the world. "I'm so very, very happy."

There was a pause when neither of them said anything, then Spotted Eagle leaned on one elbow and gazed over at Jolena. "I know your true father," he said suddenly, without warning.

Jolena's eyes flew open and she looked up at Spotted Eagle, her eyes wide and imploring.

Chapter Sixteen

Stunned, Jolena gazed into Spotted Eagle's eyes, then suddenly came to her senses. Instead of reacting with curiosity to his statement, anger was suddenly her main emotion. He had surely known from the very beginning who her father was, and he had chosen not to tell her!

She wanted nothing more at this moment than to know who her father was and where she could find him, but her anger with Spotted Eagle seemed to blind her to all logic. She felt as though he had played a game with her, by knowing all along something that would make her heart sing, and yet not telling her.

She wondered now if all words that he had said to her were just part of a game!

Heatedly, she gathered her clothes up from the ground and moved quickly to her feet, turning her back to Spotted Eagle. She could feel his eyes on her as she hurriedly dressed, surely as stunned by her attitude as she had been by his sudden decision to tell her secrets about herself, her family, and her past.

Her heart cried out to turn to him and plead with him to tell her everything. But the stubborn side of her made her remain quiet, knowing that if Spotted Eagle knew these answers, so would someone else.

Perhaps even Two Ridges!

Surely that was the reason he always stared at her!

Yet if he knew, why would he, also, not share these wonderful things with her?

She had the right to know!

Sudden, tight fingers on her shoulders made Jolena's insides stiffen. Her lips parted and her eyes widened as Spotted Eagle quickly spun her around to face him, his eyes two dark, angry pits as he glared down at her.

"I was wrong to tell you that I know your true father?" he said, his voice drawn. "That I even knew your mother?"

Jolena winced as his grip on her shoulders tightened, yet she soon forgot the pain when she absorbed his words—he had even known her true mother! It was hard not to blurt out all sorts of questions to him, yet still she could not get over being upset with him over having not told her these truths as soon as he realized who she was.

"It is not what you told me, or profess to tell

me," she finally said, her throat dry. "It is *when* you chose to tell me. Why did you wait so long? I find that very hard to understand. Did you enjoy keeping secrets from me?"

She paused and peered more intensely up at him. "How do you even know who my true parents are?" she said, her fingers trembling, her voice breaking with emotion.

Spotted Eagle eased his fingers from her shoulders. He touched her cheek gently with a hand.

"The moment I first laid eyes on you, I knew you must be the daughter of Sweet Dove and Brown Elk," he said, his thumb caressing the flesh beneath her chin. "Yet do you not also see this as perhaps too much coincidence? I wanted to study you and be certain before I told you."

Deep down inside himself, he knew that was not totally true. The truth had more to do with Sweet Dove than anything else. If Jolena ever discovered his boyhood feelings for Sweet Dove and that Jolena was the mirror image of her mother, would she believe that it was she he loved, instead of a memory—perhaps the spirit of a woman who had come back to him?

He doubted it.

"You . . . knew my mother . . . ?" Jolena asked, her voice trembling at the thought. Perhaps Spotted Eagle had even spoken to her mother from time to time when he was a young boy.

For a moment, Spotted Eagle felt trapped between memories and reality.

To delay responding to Jolena's answer, he reached for his clothes and began dressing.

"Spotted Eagle, please tell me," Jolena pleaded, frustration gripping her. "I want to know everything. I have wanted to know these things since I first discovered that my childhood playmates' skin coloring differed from mine and I forced answers from my parents—answers that revealed to me that I am Indian, not white!"

Nervously running his long, lean fingers through his hair, Spotted Eagle gazed down at Jolena. "You turned from me earlier when I was ready to reveal all truths to you," he said. "Now you are pleading with me for these answers? Why is that?"

"It is only because I could not understand why you didn't tell me the moment you discovered who my true parents were," Jolena responded. "I . . . thought you were playing some sort of game with me. Now I can tell it is more than that. Until now, something has kept you from revealing the truth to me. What has changed *your* mind?"

"The commitment that is building between us," Spotted Eagle said, reaching for her hands and holding them lovingly with his. "There should be no secrets between a man and woman who are contemplating marriage."

"Are we?" Jolena said, her voice soft. "Are we truly contemplating marriage?"

"It is my deep desire to have you as my *nit-o-ke-man*—my wife," Spotted Eagle said, drawing her into his embrace. "Let me care for you. Let us share in everything we do, and it is my solemn promise to you that there will be no more secrets between us."

"There is only one more thing in life that I want as badly as I want to marry you," Jolena said, swallowing hard as she leaned back enough to be able to look into his dark eyes. "Spotted Eagle, you mentioned my parents' names. You have known them. I know my mother is dead. But what of my true father?"

"Your true father, Brown Elk, is well and soon I will take you to him," Spotted Eagle said. "I will do it tomorrow at the early sun's rising, if you so wish."

Jolena eased from his arms and began a slow pacing, her eyes troubled. She was eager to see her true father and feel the embrace of her true people, yet . . . yet she had another father, one with whom her life had been shared!

Already she had chosen, by accepting Spotted Eagle's proposal of marriage, not to live with him anymore.

How would he understand any of this, especially that she would forget her loyalties to him after he had given her everything in life that was good?

She stopped and turned toward Spotted Eagle, knowing what she must do, even though delaying meeting with her true father was eating away at her. "No," she said, her voice almost failing her because her emotions were running so sharply through her. "I must continue searching for the elusive, rare butterfly. Once I find it and can send it back to my father in Saint Louis with Kirk, along with the other specimens that I have caught for my father's collection, then I will feel that I have in part repaid my white father for being so good to me."

She paused and her eyes beamed up into Spotted Eagle's. "Then I will feel free to go to my true father and reveal my identity to him," she murmured. "It will be a day of miracles, Spotted Eagle, that after all these years, I will finally be able to embrace my true father and my true people."

Then she became solemn again. "You have not yet told me how you knew who I was," she said softly. "Does someone else know? Did they point me out to you, saying that I was the daughter of Brown Elk?"

Then her eyes widened and she spoke again before Spotted Eagle had the chance to answer. "Am I Blackfoot like you?" she asked, her voice anxious.

"Very much so," Spotted Eagle said, drawing her close and hugging her tightly.

"That is wonderful," Jolena sighed, clinging to him. "Now, darling, tell me how you knew who I was?"

She could feel Spotted Eagle stiffen somewhat and could feel the sudden hammering of his heart against her cheek.

She now feared the answer, more than wanting to hear it!

"How?" Spotted Eagle eased her from his arms and took her hands, leading her down onto the softness of a layer of moss that lined the riverbank. "As I said, there will be no more secrets between us. I will tell you everything."

He began his tale, beginning when he was nine and his infatuation for an older woman had begun. Except for having shared this with Two Ridges, he had kept his secret hidden within the depths of his heart. He told Jolena of his feelings for Sweet Dove and how he had felt when word had been received of her death and that her child had been taken from her by an unknown person.

He told Jolena about having gone to his favorite private spot where he had prayed to fires of the sun for Sweet Dove's child, praying that those who took the child would give her much love.

He told Jolena how long he had mourned the loss of Sweet Dove, how in the past he had experienced a strange sort of sinking feeling when he saw her in his mind's eye, so beautiful and alive, so sweet.

"You no longer get that sinking feeling when you think of my mother?" Jolena asked softly. "Why, Spotted Eagle?"

Spotted Eagle looked away from her, then gazed into her eyes again. "Why?" he repeated, placing a gentle hand on her cheek. "Because of you. When you entered my life, many things changed for me."

"Oh, I see, I—I took the place of my mother in your heart," Jolena said, blinking her eyes up at him.

"More than that," Spotted Eagle said, his eyes again shifting away from her.

"Oh, Lord," Jolena said softly, her voice drawn. "Now I think I know why you knew who I was.

When you look at me, you see my mother! That's it, isn't it, Spotted Eagle? In your eyes and heart I *am* my mother!"

"That is not so," Spotted Eagle said quickly as he turned around to face her. "My feelings for you are different in every way. My feelings for your mother were those of an adolescent. It was merely an infatuation. My feelings for you are those of a man, true and deep."

"But you can't help seeing my mother when you look at me," Jolena said, her voice breaking. "I want to be loved for myself, not because I am the mirror image of someone else."

"It is true that at first, when I looked at you, my feelings were the same as that young boy whose heart ached for an older woman," Spotted Eagle tried to explain. "But as I grew to know you, someone different from your mother in so many ways, it was *you* who moved me into a man's feelings. Your mother is now a pleasant memory. You are here, quite real, and wonderful."

"When we have been making love, have you ever wished it were my mother instead of me?" Jolena could not resist asking. "Have you ever pretended I was she?"

Spotted Eagle's jaw tightened and his eyes flared with a sudden anger. "I have not loved a memory while I held you in my arms," he said tersely. "Never will I. I love you. Forever and ever, I shall love only you."

"It would break my heart if it were otherwise," Jolena said, flinging herself into his arms. As she laid her cheek against his powerful chest, she began her own confessions. "Darling, I knew you before we met, also."

"And how is that possible?" he asked, stroking her thick, long hair.

"I do not understand how that could be possible," she murmured. "But it is true that when I saw you I was stunned because I had seen your face before—in dreams."

He placed his fingers to her shoulders and eased her back from him so that their eyes met and held. "You say you dreamed of me?" he said wonderingly. "You saw my exact facial features in your dreams?"

"Yes, many times," she murmured. "And yet I still do not see how that can be so."

Spotted Eagle smiled softly down at her. "There are ways," he said, nodding. "You are Blackfoot. Many things are foretold in the dreams of the Blackfoot!"

"Truly?" she asked, her eyes wide. "Please tell me how. I have had many dreams, foretelling many things. Sometimes it has frightened me to have such . . . such abilities."

"You should not be frightened by a gift that has been handed down from generation to generation of Blackfoot," he said, drawing her into his embrace once again. He held her close, breathing in the sweet fragrance of her hair as he placed his cheek against it. "Our people, the Blackfoot, are firm believers in dreams. These, it is said, are sent by the Sun to enable us to look ahead, to tell what is going to happen. A dream, especially if it is a strong one—that is, if the dream is very clear and vivid—is almost always obeyed."

He paused, then continued, "An animal or object which appears to a boy or man who is trying to dream for power is, it has been said, regarded thereafter as his secret helper, his medicine, and is usually called his vision dream—*Nits-o-kan.*"

"I have obeyed the commands of my midnight dream," Jolena said, clinging to him. "I have followed its bidding and have found you, my darling."

Then a silent panic seized her, recalling the dream in which Spotted Eagle died, fearing that it might come true also. She leaned into his arms and held him much more tightly, wanting never to let him go.

The night was wrapped in shadows, with shreds of mist clinging to the trees overhead, as Jolena and Spotted Eagle began walking back toward their campsite. Spotted Eagle stopped when the moonlight revealed something that lay in their path. Jolena followed Spotted Eagle's eyes to a feather that had surely fallen from the wing of an eagle. It was perhaps the largest one that she had ever seen, and its colors were a beautiful soft gray, touched by streaks of white.

Spotted Eagle stooped and picked up the feather, then handed it to Jolena. "Have I told you before that the wing of a bird is a symbol of thoughts that fly very high?" he said softly.

"Whether or not you have, I could hear it over and over again," Jolena said softly. "That's a beautiful saying."

She held the feather to her heart and walked leisurely along with Spotted Eagle again, the campfire throwing its golden light through a break in the trees a short distance away.

Jolena leaned closer to Spotted Eagle, not wanting these special moments to end.

Chapter Seventeen

The next day, the wagons continued onward. Jolena was filled with an anticipation she had never known before.

And why shouldn't she be feeling this way? she argued to herself. She was perhaps only days away from meeting her true father.

Oh, but how simple it would be to abandon this expedition and hurry onward with the rest of her life instead of waiting until she completed her mission for her ailing white father.

It was hard to sit on the wagon beside Kirk as though nothing had happened, while at the same moment her heart was beating out each and every minute of the day, bringing her closer to that time when she would say an awkward farewell to him.

He would not leave her all that easily, she

knew. He would try to fill her mind with doubts about the life that lay ahead of her in an Indian village.

And she knew that most of his arguments would be valid ones. In her lifetime, she had known only luxuries. She knew that living in a tepee had to be far from luxurious and comfortable.

Being with Spotted Eagle would make up for everything else, but she dreaded trying to convince her brother of this. Often he was even more stubborn than she. . . .

"You're more quiet than usual," Kirk said, allowing the reins to go somewhat slack in his hands as he gave Jolena a studious stare. "Why is that? What's on your mind?"

His lips curved into an angry pout when she smiled weakly at him, offering him no explanation. "How foolish of me to have asked," he said heatedly. "I already know the answer, don't I?"

He turned his gaze ahead, focusing on the straight back of Spotted Eagle as he rode his magnificent stallion only a few feet ahead of the wagon, then turned angry eyes at his sister again.

"*He's* the cause of your strange behavior," he said in a low hiss. "You've allowed yourself to fall in love with him, haven't you?"

"Kirk, I don't think you want to continue with this debate," Jolena finally said, her voice strained. "Just concentrate on getting the wagon through the forest. I'd like to find that elusive butterfly today so that I—"

She caught herself before saying what her heart was feeling.

"So that you can what?" Kirk said, forking an eyebrow.

Jolena flipped her hair back from her shoulders. "Kirk, stop prodding me with questions," she said, giving him an annoyed stare. "You may cause us not to see the two special butterflies we seek."

"Two special butterflies?" Kirk said, once again looking straight ahead. He flicked the reins, snapping them along the backs of the two mules attached to his wagon. "Now you are looking especially for two, not just the *euphaedra?*"

"I am intrigued by the *nymphalid*, as well," Jolena said, scoffing now at Spotted Eagle's warnings that the *nymphalid* was bad luck.

It *was* true that she had fallen over the cliff while chasing the butterfly. But to actually believe that it had teased her over the cliff purposely had to be ridiculous.

She wanted the *nymphalid* now more than ever.

While her father admired it, Kirk could be telling him the special story about it. . . .

Yet, on second thought, she doubted that her brother would tell her father about the incident. Kirk had not attempted to save her. He would not want to give the credit to Spotted Eagle, who would by that time have become Kirk's arch-enemy for having stolen Jolena away from him and his father.

"I think it's best that you concentrate on something besides that damn *nymphalid*," Kirk grumbled. "I'll never forget that it is the cause for your having fallen over the cliff."

He cast her a sheepish look. "I should've tried to save you," he said, his voice drawn. "But my feet would not carry me to the edge of the cliff. And my heart was beating so hard, I felt dizzy. I . . . surely would have fallen over the side also, had I leaned even that one inch over it. And you know my fear of heights, sis."

Jolena hesitated a moment, feeling that no excuse would ever make up for his not having attempted to save her.

Yet she was not one to hold a grudge.

She patted Kirk's knee. "Yes, I know," she murmured. "Let's not speak of it anymore. I'm alive. That is all that should matter."

Kirk swallowed hard, nodded, then silence fell between him and Jolena as the wagon lumbered on beneath the trees.

Although the sun was nearly at its mid-point in the sky, there was a deceptive silvery light in the air. The sunshine weaved through the thick foliage overhead, melting into the gray, steaming mist that gave body to shadow and made phantoms of solid objects.

As the forest was left behind and the wagons and their two Blackfoot guides on horseback moved out into open land, the mist began clearing. Jolena caught glimpses of the blue sky overhead.

Jolena sighed, enjoying the changes around her. The valley in which she was now traveling was refreshed from the last night's heavy dew, the grass glistening as if in the first flush of spring. The air seemed washed clean and sparkling clear with crystalline sharpness. Birds soared overhead, giving off their strange calls, their wings casting shadows across the land beneath them.

And then the valley stretched out to mountain peaks and more valleys. As the wagon went higher and higher, now on narrow canyon paths, Jolena's pulse began to race. Suddenly she began to see butterflies flitting around everywhere, their colors brilliant as the clouds melted away in the sky overhead, spilling the sun's rays down to create bright and certain light in which to see the butterflies more clearly.

Jolena's heart lurched when her eyes caught sight of the *euphaedra*, which had finally come out of hiding! "Kirk, stop!" she shouted, waving her arms in the air frantically. "I've seen it."

Kirk yanked the reins and stopped the mules, but he showed no signs of being happy about Jolena's announcement. The wagon was in a precarious place, a ledge of rock on one side, a sheer drop on the other, with barely enough space for anyone to move safely around.

Jolena already had the butterfly net in her hand. "Get the jar and follow me, Kirk," she said, her eyes bright with excitement. If she could catch this butterfly, she would forget the other one, after all. Today could be the final day of the expedition and tomorrow—oh, tomorrow, she might be able to go to her true father and reveal herself to him. She would be able to be with her true people!

"Sis, this isn't wise," Kirk said, not budging

from the seat. "This isn't a safe place to go butter-fly catching."

"Kirk, I *saw* it," Jolena insisted, annoyed at Kirk's further proof of cowardice. "Get the jar and let's go!"

Her eyes caught sight of something else as it flitted only a few inches past her nose. She gasped and her knees grew weak, realizing that the *nymphalid* was there again, teasing her again.

"I'm going to catch that butterfly also," she said, sliding easily from her seat, watching her feet as they reached the slippery rocks that gave her anything but sure footing. She did not look past her feet, for she knew that the steep drop would take her breath away.

She gave Kirk a quick glance, remembering that he was afraid of heights. "Don't get out on your side," she hastily warned. "Stay over there. I'll come to you."

"This is damn foolish," Kirk argued, yet he knew that he had no choice but to join her or look the fool again in his sister's eyes.

He reached beneath the seat and grabbed the bottle that already had a piece of cotton soaked with alcohol in it. Grumbling, he left the wagon.

When Jolena came to him, he began following her, catching glimpses over his shoulder of the other lepidopterists busy swinging their nets, catching everything but the two that Jolena was so determined to snare.

"Up there!" Jolena shouted, pointing up the steep side of the bluff as it loomed overhead.

"I've got to climb up there and get it!"

Spotted Eagle had been watching everything with caution, knowing that if he should show too much concern for her, Kirk could cause much trouble for them.

To save Jolena undue embarrassment, Spotted Eagle had stood by, silent until now. But when he heard Jolena say that she was going to climb the side of the cliff, that was all the fuel he needed to go after her.

"Care for my horse," he said, giving his reins over to Two Ridges.

Two Ridges had been watching Jolena with concern also and did not like the idea that Spotted Eagle was going to once again get the glory for saving her from what might be a close brush with death. If she attempted climbing the side of the cliff and lost her balance, she might not just fall to the narrow path. She might miss it and plummet to her death below, where rocks jutted out in cone-shaped peaks, waiting to pierce her body like sharpened lances.

Spotted Eagle went to Jolena and grabbed her by one wrist, stopping her as she walked determinedly away from Kirk. "I cannot allow you to do that," he said, ignoring the looks and frowns of everyone who now stood by watching. "It is too dangerous."

Jolena gazed up at him, her lips parted with surprise that he would come to her in such a way, knowing how it must look to everyone else.

Yet he was their guide, looking out for their interest. She hoped that everyone would see that as the reason he had come to her with the commands of a lover!

Frustrated and angry, Kirk frowned at Spotted Eagle, then looked slowly over at Jolena. There was clearly something between his sister and this Blackfoot guide, and it tore at his heart. This drove him into doing something which under other conditions he would never have attempted.

He set his jar aside and went to Jolena, grabbing her net away from her.

"I'll get *both* butterflies for you," he said, his voice tight.

Jolena reached a hand out to Kirk in an effort to stop him, but Spotted Eagle would not allow her to.

As the *nymphalid* fluttered higher and higher along the sides of the steep slope of rock, Jolena held her breath, her heart pounding as fear suddenly gripped her. The damnable butterfly was behaving in a teasing fashion again, but this time it was Kirk who was the recipient of its sultry charm.

Perhaps there *was* something to the myth that the butterfly caused bad luck. The thought sent icy shivers up and down Jolena's flesh.

"Kirk, don't!" she cried, but it was already too late. Kirk was fitting his feet in tiny holes along the side of the rock wall. As one hand searched for something solid to grab, the other firmly gripped the handle of the net.

Scarcely breathing, Jolena watched as Kirk climbed higher, his eyes watching the *nymphalid* fluttering closer and closer to his face.

"The damn thing!" he shouted, turning to give Jolena a look of frustration. "How can I catch it if it continues trying to land on my nose!"

Just as he made eye contact with Jolena, the butterfly began flapping its wings against Kirk's face, over and over again. Jolena's heart sank as she watched Kirk momentarily forget that he was holding on to the sheet of rock to keep himself from falling. Instinct led him to slap at the butterfly, and when he did, his body fell backward away from the wall, plummeting quickly toward the rock path below.

"Oh, Lord," Jolena whispered, her eyes wide and terrified as she watched Kirk land clumsily on the rock, his head making a strange thud as it hit.

Wrenching her wrist out of Spotted Eagle's firm grip, she ran to Kirk and fell to her knees beside him. She covered her mouth with her hands as she watched blood trickle from the corner of her brother's mouth, concerned over how quietly he lay—had he only been rendered unconscious by the fall? Would he wake soon?

Tears rushed down Jolena's cheeks, and she was filled with guilt for having neglected Kirk's attentions of late and actually keeping her distance from him when they had made camp so he would not preach to her against the Indians.

"Oh, Kirk," Jolena sobbed. She started to reach out to cradle his head on her lap, but stopped when Spotted Eagle knelt down beside her, a canteen in his hand.

Wide-eyed, Jolena watched as Spotted Eagle

emptied the water from the canteen onto Kirk's face, then gasped with happiness as Kirk's eyes began to flutter open, his hand reaching for the throbbing knot that was forming on the back of his head.

"What happened?" Kirk asked, gazing questioningly up into Jolena's eyes, then past her at Spotted Eagle, who was screwing the top back onto his canteen.

Jolena did not take the time to answer him. She leaned down and gave him a big hug. "Thank God you're all right," she said, sobbing as she cradled his head close to her bosom. "That damn butterfly. I never want to see it again, much less try and catch it. Kirk, I'm sure it meant for you to die!"

Kirk eased from her comforting arms and moved to a sitting position. "Hogwash," he said, yet his insides were cold with the memory of the butterfly attacking him, as though purposely. "Butterflies have no sense of logic. Something frightened it into thrashing itself against me. That's all."

Jolena placed a gentle hand to his elbow and helped him up from the ground. "Are you truly all right?" she murmured. "You had quite a fall."

Kirk looked at Jolena. "I'd say it was worth it," he said, smiling softly. "Seems I've got my sister back."

Jolena smiled weakly at him, knowing that it did appear that way, yet she knew that this closeness was only temporary.

Even after they continued on with their journey and made camp for the night, Jolena continued to pamper Kirk with all sorts of attention. She was thankful that he was all right, and she could not help but feel somewhat guilty for how she would soon abandon him. So for now, at least, she was trying to make up to him all at once.

"Here's another cup of coffee," Jolena said as she brought the tin cup back to Kirk, where he was leaning his back against the trunk of a tree, resting before the slowly burning embers of a campfire. "Can I get anything else for you? There's plenty of rabbit left. Would you care for more?"

"Sis, sit right down here beside me," Kirk said, patting the blanket that was spread out beneath him. "All I need is you."

Jolena lifted the hem of her travel skirt and plopped down beside Kirk. When he reached an arm around her waist, drawing her close, she allowed it. They sat quietly watching the fire as they had so often as children in their granite fireplace in their plush parlor in Saint Louis.

"We've shared so much," Kirk said, his voice thick with melancholy. "Remember how we used to share our dreams? Do you wish to share them again, sis? I . . . I feel as though I am losing you. As each day passes, I sense I have lost a little more of you to this land of your ancestors."

He reached for one of her hands and clutched hard to it. "Oh, God, Jolena, please don't let it happen," he pleaded. "No matter the color of your skin, in every sense of the word you are my sister. You are my best friend."

"I know," Jolena murmured, easing into his embrace. "I know, Kirk."

She hugged him as though it might be her last chance to do so.

She wanted to whisper to him that she was sorry for the decisions that she had recently made in her life that would sorely affect his. She wanted to beg him to understand, yet she felt that this was not the time—if ever there would be a right time.

Spotted Eagle watched, but did not grow jealous at the sight of his woman being hugged by another man. He could see the desperation in the brother and sister's embrace.

And he understood why.

Without Kirk being aware of it, it was the beginning of the farewell between him and his beloved sister.

Spotted Eagle glanced over at Two Ridges, who sat sullenly at his right side, staring aimlessly into the fire. Spotted Eagle had not yet told Two Ridges the truth about Jolena—that she was his true sister. He wanted to savor the secret that was now only Jolena's and Spotted Eagle's for as long as possible.

And he feared that a chain reaction might be started should he reveal the news to Two Ridges or Jolena too soon. Kirk Edmonds would then know also and would realize that Jolena's days and hours with him were numbered.

It was best delayed, this telling of truths that could hurt and possibly jeopardize Spotted Eagle's future with Jolena. Kirk could become crazed enough with the knowing and steal Jolena away, forcing her on the large, white canoe that would take her back to Saint Louis, where she would be lost to Spotted Eagle forever.

He nodded, knowing without a shadow of a doubt that this secret was best left alone, for now.

Chapter Eighteen

The next morning, a mist filled the air, so that in the uncertain light objects seemed shrouded in mystery as the wagons moved slowly alongside a steep cliff, then momentarily away from it as the mules ambled along, squealing as the wagoners swore at them and uncoiled and snapped their whips like fusillades of rifle fire over their heads.

Jolena clung to her wagon seat, fear entering her heart as black storm clouds began gathering more thickly in the sky overhead and lightning moved in bright zigzags between them.

"Kirk, I don't like the looks of the sky," Jolena said, breaking the silence between them.

She looked over at Kirk, whose lips were pursed and whose eyes squinted angrily as he stared ahead, tending to his team of stubborn mules.

"Kirk, did you hear what I said?" Jolena persisted. "It seems as though you are in a different world today. Is it because of what happened yesterday? Because of your fall?"

She glanced at the purple knot on his head, knowing that it must be throbbing painfully. Kirk had not allowed Spotted Eagle anywhere near him when Spotted Eagle had brought herbs gathered from the forest to place upon the wound. Even though Kirk had not been told anything about Jolena's plans to stay with Spotted Eagle when the time came for everyone else to return to Saint Louis, Kirk seemed to sense it. When Spotted Eagle had offered to help him, Kirk had shunned him.

"It's this whole damn mess of an expedition," Kirk finally said in a low grumble. He gave Jolena a frowning glare. "I've had enough. I want to return to Saint Louis. Both you and I have almost lost our lives trying to find that damnable butterfly. And now it's not only the *euphaedra* that you are so obsessed with, it's also the *nymphalid*."

Kirk paused, his eyes locked momentarily with Jolena's. Then he looked ahead again, watching the procession of the wagons that were traveling in front of him and Jolena today, instead of following. Somehow he felt safer lagging behind instead of being the lead wagon.

Jolena started to comment on what her brother had said, but stopped when he began talking again in a monotone.

"If you ask me, sis, the *nymphalid* is living up to its legend," Kirk said exasperatedly. "It has not only almost teased you to your death, but also me. I don't want to be around when it appears again, as though out of nowhere, with its teasings."

He gazed at Jolena again, his eyes pleading. "Let's turn around right now, Jolena, and return to Saint Louis," he said softly. "Once father hears the dangers we put ourselves in to catch the butterfly of his obsession, he will know that our decision to return home was right. He would not want it any other way."

Jolena reached a hand over and patted Kirk's knee. "I know that what you experienced yesterday was frightening," she murmured. "And when I almost plummeted to my death, I was petrified. But both times it was an accident—not the doings of a butterfly. Surely nothing else will happen."

She moved her hand away from him and clung to the wagon seat again when the wheels sank into a pothole, then rolled free again, the wagon swaying dangerously from side to side from the jolt.

"I can't return to Saint Louis, Kirk," she said, forced to tell him truths that would hurt him. But she could not continue with this charade. If he was determined to return to Saint Louis this soon, she had no choice but to tell him that she would not be aboard the riverboat with him, no matter when he chose to travel on it again.

Kirk gave her a quick, wide-eyed glance. "What . . . do you mean?" he said, his voice drawn.

Jolena started to speak, but was stopped when rain began pouring from the sky in blinding sheets, as though someone overhead in the thick clouds was overturning monstrous buckets of water onto the travelers.

When a sudden bolt of lightning splintered a tree close by, there was nothing to be done about the mules that were just as quickly spooked.

Jolena screamed.

The mules attached to all of the wagons began squealing and scrambling in all directions. The wagoners cursed and snapped their whips along the backs of the confused, frightened mules, causing the animals to strain even more desperately at their harnesses.

The chains clanked.

The axles groaned as the mules turned in a frenzy and began running blindly toward the edge of the cliff.

Spotted Eagle had been lagging behind on his stallion, discussing the day's plans with Two Ridges, when the storm broke and everything around him became a frenzied mass.

Stunned, he watched through the blinding rain as the mules began running toward the cliff. His insides froze as first one wagon plunged over the side, then another.

And even when Jolena's wagon went over the side of the cliff and he felt as though his heart leapt from inside him, he was unable to do anything since it had all happened so quickly. In one wink of an eye his woman was lost to him!

"Can it be that what we saw is real?" Two

Ridges said, in his voice a panic. He reached over and clasped Spotted Eagle's arm. "*Hai-yah!* Tell me that what I saw is not real! Tell me, Spotted Eagle, that it was not real!"

Spotted Eagle yanked his arm away, sank his heels into the flanks of his horse, and rode off in a hard gallop toward the scene. His pulse raced, and within his heart there was an ache far worse than he had experienced when he heard of Sweet Dove's passing.

This time he had lost *his* woman—the woman who was his future, the mother of children that would now never be born of their love!

Tears scorched Spotted Eagle's cheeks. Dismounting in one leap when he reached the cliff, he clung to the horse's reins as he dared to take a step closer so that he could look down upon the wreckage below him. He could scarcely summon up the courage to look over the cliff and see her broken body.

Yet he could not turn away until he knew for certain that she *was* lying among her friends and brother, dead. . . .

Two Ridges was still too stupefied by the suddenness of what had happened to move. He watched with bated breath as Spotted Eagle took another step closer to the edge of the cliff, waiting for his friend to emit a loud cry of despair.

Not wanting to experience such a moment, Two Ridges turned his eyes away from his friend, trying to focus them on something else that might make him forget that horrible sight of Jolena's wagon plunging over the cliff. Two Ridges swept his eyes slowly around him. The rain was now only a slight drizzle, making the scene more visible than only moments ago. He still refused to look Spotted Eagle's way, although he wondered why his friend was so quiet, as though his eyes had not yet found the woman of his desire.

This gave Two Ridges a soft ray of hope within his heart—that perhaps his copper princess had not truly died after all and that what he had seen had been a mirage caused by the iridescent flashing of the lightning combined with the blinding haze of the rain.

His heart thudding at the thought, Two Ridges started to dismount and go to see for himself that perhaps what he and his friend had thought they had seen had not been real at all.

But just as he was swinging his leg over his saddle, something caught his attention.

"Jolena?" he whispered harshly, his pulse now pounding in his ears at the sight of a slight hand lying on the ground, stretching out from behind a thickly leafed bush.

"Can it be?" Two Ridges mumbled to himself. Could that be Jolena? Had she been thrown free?

In his anxiousness to see if it were true, he started to shout at Spotted Eagle, but something wicked inside him told him not to—told him that this could be the perfect opportunity to do as *he* pleased, for a change.

If this was Jolena, he could have her all to himself!

He would carry her away and treat her wounds.

She would be so grateful to this Blackfoot warrior that she would be his, instead of Spotted Eagle's.

The thought dizzied him as he jumped to the ground and ran stealthily toward the bush. When he stepped quickly behind it, everything within him mellowed at the sight of Jolena lying there, unconscious, but obviously not injured all that badly.

Smiling to himself, Two Ridges knew that Jolena's unconscious state gave him the opportunity he needed to carry her away without alerting Spotted Eagle to his friend's deceit. He did not even allow himself to consider the end results of such a deceit.

But having Jolena as his own was well worth any sacrifice. Two Ridges swept her up into his arms and carried her limp body to his horse.

Casting quick glances Spotted Eagle's way as he now knelt at the edge of the cliff, obviously praying for the soul of his woman, Two Ridges placed Jolena across his saddle and swung himself into it.

Still cautiously watching Spotted Eagle, Two Ridges eased Jolena onto his lap and leaned her head against his chest, holding her in place with one of his powerful arms, while with his free hand he gripped the reins and urged his horse quietly around.

His heart pounding, Two Ridges felt blessed that soft moss cushioned the sound of his horse's hooves as they moved onward. Two Ridges knew where he would go. There was a secret cave that he knew. Never had he shared the location of this cave with Spotted Eagle or any of his other friends. It had been Two Ridges' secret place to play as a child and pray as an adult.

Jolena would be the only one to share his secret.

Moving into the shadows of the forest, Two Ridges sighed with relief. Sinking his knees into the sides of his horse, he sent it quickly onward. When Jolena moaned and moved slightly in his arms, his insides melted as he glanced down at her. He studied her features, finding them beautiful and alluring, yet now that he was this close, there seemed something different about her from the beauty he had admired in her at arm's length.

It was only a slight resemblance that he was seeing, yet it was there—a look in her sleep that he had seen often when his very own father lay sleeping.

There was something about the way she held her lips, the way she seemed to be smiling even while asleep. . . .

He had admired that trait in his father, whose heart was always so kind to everyone, even strangers, that his kindness had always followed him as he fell asleep.

This gave Two Ridges a strange foreboding inside his heart, yet he scoffed and cast these feelings aside, knowing that although this woman was Indian in all of her features, she was not related to anyone that Two Ridges knew!

Most certainly Jolena was not the daughter of his father!

A sudden thought gripped Two Ridges' insides then, and he recalled the story of his father's first wife and how a child had been taken from her. No one had ever seen the child again, nor had it been known if it was a boy or a girl.

No one even knew if the child was still alive!

"This is not my father's daughter," Two Ridges said, convincing himself that she wasn't.

The reason this woman smiled in her sleep was only because she was kind and sweet in all ways possible!

She was what he wanted in a wife, even if he won her love at the same time that he betrayed his friend!

Clutching her to him, as though his own life depended on it, Two Ridges rode relentlessly onward, hoping to reach the cave before Spotted Eagle discovered him gone.

Spotted Eagle's eyes scanned the land below him, his heart bleeding as he saw the broken, twisted bodies and debris scattered everywhere. There was no way to identify those who were dead without seeing them up close.

His head bent low, he moved slowly to his feet and without much thought, too filled with remorse to think about anything but his beloved woman, he swung himself into his saddle and wheeled his horse around to seek a path that would take him to the bottom of the cliff.

Between him and Two Ridges, a way would be found!

Raising his head to tell Two Ridges to help

him at this time of his deep despair, Spotted Eagle's lips parted in a surprised gasp when he discovered that his young friend was no longer there.

"What would make him leave?" he whispered to himself, peering ahead, hoping to see his friend waiting farther up the path, yet he saw no sign of him anywhere.

Puzzled and disappointed, yet not wanting to take any more time wondering about a friend who would abandon him at such a time as this, Spotted Eagle set his jaw hard and searched until he found the safest way to travel down the steep incline.

Holding his reins tightly, and locking his knees to the sides of his horse to steady himself as his stallion's hooves began slipping and sliding on the loose rock beneath them, Spotted Eagle determinedly moved lower and lower until he reached the place where broken bodies, scattered journals, and pieces and wheels of wagons were strewn about.

There was not a sound to be heard as Spotted Eagle dismounted. The birds in the trees had even ceased to sing as the fires of the sun poured down from the heavens on the death scene spread around before Spotted Eagle's tear-filled eyes.

Stiffly he went from body to body, gasping at the sight of those who were so bloodied and smashed it was impossible to identify them.

The clothes on each victim were so ripped and torn and covered with blood that Spotted

Eagle could not even use that means to identify his woman.

He shouted to the heavens a cry of despair, devastated to know that Jolena was gone from him so quickly!

After searching for a while longer, desperate for any clues as to which one might be Jolena, Spotted Eagle finally gave up, feeling that he had no other recourse but to leave the death scene.

Jolena and Kirk's bodies were unidentifiable.

There was no way to separate them from the others, to give them a proper burial.

All that he wanted now was to escape, to put this horror from his mind, yet he knew he never would be able to forget!

It was there forever, like leaves carved into stone as they become fossilized with age!

In a daze, he mounted his horse again. With his head hanging and his heart and soul empty, he sent his horse up the side of the steep incline again. Surely Two Ridges would be there now, waiting for him. It made no sense that his friend would leave him at such a time.

If ever Spotted Eagle needed a friend, it was now.

Finally back on solid ground, the shadows of the forest on one side of him, the sheer cliff on the other, Spotted Eagle placed a hand over his eyes to shield them from the blinding rays of the sun, scanning the land for his friend.

Again his jaw tightened, now seeing Two Ridges as a coward, one who rode from death instead of looking it straight in the eye!

But too caught up in sadness, Spotted Eagle gave Two Ridges no more thought and rode off with hunched shoulders toward his village.

Never had he felt so alone as now. It was as though he had lost Sweet Dove a second time— and he knew that this time he would never get over the loss!

Chapter Nineteen

Moaning, her whole body aching, Jolena slowly opened her eyes. The embers of a fire glowed warm beside her and the aroma of cooked rabbit wafted to her nose from the spit it hung on, low over the fire, dripping its tantalizing juices into the glowing coals beneath it.

Feeling around her with her hands, she soon realized that she was lying on a layer of blankets.

Her gaze moved upward, but she could see no stars, no sky, no moon.

"Where am I?" she whispered, leaning up on one elbow, moaning again as she realized how much more she ached with the effort of moving. How did she get here? Why was she aching so badly?

Moving slowly to a sitting position, she

looked more carefully around her. When she spied someone lying across the fire from her, obviously asleep, she sucked in a wild breath of relief, thinking it was Spotted Eagle.

Her sigh drew Two Ridges awake, and he bolted to a sitting position, remembering that he had not bound Jolena's wrists and ankles. She would not have had a chance to flee him while he stayed awake, guarding her, but he had not counted on being weary enough to go to sleep so easily.

When he saw that the fire had died down only to embers, he realized just how long he had been asleep.

Too long.

He was lucky that Jolena was still there.

Jolena gasped and grabbed a blanket protectively around her when she discovered that she was not with Spotted Eagle at all! She was staring over the embers at Two Ridges.

Her pulse raced as fear crept into her heart, and she looked wildly around her, realizing that she was in a cave, with no memory at all of how she might have gotten there.

Not seeing any sign of Spotted Eagle anywhere, Jolena glared over at Two Ridges. "I do not have to ask how I got here," she said in a hiss. "You brought me. How could Spotted Eagle have allowed it? Where is he now?"

Before Two Ridges had the chance to respond, what had happened during the storm began coming to Jolena in flashes, as though bolts of lightning were going off and on inside her brain. Each flash brought up new memories that made her heart seem to stop still within her body and her throat to constrict. Everything was so vivid to her in her mind's eye that she could not scream or even talk.

The blinding rain!

The lurid flashes of lightning!

The frightened, wild-eyed mules!

Her screams as she watched the other wagons plunging over the sides of the cliff.

She held her face in her hands as she began sobbing. Then something else came to her, flooding her memory. She thought she had felt strong arms around her waist, dragging her from the wagon just before it toppled over the cliff.

But she now realized it had to have been a savage illusion. The moment she hit the ground, she had been knocked unconscious from the force of the fall.

She lifted sorrowful eyes up at Two Ridges, unable to remember who had saved her.

"Who else survived but the two of us?" she demanded, moving to her knees, yet still clutching the blanket around her shoulders. "Two Ridges, tell me who lived . . . and who died."

Two Ridges moved to his feet and stepped around the fire, squatting down onto his haunches before her. "We are the only survivors," he said, the lie slipping across his lips easier than he would have imagined. "I have brought you to a cave. I have built you a fire for warmth and have prepared food for you.

Perhaps it is best now if you eat, not talk. You will need your strength to travel onward to my village."

He knew that he could never take her to his village—not as long as Spotted Eagle was alive! Spotted Eagle would take her away from him and condemn Two Ridges in the eyes of their people!

There was only one solution.

Two Ridges would have to ambush Spotted Eagle and kill him, so that Two Ridges would not have to live the life of a banished Blackfoot. He wanted to take his copper princess to his people and show her off to them. They would see why she would cause him never to take another woman to his bed.

She was the most beautiful of all the women he had ever known! He ached to touch her copper skin. He ached to bury his nose in the depths of her midnight-black hair, to smell its fragrance. His mouth wanted to know the sweetness of her lips.

But he knew that he would first have to gain her trust to have these pleasures!

Jolena was stunned numb with the news that she and Two Ridges were the only two of the expedition to come out of this tragedy alive.

She closed her eyes and sobbed out Kirk's name, then her beloved Spotted Eagle's.

She crumpled down onto the blankets and curled into a ball, still crying, her eyes closed, her heart shredding into a million pieces of despair.

When a warm hand touched her face, she thought it was Spotted Eagle's, so much did she want it to be so. She leaned into the palm of the hand, sobbing softly.

When she opened her eyes, she lurched back wildly away from Two Ridges, jolted back to her senses.

"Allow me to comfort you," Two Ridges said, placing a hand to her wrist, attempting to draw her into a sitting position next to him. "For a moment you allowed it. *Ok-yi*, come. *Kyi*. Let me hold you. Cry until all of your sadness is washed from inside you."

"No," Jolena said, choking back another sob. "I'm fine. I don't need anyone. I'm going to be fine."

"You need not suffer through this alone," Two Ridges said, drawing her closer to him as he still held tightly to her wrist. "I was Spotted Eagle's best friend. He would want you to seek comfort in my arms."

"Please leave me be," Jolena said, yanking her wrist free. "I need no one. No one, do you hear?"

His eyes narrowing, Two Ridges moved away from her and resumed his place before the dying embers on the opposite side of the fire from Jolena. His eyes never left her as he placed more wood on the coals of the fire, and the flames soon ate away at the dry timber.

Jolena stared into the flames, trembling from the coldness she felt inside over her losses.

Her brother! Her wonderful Spotted Eagle!

All of the others of the expedition of whom she had become so fond!

And her beloved journals and her precious butterfly collection!

"Everything is lost to me," she whispered, tears again splashing from her eyes. "Everything."

Returning to her soft pallet of blankets, she stretched out onto them, meticulously covering herself with another one. When she closed her eyes, she found that there was too much there in her mind's eye that continued troubling her . . . the damnable *Nymphalid* butterfly that was known to portend death! And the damnable dream in which Spotted Eagle had died!

Although Spotted Eagle had not died from an arrow's wound, he was dead just the same.

She now wished that she had listened to Kirk and had turned back toward Fort Chance, leaving the butterfly to tease and cause death to someone else.

"Oh, why didn't I listen to Kirk?" she cried softly, pummeling her fists into the blankets. "Why? Why?"

She had been so caught up in her grief that Jolena had not heard Two Ridges coming toward her again, had not been aware of him lying quietly down onto the blanket beside her. . . .

Only when he scooted beneath her blanket and placed his body behind hers was she aware that he was there, his breath now hot on the nape of her neck as his fingers lifted her hair so that he could kiss her sweet, soft flesh.

Jolena's eyes opened wildly and her heart

skipped a beat when she felt the most identifiable largeness of his manhood through the material of his breeches and her skirt as he began gyrating himself against her from behind.

She was so shocked by his actions that she was momentarily rendered speechless and seemingly helpless. She lay there, scarcely breathing, as one of his hands moved around and cupped one of her breasts through the cotton fabric of her blouse.

In a flash, the blanket was thrown aside and Two Ridges was atop her, his mouth seeking her lips, his hands slipping quickly up the inside of her skirt.

"I will make you forget everything but the pleasure that you will receive from my lovemaking," Two Ridges whispered huskily against her cheek, his lips quickly claiming hers in a frenzied kiss.

With one shove, she pushed Two Ridges away from her.

She scrambled to her feet, and as he jumped to his feet and towered over her, she started to run. He grabbed her by the waist and spun her around so that she was held immobile against his body as he lowered her again to the blankets.

"This is what you would do while your best friend lies dead?" Jolena cried, stricken with a sudden fear when she gazed up into eyes that were anything but friendly.

She shoved at his chest. "Why are you doing this to me?" she cried. "Please let me go. Please don't do this!"

"I cannot stop myself from wanting you," Two

Ridges said, a strangled sob leaping from his throat.

His gaze moved over her face, suddenly realizing again that there was something about her that was too familiar.

This made him come to his senses.

He moved quickly away from Jolena, then shamefully hung his face in his hands.

Too frightened to trust his sudden change of mood, Jolena knew that she must not take any chance of his changing his mind again and continuing with his plan of raping her.

Wildly, she gazed around her for something with which to protect herself against this Blackfoot Indian seemingly crazed by runaway lusts and desires!

Breathing hard, her eyes fell upon a rock near where she sat.

Without any further thought, she grabbed the rock and brought it down hard upon Two Ridges' head.

When the rock made contact with his skull, Jolena recoiled and looked away.

When she slowly turned her eyes around a moment later, Two Ridges lay perfectly quiet beside the fire. Jolena covered her mouth with her hands, gasping as she stared at him. His eyes were closed. Blood was curling down across his brow from the wound she had inflicted on his head.

He was breathing raspily.

"I've got to get out of here," Jolena said, looking desperately around her.

She gazed again at Two Ridges, then gulped back a fast-forming knot in her throat. What if he died? She hadn't wanted to kill him. Why had he forced her to do this terrible thing to him?

She moved shakily to her feet and began inching backward, away from Two Ridges, fearing more that he might wake up than that he should not wake up at all.

He had reason now to do more than rape her.

He might even kill her!

Remembering the dangers that lurked in the forest, and realizing that she could wander alone for days before finding any sort of civilization, Jolena stopped and gazed down at Two Ridges' knife. She was afraid to try and get it, fearing that he might wake up the very moment she was leaning down over him. She closed her eyes at the thought of him grabbing her and forcing himself on her again!

Then she opened her eyes again slowly, knowing that her life now depended on her taking many risks.

Leaning down, she moved her trembling fingers to Two Ridges' sheathed knife at his right side. She watched his eyes as she quickly grabbed the handle and brought the knife out of its sheath.

Her heart thumping wildly, Jolena turned her attention to the food dripping its juices into the fire. Her mouth watered suddenly for she had not realized until this moment just how hungry she was.

"To survive, I must eat," she whispered, stepping up to the browned morsel, very deliberately cutting several wide strips of the meat away, then thrusting them into the depths of her skirt pocket.

"And warmth," she whispered, spying the blankets upon which Two Ridges still lay. She must take at least one of those blankets.

With one hand, she poised the knife above Two Ridges, ready for the death plunge should he awaken while she was slowly rolling his body off the blankets.

When he was successfully moved over onto his stomach, his face pointing away from Jolena, she grabbed the blanket, then took off in a mad dash toward where she thought the mouth of the cave might be.

The pitch darkness of the cavern slowed her escape. She found her way by keeping her back against the one side of the cave and inching herself along. She was glad when she finally saw the light of the moon as it made a path of silver just inside the entrance of the cave.

Jolena broke into a run again, tears filling her eyes with renewed thoughts of Spotted Eagle and Kirk. She felt empty with loneliness.

How could she bear such losses? Her future was bleak. Without Spotted Eagle's arms and strength to guide her into the future, how could she exist?

She felt useless now, utterly useless.

Running out into the clear, clean air of night, Jolena moved relentlessly onward, knowing she must put much distance between herself and Two Ridges. When he came to and found her gone, he would surely not leave a stone unturned to find her again.

And if he found her, what then?

Would he kill her?

Or continue where he had left off—and *rape* her?

Both thoughts sent chills racing up and down her spine.

"His horse!" she cried. "Why didn't I think to get his horse?"

But she had been too eager to get as far from him as she could, and since she had not seen the horse, it had not come to her mind to take it.

Stopping to draw the blanket over her shoulders, she looked in all directions, wondering which route would get her to civilization the fastest.

Fort Chance was many miles away, and she knew not where the Blackfoot village might be.

It truly didn't matter which way she went. Spotted Eagle would not be there.

She gazed through a break in the trees overhead and stared at the flecks of stars blinking down at her. "Oh, Lord, why did this have to happen?" she prayed. "Why was I allowed to fall so madly in love, and then have to learn how to live without him? Why, Lord? What have I done to deserve this?"

She lowered her eyes and gazed cautiously around her. The only sounds were frogs fairly cracking the air with their noise. The night was filled with a queer, luminous darkness. It was like velvet, soft yet heavy, but the moonlight

234

enabled her to dimly see the different objects all around her.

The forest, always a thing of mystery at night, stood as though ready to enfold her within its dark arms, chilling her with terror at the prospect of never being found.

She shuddered at the thought of being attacked by a panther, wolf, or bear. A coyote's sudden long howl from somewhere in the distance startled Jolena into a mad run. She stumbled through the darkness, soon discovering that all the forces of nature seemed pitted against her. The bushes were so close-set that they tangled her progress slowed to that of a snail. When she stepped from the forest onto a stretch of open meadow, only then could she run again as the moon now lighted the mountains looming ahead of her.

Tears streamed down her cheeks again at the thought of the sheer drop from the cliff that had taken the lives of so many.

"Spotted Eagle," she cried mournfully aloud, her voice echoing back at her, hauntingly over and over again.

A horse whinnying stirred Two Ridges awake. He blinked his eyes nervously and reached a hand to his throbbing head, suddenly recalling what had happened.

Angry at himself for allowing a mere woman to take advantage of him, he moved quickly to his feet.

The fire was almost out. Smoldering ashes gave off only enough light for Two Ridges to see that he was quite alone.

He kicked at some loose rock at his feet. "She escaped!" he hissed between clenched teeth. "*Hai-yah*, she escaped!"

Dizzy from a severe headache, Two Ridges stumbled through the gray darkness until he found his horse, which had been secured in the farther depths of the cave, where a stream meandered into the cavern through cracks and crevices.

Flinging his saddle onto his horse, Two Ridges tried to decide what he must do. If he didn't find Jolena before Spotted Eagle found her, she would tell Spotted Eagle everything!

Taking the reins, he led his horse through the dank darkness of the cave. To keep his honor intact, Two Ridges knew, either Spotted Eagle or Jolena must die. Or both.

Frowning, he led his horse out into the open space where daylight was breaking along the horizon. Swinging himself into the saddle, he knew that he would be killing whomever he came across first, whether it was his long-time friend or the woman who he now knew would never be his.

He sank his heels into the flanks of his horse and rode into the shadows of the forest.

Chapter Twenty

The loss of her brother and Spotted Eagle lying heavy on her heart, Jolena walked aimlessly onward, relieved that it was now daylight so it would be easier for her to keep watch for dangerous animals. In her mind's eye, she kept reliving the night the panther had stalked her.

But Spotted Eagle had been there for her then!

Now she was solely dependant on herself. She hoped she would come upon travelers or perhaps even find herself in a Blackfoot village.

Bone-tired and sleepy, Jolena found it hard to move one foot ahead of the other. She was traveling through a wilderness that was not easily traversed. If she wasn't going through dark forests with close thickets and rapid streams, she was walking along cliffs with sheer drop-offs and wildly flung rocks.

Presently she found herself in a wide, shallow valley that was thickly timbered, where cottonwoods and rocks and silent streams joined together to create a tranquil setting.

In the distance, Jolena could see great numbers of deer, elk, and mountain sheep on the hillsides.

Then a jackrabbit bounced past her, so close she could have reached out and touched it.

Jolena paused, sighing. She wiped beads of perspiration from her brow as she leaned against the trunk of a cottonwood. She closed her eyes and listened to the whisper of the leaves above her. If she did not know better, she would think she was listening to the sound of a peaceful, slow rain falling softly from the sky.

She envisioned herself back in Saint Louis and recalled how she had listened to the sounds of the one giant cottonwood tree that stood just outside her bedroom window. On days when she was caught up in wondering about her heritage, and where her true father might be, she had listened to the cottonwood tree, allowing it to soothe her in her moments of loneliness for a life that she had been denied.

Her stomach rumbled, and the gnawing ache at the pit of it drew Jolena's eyes back open. She knew that she must travel onward, if not to find civilization of some sort, at least to find food. She had been able to quench her thirst in the clear, sparkling streams, and an occasional blackberry bush had offered her some respite from her hunger as she had gobbled up handsful of the berries.

But now, even that meal was far behind her and she knew that she must eat soon or collapse from weakness.

She could feel it already beginning—the trembling in her knees and the slight dizziness.

"I must move onward," she whispered, pushing her way through knee-high prairie grass. "I must. I must."

The sun seemed to be branding her as it beamed its heated rays down upon her. She wished the day away, hungering for the cooler breezes of evening, yet fearing the unknown again in the deep, purple shadows of night.

Jolena stopped to take a quavering breath, and to use the hem of her skirt to sponge the perspiration from her face. As she dropped the skirt down again, something grabbed her attention. Her heart seemed to skip several beats when again she heard something wafting through the air.

"Is that children's laughter?" she whispered, then stiffened when she heard the faint barking of dogs and neighing of horses.

Then she crinkled her nose as she picked up the wonderful aroma of meat roasting over an open fire.

All of these things could only mean one thing.

She was nearing either a settler's cabin—or an Indian village!

The thought of finally finding someone—any-one—out here in the middle of nowhere gave Jolena the incentive she needed to go that one more mile, if needed, to finally be safe from the dangers of being alone, and to *eat*. Each step she took now was a true effort, as though it just might be her last.

Suddenly she saw them!

Her eyes grew wide and her heartbeat went wild with the discovery.

Through the cottonwoods she could see dark, smoke-blackened tepees, their peaks releasing drifting, lazy smoke up into the breeze. Every open place in the valley was covered with tepees!

The hills close by the village were dotted with horses grazing in a large, wide corral.

She shifted her gaze and watched children scampering about barefoot and in brief breech-clouts, chasing one another in what seemed mock battles, with limbs for lances and rifles.

Dogs followed on their heels, yapping.

Jolena stepped behind a tree, suddenly fear-ful of approaching an Indian village alone. She watched with a shallow breath as women came into view, stooping, tying and hauling their gath-ered wood that would feed their fires tonight.

Jolena looked past these women at the blue smoke of the cooking fires rising into the still air in little columns from the tepees, soon dis-appearing into nothingness.

Her eyes widened, and her stomach growled again at the sight of meat cooking on a spit over a large, outdoor fire in the center of the village.

She knew that she had no choice but to go on into the village. She eased from behind the tree, ready to approach the women, but found them gone, and also the children and dogs that had been with them.

Sighing heavily, Jolena moved on toward the village, casting all fears aside, not allowing herself to think they might be enemies, instead of the friendly Blackfoot. If they were the Cree, Sioux, Crow, or Snake she did not know how she would be received. She did know that Spotted Eagle had been accompanying the expedition of lepidopterists in part because of the danger of a Cree attack. He had most definitely seen the Cree as his enemy and the enemy of white people.

Bringing Spotted Eagle to the surface of her memory again made a sad longing wash through her. She wiped tears from her eyes and trudged onward, soon reaching the outer edge of the village.

Limping slightly, Jolena moved toward the closest dwelling, a colorful tepee made from buffalo hides with strange medicine animals painted on it, knowing that it should not matter which one she approached for assistance.

As she circled around the tepee from behind, she stopped when she discovered an older man sitting in front of the tepee on a blanket, polishing his arrow shafts by passing them through holes drilled in a thin, flat rock. She had been so quiet in her approach that he had not yet discovered her there, which gave her time to study him and to guess whether or not he might be friendly enough to approach.

This man, who wore a vest of puma skin and fringed buckskin trousers had a great, arching chest and immense shoulders. His hair was black and thick and hung in braids down his massive, straight back. His face had lines of force and intelligence. She felt suddenly awed in his majestic presence and wondered if he might be someone of great importance.

Her eyes stopped on his moccasins, causing her heart to jump with relief.

They were black!

The Blackfoot were the only Indians known to wear black moccasins. That had to mean that she was in a friendly camp of Indians!

She turned her eyes slowly around her, deciding that this man was surely not the chief of this village, for farther into the village sat a much larger tepee positioned on a knoll that overlooked the others, as she imagined a chief's tepee would be.

A shuffling sound and a gasp drew Jolena's head around in a jerk. She swallowed hard and placed a hand at her throat when she found the older man staring at her, his eyes full of questions as he gazed intensely at her face—as though perhaps he knew it well already!

Brown Elk began inching backward, away from Jolena, then was forced to stop when his back came into contact with the cowhide fabric of his tepee. His heart was thudding wildly and he was feeling faint, for never had he expected to see that face again—not until he joined his beloved wives in the land of the hereafter!

"How . . . can . . . it be?" he finally stammered.

Jolena had already experienced such a reaction from another Blackfoot—Spotted Eagle!

He had also looked at her as though seeing a ghost, thinking that she was her mother!

That had to mean that this man also recognized the resemblance, which had to mean that he was surely from the same tribe, the same village, perhaps the same dwelling!

"Are you Brown Elk?" she blurted out, hoping he would understand her. She might be looking upon the face of her true father for the first time in her life! It did not seem possible, yet there it was in the way he was reacting to her knowledge of his name!

"My name is Brown Elk," he said in English, his voice drawn. "And yours? What are you called? Where did you come from? Why are you here? How do you know my name?"

His gaze swept over her again, raising an eyebrow at the way she was dressed. It was obvious that she was an Indian, yet she was dressed as a white woman!

He looked at her again with wild, wondering eyes, knowing of only one way all of this could be possible!

She was the mirror image of Sweet Dove.

She was . . . his *daughter!*

It was as though it had been destined for them to meet in such a way!

After all these years of wondering, Jolena was in

the presence of her true father, and now she didn't know what to do next.

She so badly wanted to move into his arms and cling to him, to take from him the comfort that she needed now to get her past her grieving for Spotted Eagle and Kirk.

But she knew that she had to hold herself in check. Just because he was her father by blood did not make them instantly love each other as daughter and father! Love would surely have to grow between them.

He was a father who would have to accept that the baby he had been denied was suddenly a grown woman.

"You are Brown Elk," Jolena said, her voice trembling as much as her knees and fingers. "I am called Jolena by the white community, but I am not sure what Blackfoot name you would have called me had I not been taken by white people instead of being left for you to find on the day my mother sacrificed her life to give me mine."

Brown Elk's shoulders swayed with the absolute knowledge now that this *was* his daughter, the child he had mourned. Even after his second wife had given birth to Two Ridges, this son had not been enough to erase the sadness of having lost his other child.

When his second wife had died from a feverish malady, he had not married again, but resumed trying to ease his haunting thoughts of where his first child was, and whether or not the child was even alive!

And now he was blessed! His daughter had returned to him.

After all these years, his pleas and prayers to the fires of the sun had finally been answered.

Brown Elk reached his arms out for Jolena. "*Ok-yi,* come to me, daughter," he said thickly, fighting back the urge to cry that made men look like women in the eyes of those who witnessed such a weakness. "Let me fill my arms and heart with you. This has been denied me long enough."

Sobbing with joy, Jolena eased herself into his thick, muscular arms. She hugged him tightly, reveling in the wonder of the moment. "I never thought this would happen," she cried, turning her dark eyes up to him. "I have dreamed it. Oh, how many times I have dreamed it. I've prayed for this. It took a long time, but God finally answered my prayers."

Brown Elk placed his fingers at her waist and eased her slightly away from him, enabling him to get a good look at her. "I, too, have prayed," he said. "The Blackfoot creator, *Napi,* has heard my prayers. He has finally granted them true."

They gazed smilingly at one another a few moments longer, then Brown Elk frowned. "How is it that you are alone?" he said, his voice drawn. He swept his eyes over her, seeing her complete disarray.

Then he gazed into her eyes. "How did you find this Blackfoot village?" he said softly. "How long have you been wandering, looking for it?"

Jolena was catapulted back to the tragic accident. She lowered her eyes, truly not wanting to talk about it.

Not the death of those she loved!

Nor of Two Ridges' deceit of a friend—and near rape of his friend's woman!

All of this caused a bitter ache to circle her heart, yet she knew that she must tell at least part of the tragedy.

She would not reveal Two Ridges' true nature to his people. That would happen soon enough, when he returned to the village and saw that she was there! He would not know if she had or had not told what he had done.

This would make him react strangely enough in front of his people so that they would ask what was the cause of his behavior. She would stand back, smiling smugly when he tried to invent a lie that might free him of all blame and shame!

"You show such pain in your eyes," Brown Elk said as he placed a forefinger beneath Jolena's chin, forcing her eyes to lock with his. "What has happened? You can tell your father."

Then his eyes widened with horror as he once again swept them over Jolena, remembering that Spotted Eagle and Two Ridges had gone to guide a group of white people. Lepidopterists, he believed they were called. Could his daughter have been among those people? If so, where was Spotted Eagle and Two Ridges? They had been hired as guides!

"Spotted Eagle and Two Ridges?" he cried. "Do you know these two Blackfoot?"

Jolena felt her throat become constricted at the

mention of those names. "How would you know that I did?" she said in almost a whisper.

"Then you *are* in the Montana Territory seeking butterflies?" Brown Elk said, his voice guarded.

"Yes, I was," Jolena said, finding it difficult to speak about it without reliving in her mind's eye all over again the tragedy of it all.

Brown Elk placed his fingers to her shoulders. "You say that as though you are no longer a part of the expedition," he said, his voice drawn. He glanced at her disheveled clothes again and at her tangled hair, suddenly feeling as if he was drowning inside at the thought of what this all meant.

"Where is Two Ridges?" he said in a rush of words. "Where is Spotted Eagle?"

Jolena stared up at him, realizing that he had guessed what had happened, and she dreaded having to tell him that what he feared was in part true.

One Blackfoot warrior was dead.

The other . . .

Oh, God, what *could* she say about the other?

This moment, when she should be happy to have finally found her true father and true people, she felt trapped—trapped by someone else's lies and deceits and lusts.

Chapter Twenty-One

The sudden alarm in Brown Elk's eyes made Jolena aware that he perhaps knew her answer before she spoke the words out loud.

Even though talking of Spotted Eagle's death would tear her heart apart, Jolena knew that she had no choice but to tell her Blackfoot father the truth. She owed him so much for having been denied his daughter for the first eighteen years of her life, and she never wanted to be anything but truthful with him.

"Spotted Eagle and Two Ridges were doing well their task of keeping the expedition from harm," she said, swallowing hard. She nervously clasped her hands behind her. "But there was nothing they could do about the fierce lightning. It caused the mules and horses to go wild," she said in a rush of words.

She lowered her eyes, finding it even harder than she had at first imagined to tell the rest. It wasn't that she had actually seen Spotted Eagle's horse become spooked enough to carry Spotted Eagle over the cliff. She knew it to be true because Two Ridges had told her that it had happened.

Her heart skipped a beat. What if Two Ridges had been telling a lie, in hopes that she would lean on him for protection in the absence of her beloved Spotted Eagle?

Then she felt foolish for such a thought.

Even Two Ridges could not be that vindictive.

She had to accept that Spotted Eagle was gone—forever.

Hands gripping her shoulders, almost painfully, caused Jolena to look suddenly up, finding her Blackfoot father's dark eyes silently pleading with her.

"Tell me the rest," Brown Elk said, his voice drawn. "Did Two Ridges and Spotted Eagle lose control of their horses? Were they thrown and trampled to death? Tell me. I must know the fate of my son, Two Ridges!"

Everything that Brown Elk was saying was lost to Jolena except that he had called Two Ridges his son!

Jolena become numb inside to know that Two Ridges was kin to her by blood!

They had the same father!

That meant that although Two Ridges certainly had not known it, he had fallen in love with his sister!

The thought sickened her, and the only thing that helped her keep her sanity was that neither of them had known that when they were together they should have been rejoicing over a brother and sister having finally found one another!

Now she pitied Two Ridges more than she could ever hate him.

She even pitied herself, for never could she love Two Ridges as a sister loves a brother.

He had made that impossible!

"Two Ridges is all right," Jolena said, searching within her scrambled brain for a way to tell him that she knew he was alive without actually being forced to tell him how she knew and the circumstances of how she had escaped from her captor—Brown Elk's very own son!

"Before I was thrown from the wagon and rendered unconscious I—I saw Two Ridges jump from his horse before it plunged over a steep cliff . . . along with the others," she murmured, lowering her eyes. She hated to lie, and she cursed Two Ridges for having caused her to!

"My son is alive," Brown Elk said, showing his relief as he sighed, then asked, "Spotted Eagle?" He implored Jolena with another look of concern. "You saw Spotted Eagle plunge to his death?"

"No, I did not witness it, but—but I believe that it is so," Jolena said softly. "Were he alive, he would be here now. As for Two Ridges, he most surely did not see me thrown from the wagon. When he was forced to travel without a horse, I am sure he began walking even then toward the village. I do not know why I arrived before him. Perhaps he stopped to rest, or . . . to pray."

She hated Two Ridges more by the minute for putting her in the position of having to add lie upon lie. Two Ridges had told her that he had seen Spotted Eagle fall to his death, yet she could not tell her Blackfoot father that Two Ridges had told her this without having to explain why she had been with Two Ridges, while she was trying to pretend that she had not been with him at all.

She circled her hands into tight fists at her sides, finding this awkward and confusing and hating it because she wanted to be free of all emotions except for being happy at finally having found her true father—and sad for having lost the only man she could ever love!

"It is not certain that either warrior is dead," Brown Elk said, hope showing in the depths of his eyes as he smiled at Jolena. "Let me take you to your true people and let them see this daughter of mine who has never forgotten her father. I will introduce you and then tell Chief Gray Bear the news of his son, Spotted Eagle. We will then send out many of our warriors to search for both missing sons."

Jolena could not help but hope, after seeing her Blackfoot father's calm reaction to the news, that perhaps Spotted Eagle was alive after all. A gentle peace seemed to embrace her as she allowed herself to believe that Two

Ridges had lied to her about Spotted Eagle's death!

Oh, but if only he *were* alive!

Jolena walked beside her Blackfoot father, absorbing everything around her, feeling strangely as though she had been in this place before. It was eerie how she felt that she had seen the same hides pinned out to dry outside the dwellings and how she had seen the same tepees, and the tepee paintings showing the exploits of the husbands.

Her gaze fell upon the rawhide shields that hung from tripods outside many of the tepees. Her curiosity having led her to study Indians, she knew that the shields were ceremonially turned by the owner several times a day to face the sun.

As they came closer to the activity of the village, she saw some women outside cooking in brass buckets which they had obtained through barter with the Pawnee of the North, who in turn had procured them from white traders. Old men sat in the sunshine and contemplatively smoked the aromatic mixture of tobacco leaves and bark they called *kinnikinick*.

Soon Jolena became aware that everyone had become quiet as their eyes discovered her at Brown Elk's side. The children hid behind the buckskin skirts of their mothers. Some women went back inside their dwellings, their large, dark eyes visible as the corners of their entrance flaps, which were drawn slowly aside so they could see this stranger who was of their same skin coloring, yet dressed as a white person.

Realizing how disheveled she was, Jolena

reached a hand to her hair, groaning when she found nothing but witches' knots and tangles.

Her gaze then swept down the full length of herself, seeing the rips and tears of her travel skirt and the soiling of her blouse that now looked more muddied gray than white.

When Jolena and Brown Elk reached the largest, most beautifully decorated tepee of all, decorated with buffalo tails and brightly painted pictures of animals on the outside, her knees weakened when the entrance flap was raised and an elderly man, all stooped and thin in a long and flowing buckskin robe, came from the tepee, leaning heavily on a staff. As she gazed up at him and found herself lost in his midnight-dark eyes, she surmised that this was Spotted Eagle's chieftain father and felt humble in his presence.

He stared intensely at her, his lips parting in a slight gasp, and Jolena was quickly aware that he also saw her mother in her features.

"You who resemble someone of our people's past goes by what name?" Chief Gray Bear finally said in a weak voice. He gazed at Brown Elk. "Where did you find her? Brown Elk, how can this be? Your wife's grave lies just beyond that rise. How can she be here?"

"My wife Sweet Dove is always with me in spirit," Brown Elk said softly. He placed an arm around Jolena's waist and drew her to his side. "This is my *ni-tun*—my daughter. She has no Blackfoot name. She was given the name Jolena by those who took her from her homeland eighteen summers ago!"

His eyes wide, Chief Gray Bear took a shaky step toward Jolena. "It is truly you?" he said, reaching his free hand to her cheek, guardedly touching it. "After all these years, you have come home to your father and people? How did you know to do this? How did you know about us?"

"For so long I didn't," Jolena said, trembling beneath his gentle touch and recalling how often Spotted Eagle had also touched her there with such feelings. Missing him so much at this moment, her whole body ached from despair and acute loneliness.

"From the time I was old enough, I knew the difference between myself and my playmates," she continued softly. "But only recently did I discover my true heritage."

She lowered her eyes and swallowed hard. "Spotted Eagle saw my resemblance to my mother and explained everything to me," she said softly, then raised her eyes again slowly. "Only then did I know that I was Blackfoot and that my father wås Brown Elk."

Chief Gray Bear forked an eyebrow. "You know my son?" he said. He looked past her, then into her eyes again. "I do not see him here. He did not accompany you here, to introduce you to your true people?"

Jolena cast her Blackfoot father a troubled glance, seeking assistance in explaining to a father that his son might be dead!

Brown Elk drew her closer to his side, giving her the comfort that she was seeking. He explained to Gray Bear what had happened, though he found it hard to explain away his own son's absence since he should have arrived back at the village by now.

Chief Gray Bear leaned more heavily into his cane, the grief and concern thick in his eyes and his voice as he spoke. "We will not begin mourning my son until his body has been brought to his people as proof of his death," he said. "I will send many warriors to search for both our sons. I will speak to the fires of the sun to bring them home safely to us."

Then Chief Gray Bear raised a hand in the air and motioned for his people to come forth. Everyone obeyed and came and stood quietly behind Jolena and Brown Elk. Brown Elk urged her around to face them, as Chief Gray Bear addressed them.

"One of our people has returned to us!" Chief Gray Bear shouted, as best his voice would carry in his weakened state of health. "Look upon her! You will see Sweet Dove in her features! She is the daughter of Brown Elk and Sweet Dove! She has come home to us!"

Now Jolena understood why so many of the women had fled for shelter inside their tepees when they had gotten a better look at her. The older women remembered Sweet Dove as though she were alive only yesterday!

They surely thought she had risen from the dead!

Now that Jolena's true identity had been explained to them, they all came to her in clusters, some smiling, some touching, some hugging.

Chief Gray Bear came to Jolena and himself

embraced her. "There should be a great feast to celebrate your return to us," he said, stepping away from her. His eyes were hauntingly dark as he peered down at her. "But you understand that while my son is missing there can be no celebration?"

"Yes, I understand," she murmured, deep within herself wishing that she could tell him that she understood more than he realized. She wanted to share her feelings with this elderly, ailing man, about a son whom he apparently idolized. She wanted to tell Chief Gray Bear that she loved him as much!

But she knew that this was not the time—even that the time might never be afforded her.

If Spotted Eagle were truly dead, their feelings for one another would be kept a secret, stored safely within the soft confines of Jolena's heart, to enjoy on those nights when she allowed herself to close her eyes and pretend he was there with her again.

"Let us go inside my dwelling," Brown Elk said, again placing a protective arm around Jolena's waist and whisking her away from the others. "There you will eat and be given clothes of our people."

Only for an instant did Jolena think about the father who had raised and nourished her. The wonder of being with her true father was washing all thoughts of her past life slowly away.

"That sounds wonderful," Jolena said, smiling at him. Over her shoulder she watched several warriors mount their proud steeds and ride away.

Her smile waned, knowing where they were going.

She closed her eyes and gave a silent prayer that Two Ridges had been lying about Spotted Eagle and that he would be found alive and well.

"White woman's attire should have never clothed you," said Brown Elk, his voice breaking. "Never shall it again."

The hurt in her father's voice drew Jolena's thoughts back to him. At this moment, he deserved her full attention and devotion. He had been denied these things for far too long.

She followed him inside his tepee, where she began to absorb everything as though her mind were a sponge, wanting to quickly learn everything that had been denied her, to make up for lost time.

She already felt deep inside her soul that this was where she belonged!

Oh, but if only Spotted Eagle could have been a part of this discovery of herself as she was truly meant to be!

Knowing that if she labored over thoughts of Spotted Eagle much longer, she would not be able to keep from weeping, she held her chin proudly high as her father helped her down onto a couch softened with a cushion of buffalo robes beside the fire in the firepit.

As Brown Elk placed more wood on the fire, Jolena gazed around her again. The inside walls of the tepee were made of brightly painted cowhide, reaching from the ground to a height of five or six feet. The paintings portrayed the various battles and adventures in which her father had taken part. An air space about two or three inches thick had been left between the inner lining and the lodge covering. The air rushing up through it from the outside made a draft which aided the large flap at the top to free the lodge of smoke.

Three couches were positioned around the fire. At the foot and head of every couch, a mat made of straight, peeled willow twigs, fastened side by side, was suspended on a tripod so that between the couches spaces were left as convenient places to store articles which were not in use.

The earth flooring of the lodge had been swept fantastically clean, and domestic paraphernalia— worn, gray millstones, gourds, baskets, and clay pots—sat neatly in place along the walls.

Jolena's eyes were drawn to an exhibit of warring attire and weapons, which was most impressive as the fire cast its dancing shadows upon the bows and arrows, the lances decorated with many colorful feathers, and the rifles with their shining barrels.

She looked for signs of women's attire or needlework, seeing nothing of the kind, which had to mean that her father no longer had a wife.

Jolena was reminded of her hunger when several lovely Blackfoot maidens came into the tepee carrying an assortment of food on wood platters and in large kettles. She did not have to be asked twice to partake of the food and was soon stuffing her mouth with pemmican made of berries and dried back fat of buffalo, rabbit stew with delicious chunks of carrots and cabbage floating around in the rich liquid, and many other things that she did not take the time to ask the ingredients.

She did not even notice that her father was not eating, instead amusedly watching her. She seemed to have lost all of her delicate table manners as she continued stuffing her mouth with food until she suddenly realized that she could not eat another bite.

Jolena did not have the time to feel embarrassed over her ill manners. Something else—another generous offering from more women—made her breath catch in her throat.

"Those are for you," Brown Elk said, rising. He walked toward the entrance flap. "I will leave as you dress yourself as a Blackfoot woman should be dressed."

"Thank you for everything," Jolena said, smiling up at her father as he gave her a glance over his shoulder, then stepped outside, leaving her alone with the women.

"I shall bathe and dress you, and Moon Flower will braid your hair," a woman named Crying Wind said as she brought a large basin of steaming water into the tepee.

Feeling pampered and enjoying it, Jolena shed her clothes and allowed the women to do as they pleased with her. First her hair was washed in water perfumed with what smelled like pine needles. Then, as she was being washed with a soft cloth, she gazed down at the clothes that she would soon be wearing.

She silently admired the smock made from tanned buffalo skins, the milk teeth of an elk fastened in a row around the neck of the dress. There was also a pair of leggings that would reach to her knees, also made of tanned skins.

The black moccasins that sat beside the dress and leggings were made from tanned buffalo skin with parfleche soles which greatly increased their durability. They were ornamented over the toes with a three-pronged figure worked in porcupine quills and beads, the three prongs representing the three divisions, or tribes, of the Blackfoot nation.

After Jolena was dressed and her hair was braided, she gazed down at herself, again finding it strange how she felt as though she had lived this all before!

One by one, the Blackfoot women filed out of the tepee. Brown Elk soon entered. When he gazed over at Jolena, tears flooded his eyes, for he felt suddenly that he was once again the young man who had taken Sweet Dove as his bride.

"Father?" Jolena whispered, feeling no awkwardness in calling him that. It seemed so very natural and most definitely right! "Do you approve? Do I now look Blackfoot?"

"You called me Father," Brown Elk said, his voice filled with emotion. "It has been many years of waiting to hear such words from my daughter."

Then he nodded as his gaze swept over her. "Does this father approve of how you look?" he said, his voice breaking. "He approves. And do you look Blackfoot? Very!"

A sob lodged in Jolena's throat as she went to her Blackfoot father and flung herself into his arms. "Oh, Father, I love you so naturally, as though we have never been apart," she cried.

Brown Elk held her near and dear to his heart. "We are together now, but one day you will leave my dwelling again," he said remorsefully.

Jolena eased back from him and gazed into his eyes. "Never shall I," she said, her voice determined.

"You are a beautiful woman who will bring many men to my door to court you," Brown Elk said, smiling gently down at her. "You will make a choice and then share a tepee with your husband, not your father."

Jolena's heart seemed to drop to her feet at the mention of her marrying someone. All her dreams and plans for marriage had died the day Spotted Eagle had been taken from her! She did not even like to think about it, much less talk about it!

Deep down inside herself, where her desires were formed, she knew that no man would ever take Spotted Eagle's place in her life.

She eased into her father's arms again. She closed her eyes, silently praying to her Lord that Two Ridges had been lying and that Spotted Eagle was still alive.

Soon. Soon she would know. . . .

Chapter Twenty-Two

The sun was lowering behind the mountains in the distance. Purple shadows filled the empty spaces of the forest as Spotted Eagle rode relentlessly onward. He had not returned to the village right away. He had needed time alone, to commune with the Sun and Old Man, for only they knew his feelings about losing the only woman he would ever love.

Spotted Eagle was now on his way home, to find solace in the quiet cocoon of his dwelling.

Life had struck him so many hard blows! All of his relatives, except his beloved chieftain father, had gone to the Sand Hills, the shadow land and place of ghosts, the Blackfoot's future world.

And now also his woman.

His period of mourning for Jolena would be long and painful!

He was not even sure if he could ever not mourn the death of his beloved Jolena!

He *did* know for certain that he would never allow any other woman to warm his blankets at night.

He even accepted the fact that he would not have a son to follow in his footsteps into chieftainship. This honor would have to be passed on to someone else's son.

Perhaps Two Ridges'.

Spotted Eagle frowned when he thought of how Two Ridges loved women—*all* women. It would be hard for his virile friend to choose among those many to whom he had shown special attention.

"He is yet young," Spotted Eagle whispered to himself. "And best that he has not yet made a choice. I made mine, and I have now lost her!"

Then he frowned, wondering how he could ever again have a pleasant thought about Two Ridges, who had deserted Spotted Eagle! It would be hard for Spotted Eagle ever to understand why!

His head bent, his shoulders slouched, Spotted Eagle rode onward, now unthinking, for to think was to hurt. No matter how hard he tried, he could not stop thinking about Jolena for long.

Everything led back to her.

The rustling of dried and rotted leaves beneath the umbrella of trees at Spotted Eagle's right drew his head up with alarm. His hand went automatically to the rifleboot at the side of his horse.

His fingers did not even have a chance to make contact with the rifle before he saw his arch-enemy, the Cree warrior Long Nose, notching an arrow onto his bow and taking a steady aim at Spotted Eagle.

Another sound alerted Spotted Eagle to yet another presence in the forest. Gasping, Spotted Eagle watched Two Ridges ride toward him, in his hand an upraised knife. Two Ridges glared at Spotted Eagle, his jaw clenched tight with hatred. It dawned on Spotted Eagle that his best friend was attacking him!

Stunned by Two Ridges' behavior, he forgot all about Long Nose. Two Ridges was closer. His knife would find Spotted Eagle's heart before the Cree's arrow did.

Spotted Eagle glanced from the Cree to Two Ridges as Two Ridges came closer. Then Spotted Eagle gasped and cried out when unknowingly Two Ridges blocked Long Nose's way, spoiling the renegade Cree's shot.

Just as Two Ridges rode up next to Spotted Eagle, his arm poised for the death blow, Spotted Eagle heard the sharp twang of a bow as Long Nose let loose his arrow. Spotted Eagle's body lurched, responding as though the arrow were piercing his own body as he watched it enter Two Ridges' back.

The knife fell from Two Ridges' hand as Two Ridges swayed, then toppled off his horse onto the ground, scarcely breathing.

Stunned, Spotted Eagle stared down at Two Ridges, unable to move. His thoughts centered only on his former friend, who lay dying, and on Two Ridges' obvious intention to kill him. Spotted Eagle forgot to worry about the Cree who had shot one Blackfoot while planning to kill the other!

Two Ridges' life's blood poured from his wound, staining the leaves on which he lay a scarlet red.

A lone gun blast filled the air, drawing Spotted Eagle out of his stunned reverie to remember the Cree and the Cree's reason for being there—to kill Spotted Eagle, his enemy!

Spotted Eagle watched Long Nose crumple to the ground, wildly clutching at a bloody wound on his bare chest, then gaped openly at several Blackfoot warriors from his village as they came riding up, one of their rifles smoking from the shot that had killed the renegade Cree.

"Spotted Eagle!" Double Runner said, quickly dismounting, while the others went to Two Ridges' aid, kneeling down around him. "We have been searching for you. We feared you were dead."

Double Runner glanced down at Two Ridges, then up at Spotted Eagle again. "The Cree shot arrow off at Two Ridges before we could stop him," he said. "We did not arrive soon enough."

Knowing that his warriors had not arrived soon enough to see that Two Ridges had planned to kill him, Spotted Eagle found it hard to respond to Double Runner.

Instead, his head swimming with so many questions, especially about Two Ridges, and seeing that Two Ridges would not last much longer, Spotted Eagle quickly dismounted and fell to his knees beside Two Ridges. He looked at his warriors, one by one. "Leave me to speak alone with Two Ridges," he said thickly.

The warriors nodded and went back to their horses, walking them away from Spotted Eagle and Two Ridges.

Spotted Eagle's first thoughts were to make Two Ridges more comfortable. He studied the arrow, then steadied his hands and placed them to it and snapped it in two. It was lance-shaped instead of barbed, so he managed to draw it out completely instead of having to leave a portion of it imbedded in Two Ridges' back.

When Two Ridges emitted a guttural groan of pain, Spotted Eagle frowned down at him, still wondering what could have caused his friend to become his enemy!

"Your knife did not have a mind of its own," Spotted Eagle said, tossing the broken arrow aside. He lifted Two Ridges' head from the ground so that their eyes could meet and hold. "You were in full command. Why did you choose to use it on your best friend?"

"Before I die, forgive me," Two Ridges said, reaching to clutch desperately onto Spotted Eagle's arm. His voice was so weak that only Spotted Eagle was able to hear him. "Because of a woman I did this! Only because of a woman would I go against my best friend! Never have I found a woman who was special enough to risk a friendship over. Not until . . . Jolena."

"Jolena?" Spotted Eagle gasped. "You did this because of Jolena? You . . . fell in love with my woman?"

"As you did, I could not help but fall under her spell," Two Ridges said, choking as blood began seeping from the corners of his mouth. "I was cursed, it seems, the moment I chose to win her love, no matter what I had to do, even if it meant losing a friend."

"You loved her enough to want to see Spotted Eagle dead?" Spotted Eagle said, his heart aching to know these truths, yet now regretting having kept a certain truth from Two Ridges! If Spotted Eagle had not selfishly kept the secret of Jolena's parentage from Two Ridges, her very own brother, then none of this would have happened!

But never would Spotted Eagle have guessed that Two Ridges was capable of such a fiendish act as this, no matter what truths that had been kept from him. Spotted Eagle had always thought that Two Ridges was a man of strict honor, capable only of undoubted truthfulness and unbounded generosity. The love for a woman had changed him overnight, it seemed!

"Forgive . . . me . . ." Two Ridges begged, his eyes slowly closing.

Spotted Eagle had no chance to respond. Two Ridges took a wild gasp for air, then died.

Filled with many tumultuous emotions, Spotted Eagle stared down at Two Ridges, finding all of this hard to comprehend. This young man whose future was so bright was now dead, everything gone so quickly from his grasp! Spotted

Eagle had often teased his friend that his passion for women would be the death of him.

But never had he actually meant it! It had been a way of teasing Two Ridges over his wandering eye and heart!

Spotted Eagle had actually envied Two Ridges' lighthearted mood towards women and his skill at teasing and loving so many!

Now there was nothing to envy.

A sudden thought came to him—how would Two Ridges' father feel if he knew the full truth of what had happened here today? It would devastate a man such as Brown Elk to know that his son had brought such dishonor to himself!

It had to be kept from him, so that Brown Elk could mourn his son without shame clouding his memories of a son he had idolized.

"I will rightfully keep this secret," Spotted Eagle whispered, slowly laying Two Ridges' head back on the ground. "I was wrong to keep the secret to myself that Jolena was your sister. But I must keep secrets again! Never will I allow your father to know the treacherous son that you were. You do not deserve such loyalty from Spotted Eagle, but your kind and generous father does!"

Rising slowly to his full height, Spotted Eagle gazed down at Two Ridges a moment longer, then walked away toward his waiting warriors. When he reached them, he looked solemnly from one to the other.

"He is gone from us," he said, almost choking on the words and the actuality of what Two Ridges had planned to do.

And why would Two Ridges want to do such a thing?

He surely had to know that Jolena was dead!

That had to mean that his hatred for Spotted Eagle ran even more deeply than jealousy for a woman, and that was something that Spotted Eagle could hardly accept.

Only yesterday he and Two Ridges were riding side by side, talking and laughing as friends do.

There had been no sign then of Two Ridges having hated him.

"The news we take to Brown Elk will take away the joy of his having just discovered that he has a daughter, and that she is alive and well," Double Runner said gloomily. "Sad it is, that he gains a daughter, then loses a son."

Spotted Eagle's heart did a strange leap at Double Runner's mention of Brown Elk's daughter.

There was only one daughter!

Jolena!

And Double Runner was talking about her as though she were alive, as though he had met her!

This had to mean only one thing—that Jolena was in his Blackfoot village!

"What are you saying about a daughter?" Spotted Eagle said, clasping his fingers to Double Runner's shoulders. "About Brown Elk's daughter?"

"While you were away, she came into our village," Double Runner said softly. "She was the one who told us that you might be dead. Your father sent a search party out looking for you, in hopes that you would still be alive. It was with happy hearts that we found that you were."

Double Runner glanced over his shoulder at Two Ridges. "Had we arrived sooner, we would make two fathers happy upon our return to our village," he said sadly.

Spotted Eagle was only half-hearing what Double Runner was saying. His heart was thumping wildly with joy over knowing that his woman was alive after all.

And she had even found her way to her people's village!

Everything would now be perfect if not for . . .

He turned and stared down at Two Ridges, still finding it hard to believe that Two Ridges would go so far as to kill his best friend.

Yes, he nodded to himself—there had to be more to it than that.

But he doubted he would ever find the answers now that Two Ridges was no longer able to give them to him.

Anxious to go to Jolena, to take her into his arms and hug her to him, feeling the warm, sweet press of her body next to his as full proof that she was, indeed, alive, Spotted Eagle walked briskly to his horse and swung himself into his saddle.

"Double Runner, secure Two Ridges on your horse," he said, his voice solemn. He gazed at one of his other warriors. "Wolf Tail, go and find his horse. Take it and the Cree's with you to the village."

Not waiting for Two Ridges to be secured on the horse, his every heartbeat counting the minutes until he saw Jolena again, Spotted Eagle swung his horse around and began thundering through the forest. He was glad when he reached the open spaces of a meadow, giving him more freedom to send his horse into a hard gallop.

As the sun was replaced in the sky by a round globe of moon, Spotted Eagle caught the reflection of a fire in the black velvet sky just up ahead and knew that he would soon be in his village. His pulse raced and his eyes grew anxious as he sent his horse into an even harder gallop, breathless now as he entered the outer fringes of the village.

He eased his mount into a soft trot and moved past the outdoor communal fire that blazed all night in the center of his village to help discourage the wild animals from coming near the Blackfoot people as they slept.

When Jolena's father's tepee came into sight, Spotted Eagle's heart seemed to skip a beat, for standing just outside the tepee, studying the heavens, was his woman!

Inhaling a quavering breath, he stared at this woman who only a short time ago he had thought was lost to him forever! Here she was, as though an offering to him, or an answer to his prayers to the fires of the sun!

And never had she looked lovelier!

Beneath the splash of the moonlight, she stood like a copper princess attired in the clothing of the Blackfoot. Her long, dark hair was hanging free and fluttering around her shoulders in the gentle breeze. Her expression was filled with sadness as she gazed upward, and as Spotted Eagle drew his mount to a halt and dismounted, he could see tears streaming down her cheeks.

Jolena was so caught up in her feelings that she had not heard the horse's approach, nor did she hear Spotted Eagle now as he dropped his reins and left the horse behind as he walked toward her.

Feeling as though he were being swallowed whole by his thunderous heartbeats, Spotted Eagle took one more step, then stopped and trembled when she turned sudden eyes to him and discovered him standing there.

Jolena's heart seemed to leap into her throat. She became dizzy from the surprise of finding Spotted Eagle there. She was so stunned, she could not speak, nor could she move! She had just been praying that he would be all right and that he would come to her.

And there he was, as big as life itself, standing so close, his eyes brimming with his own tears of happiness!

"Jolena?" Spotted Eagle said softly.

"Spotted Eagle?" Jolena said softly.

Then both broke into a run and flung themselves into each other's arms.

Jolena sobbed as she clung to Spotted Eagle.

Spotted Eagle clung to her as though, if he let her go, he would discover that this had all been a figment of his imagination—a savage illusion!

"You are really here," Jolena cried, gazing up at him. "Oh, darling. You did not die?"

"I did not die, nor did you," Spotted Eagle said, laughing softly as his hands now moved gently over her face, his forefinger stopping at her lips, tracing them. "My woman, I thought you died with the others."

"I was thrown from the wagon before it went over the cliff," Jolena said, placing a hand to one of his cheeks, testing to see if he were real. "And you?"

"It all happened so quickly that I was forced to watch, instead of to act," Spotted Eagle said, again drawing her into his embrace, hugging her to him. "I thought you were with the others. I . . . I went down to the foot of the cliff and looked for you. I could not find you. And there was no way to tell if you were there or not. Most of the bodies were unidentifiable."

A shudder soared through Jolena at the thought of what he was describing. "My brother?" she whispered, daring to seek the truth, not sure if she could face it if she found out that Kirk was truly dead.

"Could you tell if Kirk . . ." she began.

"No," Spotted Eagle said, placing a finger to her lips, stopping her next words. "I do not know the fate of your brother."

He held her away from him and gazed into her eyes. "Did you walk all the way here from the site of the wreckage?" he asked. "I do not see how you did. That is a long way to travel by foot."

Jolena was not sure how to tell him about Two Ridges and what he had tried to do. Two Ridges was supposed to be Spotted Eagle's best friend. She did not want to be the one to tell Spotted Eagle of a best friend's deceit!

Before she decided what to say, or how, the warriors bringing Two Ridges' body back to his people came riding into the village.

The arrival of many horses into the village brought the people outside. Chief Gray Bear came from his tepee ahead of the others. There was a happy, joyous reunion of father and son as Spotted Eagle and his father embraced.

And then Jolena saw Two Ridges. The moon was so bright that she quickly recognized him. She placed her hands over her mouth to stifle a scream when she discovered Two Ridges' bloody back as he lay across the horse on his stomach.

Jolena then gazed quickly up at Spotted Eagle, questioning him silently with her eyes.

"A Cree's arrow that was meant for Spotted Eagle killed Two Ridges instead," Spotted Eagle said sullenly.

Jolena was rendered even more speechless, now recalling her dream in which Spotted Eagle had died from an arrow's wound.

"Two Ridges saved your life?" Jolena blurted out, finding that hard to believe now that she knew of Two Ridge's darker side.

Having decided not to tell anyone the truth about Two Ridges' attempt to kill him, Spotted Eagle's jaw tightened and his lips became tightly pursed.

"Spotted Eagle, why don't you answer me?" Jolena murmured, then grew cold inside, thinking she already knew the answer without his actually saying the words.

Footsteps behind her drew her thoughts and her pity elsewhere. She watched Brown Elk's expression as he stepped into the moonlight just as Two Ridges' body was lifted from the horse and was carried toward him.

Chapter Twenty-Three

Everyone stepped aside as Brown Elk moved at a dignified pace toward the horse on which his son lay. He made no sound as he lifted Two Ridges from the horse and carried him in his arms toward his dwelling, stopping before entering his tepee to gaze up into Spotted Eagle's eyes.

"Did my son die with courage?" Brown Elk asked softly, his eyes hazed with a sadness that he was trying to keep within himself.

Spotted Eagle's insides stiffened, feeling everyone's eyes on him, especially Jolena's as she shifted hers upward, gazing up at him as she awaited his response.

Although Spotted Eagle was a man of truth and honesty, this time he had to lie, for to tell the truth meant causing pain that was not necessary.

"He died with both honor and courage," Spotted Eagle said, his voice drawn. "Your son died in place of Spotted Eagle, for Long Nose's arrow was meant for me, not your son."

"He died so that you could live?" Brown Elk said, his voice breaking. He lowered his eyes. "My son died for a good purpose then. He keeps the son of Chief Gray Bear alive so that he can one day be chief of our people!"

Jolena listened to everything that was being said, realizing that most was false. She knew the evil that lurked within Two Ridges' heart. She could never see him as courageous or one who might do an honorable deed for the man who stood in the way of his having the woman of his desire.

Jolena had to believe that Spotted Eagle was covering up some horrible truth. She could see it in his eyes, in how they had wavered as he spoke to Brown Elk. She had heard it in his voice, that what he had said was pretense, surely to save hurting Brown Elk.

For now she held her tongue. But later she would question Spotted Eagle about it.

She could also no longer keep to herself the horrible secret of what Two Ridges had attempted to do to her.

"Let me help you with your son," Spotted Eagle said, moving closer to Brown Elk. "Let me carry him inside your dwelling for you."

Brown Elk firmed his hold on his son. "No," he said firmly. "I need time alone with my son, and then I will go to a high place away from the village for my private mourning."

Brown Elk shifted his gaze to Jolena. "Tomorrow you will prepare your brother for burial," he said softly. He lifted his eyes to Spotted Eagle again. "Tonight take my daughter with you and see to her comfort. She has spoken well of you, Spotted Eagle. It is good that she has found a friend in you, just as my son also saw you as a devoted friend. The friendship between our families will become even closer as we all become more acquainted with my daughter."

Jolena was filled with dread at what Brown Elk had said—that she would be preparing Two Ridges for his burial!

How could she? She could hardly stand to be near him when he was alive, much less now when he was dead!

Brown Elk smiled down at Jolena. "I spoke to you of warriors coming to my door to court you?" he said softly. "Perhaps there is no need to look further for a perfect husband. Spotted Eagle would make the best of husbands for my daughter."

Jolena's lips parted in surprise, and her heart pounded as she felt a blush rush to her cheeks. Although she had just been filled with an apprehensive dread for what would be expected of her tomorrow, everything else in her new life seemed to be falling into place easily.

She had found her true father. She was loved by a wonderful man. Her father had even blessed their union without knowing it!

The only missing ingredient in her happiness was her relationship with Two Ridges. If only she and he could have known each other as brother and sister!

His attraction to her had surely been because he had misinterpreted their natural close feelings as lust!

She shook her head slightly, sorrowful for that part of her life that she would never know—of sisterly affection for a brother other than Kirk.

Kirk! she thought desperately to herself. So much had been happening, her sadness about Kirk had slipped from her mind!

She turned her eyes up to Spotted Eagle, wanting to beg him to go and look for her missing brother. If she and Spotted Eagle had survived the storm, perhaps Kirk had been as lucky!

But now was not the time to bring up one brother when another was lying dead and being mourned by her true father.

Later, when she and Spotted Eagle were alone, she would then talk of another brother.

Everything became quiet as the renegade Cree's horse was brought close for Brown Elk to see and to accept as his.

"This is the horse of the Cree renegade who killed my son?" Brown Elk said, his gaze moving slowly over the white stallion, seeing its sleekness and its worth.

"Yes," Double Runner said solemnly. "It is yours now. The Cree loses not only his life, but his means of travel to the Sand Hills."

Brown Elk nodded his approval, then turned and went inside his tepee.

Quiet, their heads bowed, the people turned and went to their own dwellings.

Gray Bear gave Spotted Eagle a father's hug, stared down at Jolena questioningly for a moment, then wandered away toward his own dwelling.

Spotted Eagle placed an arm around Jolena's waist and ushered her to his tepee at the far edge of the village, where a meandering stream passed behind it, silver in the moonlight.

As Spotted Eagle held the buckskin entrance flap aside, Jolena paused and grew even more somber and quiet when she heard the sudden sorrowful wails of her father. She cringed and tried to close her ears to the sound, but nothing stopped the mourning cries from reaching her.

"*Oh, ah! No-ko-I! Ah, Ah! No-ko-I!* My son! My son!" cried Brown Elk, over and over again, filling the still night air with the sound, as though thousands of arrows were piercing it.

Spotted Eagle placed a firm arm around Jolena's waist and whisked her inside his tepee.

Wiping tears from her eyes, Jolena found two Indian women there. One was readying the fire, while the other held a large black kettle with pleasant aromas wafting from it.

Spotted Eagle gestured toward a couch cushioned with pelts beside a fire that was now taking hold, sending its flames around the logs, as though in a sensuous caress.

Jolena sat down. Recognizing one of the two

women as Moon Flower, she found it easy to smile as the women cast her humble glances just before leaving Jolena and Spotted Eagle alone.

After the women left, Spotted Eagle sat down beside Jolena. Taking two wooden bowls that had been placed close to the fire, he ladled out enough soup for them both, then handed a bowl and wooden spoon to Jolena.

"Eat," he said softly. "Sometimes it is good to feed the physical body at times like this, if not the soul."

Jolena nodded and took the bowl and spoon. Without reluctance she began sipping the soup from the spoon, finding it rich and delicious, and in a way it filled part of that empty void that the day's events had caused. Her gaze swept around her. Spotted Eagle's lodge was the same as her father's—very large and handsome, well supplied with parfleches, saddles, food, robes, and bowls. It was comfortable and cozy, what Jolena would have expected in the lodge of her Blackfoot warrior.

Spotted Eagle ate in silence, then set his empty bowl aside as Jolena set hers down on the floor at her right side.

"Tell me how you happened to find our village of Blackfoot," Spotted Eagle then asked, not able to hold in the questions that were eating away at him any longer. "Tell me what you know about Two Ridges' feeling toward you."

Jolena turned her eyes slowly to Spotted Eagle. "I, too, have questions," she murmured. "And, darling, do you remember how we have both said that we should never keep secrets from each other? I will tell you things that need to be said, if you will also empty your heart of feelings that are troubling you."

"About Two Ridges?" Spotted Eagle said, stretching one long, lean leg out before him, leaning back so that he was resting on his right elbow.

"Yes, about Two Ridges," Jolena said, swallowing hard.

"Besides myself, you are the only one that will know the truth," Spotted Eagle said, his voice drawn.

"And you know that it will go no farther," Jolena said, moving to her knees beside him. She gazed intensely into Spotted Eagle's eyes. "Darling, what I have to say can hurt you deeply."

"The hurt is already there," Spotted Eagle said. "*Kyi.* I know of Two Ridges' feelings toward you. I know that he intended to kill me because of you, yet I find it hard to know the exact reason he felt that this was necessary."

Jolena lowered her eyes and again swallowed hard, trying to find the courage to tell him what she needed to thrust from within her, so that she could enjoy some semblance of peace again. She wanted to be free to be happy with her beloved warrior and to be a part of her true people.

She raised her chin and looked Spotted Eagle square in the eye again. "I was thrown from my wagon on the day of the accident," she explained. "Two Ridges found me before you did. He took me to a cave."

She was finding the story difficult to tell, because telling it seemed the same as reliving it.

But she finally found the courage to continue.

"Two Ridges was gentle at first," she said, her voice soft and quavering. "But then . . . then he began kissing and touching me. He tried to rape me, Spotted Eagle. I . . . found a rock. I hit him over the head, then escaped."

A quick rage heated up Spotted Eagle's insides. His eyes were lit with fire as he sat up and reached for Jolena's hands and clutched them tightly. "He did that?" he said, his jaw tight. "Two Ridges was capable of even that sort of deceit?"

"You wondered what would make him feel that it was necessary to kill you?" Jolena said, tears streaming down her cheeks. "He could not face you knowing the truth, and he knew that I would tell you if ever I had the chance. He had to know that it would be either you or he who would die. I don't guess he liked the odds. By ambushing you, he was going to be sure that you died, instead of him."

She leaned closer to him. "That's how it happened, isn't it?" she softly cried. "He was going to kill you and accidentally got in the way of the Cree's arrow? He would have never stopped the arrow on purpose. He would have allowed the Cree to kill you to keep from having to do it himself."

"You are right," Spotted Eagle acknowledged, releasing her hands. He leaned over the fire and stacked more wood onto the flames. "Two Ridges did not know of the Cree's presence. When Two

Ridges raised his knife to kill me, the Cree's arrow is what stopped him from taking my life."

He turned back to Jolena and placed his hands at her waist, slowly drawing her to him. "Had my warriors not arrived when they did, the Cree would have sent another arrow into the air, and that one would have found its true mark. I would have joined Two Ridges on the long walk to the Sand Hills."

Jolena flung herself into his arms. She clung tightly to him. "I could hardly bear it when I thought that you had died," she sobbed. "Two Ridges had almost convinced me that you were dead. I didn't want to accept what he said as true. But there was no proof that you weren't. When I rendered him unconscious I started working my way through the forest, but only half-heartedly, for without you, nothing seemed important to me anymore."

"You should never allow yourself to feel hollow with despair," Spotted Eagle said, stroking her long, thick hair. "I made the same mistake when I thought you were dead. And now do you see? *Hai-yah!* We despaired for naught. It was emotion wasted! One must always have faith and hope. Despair is a worthless emotion!"

"It is easy to condemn such feelings," Jolena said, leaning back, gazing up at him. "But when I thought you were dead, I could not help it. My world has become you. You are my life—my every heartbeat. Should you die, I would be only half alive!"

He framed her face between his hands and

drew her lips to his. When he kissed her, it was not from hungry passion, but sweetness and lightness, matching the mood they both were feeling.

Remembering what her Blackfoot father had said about having to prepare Two Ridges for burial made Jolena draw away from Spotted Eagle. She gazed up at him with wide, woeful eyes.

"Why should I be expected to prepare Two Ridges' body for burial?" she asked, shivering. "Spotted Eagle, the thought of doing that curdles my blood. How could I be expected to forget how he tried to rape me? How?"

"There are times when one must put other people's feelings before one's own," Spotted Eagle said, gently placing a hand to her cheek. "Now is such a time for your Blackfoot father."

"But why should I?" Jolena said, more in a whine than she wished it to sound. "Two Ridges and I shared the same blood, but that is all."

"And that is my fault," Spotted Eagle said, turning his face away from her to stare into the dancing flames of the fire. "Had I been truthful with Two Ridges, he would not be dead now. He would be celebrating having a sister. You would share *that*. Knowing that you were blood kin!"

"Why *didn't* you tell him?" Jolena said, moving around in front of him. She leaned up on her knees, so that she could look directly into Spotted Eagle's eyes. "Didn't you think that he would welcome such news?"

"I am not sure how he would have accepted the truth, had it been told him," Spotted Eagle said.

285

"I believe that he had strong feelings of a man for a woman for you and never would have been able to sort through them and find those meant only for a sister."

He paused and lowered his eyes, then looked up at Jolena again. "My reason for not telling him was a selfish one," he said, his voice breaking. "I did not want you to know that he was your brother, nor did I want him to know that you were his sister, fearing that too much of your time that I wanted to spend with you would be spent with your brother. He would have the answers to so many of the questions eating away at you. I wanted you all to myself for as long as I could have you. And I was wrong. Will you forgive me?"

Jolena crept closer to him and twined her arms around his neck. "Darling, there is nothing to forgive," she murmured. "The fact that you love me so much makes my heart sing."

She gave him a soft kiss, then leaned into his embrace. "There is much to be sad for," she murmured. "But also there is much to be happy for. We have found such love, you and I. And I have found my true people, especially my father. He is exactly what I thought he would be. He is a kind, dear man. How sad that he has lost a son, after discovering he has a daughter!"

Her eyes widened and she leaned away from Spotted Eagle again. "There is just so much to ask, and to say," she blurted out. "I feel that my brother Kirk is still alive. Will you send a search party out to look for him? Please, will you?"

"Soon, my love," Spotted Eagle said. "After

arrangements are made in our village for Two Ridges. Then we will focus our attention on your other brother."

"Thank you," she whispered, giving him a gentle hug.

Then she looked up at him, her eyes wavering, her insides cold again at the thought of what her Blackfoot father was expecting of her. "You did not say why I must prepare Two Ridges for burial," she said, her voice shallow. "Why must it be me? There are many others in your village who had more respect for Two Ridges than I. How can I, the woman he tried to rape, be expected to be dutiful to him?"

"No matter what he did, he *was* your brother," Spotted Eagle said. "It is the practice of the Blackfoot that the next female relative of the deceased prepare the one who has died for burial. You are the only living female relative. It is required of you to do this for your Blackfoot father."

Jolena shuddered. She dropped her gaze and slowly shook her head back and forth. "I don't think I can," she said in an almost whisper.

Spotted Eagle cupped her chin with one of his hands and raised her eyes to his again. "Yes, you can," he said firmly. "For your true father, you must."

"I don't think I can touch him! My father will know that something is wrong by my behavior."

"You must not allow that to happen," Spotted Eagle said, taking both her hands and drawing her close to him. He implored her with his dark eyes. "We must never allow your father to know the terrible truth about his son. Can you not see why? Your father might blame you for the chain of events that led his son to his death! If not for you, Two Ridges would have not become someone foreign to himself! It is best not to give the old warrior cause to resent his daughter! He deserves to have some time of happiness with a daughter he now knows is very much alive, and here to love him."

"It's all so confusing," Jolena said, tears streaming from her eyes.

"There is something else to consider," Spotted Eagle continued. "I do not want to give Brown Elk cause to doubt what I told him about how his son died," he said. "If so, I might be put to the test of truth-telling. It is not good that a next chief in line be dishonored in such a way."

"What do you mean?" Jolena asked softly. "What sort of test would you be put through?"

"It is a solemn form of affirmation, a sacred ceremony practiced by our people when someone's word is in doubt," Spotted Eagle said, rising. He began slowly pacing back and forth, his arms folded tightly across his chest. "If a man tells his companions some very improbable story, something that they find hard to believe, and they want to test him to see if he is really telling the truth, a pipe is given to a medicine man. The medicine man paints the stem red and prays over it, asking that if the man's story is true he may have long life, but if it is false that his life may end in a short time."

Spotted Eagle paused, then gazed intensely down at Jolena. "The pipe is then filled and lighted and passed to this man who is doubted. The medicine man says to him, 'Accept this pipe, but remember that, if you smoke, your story must be as sure as the hole through this stem. So your life shall be long and you shall survive. But if you have spoken falsely, your days are counted.'

He knelt down before Jolena and placed his hands on her shoulders. "This man may refuse the pipe, saying, 'I have told you the truth; it is useless to smoke this pipe,'" he explained softly. "But if he declines to smoke, no one believes what he has said and he is looked upon as having lied. If, however, he takes the pipe and smokes, everyone believes him. It is the most solemn form of oath."

"Should you be put through the test and smoke the pipe, everyone would believe that what you have said about Two Ridges' death was true," Jolena said, her eyes innocently wide. "So I see no problem."

"The problem is that *I* would know that I was lying and at such a solemn, sacred time as that, I would not be able to lie *about* the lie," he said solemnly.

Jolena nodded, understanding, and knowing that no matter how she felt about Two Ridges, she must do what she must, to keep Spotted Eagle from being put in any awkward position.

"I will do as my Blackfoot father wants," she murmured. "I will prepare Two Ridges for burial."

Chapter Twenty-Four

"Let us have no more talk about that which burdens our hearts," Spotted Eagle said, his gaze moving slowly over her. "Let us speak of things that will make us smile."

"Yes, let's," Jolena said, her heart hammering wildly as she felt the heat of Spotted Eagle's eyes moving over her, seeing her for the first time in Indian attire. She could tell by the gentleness in his eyes and the slow smile quavering on his lips that he approved of this change that had come over her in his absence.

Smoothing a hand down the front of her doeskin smock, she smiled up at Spotted Eagle. "Is it not a beautiful dress?" she said softly. "I so love it."

"Its loveliness is enhanced by the woman wearing it," Spotted Eagle said, his loins becoming hot with need of her as he gazed into Jolena's eyes. "In Blackfoot attire, you are even more beautiful than when you are wearing clothes of the white women."

He reached a hand to her hair and twined his fingers through it, tugging her closer to him. "But, my woman, you are even *more* beautiful when you have nothing on. Shall I . . . disrobe you? Or would you rather do it yourself?"

Jolena's throat was growing dry as the excitement of the moment built, yet she hesitated to follow him into this sensual bantering.

"Should we?" she said weakly. "Is this a proper time?"

"Time is precious, yet fleeting," Spotted Eagle said, his hand cupping her breast through the soft fabric of her smock. "Never should we waste a moment of our time together. Who knows of tomorrow? Tonight we are together. Let us use the moment in the way we both desire."

"I so badly want to," Jolena said, her breath catching in her throat when Spotted Eagle leaned a soft, quavering kiss to her lips, silencing her every doubt, bringing forth within her waves of rapture that began cresting, as though her passion were a tide following the command of the moon.

As he lowered her into the buffalo robes that lay on the floor beside the fire, she weakened with passion as his kisses became more demanding, his hands trembling as they disrobed her.

When even Spotted Eagle's clothes were tossed

aside, and Jolena felt his weight pressing on her body, she spread her legs and welcomed him as he quickly and magnificently filled her.

Smothered with feelings that were overwhelming her, Jolena thrashed her head back and forth as Spotted Eagle's thrusts within her became rhythmically fast, his lips moving from one of her breasts to the other.

Then he rolled away from her. Their hands began moving on each other's bodies, and they met each other, touch by precious touch.

Jolena sucked in a wild breath of rapture when Spotted Eagle laid his hand over the fronds of black curls at the juncture of her thighs, then thrust a finger inside her.

She then sought out his throbbing hardness and when she found it, she began moving her fingers over him, smiling as his body trembled with pleasure. As he stroked her, she continued moving her fingers over him.

Then Spotted Eagle moved over her again and in one deep thrust had himself deeply inside her again. He enwrapped her within his powerful arms and placed his cheek to hers. "I would be an empty shell without you," he whispered. "But while we were separated, I did not have to touch you to feel you in my mind."

"My darling, I carry you with me always within my heart," Jolena whispered back, moving her hips with him, pulling him more deeply within her as she locked her legs around him. "I love you so."

"I will pay your father a great bride price,"

Spotted Eagle said, kissing his way down to her breasts. He flicked his tongue around a nipple, drawing a guttural sigh of pleasure from deeply within Jolena. "We will marry soon."

For a moment Jolena was catapulted back to another time and another father. Bryce Edmonds had spoken often of how beautiful a bride Jolena would be in a dress of white against her copper skin. He had always counted on the day that he would have the honor of giving her away in a beautiful marriage ceremony in their church.

She had to wonder how he would react when he saw this dream shattered. She knew that he was not well enough to withstand the riverboat ride to the Montana Territory, and she knew that it would be asking the impossible of Spotted Eagle to go with her to Saint Louis to be married.

He would remind her that she was Blackfoot and must be married in the Blackfoot tradition. And she would agree without further thought. She had been denied too many Blackfoot traditions as she was growing up in a white community.

Now she wanted to absorb each and every one of them within her heart so that she could eventually not even think about the time when she was forced to follow the road of the white people instead of her own true people!

Spotted Eagle sensed that Jolena's heart was no longer in their lovemaking. He paused and leaned away from her so that their eyes could meet and hold. He placed a gentle hand to her cheek.

"What is troubling you?" he said softly. "Never

have you before been in two separate places while we were making love. Where has your mind taken you? Shall mine follow and join you, to share with you that which is taking you from me?"

Jolena swallowed hard as she gazed back at him. "I'm sorry," she murmured. "My mind wandered. It won't again."

"It will, unless you free your mind of what is worrying you," Spotted Eagle said, leaning a soft kiss to her brow. "Tell me what is in your heart. I shall help you put it behind you."

"When you mentioned marriage to me, my thoughts went to my father in Saint Louis," she murmured, casting her eyes downward. "I know that when we speak vows, it will be done in the Blackfoot tradition. My white father will be left out."

Jolena moved her eyes slowly up again. "That saddens me, Spotted Eagle," she murmured. "I feel that I owe him loyalty for how he has so devotedly raised me as his."

"I did not have to live with you to know that you were a dutiful daughter to this father," Spotted Eagle said, his eyes filled with a quiet understanding. "So you see, you have repaid him time and again for his kindness. You owe him nothing else."

Spotted Eagle ran his hands along the soft flesh of her skin, then cupped her breasts. "Would he not want you to do what makes you happy?" he said huskily.

"Yes," Jolena whispered, closing her eyes to the ecstasy as he once again began moving within her, filling her with his manly strength, awakening her to renewed heights of bliss. "And, darling, somehow he must be made to understand that *you* are what makes me happy."

"He will question it and then accept it," Spotted Eagle said. He placed a finger over her lips. "Shh. Let us not talk anymore. Let us make sunshine fill this tepee."

"I already feel its warmth," Jolena said, her pulse racing as warm surges of pleasure flooded her body. She closed her eyes. "It is such a delicious place—your arms. Hold me, darling, and never let me go."

Her whole universe seemed to start spinning as she felt herself going over the edge into ecstasy. . . .

The purple shadows seemed to have a life of their own as something moved midst them beneath the thick umbrella of trees. A throaty cough and then a groan broke the silence of the night. The lone figure stumbled blind from tree to tree, the man only half coherent after being alone in the forest for too many hours with nothing to eat but berries. Without a weapon, Kirk had not been able to make a good kill for a meal. His gun had been thrown aside as he had been thrown from the wagon and knocked unconscious just before it had tumbled over the cliff, joining those below, where death had come to so many.

"Jolena," Kirk whispered, swatting mosquitoes away from his face as a swarm began buzzing around him. "Where are you, Jolena?"

When Kirk had awakened behind a cover of bushes, he had seen no one except those who lay broken and bloody at the bottom of the cliff. He thought that he had succeeded at grabbing Jolena from the wagon. But it was hard now for him to sort through his scrambled memory as to what was real and what was imagined, perhaps during hallucinations as he clung somewhere between a conscious and unconscious state right after his fall.

He remembered very vividly how he had run desperately down the steep hillside, blinded with tears, fearing recognizing Jolena among those who had died from the fall. When he found nothing that even vaguely resembled his sister, he had searched high and low for her, finding no signs of her except for her strewn journals and destroyed butterfly collection.

After giving up on her, he had searched for his pistol. When he did not find it, he felt naked traveling through the Montana wilderness. He had lost count now of how many days and nights he had been wandering aimlessly about.

But he did know for certain that he had not come upon any civilization. He had even prayed to find the Blackfoot village. There he would have found food and lodging and perhaps those who sympathized with his plight and would go and search for his sister.

As Kirk stumbled out of the forest and into a moon-drenched meadow, he sighed and moved relentlessly onward. Brief dizzy spells caused him to weave, then he would snap out of it and be lucid again for a while.

Then he stopped with a start when he saw movement ahead of him, only a short distance away. He blinked his eyes and wiped them with the back of his hands, wondering if it were possible to see a mirage at night.

"Is it real?" he whispered, his knees wobbling as he tried to stand steady enough to gaze again into the distance.

"It is," he whispered, the discovery causing his heart to begin pounding. There were several riders approaching.

He squinted his eyes, trying to see if they were Indians or soldiers. His insides seemed to curl up into a tight knot when he recognized the riders as Indians, but he had no way of knowing which tribe! The Blackfoot were known to be friendly in these parts.

There were also known to be several Cree renegades who terrorized everyone that had two legs, no matter the color of their skin.

Kirk gazed up at the star-speckled heavens. "Lord, oh, please, Lord, let it be the Blackfoot," he whispered.

Then, knowing that he had no choice, he stood his ground and waited. When the Indians spotted him, they came riding harder, their shrieks piercing the air. This was enough for Kirk to know that they were not friendly Indians. He turned and tried to run from them, but his legs were too weak to carry him any farther. They gave way, and he crumpled to the ground.

As he lay helpless on his stomach, Kirk covered his ears with his hands to keep from hearing the pounding of the horses' hooves as they came closer and closer. He closed his eyes and held his breath as the horses made a wide circle around him, then stopped.

Kirk's heart pounded wildly as he waited for arrows to pierce his back.

When this did not happen, he slowly opened his eyes and turned over onto his back, then screamed when he found one of the gaudily painted Indians leaning over him, a knife in his hand.

When the Indian placed the knife at his throat, so close that the tip pierced his flesh and caused blood to curl from the wound, Kirk almost fainted from fright.

The Indian began speaking in a language unfamiliar to Kirk, and when Kirk talked back to him, he could tell that these Indians were unlike Spotted Eagle, who knew the art of speaking English quite well.

"You ... are ... Cree?" Kirk managed to say, saying the word Cree slowly.

The Indian who still knelt over Kirk nodded, and with his free hand doubled over his heart, pounded his chest over and over again with it. "Cree," the Indian snarled. "Cree!"

"Kirk," Kirk murmured, flashing his eyes from Indian to Indian, scarcely breathing. "I am called Kirk."

This seemed not to matter at all to the Indians. They ignored him as the one Indian grabbed his wrist and jerked him to his feet. Kirk looked wildly from Indian to Indian as his captor handed out orders to the others.

Soon Kirk's hands were tied behind him and a rope was placed around his neck. When the Indians mounted their horses again and began riding along in a slow lope, back in the direction whence they had just come, they laughed and mocked Kirk as they watched him stumble along behind the last horse of the group. Kirk gurgled strangely when the Indian who had command of his rope gave a strong tug, causing the rope to tighten around his neck.

Again the Indians laughed.

After so many tugs and near blackouts, Kirk fell senseless to the ground. He was only vaguely aware of someone poking at his side with a moccasined toe. He was only half aware of being lifted onto the back of a horse. He drifted in and out of consciousness as the Cree rode on into the night until the sky began lightening along the horizon.

Unable to stay awake any longer, Kirk drifted off into a restless sleep. When he awakened, he found himself tied to a stake in the center of a village, the object of much scrutiny as women and children edged in closer to him, touching him and ripping his clothes from him. After he was completely naked, his private parts became the object of attention.

Sticks probed at him.

Hands fondled.

Fingers pinched and hurt him.

Humiliated, Kirk closed his eyes and allowed his thoughts to wander elsewhere, to a more pleasant time, when he and Jolena were children and played hide and seek in the garden at the back of their Saint Louis mansion. He had known then that she was much different than he, but never had he allowed her to become acquainted with other Indians, for most were looked upon as savage.

Today, he was discovering just how savage some of the Indians could be.

She would never belong to this way of life, he thought.

Never!

Should she be alive, and he able to speak his mind, he would not allow it!

He screamed throatily and begged for mercy when someone placed the sharp tip of a knife at his throat. . . .

Chapter Twenty-Five

Jolena awakened with a start and gazed up at the smoke hole. She cringed when she discovered that it was morning and dreaded what was expected of her. It was her duty as the sister of Two Ridges to prepare him for burial!

Shuddering at the thought of not only having to look down at his corpse, but also having to touch him, Jolena knew that, of all of the Blackfoot customs that she knew she must learn, surely this would be the hardest for her to bear . . . or accept.

She closed her eyes and snuggled against Spotted Eagle's back, finding solace with him for just a short while longer. Through the night her dreams had been most unpleasant! In one of her dreams, as she had been preparing Two Ridges' body for burial, his eyes had suddenly opened. His hands had gripped her shoulders tightly and had made her trade places with him on his bed of thick, handsome bear pelts. In her dream, Two Ridges was preparing *her* for burial! Her throat had been as though frozen, and she was unable to cry out as Two Ridges stripped her of her clothing and had then began spreading black paint all over her body. The touch of the paint had burned her, as though it were acid.

She had awakened in a cold sweat, fearing any dream that was not pleasant. Too often her dreams had been an omen of something that had truly happened. She had dreamed of Spotted Eagle's death by a deadly arrow, and it would have come to pass had not Two Ridges been suddenly there in the path of the arrow!

She tremored at the thought of what this most recent dream might mean . . . .

"Jolena?"

A tiny woman's voice speaking her name outside the lodge caused Jolena's thoughts to return to the present, and to remember that her time had come to join others on this day of Two Ridges' burial. Late last night, before she had fallen into her restless sleep, Spotted Eagle had told her that she would not be totally alone in preparing Two Ridges' for his burial. Moon Flower would assist her.

Spotted Eagle had also told Jolena that Moon Flower had professed her love for Two Ridges more than once to their village. It was presumed by everyone that they would soon be married.

Even Spotted Eagle had for a while believed that it might come to pass, until he had witnessed his friend taking woman after woman to his blankets.

"Spotted Eagle," Jolena whispered, slightly shaking him. "Please wake up. It's time for me to go with Moon Flower."

Spotted Eagle yawned and stretched his arms above his head, then turned and faced Jolena. He placed his hands to her shoulders and brought her lips to his and kissed her. But when he found no willing response, he eased his hands from her and looked into her eyes.

"Spotted Eagle, how can I be expected to behave as though I think that Moon Flower is helping me prepare Two Ridges for burial because she was his woman when both you and I know different?" Jolena whispered. She cast the closed entrance flap another brief glance when Moon Flower persisted calling Jolena's name outside the dwelling. "Surely Moon Flower heard the rumors of Two Ridges' professed prowess."

"Moon Flower hears what she wants to hear and believes what she wants to believe," Spotted Eagle said softly. "Today she believes she belongs next to you while preparing Two Ridges' body for burial. Allow it. It will make the chore easier for you, will it not?"

"I will feel I am taking part in Two Ridges' betrayal of Moon Flower if I do this," Jolena said.

When Moon Flower said her name again,

this time sounding desperate, Jolena knew that she had no choice but to go ahead and do as Spotted Eagle suggested. She gave him a lingering, loving stare, then left their bed of blankets and furs and dressed.

Smelling the aroma of food being cooked in the other dwellings of the village, she only half-heartedly realized that she was hungry. Surely if she tried to eat anything before this terrible ordeal that lay ahead of her, she would not be able to hold it down.

Warm arms encircling her waist momentarily washed away Jolena's troubled thoughts, and when Spotted Eagle turned her around to face him, she was once again made aware of what was most important to her in life.

Spotted Eagle.

She knew that nothing would cause her to leave him—not even customs that were foreign and ugly to her!

"It will soon be tomorrow and all of this will be behind you," Spotted Eagle said softly. He lifted her chin with a finger, directing her eyes to his. "Tomorrow you will focus thoughts on the brother you have known as a brother all the winters and summers of your life. Not a brother who is buried today."

Tears of gratitude flooded Jolena's eyes to know that Spotted Eagle was so conscious of her feelings.

She leaned into his embrace and hugged him tightly, then turned and fled from the tepee, her knee-high moccasins warm against her flesh as the early morning's dampness enveloped her in a cold embrace.

With that first step outside the tepee, Jolena stopped and stared in disbelief at Moon Flower. Her eyes widened and she gasped as her gaze moved slowly over Moon Flower, seeing the lengths to which she had gone in her mourning for Two Ridges. Late last night, Moon Flower had left the camp and gone to a rise of ground near the village on which to release her sorrows for Two Ridges. There she had cried and lamented, calling Two Ridges' name over and over again.

Jolena had lain stiffly at Spotted Eagle's side, listening, unable to distinguish whether or not the way in which Moon Flower had spoken Two Ridges' name was a chant or a song. There was a certain tune to it, sung in a minor key and very doleful.

Jolena had soon surmised that this was a mourning song, the utterance of one in deep distress. It had been the sound of someone whose heart was broken.

Today Jolena saw just how much Moon Flower was distressed over Two Ridges' death! Her beautiful hair had been cut quite short, and she wore no moccasins today, standing barefoot and exposing the terribly scarred calves of her legs, on which blood had dried to the wounds.

"Let us go now, Jolena, and ready my beloved for his travels alone on the road to the Sand Hills," Moon Flower said, her voice breaking.

"We must give Two Ridges up to the Sun today."

Jolena wanted to cry out to Moon Flower that Two Ridges was not worthy of her undying devotion and love! To herself, she was cursing Two Ridges, thinking he deserved not a warrior's burial but that of a coward!

It was going to be harder than she had earlier thought to get through this day, for she was going to find it hard to stand by and watch Two Ridges being praised instead of condemned!

She knew one thing for certain. Even though they were of blood kin, she would never look on him as a brother!

She would not mourn him as a sister would mourn a dead brother!

She would proudly present herself to her Blackfoot people with her hair long and flowing, instead of cut off short, as one who mourns cuts one's hair.

She most certainly would not place a knife to her calves and scar herself!

She was certain no one would question this choice of hers. To everyone but Spotted Eagle, she was still a stranger who would not be expected to follow the set rules of her elders.

"I will do what I can," Jolena said, her voice drawn. "But you must know that I will need to be shown."

"I will be at your side at all times, directing you," Moon Flower said, taking Jolena by the elbow and ushering her away from Spotted Eagle's dwelling. "It is sad that you did not

know Two Ridges as a sister knows a brother.
It is sad that he did not know you as a brother
knows a sister. His heart was warm and big.
He would have drawn you into loving him, as
he did everyone who knew him."

"I'm sure he would have," Jolena said, noting
now the utter silence of the village. No children were running around playing. No elderly
men were sitting outside, sharing smokes and
gossip. No women were carrying wood from
the river.

It was as though time had stood still in the
Blackfoot village, perhaps waiting to resume
once the burial rituals were over.

When Jolena and Moon Flower came to Two
Ridges' tepee, Jolena hesitated, then walked
inside with the beautiful, slight Blackfoot woman. The fire in the firepit had been allowed to
die down to cold, gray ashes. Jolena shivered
and hugged herself, feeling as though she had
entered a tomb. As her eyes adjusted to the
darkness, she focused them on a body that was
lying on a couch of bear pelts.

Again she shivered, stunned to find that Two
Ridges was lying there without clothes or any
blankets to cover his nudity. When her gaze
stopped at his face and saw how white and
chalky it was, a feeling of light-headedness
swept through Jolena. She grabbed at Moon
Flower to steady herself.

"You have not seen many dead people before?" Moon Flower said, gazing at Jolena with
sorrowful eyes. "You are finding it hard to look

at your brother as he lies there with only his death mask?"

"No, I haven't experienced many deaths," Jolena whispered, fearing disturbing the dead if she spoke aloud. "But I have experienced one very painful loss. My mother."

She paused and glanced quickly at Moon Flower, feeling a need to explain which mother she was referring to, but she saw that was not necessary. Moon Flower's eyes, and it seemed her thoughts, were now solely on Two Ridges.

Jolena followed Moon Flower to Two Ridges' bed. She watched as Moon Flower went to one side of the tepee and gathered several robes up into her arms, then carried them back to Jolena.

"You must wrap your brother snugly in these," Moon Flower said, laying the robes across Jolena's outstretched arms. Moon Flower looked around her, then back into Jolena's eyes again. "While you wrap your brother, I will carry his belongings from his dwelling."

Jolena swallowed hard, then proceeded to wrap Two Ridges with first one fur robe, then another, until at least eight were fitted snugly around him.

Moon Flower came to Jolena. "Everything that Two Ridges possessed is now carried to his gravesite," she murmured. "Now, my friend, let us dismantle his tepee so that you can then use the lodge covering for his final wrap."

Jolena's eyes widened. "That is required?"

she whispered harshly. "That you and I tear down the tepee while Two Ridges still lies within the circle of its base?"

"That is how it is done," Moon Flower said, nodding.

Sighing heavily, Jolena followed along after Moon Flower and began loosening the buckskin straps that held the tepee securely to the lodge poles. A short time later, everything was dismantled and Two Ridges' body lay beneath the lodge poles that still stood in their original shape, before the skins were wrapped around them.

Jolena felt a coldness rush over her flesh as she gazed slowly around her at the bare lodge poles, thinking they looked like the skeleton of a dead lodge.

The sudden drone of a drum began somewhere in the distance. Mournful songs and chants filled the air as people filed one by one from their dwellings and came to stand in a wide circle around Two Ridges' demolished tepee.

Jolena gasped when her Blackfoot father came into view, walking solemnly from the purple shadows of the forest on the one side of the village. In his mourning, he had painted himself black and had cut off his long, thick braids, and had discarded his leggings, revealing that he, also, had scarified his legs.

Jolena's attention was drawn back to Moon Flower, as Moon Flower grunted and groaned with the weight of the skins that had been taken from the lodge poles of the tepee.

Jolena went to her rescue, and between them they were finally able to get Two Ridges' body wrapped, then laced with rawhide ropes.

Spotted Eagle and several warriors came into view. Solemnly, they went to Two Ridges' body. Some stood at his head, others at his feet. Spotted Eagle nodded, giving a silent order to the warriors to help him carry Two Ridges to his burial site.

Jolena fell back from the others, feeling that her duty to her brother had been done. She wanted to comfort Moon Flower, who was walking beside her crying and wailing. But she felt too awkward even being there, much less trying to give anyone any comfort.

The procession walked into the forest and slowly through it until it came to a hill, upon which stood a lone tree. Upon its branches had been arranged a platform of lodge poles.

The bundle was placed on the platform, along with Two Ridges' favorite weapons, his medicine bundle, and his war clothing.

Jolena had solemnly watched how reverently everyone then passed beneath the platform, placing their gifts on the ground beneath it.

When Jolena heard a commotion behind her, she turned with a start and watched, puzzled, as a young brave came walking toward Brown Elk, a rope leading Two Ridges' magnificent horse behind him.

Brown Elk took possession of the horse and

led it beneath the platform upon which lay his only son.

Jolena felt faint when, without hesitation, her Blackfoot father drew a sharp knife from a sheath at his side and plunged it into the horse, over and over again, until it was dead and lying in a pool of blood on the ground beneath him.

Scarcely breathing, her eyes wide, Jolena then watched Brown Elk replace the knife in its sheath, then hold his outstretched hands up to Two Ridges' bundled body.

"*No-ko-i*, my son, now you will have your favorite horse to ride on your journey to the Sand Hills," he cried. "And to use after arriving there!"

There was a pause, then everyone turned and walked slowly back toward their village. Spotted Eagle took Jolena by the elbow, ushering her away from the burial site. She looked over her shoulder, watching her father as he walked in another direction.

"He will mourn alone for a while, then come to you as a father again," Spotted Eagle said softly. "When he comes to you then, all thoughts of a son will be forgotten. He has a daughter now to fill the empty spaces in his heart that the death of his son has left."

"I just want this day to be over," Jolena said, tears flooding her eyes. "Take me home, Spotted Eagle. I want you to hold me."

"I will hold you until your tears are washed from your eyes—and hold you even longer, if you so desire," Spotted Eagle said, placing an arm around her waist and drawing her protectively to his side. "My woman, I will always be there to hold you. Always."

"How did I ever exist without you?" Jolena murmured, a sob catching in her throat. "Surely I wandered through each day only half aware of things around me!"

"I feel the same," Spotted Eagle said. "Until you, there was truly no purpose to my life."

"But now we have forever, don't we?" Jolena said, gazing raptly up at him.

"Forever," Spotted Eagle said, nodding. In his heart, he was thinking about what he had planned for tomorrow—that he would be searching for Kirk, knowing that to do so would be placing him and his many warriors in danger.

The Cree renegades were always out there, always waiting for a reason to kill their neighboring enemy, the Blackfoot!

Tomorrow they would perhaps have that chance, for Spotted Eagle knew that his search for Kirk could take him into Cree country.

He planned to send scouts out tonight, hopefully to find evidence of Kirk's whereabouts—or the Crees'—without meeting danger head on.

"You are so suddenly quiet," Jolena said, glancing up at him. "Why are you, darling?"

"No reason," Spotted Eagle said, forcing himself to sound nonchalant. "No reason at all."

Something in the way he spoke and looked made Jolena not believe him all that easily.

But she did not want to cloud her thoughts

with doubts and wonder again. For now she just wanted to go to Spotted Eagle's tepee and hide there from all the rest of humanity, at least for the rest of the afternoon and tonight.

She dreaded tomorrow, fearing that Kirk might be found—and that he would be dead.

But she wanted to face that when it happened.

Not now, when her heart was already so scarred from today's activities.

Chapter Twenty-Six

The sun had gone to his lodge behind the mountains, disappearing behind the sharp-pointed peaks. In the fading light, the far-stretching prairie was turning dark. In the valley, sparsely timbered with quaking aspens and cottonwoods, a lone voice could be heard in the Blackfoot village, from a hilltop a short distance away.

Jolena clasped a blanket around her shoulders as she sat quietly beside Spotted Eagle's fire in his tepee, haunted by too many things to eat her evening meal. As soup simmered over the fire in a black pot, she was only faintly aware of the tantalizing fragrance of buffalo meat cooking with large chunks of vegetables.

Spotted Eagle had sent scouts ahead to look

for Kirk. They had returned earlier in the afternoon with the news that he was being held captive in a Cree camp.

Jolena was joyous that her brother was alive, yet feared for his treatment at the hands of the Cree.

And now she was worried over Spotted Eagle, who was readying himself to go and rescue Kirk. He had left her early this day to take his medicine sweat and to prepare himself for a possible confrontation with the renegade Indians. He had even appointed a medicine pipe man to make medicine for him during his absence.

Spotted Eagle had chosen the warriors who would make up his war party. These warriors and himself had already gotten together and sung the wolf song. Their sweat lodge was then built and, unclothed, they entered it. With them came an elderly Blackfoot, Clouds Make Thunder, a medicine pipe man, who had always been a good, revered warrior.

The long-stemmed medicine pipe was filled. The warriors each asked Clouds Make Thunder to pray for them, that they might have good luck and accomplish what they desired.

Clouds Make Thunder prayed and sang and poured water on hot stones in the center of the sweat lodge, causing the warriors to sweat profusely.

Clouds Make Thunder then offered Spotted Eagle a new medicine bundle, to give him strength and courage for the time ahead and to bind him with the spirits who would carry his life in their mouths.

The bundle was formed from the head of a coyote, its jaws sewn together with sinew; from the jowls hung a few small locks of hair wrapped in red cloth. From the back of the head was suspended a round loop of willow, wrapped tightly in rawhide, to which was tied a fully stuffed war eagle.

After the ceremony was over, the warriors, all dripping with perspiration, ran to the river and plunged in, singing war songs.

Jolena gazed up at the smoke hole in the ceiling, shuddering when she discovered that the sunset's brilliant orange splash had faded from the sky, which meant that Spotted Eagle would soon leave the village. He had explained to her that he would be riding with his warriors from the village just after sunset, for it was a foolish warrior who traveled in the day when war parties might be out.

To busy her hands, Jolena leaned over and tossed some small twigs into the low flames of the fire. Then she straightened her back and stiffened. She glanced quickly toward the closed entrance flap of the tepee when she heard the thundering of many horses' hooves leaving the village, Spotted Eagle's voice the loudest of them all as he sang a song of war.

"Return to me with speed," Jolena whispered to herself, reaching a trembling hand toward the entrance flap. "I love you. Oh, how I love you."

Again she gazed into the flames of the fire, the horses' thunder having at least for a moment drowned out the mourning cries of her Blackfoot father as he sat on his high place, alone and distraught over the death of his one and only son. Through the long day, her father had sat on a nearby hill, mourning, his songs and wails filled with much sadness.

Jolena buried her face in her hands, her heart touched by the wailing. She still could not find it in her heart to mourn with him, but she did mourn *for* him!

Jolena moved her hands from her face and slowly lifted her eyes, her pulse racing. She leaned her ear toward the entrance flap, now scarcely breathing, realizing that suddenly she no longer heard her father's mourning cries. Everything outside was quiet except for an occasional bark from a dog, or cries from a child fighting off the urge to sleep.

A fire outside threw a square of flickering light on the outside of the tepee and then she saw the outline of someone standing over the fire, feeding wood into the flames.

"Is that my father?" Jolena whispered, pushing herself up from her couch of skins. "Is that him beside the communal fire?"

Keeping the blanket around her shoulders, clasping it together with a hand, Jolena went to the entrance flap and peered outside, disappointed that the person she had seen tending to the fire was not her father at all. Four Bears, a handsome, middle-aged Blackfoot, turned Jolena's way and nodded a grim and silent hello, then sauntered off into the night toward his own tepee, where his wife and daughter waited for him.

Sighing, Jolena decided to wait outside for a while longer to see if her father's silence might mean that he was placing his sadness for a son behind him to join a daughter who was very much alive.

The night breeze carried a chill, but the blanket lent warmth to Jolena's shoulders. She looked heavenward and watched the play of stars in the velvety black sky. She could make out the big and little dipper and other constellations, especially that which the Blackfoot called *The Seven Persons,* the constellation of the Great Bear. Tonight it seemed overpoweringly bright, as if it were an omen.

"Daughter?" Brown Elk said as he came to Jolena out of the darkness, his face still painted black with mourning. "You wait for your father in the cold?" He came to her and placed a hand to her elbow, ushering her away from Spotted Eagle's dwelling to his own.

Jolena expected to find his tepee cold and without the fragrance of food, but someone had kept the fire burning and had made sure food awaited his return from his long hours of mourning. She expected the one who was so thoughtful and kind was Moon Flower. Her kindness was spread around, it seemed, to everyone who needed it. Even while she mourned for Two Ridges, she was putting her feelings second to others who mourned even more deeply.

Brown Elk nodded toward his couch, which was cushioned with many plush furs. "Sit," he said, helping her down onto it. "We will talk after I remove the mourning paint from my face."

"You must be starved," Jolena said, watching him as he poured water from a jug into a wooden basin, then began splashing his face with the water. "The stew smells delicious. While you wash your face, I will dip some stew into a bowl."

"Dip stew into two bowls," Brown Elk said, scrubbing his face with his hands, watching the water turn black with the discarded paint. "Am I right to think you have not eaten enough to keep your strength? Your heart is troubled too much to enjoy the taste of food on your tongue?"

"Yes, something like that," Jolena said, marveling over how he could measure her mood so well. She ladled stew into two bowls and set them aside until he came and sat down beside her.

She didn't hesitate to eat once he began, not having realized that she was so hungry until she got that first bite between her lips. She ate ravenously, then set her bowl aside as he scraped the last morsel of carrot from his bowl with his fingers.

Brown Elk then set his bowl aside and turned his dark eyes to Jolena. "It is written on your face that too much worries you," he said. He placed a gentle hand to her shoulder. "Do not fret over your white brother. Spotted Eagle will return him to you. And do not worry over Spotted Eagle. He is brave but cautious, and he has strong medicine. Some say that he is related to the ghosts and that they help him."

"Truly?" Jolena said, her eyes wide.

Brown Elk dropped his hand to his lap. "You see, my daughter?" he said, chuckling. "This wizened old man knows what to say to draw a daughter out of herself." His eyes twinkled into hers. "The mere mention of Spotted Eagle did not do it, but the wonder of what I said about him is what helped draw your thoughts away from that which torments you."

"Do people truly say that he is related to ghosts and that they help him?" Jolena asked, her eyes still filled with wonder.

"Perhaps," Brown Elk said, shrugging. "It was just something that came to me that I thought might draw your attention. It worked, did it not?"

Jolena laughed softly, now realizing that what he said was not at all true, but it had seemed something that might be. Spotted Eagle seemed the sort to be able to do anything and to be anything he desired.

"Yes, it worked," she murmured. "And I appreciate it. I *am* concerned over Spotted Eagle and my brother's welfare. Both are precious to me."

"Then I was right earlier to assume your feelings for Spotted Eagle are those that a woman feels for a man when she wishes to speak vows of forever with him?" Brown Elk said, leaning over to push another limb into the flesh-warming fire.

"Yes, I have many wonderful feelings for Spotted Eagle," Jolena said, finding it easy to talk with this man who until a few days ago had been a stranger to her. She was so glad that the Blackfoot of this village had associated enough with white people that they could speak her language. If not, she would have felt like a stranger in a foreign country!

"And I approve," Brown Elk said, settling back down onto his couch again. He folded his arms comfortably across his chest. "He need not pay me a large bride price for you, for I can see that he already has you locked within his heart, as he is locked within yours."

Jolena moved from the couch onto to her knees before Brown Elk. "Father, it is so strange how it happened," she murmured, her eyes sparkling into his. "I saw Spotted Eagle in my dreams before I ever met him face to face! When I told Spotted Eagle this, he explained the importance of dreams to the Blackfoot. I feel so blessed, Father, to be Blackfoot and to be here to learn everything that a Blackfoot woman should know."

"You will learn easily," Brown Elk said, smiling at her. "Already you know much."

"And how do you feel about my dreams?" Jolena said anxiously. "And that they for the most part come true?"

Brown Elk framed her delicate, copper face between his hands. "I, too, am gifted with dreaming," he said, his voice low and comforting. "You see, my daughter, I dreamed of you often before you came to me in the flesh."

"You did?" Jolena said, gasping. "Truly you did?"

"It is true that I did," Brown Elk said. "But you see, my daughter, until you came to the village and showed yourself to me, when I dreamed of you I thought the dreams were of your mother! Now I know they were, in truth, of *you!*"

He drew her to him and cradled her close. "This father missed you," he said, his voice breaking. "You are so like your mother, my beautiful bride, my reason for breathing. But you are real and dear to me, forevermore, *Ni-tun*, as my daughter. Your mother is just a sweet memory that I have tucked away now inside my heart."

"Would you mind terribly telling me about my mother?" Jolena asked, easing from his arms. "If you would rather not, I would understand. You have just a short while ago left your place of mourning, where you mourned a son. I would understand if it is too soon to talk of someone else for whom you have sung your mourning songs."

"It would please me to acquaint you with your mother," Brown Elk said, his voice trailing off into silence as he gazed into the flames of the fire.

Jolena crept back onto her couch, feeling awkward in this silence. She stole a glance at her father's face and noticed again its texture, then noticed something new since he had lost a son—the sagging lower lids of his level, assured eyes. Yet nothing had changed about his uncompromising, self-willed mouth.

After a long moment of peaceful silence, Brown Elk began to talk. "There are many winters in this old man," he said. "But once I was young, and I had a young wife. Her name was Sweet Dove, the most beautiful woman of the Blackfoot, Cree, Crow, and Snake tribes of the Montana Territory. When she agreed to become my wife, I gave a celebration that lasted for many days and nights."

He swallowed hard. "We spent many nights sharing blanket warmth, and then she told me she was with child," he said, giving Jolena a proud smile. "Never was a Blackfoot warrior as happy as when that announcement was made to me. I pampered my woman, and every night I spoke to my child through the walls of my wife's stomach. I told my child that this father already loved her very much."

He looked quickly away as tears began silvering his eyes. "Yes, even then I saw the child as a daughter," he said, his voice trailing away. "And then came the day for this child to be born. Foolishly I allowed my wife to go from this village to have the child alone, as Blackfoot wives do. Never did the life of my child seem threatened, nor that of my wife. Sweet Dove was healthy and strong. But not strong enough, it seems."

Brown Elk rested his face in his hands and began shaking his head back and forth mournfully. "She must have suffered much before she released the child from her womb," he said, his voice drawn. "The blood . . . there was so much blood when she was found. . . ."

Jolena moved to her father and took his hands from his face and leaned into his arms. "No more," she cried. "Please don't say any more. It isn't fair of me to ask you to go through this again, as though it were today instead of eighteen summers ago. Please say no more, Father."

In her mind's eye, Jolena was trying desperately to block out the sight of her mother lying in a pool of her life's blood without feeling to blame, even though she had been a mere babe, innocent of everything as she had lain beside her dying mother, who had given her life to give birth to her. She was so glad that her Blackfoot father did not see her as the cause of his wife's death.

Jolena clenched her eyelids closed, having learned something from this experience. She knew that whenever she was heavy with child, she would most definitely break away from the old tradition of going from the village to give birth to the child alone! She would want her beloved Spotted Eagle at her side during her time of labor and birthing. She would not let history repeat itself.

Her eyes fluttered open, realizing where her thoughts had just taken her! She was marveling at how she could think that far ahead and consider children with Spotted Eagle when she wasn't even yet his wife!

Someone crying just outside the tepee drew Jolena and Brown Elk apart. They both rushed to their feet and went to the entrance. Jolena watched anxiously as her father lifted the flap, gasping when she found Moon Flower there, trembling and crying.

"I have been banished from my parents' lodge," Moon Flower said, sobbing as she gazed from Jolena to Brown Elk. "Where can I go? What am

I to do? My parents disown me."

Brown Elk reached quickly to Moon Flower. He placed an arm around her waist and drew her into the tepee. "Tell us what has happened to cause such trouble between yourself and your parents," he said, helping her down onto the couch cushioned with many pelts.

Jolena followed and sat down on one side of Moon Flower as her father sat down on the other side of the distraught young woman.

Moon Flower buried her face in her hands, her whole body shaking as she continued crying. "I told my parents that I was with child!" she cried. "I asked for their pity and . . . told them that a child born to me now would be born of a daughter still unmarried!"

"You are with child?" Jolena said, trying to keep the alarm that she was feeling from her voice. She knew of Moon Flower's love for Two Ridges. The child could be none other than his!

"Yes, and I am proud, not ashamed!" Moon Flower said, giving Jolena a defiant look. "Had Two Ridges not died, he would have married me! I . . . had not found the courage yet to tell him about the . . . child."

She lowered her eyes and wept again. "And never shall I be able to!" she wailed.

"You did not have the courage also to tell your parents until now?" Brown Elk said, reaching a hand to Moon Flower's brow, smoothing some fallen dark locks of hair back into place.

"I did not want to tell them until I had exchanged vows with Two Ridges and then the pregnancy would be legitimate in the eyes of my parents and my people," Moon Flower said, sniffling as she wiped her nose with the back of a hand. "I had thought to run away after his burial and stay away until I had the child. I did not think my parents could turn their backs on a daughter who was offering a tiny child to its grandparents for loving and understanding. But today I could not bear the thought of leaving, nor could I bear the thought of carrying this burden within my heart any longer. I revealed the truth of my condition to my mother and father, and neither embraced the knowing. Both are ashamed and they pointed to the door and ordered me to leave."

Knowing that Two Ridges had never had any true feelings for Moon Flower, Jolena was torn in her feelings about knowing that the child Moon Flower was carrying was his.

Now a part of this horrible man would be alive forever!

Yet she could not shun this woman whose life had been altered forever by Two Ridges' need to conquer as many women as he could to prove his prowess.

This woman had not been as lucky as Jolena— to find a man who was honorable in every way!

Also, this unborn child was in part related to Jolena! She would be the child's aunt!

She glanced at her father, seeing how he wore this knowledge heavy in the depths of his eyes— to know that a son had fathered a child and had not wed the woman first!

She could see a mixture of alarm and shame in

his expression and was glad when he opened his arms to Moon Flower, surely ready to accept this woman into his life as he would his grandchild once it was born.

"You need go no farther than my tepee," Brown Elk said, embracing Moon Flower as she clung desperately to him. "I shall take over the duties of my son. You will live with me. The child will have a place to live. Your child will be dearly loved."

"Oh, thank you, thank you," Moon Flower sobbed. "I promise that I will find many ways to repay your kindness."

"You need not worry about repayment," Brown Elk said, patting her back. "That you were honest enough to reveal the truth to me, the unborn child's grandparent, is payment enough. Should you have left the village, never would I have been given the chance to hold my grandchild, nor to give it the love it deserves from a grandparent."

He paused, then said, "Your mother and father will envy this grandparent when they see he holds the child up on the day of its birth for all to see!"

Jolena wiped tears from her eyes, thankful to have been a witness to her father's deep emotions and compassion tonight.

This made it easier not to be so torn between loyalties where fathers were concerned!

She now understood the depths of his hurt when she had been denied him those eighteen summers ago and all the years since.

She had so much to make up to him.

And she would—in many lovely ways.

Chapter Twenty-Seven

Although he had hoped that warring wouldn't be required to rescue Kirk, Spotted Eagle feared nothing and was always ready to fight.

He had put on a necklace of bear claws, a belt of bear fur, and around his head a band of fur. He was now ready for whatever the night hours brought him.

The moon was high in the sky, casting its silver light down upon many glittering lances and brightly polished weapons as Spotted Eagle and his warriors moved with the precision of clockwork and the pride of veterans through the hills and ravines so that they could not be seen.

Spotted Eagle had sent Double Runner far ahead to check on the Cree camp where Kirk was being held captive. When Spotted Eagle spied Double Runner up ahead, returning, he sank his heels into the flanks of his powerful steed and broke away from the others, riding to meet Double Runner's approach.

Each man reined his horse to a stop alongside the other.

"What news have you brought back to me?" Spotted Eagle asked, wary when he saw that his scout was wearing a frown instead of the look of excited wariness that always came into Double Runner's eyes before going into an enemy's village.

"I found the camping place of the Cree war party deserted," Double Runner said in a low rumble of a voice.

Spotted Eagle's spine stiffened. "And what of Jolena's white brother?" he said, his eyes lit with a sudden, angry fire at the possibility that he had been duped by his enemy!

"He is no longer a captive of the Cree," Double Runner said.

"If you did not see the Cree, how do you know the fate of the white man?" Spotted Eagle said, forking an eyebrow as he leaned closer to Double Runner.

"The white man still hangs on the stake, alone where the campsite has been deserted," Double Runner explained. "I did not venture to go to him alone. I fear this might be a trap."

"Yes, a trap," Spotted Eagle said, rubbing his chin thoughtfully. Then he looked over his shoulder at his warriors as they rode up behind him and drew rein, waiting to see what his next command might be. "We shall see. We will be prepared for an ambush, if one is planned."

He explained everything to his warriors and then they all rode cautiously onward, eyes darting around them, watching guardedly for any movements.

Spotted Eagle gazed heavenward, noticing that the moon was now hidden behind a thick, black cloud.

Spotted Eagle and his companions traveled onward, and when they came close to the Crees' abandoned campsite, they rode up in a ravine behind it and brought their horses to a halt.

Dismounting, Spotted Eagle secured his horse's reins to a low tree limb, his warriors following his lead. With his quiver of arrows secured to his back, and clutching his bow, keeping the weapons ready in case they were needed, Spotted Eagle crept into a large bunch of rye grass to hide as he surveyed the abandoned camp with slow, intense eyes.

He could tell that the Cree had torn down the lodges and packed their dog travois in haste, for they had packed in such a hurry that they had left many little things lying in camp.

Spotted Eagle could see knives, awls, bone needles, and moccasins scattered around on the packed earth.

When the cloud finally scurried on past, and the moon's glow again illumined everything as though it were morning, it revealed the stake on which Kirk was tied, his head bowed, motionless.

Double Runner eased himself closer to Spotted Eagle. "He is dead?" he whispered, the rifle barrel he carried shining beneath the moon's bright rays.

Fearing its reflection might cast itself where it did not belong—perhaps in the eye of a Cree waiting to ambush those who would rescue the white man, Spotted Eagle placed his hand onto Double Runner's rifle and quickly lowered it to his scout's side.

"We might be dead if you do not use more caution," Spotted Eagle warned, glaring at Double Runner. "Even you think this might be a trap. Act accordingly."

Double Runner nodded, then peered at Kirk again. "And what do we do now?" he whispered.

Spotted Eagle looked over his shoulder at his other warriors. He made a wide swing in the air with his free hand. "Everyone spread," he flatly ordered. "Go with much care as you surround this campsite. If you find the Cree, silence them with your knives before they can alert others. For this a rifle is useless. Take your knives!"

"Your rifle will guard this warrior as he goes into the camp alone," he said to Double Runner. "If you soon see that there is no threat of a Cree ambush, come to me and help me with the white man. If he is alive, he will need nourishment quickly and a travois made for his return to our village. You will help Spotted Eagle do these things. Do you understand?"

Double Runner nodded.

Spotted Eagle waited until he thought that his men should be in a wide circle around the abandoned camp, then crept out into the open, an arrow notched to his bow. With wary eyes, he kept a guarded look on all sides of him as he moved toward Kirk.

When he came closer to Kirk, he realized now how the Cree had gone about preparing their white captive for the stake. They had smoothed a cottonwood tree by taking off the bark and had painted it black. They had then stood Kirk against it and fastened him there with a great many ropes.

After they had Kirk secured enough so that he could not move, they had painted his face black.

Spotted Eagle could even now hear how the Cree renegades would have made a prayer, giving Kirk to the Sun.

And they had left him for the Sun, sky, moon and any animals that might happen along.

Spotted Eagle took the last step to stand in front of Kirk, shuddering at his appearance and the many small wounds that had been inflicted by the Cree women and children. Before he had lapsed into a deep sleep, he had suffered much at the hands of his abductors!

Thinking of Jolena waiting back at his village, Spotted Eagle hesitated to place a finger to the vein at Kirk's neck, fearing that he would discover that her white brother had not lived through the ordeal. But he had to know.

Lifting his free hand to Kirk's blackened neck, Spotted Eagle sought for a pulse, for a moment fearing there was none.

Then he smiled and nodded, finally finding one, even though faint and slow.

Double Runner came to Spotted Eagle's side as his other warriors emerged from hiding, one by one. There seemed to be no Cree anywhere. As Cree war parties were wont to do, they had moved onward to wreak havoc elsewhere.

"Is he alive?" Double Runner asked, leaning close to Kirk studying him.

"*Kyi.* Barely," Spotted Eagle grumbled, laying his bow on the ground. He drew his huge knife from its sheath at his right side. "Lay your rifle aside, Double Runner. As I cut this man's ropes, you catch him."

Spotted Eagle gazed around at his other warriors. "A travois must be prepared," he ordered them. "*Hai-yah!* Quickly! We must not tempt fate by remaining here any longer than is required to prepare this man for traveling back to our village. Among us, we should have plenty of robes and skins for his bedding!"

Everyone scurried into action as Spotted Eagle moved his knife toward the first rope, then stopped with a start when Kirk slowly began lifting his head, his eyes soon finding Spotted Eagle's.

"Thank God," Kirk whispered raspily, his throat dry and parched. "I . . . wouldn't have lasted another hour. Thank you, Spotted Eagle. Thank . . . you."

Kirk's head lowered again and his eyes closed. Spotted Eagle hurriedly cut the ropes and soon Kirk was free. Wounded and weak, he fell to the ground before Double Runner or Spotted Eagle could catch him.

Spotted Eagle slipped his knife back into its sheath and fell to his knees beside Kirk. He began rubbing his limbs in an effort to put life back into them.

Kirk slowly opened his eyes again. "You would do all of this for me?" he said in a raspy whisper.

"I do this for your sister," Spotted Eagle said, his voice drawn.

Spotted Eagle continued rubbing Kirk's limbs for a while longer, then lifted him up into his arms and carried him to a place where he had seen many sarvis berries. After laying Kirk down beside the bushes that were heavy-laden with fruit, he broke off great branches of it. He plucked a large, ripe berry from the branch and held it to Kirk's mouth.

"To get strength, eat," he said softly. "These will quench your thirst as well as your hunger."

Kirk choked on the first berry, then once his throat was reacquainted with food and liquid, he ate them as quickly as Spotted Eagle could get them into his mouth.

Spotted Eagle broke off more branches full of the ripe berries and continued feeding them to Kirk until a travois was completed and attached by long poles behind his stallion, several knots in the rawhide thongs securing the travois poles to the horse's saddle.

"*Tsis-i*—come, white brother. We will leave now," Spotted Eagle said, once again lifting Kirk into his arms and carrying him to the travois. "Soon you will be with your sister again."

Spotted Eagle laid Kirk on a bed of pelts, then wrapped him securely with the hides of the medicine animal, the great bear.

Giving Kirk another lingering stare, seeing that he was asleep again, Spotted Eagle then swung himself into his saddle. With a raised hand, he gave the silent order to head back toward their village.

Double Runner rode on ahead of the others, his eyes ever watchful for an ambush, grateful to find the path quiet and peaceful for their return to their people.

Spotted Eagle rode in a soft lope, to make the ride as comfortable as possible for Jolena's brother as the poles of the travois bounced and jostled through tall grasses and along rock-strewn coulees. He had not taken the time to remove the black paint from Kirk's body, afraid that allowing time for that might give any passing war party the opportunity to attack.

Spotted Eagle was glad that he had not been forced to attack a Cree camp filled with women and children just to rescue a white man. Although the Cree were responsible for Two Ridges' death, Spotted Eagle could not blame them all for the act of one man—Long Nose! Nor could he blame the others for what this particular band of renegades had chosen to do to Kirk.

It was not for Spotted Eagle to know why they did any of these things, but always to guard against other attempts!

The morning came with a faint tint of pink to the sky as Spotted Eagle rode into his village. The sound of their horses drew the Blackfoot people from their tepees, Jolena among them as she clutched a blanket around her shoulders.

Jolena's eyes were wide and her pulse raced as she ran from her father's tepee, half stumbling in her eagerness to get to Spotted Eagle and the travois that he pulled behind his horse.

When she reached the travois and Spotted Eagle stopped his horse, Jolena fell to her knees and gasped with shock when she found herself looking down at Kirk, his face the only thing visible. She was stunned speechless by the black paint that had been applied to his face and his apparent lifelessness.

"Kirk," Jolena whispered, gently framing his face between her fingers. Tears sprang from her eyes. "Oh, Kirk, what did they do to you?"

Spotted Eagle dismounted and knelt down at Jolena's side. A comforting arm slipped around her waist as he gazed at her. "He is alive, but weak," he explained softly. "And the paint you see is always placed on Cree captives. It will wash easily away. But there are other things than paint that I must warn you about."

Jolena glanced quickly at Spotted Eagle, his warning causing fear to enter her heart. "What else is there?" she said, her voice drawn. She eased her hands from Kirk's face and clutched them together nervously on her lap.

"You shall see soon enough," Spotted Eagle said, slowly unfolding the covering of bear pelts.

He could feel the tension in the air behind and all around him as the Blackfoot people inched closer, watching.

He could hear Jolena's shallow breathing.

Out of the corner of his eye he saw his chieftain father come walking slowly and heavily toward him, supporting himself with his tall shaft.

Brown Elk and Moon Flower also came and stood behind Jolena, Brown Elk's hand on her shoulder as a reminder of his nearness and to show his love for her.

Kirk slowly opened his eyes. At first everything seemed a blur to him, but when he began focusing his eyes, they widened with relief when he found Jolena there, gazing down at him.

"Sis," Kirk said in a raspy whisper. "I'm going to be fine. Don't cry. Please . . . don't . . . cry."

Jolena forced a smile and again placed a gentle hand on his cheek. "I can't help but cry," she murmured. "I thought you were dead. But here you are, Kirk, as fine as a fiddle."

"I . . . wouldn't say . . . that," Kirk said, laughing softly. "But I will be soon. I promise."

When the last of the bear pelts was laid aside, revealing the paint that covered every inch of Kirk's body and the wounds that were scattered across his legs, abdomen, and arms, Jolena felt a bitterness rise into her throat and the urge to retch quickly overwhelmed her.

She swallowed hard, over and over again, until the bitterness subsided. She took the blanket from around her shoulders and quickly placed it over her brother.

Then she gave Spotted Eagle a pleading look. "Please take him to your tepee," she murmured. "There I will care for him until he is well again."

She looked over her shoulder at her Blackfoot father. He had heard and nodded his head in a silent understanding of her decision to be in Spotted Eagle's dwelling instead of his. He had had a dream this last evening of a beautiful wedding—of his daughter dressed in the finest Blackfoot clothes as she joined her heart with Spotted Eagle's for eternity.

He had given her to Spotted Eagle without hesitation, for he was the finest of warriors, filled with compassion, courage, and love for humanity.

Spotted Eagle would make a perfect father for Brown Elk's grandchildren!

Spotted Eagle leaned over Kirk and gently lifted him into his arms. As his people made way for him to go to his dwelling, Spotted Eagle carried the slight white man with Jolena walking beside him, her eyes never leaving her brother's face.

When they were inside the tepee and Kirk was comfortably close to the fire on a pallet of furs, Jolena hurriedly bathed the paint from his flesh. She then sat back and silently watched as Spotted Eagle ever so gently doctored Kirk's wounds with a herbal mixture that smelled pleasant enough and surely took the pain away, for Kirk sighed heavily and closed his eyes as he allowed it to be applied to his flesh.

When this also was done, Jolena slipped a robe around Kirk's shoulders as Spotted Eagle lifted him up to make it possible.

Moon Flower entered the tepee carrying a smoking pot that sent off a pleasant fragrance of cooked vegetables and meats. "Allow me to help?" she murmured, settling down beside Kirk on the opposite side from where Jolena and Spotted Eagle sat their vigil.

Kirk turned his eyes to Moon Flower, and his lips parted in a slight gasp when he gazed up at her delicate loveliness.

"I am Moon Flower," she murmured, setting the pot of soup down beside her. "Allow me to feed you?"

"Please ... do ..." Kirk said, smiling up at her. He tried to lean on one elbow, but toppled back down, too weak just yet to make even the slightest attempt to fend for himself.

Jolena reached behind her for a wooden bowl and spoon and handed them to Moon Flower, smiling a silent thank-you for her assistance.

Moon Flower ladled some soup into the bowl, then sank the spoon into it, soon placing it to Kirk's lips. "First the broth," she murmured. "Then later you can eat vegetables, then meat."

Spotted Eagle placed a hand beneath Kirk's head and lifted it slightly from the pallet, enabling him to swallow more easily.

Kirk sipped the broth from the spoon, his eyes never leaving Moon Flower, touched not only by her loveliness, but by her kindnesses. "You are as beautiful as your name," he said as he turned his lips a fraction from the proffered broth.

Jolena sighed deeply with relief. Seeing Kirk actually flirting, especially with a Blackfoot maiden, made her realize that her brother was going to be all right.

Jolena leaned into Spotted Eagle's embrace and watched the closeness and admiration growing between her brother and Moon Flower, who just recently had lost so much. First Two Ridges, and then her parents' love and affection. Perhaps now Moon Flower would be able to carry her child with a happy heart.

Jolena's breath caught in her throat when she recalled that Moon Flower was pregnant.

Oh, Lord, Jolena despaired to herself. How could she have forgotten that Moon Flower was pregnant? Surely when Kirk discovered that this beautiful woman was carrying another man's child inside her, he would turn his back on her.

"Tomorrow you will be much better," Moon Flower was saying to Kirk. "Soon you will be well enough to take walks in the forest with Moon Flower. You will be taught many things about nature and the way it is used by the Blackfoot."

"While I am healing, I can stay here at the Blackfoot village," Kirk said softly. "But then I must think of returning to Saint Louis."

He cast Jolena a wavering glance. "My sister, also, must see the need to return to Saint Louis," he murmured. "We have a father there who is anxiously awaiting our arrival."

Chapter Twenty-Eight

Buffalo had been spotted and it was decided to make a run. Throughout the Blackfoot village, men and women were readying themselves for the short journey to the great *pis-kun* that the warriors had built very high and strong at the foot of a towering cliff, so that no buffalo could escape.

Jolena was lost in thought as she bathed her brother's brow with a cool cloth. Spotted Eagle was preparing to leave for the hunt. He had refused to eat and was now sorting through his bundles for the clothes that he wanted to wear during the hunt.

Jolena was remembering how he had talked to her of the buffalo hunt late last evening, after Moon Flower had returned to Jolena's father's tepee for the night and Kirk had fallen into a comfortable enough sleep.

Before a slow-burning fire, Spotted Eagle had told Jolena that a *pis-kun* was one of the Blackfoot's ingenious methods to ensure the taking of buffalo in large numbers at one time. This was a large corral, or enclosure, built out from the foot of a perpendicular cliff and formed of natural banks, rocks, and brush—anything, in fact, to make a close, high barrier.

From the top of the cliff, directly over the *pis-kun*, two long lines of piled-up rock and brush extended far out on the prairie, ever diverging from each other like the arms of the letter V, the opening over the *pis-kun* being at the angle.

Jolena had also been told that soon Clouds Make Thunder, who was to lead the buffalo to the cliff, would be ready to leave this morning without eating or drinking and would order his woman not to leave the lodge, nor even to look out, until he returned. While he was gone, she should keep burning sweet grass and should pray to the Sun for his success and safety.

Those who would join the hunt today would be alerted when he was ready to leave and would follow him to the *pis-kun* and conceal themselves behind the rocks and bushes which formed the V.

Clouds Make Thunder would then put on a headdress made of the head of a buffalo, and a robe, and start out to approach the animals, carrying his "medicine", a large rattle ornamented with beaver claws and bright feathers. When he got near the herd, he would move about until he

343

attracted the attention of some of the buffalo, and when they began to look at him, he would ride slowly away, toward the entrance of the chute of rocks and bushes.

The buffalo would follow, and as they did, the medicine man would gradually increase his pace.

Finally, when the buffalo were well within the chute, the people would begin to rise up from behind the rock piles which the herd had passed and shout and wave their robes. This would frighten the last buffalo, which would push forward on the others, and before long the whole herd would be running at headlong speed toward the precipice, the rock piles directing them to the point over the enclosure.

When they reached it, most of the animals would be pushed over by those behind them, and usually even the last of the band would plunge blindly down into the *pis-kun*.

Many would be killed outright by the fall.

Others would have broken legs or broken backs, while some would be uninjured.

The barricade, however, would prevent them from escaping, and all would soon be killed by Blackfoot arrows.

The women would then approach and prepare the buffalo to take back with them to the village.

Jolena dropped the cloth back into the basin of water and rose to her feet. She went to Spotted Eagle, who was smiling as he held a particular pair of leggings out before him, gazing proudly at them.

"Let me go with you, Spotted Eagle," Jolena

asked, moving to his side and kissing his cheek. "Please? I so badly want to observe how everything is done instead of just being told. I could help. Please allow it."

"There is time to teach you," Spotted Eagle said, still gazing proudly at his leggings. "I have made much meat in my time. So shall you, my woman, once you have become my wife. You will always remember that the buffalo is a smart animal and that he is meant for the people. He is their food and shelter."

When Kirk coughed, Jolena jumped with alarm and her thoughts were suddenly only of him. She hurried back to him, and when she found that he was finally awake, she smoothed her hand over his brow and smiled down at him.

"How are you this morning?" she murmured. "Are you hungry? Moon Flower has brought a fresh pot of soup, especially for you."

Kirk leaned on one elbow, gazing around him. "Where is she?" he asked, his voice sounding stronger.

"It's early morning," Jolena said, reaching for a bowl and spoon and placing these on the mat beside Kirk. "Moon Flower will be here soon."

Kirk smiled and moved to a sitting position, then his smile faded as Spotted Eagle came and stood over him.

"Soon you will be strong enough to travel to the river, to ride on the large white canoe back to Saint Louis," Spotted Eagle said, his eyes narrowing as he gazed down at Kirk, knowing that he must get this brother out of Jolena's life as soon as possible. As long as Kirk was there, he was a reminder to Jolena of the life that she had left behind, where the dwellings were large and elaborate, and where her white father awaited her return.

"Do you see me as a threat?" Kirk taunted, soon regretting his words when he heard Jolena's gasp of horror. He accepted the bowl of soup that Jolena angrily shoved into his hands.

"I'll be gone soon enough," Kirk then grumbled.

Kirk gave Jolena a half glance, then looked quickly away from her again. "At least *I* haven't forgotten where my loyalties lie," he said in a low grumble.

Jolena shoved a spoon into his free hand. "I think you'd best eat instead of talk," she said, her voice drawn.

She gave Spotted Eagle an apologetic look, then rose and went to him as he moved away from the fire, still holding his leggings instead of changing into them.

"He is less than grateful to this Blackfoot warrior who is sharing his lodge and medicine with him," Spotted Eagle said, turning to glare down at Jolena.

"My brother is afraid of losing me," Jolena said, resting a hand on his arm. "That's all. Please try and understand."

"I never understand rudeness," Spotted Eagle said in a low rumble.

"Yes, my brother can be *that*," Jolena said, sighing heavily. "But put yourself in his place,

Spotted Eagle. What if you had a sister and a white man wanted her? Would you accept it without resenting that man?"

"Spotted Eagle always thinks before he speaks!" Spotted Eagle said, casting Kirk a sour glance over Jolena's shoulder. "This brother of yours could still be in the abandoned Cree camp. Instead, he is in Spotted Eagle's dwelling, sleeping on Spotted Eagle's pelts, eating from Spotted Eagle's bowls, and taking away Spotted Eagle's privacy."

Spotted Eagle leaned down close to Jolena's face. He gazed intensely into her eyes. "We cannot make love while your brother is here," he said, his jaw tight. "Should Spotted Eagle be happy? No! But he does not speak of this to your brother. I show respect to those who are not well. It is hard, yet I do it just the same!"

Before Jolena could respond, Spotted Eagle continued, "Tomorrow your brother will be taken to the river and warriors will stay with him until the large canoe comes for him," Spotted Eagle said, his voice firm. "Today is as far as my generosity goes toward him!"

Jolena's lips parted and her eyes grew wide. "But what if he is not strong enough?" she asked, her voice tremulous. "Spotted Eagle, he's gone through a terrible ordeal."

"If he is any kind of a man, he will survive," Spotted Eagle said. He slung his leggings over his arm and clasped her shoulder. "For us it is important that he get on with his life, so we can get on with ours. And that is the way it will be."

Moon Flower came into the tepee, chattering as she moved to her knees beside the pallet of furs on which Kirk lay.

"You are eating?" she said, clasping her hands in her lap. Her eyes beamed. "You like my food? I cooked it slow through the night." She giggled. "Brown Elk chided me this morning, telling me that the smell kept his stomach growling all night and kept him awake."

"I can see why it would," Kirk said, laughing softly. "It not only smells delicious, it tastes good." He set his empty bowl aside and placed a gentle hand on Moon Flower's cheek. "Thank you. I truly appreciate your continued kindness to me."

Moon Flower blushed and lowered her eyes, then stiffened when Kirk asked a question that seemed to cut deep into her soul.

"Are you married?" Kirk said, groaning as sitting up took much effort. "Such a beautiful lady should have many men fighting over her."

When Moon Flower could not find the words to speak of the recent tragedy, Jolena went to her rescue. "Kirk, there was one man," she said. "Two Ridges. But he's dead."

Kirk paled as he looked up at Jolena. "Two Ridges—the one who rode with the expedition as a guide? He is dead?" he said, gasping. "When? How?"

"As you know, the Cree are a problem in this region," Jolena murmured.

"The Cree killed him?" Kirk said, his eyes wide.

"Yes, instantly," Jolena said, swallowing hard

as she shifted her eyes over to Moon Flower.

Kirk grew solemn and quiet.

Moon Flower saw how Kirk was withdrawing into himself and made moves to stop him. "But you are alive," she said, taking his hands. "Although tortured and left to die, you are alive, and on the road to complete recovery. So let us not think anymore on the Cree or their evil. Let us feel blessed that you are alive."

Moon Flower looked over her shoulder at the simmering soup, then anxiously into Kirk's eyes again. "More soup?" she murmured. "I shall feed you."

Kirk smiled and nodded. "More soup," he said. "But I can feed myself. It is best that I not learn to lean on anyone else while in this wild country."

"After you eat, walk with me outside," Moon Flower said, ladling more soup into Kirk's bowl. "It is important that the strength returns to your legs."

Kirk gave Spotted Eagle a glowering look. "Yes, you couldn't be more right about that," he said.

Suddenly Kirk pulled a blanket around him and pushed himself into a standing position. He swayed slightly, then steadied himself and gave Spotted Eagle a look of triumph.

Jolena watched, in awe of her brother, yet she was torn between pride in seeing him conquer the need to stand and fear that he felt the need to prove something to Spotted Eagle. If he was strong enough, he would be sent away tomorrow, and she knew that he would not want to leave without her.

She looked slowly up at Spotted Eagle, regretting that she had been put in the middle of these two men, and the two ways of life she was choosing between.

And there were two other men that were a part of her decision! Her two fathers! She owed both of them loyalty! But deep within her heart she had already made her choice. She would stay with Spotted Eagle, no matter what the cost. . . .

Spotted Eagle laid his hunting leggings aside and knelt down over his bundle of clothes and began sorting through them again. Jolena watched as he laid a complete set of buckskins on the floor at his side, then sorted through his many pairs of black moccasins, finally choosing a pair.

When he took all of this up into his arms and walked stiffly to Kirk, shoving them into his hands and arms, Jolena's eyes widened.

"You now have traveling clothes to get you to the large white canoe," Spotted Eagle said, folding his arms tightly across his chest. "Put them on, and if they fit your body, they are yours. A gift from Spotted Eagle to the white brother of Jolena."

Everything was silent for a moment, then Kirk flung the blanket from around him and struggled into the clothes. After he was fully dressed, he went to Jolena and gazed down at her. "Are you as eager to see me go as he?" he asked thickly.

"You know that I'm not," Jolena said, swallowing back a sob that was lodged in her throat. "But, Kirk, if you are well enough, it is best that you do leave as soon as possible."

"And you?" Kirk said, his voice breaking.

"You know the answer without asking," Jolena said, pleading up at Kirk with her dark, wide eyes.

"I want to hear you say it," Kirk said, placing his hands at her shoulders, slightly shaking her. "Damn it, Jolena, let me hear you say it."

Spotted Eagle had seen enough and could not stand silently by any longer. He went to Kirk and easily slipped Kirk's hands from Jolena's shoulder.

"I will speak for my woman," Spotted Eagle said, his eyes lit with fire as he glared into Kirk's. "She will not be returning with you to Saint Louis. Try and understand, white brother, when I say that although you have loved her longer than I, you will have to let her go. She belongs now to her true people and to this man who loves her more than life itself."

Kirk's lips parted in a strangled gasp, then he wrenched himself away from Spotted Eagle and turned to Jolena again. "Do you forget so easily everything in your past?" he said. "Can you toss me and father aside as though we are no better than strangers to you? Do you forget why you came to the Montana Territory? Do you fail to see, or comprehend, the disappointment father will feel when you do not return home? I am not sure he can live with too many disappointments at once."

A breeze into the tepee caused by someone lifting the entrance flap made all eyes turn that way.

Brown Elk came walking heavily into the dwelling, his eyes on Kirk. "Do not speak to my daughter in such a chastising tone as that," he said, frowning at Kirk. "This father, her *true* father, warns you against such behavior."

Kirk was stunned speechless, then spoke in a drawn manner as he gazed at Brown Elk. "Spotted Eagle spoke of Jolena's true people, which I know now is Blackfoot," he said. "And I knew that she hoped to find her true father. You are he ... ?"

"Very much so," Brown Elk said, lifting his chin proudly. Then he placed a firm hand on Kirk's shoulder. "You will come with me now. There is no room any longer in Spotted Eagle's dwelling for you. You will come to my tepee until you are able to travel to the large white canoe for your travels back to Saint Louis."

For a moment, Kirk stood as though frozen to the floor, then started backing up, as though trapped. "Jolena, help me to understand all of this," he said, his voice tiny and desperate. He gave a pleading stare to Moon Flower and reached a hand to her. "Moon Flower, help me ..."

Moon Flower stepped up beside Brown Elk and gave Kirk a firm, unwavering stare, showing her loyalty to a man who had taken her in after she had been banished by her parents.

Jolena went to Brown Elk and gave him a soft kiss on the cheek, then went and stood beside Spotted Eagle, showing *her* choice of loyalties. "Kirk, Spotted Eagle and I are going to be married as soon as possible," she said, her heart pounding as she watched her brother's eyes become misty with tears.

She went to Kirk and embraced him. "Kirk, I love you," she whispered. "Please love me no less now that I have found my true place in life. Help me where our father is concerned. Only you will be able to make him understand."

Kirk gave her a pitying look, then brushed past her and went outside.

Moon Flower shuffled her feet nervously, then went after Kirk.

Brown Elk went to Jolena and enfolded her within his arms. "My daughter, *Kye*, life becomes confused, then it passes, and tomorrow comes with smiles and sunshine," he said, patting her back. "I will go to your white brother. I will talk with him again. He will see what is best for you, his sister—and that is for you to stay with your true people and have many children in the image of the Blackfoot."

Jolena reveled in her true father's closeness, then stepped back to Spotted Eagle's side as Brown Elk departed with dignity from the tepee.

Spotted Eagle turned to Jolena. "Everything that I said to your brother had to be said," he assured her. "It is best for you. It is best for him. It is best for this Blackfoot warrior who loves you."

Jolena's eyes filled with tears as she melted into Spotted Eagle's arms. "Hold me," she cried. "Oh, darling, hold me."

Spotted Eagle held her close, then eased away from her. "Time soon comes for your man to leave for the buffalo run," he said, bending over to gather up his fancy leggings into his arms again. "You see these?"

Jolena wiped tears from her eyes and nodded as she gazed down at the leggings. She had noticed earlier how proudly he had held and gazed at them. They were beautifully embroidered with porcupine quills and bright feathers.

"These are my hunting leggings," Spotted Eagle said, slipping into them. "They are great medicine. Your man will bring home much meat for the long winter."

Jolena's thoughts were catapulted back in time, to when he had found the beautiful buffalo rock, and its meaning. "I no longer have the buffalo rock," she confessed. "It was lost to me the same day my journals and butterfly collection were destroyed. I'm so sorry, Spotted Eagle. Having it with you could have doubled your chances of a good buffalo run."

"The Sun will follow me all the day and bless my hunt," Spotted Eagle said, then knelt and began going through his bundles of clothes again.

When he rose to his feet again, with another buckskin outfit across his arms and handed these to Jolena, she looked up at him with wondering eyes, not sure why he would want her to put on the clothes of a man.

"You wear these with me to the buffalo run," he said. "I see it now that it is important that you accompany me there. You ride horses?"

"Somewhat," Jolena said, still stunned by his change of heart about allowing her to go.

Yet the more she thought about it, the more she did understand.

It was because of Kirk.

He didn't want to leave her alone with Kirk!

He *did* feel threatened by him!

"Then you will ride at my side and watch your man kill his first bull buffalo of this buffalo run," Spotted Eagle said, forcing the clothes into her hands. "Dress quickly. The sun rises steadily into the heavens. It soon will be time to go."

Her heart pounding, the excitement building within her, Jolena beamed as she scrambled into the clothes. She giggled when she looked down at how loosely the breeches fit her.

Spotted Eagle soon remedied that. He tied a rope around her waist and stood back smiling at her.

"Let us go, my woman," he said, reaching a hand out to her. "You have much to learn today."

No longer thinking about Kirk, or anything else that stood in the way of her becoming Blackfoot in all ways important to her, Jolena left the tepee hand in hand with Spotted Eagle, feeling very much alive—and needed!

Chapter Twenty-Nine

Jolena felt awkward on the black mare, yet managed to stay on the soft saddle blanket as she rode beside Spotted Eagle. The other women rode either on pack horses or on travois behind the horses ridden by their husbands.

After enough buffalo were killed, these women would do most of the butchering and transporting of the meat and hides to camp. The women who remained in the village would not be idle. All day long they would tan robes, dry meat, sew moccasins, and perform a thousand and one other tasks.

Holding securely to the reins, her knees pressed into the sides of the horse, Jolena looked around her, once again admiring the sharp contrasts of the Blackfoot country. There were far-stretching grassy prairies, affording rich pasturage for the buffalo; rough bad lands for the climbing mountain sheep, wooded buttes loved by the mule deer, and timbered river bottoms where the white-tailed deer and the elk could browse and hide.

The Blackfoot country was especially favored by the warm Chinook winds which ensured mild winters. Today the wind was so strong that Jolena had to fight it to stay in her saddle. The wind was so brisk, she could feel its force against her body, plastering her clothes against her. Her hair fluttered wildly in the wind, and her cheeks burned as the wind whipped hard against it.

Suddenly in the wind came the strong stench of the buffalo, and soon they came into sight. There seemed to be hundreds of the black animals with their long, black beards, humped backs, and large, dark eyes, grazing lazily in a field of tall grass.

Spotted Eagle wheeled his horse around and stopped, raising his hand in the air as a silent command for everyone else to stop—except for the medicine man, who was to lead the buffalo to their death.

Then came Clouds Make Thunder's final prayer for a successful buffalo run today.

"Hear me now, Sun!" he cried in a monotone that seemed to echo back at him. "Listen, above people! Listen, under-water people! Allow us to return home rich with meat."

When he was through, it seemed to Jolena that no one breathed as he broke away from the others and rode ahead of them toward the buffalo.

Jolena's eyes widened, realizing that the buffalo sensed that danger was near. Some raised their short tails and shook them and tossed their great heads and bellowed. Others pawed the dirt, snorting.

Spotted Eagle made another silent command to his people. They followed his lead, leaving their horses, travois, and dogs behind and rushing toward the bluff. Panting with exertion, the people moved upward, until they came to the top of the bluff over which the buffalo would tumble to their death.

Jolena walked beside Spotted Eagle, who was well armed with his bow and quiver of arrows. She was glad when they reached the top of the bluff and everyone quickly hid behind the piles of rocks and bushes.

Jolena knelt down beside Spotted Eagle and breathlessly waited for the medicine man. After a short while "he who leads the buffalo" was seen coming, riding his horse, shouting at the buffalo, bringing a large band after him.

Soon the buffalo were inside the lines. The people began to rise up behind them, shouting and waving their robes.

Now that she saw the buffalo close up, Jolena was too awestruck to participate. They were formidable and frightening looking animals when excited to resistance—their long, shaggy manes hanging in great profusion over their necks and shoulders, often extending down to the ground.

The cows were less ferocious, though not much less wild and frightful in their appearance.

The Blackfoot were not intimidated by the beasts, however, and soon the buffalo were jumping and tumbling over the steep precipice.

Jolena scrambled down the sides of the steep hill with the Blackfoot, and once they reached the *pis-kun*, the women and children ran up and showed themselves above its walls. By their cries they kept the buffalo that were still alive from pressing against the walls in an effort to escape.

As the surviving buffalo ran round and round within the enclosure, the warriors raised their bows and arrows.

Arrows began whizzing about Jolena, and the buffalo made loud, thundering sounds as one by one they fell to the ground, dead.

Although Jolena understood the meaning of a good Buffalo run, she was still appalled at the sight and was just about to turn her eyes away when Spotted Eagle fitted his elk-horn arrow to his bow and joined the others in the massacre. The butchering would be done in the *pis-kun*, and after this was over, the place would be cleaned out, and the heads and feet would be removed. Wolves, foxes, badgers, and other small carnivorous animals would visit the *pis-kun* and would soon make away with the entrails.

The Blackfoot would return home singing and carrying great loads of meat for the long winter ahead.

The wind blew even more fiercely now, making whining, whistling noises and whipping Jolena's hair around her face. Then something else blew against her face, momentarily blinding her.

With clawing fingers, she reached up and grabbed hold of a piece of paper that was fluttering against her face. When she saw what it was her heart did a flip-flop.

"It's a page from one of my lost journals," she whispered, staring down at the paper on which her entries were smeared, yet still legible.

Her heart skipped a beat when another page flew past her and was speared by a branch on a tree close beside her.

With wild, disbelieving eyes, she stood frozen to the ground as many more pages flew past her in the wind.

"Lord," she whispered to herself, her heart hammering against her breast as she turned and peered down the long avenue of the valley that stretched out between other high buttes on each side of it. She knew that the scene of the accident had to be many miles away, yet the wind had plucked the pages from her journal and was handing them to her today like a gift!

Jolena soon forgot the women who were now busy at work butchering the large animals. She even forgot about Spotted Eagle, who was now mingling with the other warriors, going from animal to animal to be sure they were dead before being butchered. Frantically, Jolena began running around, grabbing the pages as they blew past her, gathering them into her arms, holding them as though they were pieces of precious gold.

Then when she saw one of the pieces of cardboard fly by, on which she had pinned many of the butterflies that she had caught, she began chasing after it.

Spotted Eagle turned and saw what Jolena was doing. His heart skipped a beat when she began struggling and climbing up the steep hillside, intent on following the cardboard that he now also spied, as it seemed to be lifting as though by someone's hand, higher and higher, above Jolena's head, exactly as the *nymphalid* butterfly had done as it had teased her into danger.

Spotted Eagle's gaze shifted upward. He gasped, and his heart felt as though it had dropped to his feet when he saw one lone buffalo bull that had not followed the others over the cliff. It pranced about as though it sensed the slaughter that had occurred below him.

Spotted Eagle's gaze shifted back to Jolena, who was almost at the top of the butte, too stubborn to let the prized cardboard of butterflies get away from her. Once she got to the top and met the bull face on, she would be the one forced over the cliff to her death.

Spotted Eagle nervously notched one of his elkhorn arrows to the string of his bow and aimed, then cursed silently to himself when he found that the buffalo had moved out of eye range.

Yet Spotted Eagle could still hear the animal's loud, crazed bellows.

He could even see it in his mind's eye as it pawed angrily at the ground, fire in his eyes and rage in his heart!

Jolena breathed heavily, and her fingers were stinging as she pulled herself farther up the side of the hill. She frowned when she could no longer see the flying cardboard, then her eyes opened wildly when once again it fluttered along the ground, just at the edge of the butte overhead.

"Damn," Jolena whispered beneath her breath. "But I *shall* have it. I lost it once. But not a second time. I must have something for Kirk to take home to father."

Determination moved her onward, knowing that she now only had to reach up and grab a root that was growing out from the side of the hill and she could pull herself up onto solid ground.

Spotted Eagle cupped a hand over his mouth and shouted for Jolena. He called her name over and over again, but she still did not hear.

His muscles corded, his jaw tight, Spotted Eagle slung his bow over his shoulder and started climbing the hillside. Being more skilled at climbing, he found himself close behind Jolena just as she pulled herself up and out of sight.

Jolena was so intent on what she was after that she had not noticed Spotted Eagle climbing after her. Nor did she pay any attention to the buffalo that was eyeing her with bloodshot eyes and flaring nostrils, a hoof digging grass up by the roots as it pawed over and over again into the ground.

Her heart thumping, Jolena bent to her knees and reached for the cardboard of butterflies. When she had it finally within her fingers, she gazed down at the collection, heartbroken. Most of the butterflies were missing, and those that had survived were incomplete, only their bodies still pinned to the cardboard, or perhaps a wing or two, stripped of their colors.

"Oh, no," she whispered, slowly shaking her head back and forth. "Why didn't I realize it could be no more than this?"

"Do not move, Jolena," Spotted Eagle said, swinging himself up to solid ground.

"Do not even move your head to see what I am doing," Spotted Eagle said as he yanked the bow from his shoulder and notched an arrow onto it. "It could provoke the animal into charging me before I can send an arrow into its heart."

Jolena's throat went dry and her insides grew numb. She didn't move a muscle, but not so much because Spotted Eagle had told her not to, but because she was too frightened even to breathe.

She now heard the snorting of the buffalo.

She could hear its hoof pounding the earth as it continued to paw.

She could even feel its eyes on her.

Jolena gazed at the cliff which was only an arm's length away. If the buffalo charged before Spotted Eagle could kill it, she and Spotted Eagle would join the others at the foot of the cliff, but in a most unexpected way.

She closed her eyes and began praying. She flinched when she heard the sound of the released arrow, then sighed with relief when she heard a loud thumping sound, knowing that the animal had fallen and that she had been saved by her beloved Blackfoot warrior!

Dropping the cardboard, yet clinging to the precious sheets from her journal, Jolena turned to face Spotted Eagle. After fitting his bow back over his shoulder, he went to Jolena and framed her face between his hands, yet his eyes were on the journals that she clasped to her chest. He shifted his gaze to the cardboard on which were displayed the bits and pieces of butterflies.

He looked up at her again, glowering. "You risk your life for these useless things?" he growled. "Why?"

"For my father in Saint Louis," Jolena murmured. "Having something left of the expedition might help ease the blow of knowing that he has lost *me*."

"Would it have been worth it to him to have foolish papers only to lose his daughter altogether?" Spotted Eagle said, jerking his hands from her face. He started to take the papers from her arms, but she turned away from him.

"Please don't," she said, her voice drawn. "These are valuable."

"You must forget this part of your life if you are to become Blackfoot in all ways," Spotted Eagle reminded her.

Feeling guilty for making Spotted Eagle angry with her and for putting him in danger again for her, Jolena went to him and rested her cheek against his muscled arm. "Darling, you said that you were going to kill a buffalo bull today, and you just did," she murmured. "He will make much meat for our table."

Spotted Eagle said nothing for a moment, then turned his eyes down to her. "Lay your papers aside," he said gently. "It is time for you to learn the ways of butchering."

Jolena's smile faltered. She stepped away from Spotted Eagle, looking waveringly down at the rescued pages of her journal. She realized that Spotted Eagle was forcing her to choose between keeping the papers she'd rescued and freeing her hands to begin the butchering.

She was torn, but this time she knew what she must do, for her place was with Spotted Eagle, and if that meant more sacrifices being made to have a future with him, then she knew what she must do.

Lifting her chin proudly, Jolena opened her arms and watched the pages of her journal flutter away from her again.

Spotted Eagle went to Jolena and drew her into his embrace. "Again, you are a woman of courage," he whispered, twining his fingers through her hair.

Jolena gazed up at him. "It was not courage that made me let go, but love for my man," she said, then leaned into him as his lips crushed down upon hers in a kiss.

Chapter Thirty

A feast to celebrate the successful buffalo run would begin as the sky bade the stars and moon good-bye and welcomed old man Sun.

Jolena had slept soundly after the tiring outing, her dreams filled with wondrous moments alone with Spotted Eagle. Even now as she slept, she sighed and stretched her arms above her head as she dreamt that Spotted Eagle was kneeling over her, awakening her to an even more intense rapture than she had shared with him before as he sucked her nipples into tight nubs of pleasure and his hands swept caressingly down her body, stopping at the heart of her desire, splaying his fingers over her crown of black hair. When he thrust one of his fingers inside the warm cocoon of her femininity, Jolena gasped passionately.

As his finger moved within her, kindling the flames that were already lit inside her, she slowly opened her eyes, realizing that she was not dreaming at all—that this pleasure she was feeling was real. She found Spotted Eagle's midnight-dark eyes gazing into hers, his lips tugging into a smile when he discovered that his ploy had worked, that he had awakened her this morning to how it would be for the rest of their lives. He would greet her at each sunrise with this proof of his love.

He would make sure she never regretted having chosen his way of life over that which she had known for the first eighteen summers of her life.

In many ways he would make up to her that which she might secretly pine for.

Her heart throbbing, her insides melting with rapture, Jolena smiled softly up at Spotted Eagle and flung a leg around him, bringing him closer. She trembled with ecstasy and swallowed hard when she discovered how much even he was aroused when she felt his manhood lying thick and full against her thigh. She felt dizzy with need of him and placed her hands to the nape of his neck and drew his lips up close to hers.

Before she could kiss him, he was whispering something against her lips.

"Were your dreams good?" he teased huskily.

Jolena giggled. "Never better," she whispered back, then felt her euphoria mounting when he kissed her in a blaze of urgency, his hands cupping her breasts, his fingers pushing them up against his bare, powerful chest.

Spotted Eagle parted her legs with a knee and her body turned liquid and her breath was momentarily stolen away as he plunged his hardness within her and began his rhythmic strokes.

His arms swept around her and anchored her as he came to her, thrusting deeply. To Jolena it had seemed an eternity since they had been afforded the privacy of being together in such a way.

But never had she forgotten the golden web of magic that they spun between them as they made love.

Spotted Eagle kissed her hungrily, reveling in the sweet warm press of her body. He drank in her groans of pleasure, firing his passions— passions that had lain smoldering just beneath the surface as he waited to be with her again in this way. He felt the curl of warmth heating up and growing in his lower body, and his world melted away as he felt her hands sweep down his spine in a soft caress.

He moved his thrusts purposely slower within her, wanting to savor these moments until he could not help but allow the red-hot embers of desire explode into every cell of his body.

He clung to her and placed his lips to the slender, curving length of her throat and licked her flesh that was as sweet as honey.

His fingers dug into the soft cushion of her buttocks, holding her into the curve of his body as once again he began his eager thrusts that became faster, plunged more deeply.

Jolena's breath quickened as searing, scorching flames shot through her, her senses reeling. She sought his mouth with wild abandon and kissed him with quivering lips as she shuddered and arched, her climax sweeping through her like millions of tiny flames.

That feeling of white heat traveled through Spotted Eagle's veins as well, from the tip of his toes through the sinews of his thighs and upward, then leapt with a cry from the depths of his throat as the explosion of ecstasy rushed through him. He drew Jolena into his arms and hugged her to him as his body shook against hers, sending his seed in violent spurts of warmth into her womb.

When their pleasure was fully spent, they clung together, their breaths mingling as they once again kissed, this time without urgency, but with sweetness.

Then they rolled apart.

Jolena lay on her back beside Spotted Eagle, her cheeks flushed, her heart still throbbing from pleasure.

Spotted Eagle lay on his side, his eyes closed, not wanting to let go of this pleasure. "My woman, did reality surpass the feelings you shared with me in your dream?" he asked, reaching a hand to cup one of her breasts. "Or was it better to dream than to do?"

Jolena turned to him and traced his lips with a forefinger. "Both my dreams and being with you in reality are wonderful," she murmured. She moved to her knees and began kissing his flesh, starting with the hollow of his throat and moving slowly downward. "But, darling, you are able to do much more than my mind would ever conjure up."

She paused and gazed up at him. "And how is it for you, my darling?" she murmured. "Would you rather I leave you alone so that you can sleep and search for me in your dreams? Or would you rather open your eyes and see what I am about to do?"

Spotted Eagle thought her voice seemed more teasingly husky than he ever remembered hearing it before. He opened his eyes and gazed down at her, then sucked in a wild breath as she sank her lips over his shrunken manhood, breathing life into it again as it quickly sprang forward, thick and full.

She pleasured him in this way for a moment longer, then he rolled her onto her back and entered her again, this time rapidly reaching that ultimate of pleasure. They clung and shook and sighed when it happened, then drew quickly away when they heard the sound of drums beating out a steady rhythm outside the tepee, and heard children laughing and women singing. The aroma of cook fires wafted down from the smoke hole in the tepee.

"The village is stirring. The celebration will begin soon," Spotted Eagle said, giving Jolena a hand as he helped her up from their bed of furs. "Let us dress in our finest clothes and join the others. There will be much singing, dancing, eating, and story-telling. It will be a day that will stay fresh in one's mind when the long days and nights of winter come and everyone stays inside beside their fires."

"I'm so glad that the buffalo run was a success," Jolena said, slipping her doeskin dress over her head. She turned her back to Spotted Eagle, allowing him to brush, then braid her hair.

"Ah, yes, it was a good day for buffalo," Spotted Eagle said as he slowly, almost meditatingly, began braiding her hair. "The Blackfoot are a race of meat-eaters. While we do kill large quantities of other game, we still depend for our subsistence on the buffalo. This animal provides us with almost all that we need in the way of food, clothing, and shelter, and while we continue to have an abundance of buffalo, we shall continue living in comfort."

Her hair now braided, Jolena handed Spotted Eagle a lovely beaded necklace to place around her neck. After it was latched, she turned to him and gazed at how handsome he was in his fringed hide clothes, remembering how stunned she had been that first time she had seen him, when he seemed to have stepped right out of her dreams!

"Shall we join the others outside our tepee?" she asked softly. She had not seen Kirk since he had left Spotted Eagle's tepee in anger. As long as she had known that he was being well cared for, that had been enough to keep her from worrying needlessly about him. But now she would have to face him again.

"Your thoughts carry you far away," Spotted Eagle said, drawing Jolena out of her reverie.

"Yes, I know," Jolena said, her eyes wavering up into his. "I was thinking of Kirk and also of Moon Flower. Surely we will see them both sometime today during the long celebration."

"And it would displease you to see your white brother?" Spotted Eagle said, his eyes searching her face for answers.

"No, darling," Jolena murmured. "It's not that at all. It's just that I don't know what to expect of him when he sees me and you together. He might say things to hurt you. Please don't let his words hurt you, Spotted Eagle. They will be those of a brother who fears losing a sister. He will one day understand and wish both of us a happy future."

Spotted Eagle did not reply. He swept an arm around Jolena's waist and whisked her from the tepee. They walked slowly through the village, observing the gaiety.

Spotted Eagle's chest swelled with pride as he looked at everything and everyone. The village was such a happy place at times like this. Everywhere was heard the sound of drums and song and dancing.

"*Wo-ka-hit!* Listen," the people said. "*Wo-ka-hit!* Listen! *Mah-kwe-i-ke-tum-ok-ah-wah-hit! Ke-tuk-ka-puk-si-pim*, You are to feast! Enter my tepee with your friends!"

Here a man was lying back on a blanket just outside his tepee, singing and drumming. There a group of young men were holding a mock war dance.

The women were dressed in their best dresses, the men in their best fringed garments.

As the sun rose higher in the sky, the people came together for a dance beside the large outdoor communal fire. The men stood on one side, the women on the other. They all sang, and three drummers furnished an accompaniment. The people joined together in the dance, the women holding their arms and hands in various graceful positions.

The people then stepped aside, silent, as a group of men came to the center of attention. They wore animal-head masks, and their bodies were brightly painted. When their dance was over, the people gathered together and sat on blankets around the large fire to listen to the stories of an elderly warrior who had seen his best days. His tales were the explanations of the phenomena of life and contained many a moral for the instruction of youth.

The storyteller spoke in so much earnest, and became so entirely carried away by the tale he was relating, that he fairly trembled with excitement. He held his audience spellbound with yet more tales about the ancient gods and their miraculous doings.

And then it was time for more games!

Jolena laughed softly as she followed Spotted Eagle to a group of warriors. She could see his eagerness to challenge those of his same age. He pulled her aside as the others gathered in a circle, preparing themselves for the game, laughing amongst themselves.

"Watch as your man plays a game called *hands*," he said, smiling at her. "Let me warn you, my woman. The stakes are sometimes very high—two or three horses, or more. Some have been known to lose everything they possessed, even to their clothing."

Jolena watched as Spotted Eagle stepped away from her to join the group of a dozen men. The warriors were divided into two equal parties, one group standing facing the other. Others—women, children, and older men—pressed in behind Jolena to watch as the betting began, each person playing the game betting with the person directly opposite him. There were wagers for horses, moccasins, headbands, arrows, and prized bows.

Jolena listened for Spotted Eagle's wager, smiling when he made a simple offering of an eagle feather for someone's headband should he lose.

Two small, oblong bones were used, one of which had a black ring around it. The first man took the bones, and by skillfully moving his hands and changing the objects from one to the other, sought to make it impossible for the person opposite him to decide which hand held the marked bone.

Jolena's eyes widened, now recognizing the game as "Button, button, who's got the button?" which she had played with her friends in Saint Louis.

Now truly enjoying watching, having herself played this same game so often, Jolena watched the players' hands and listened to the various bets. Ten points, counted by sticks, won the game and the side which first got the number took the stakes.

A song was soon accompanying this game, a weird, unearthly tune sung by an old warrior. At first, it was a scarcely audible murmur, like the gentle soughing of an evening breeze, but gradually it increased in volume and reached a very high pitch, sinking quickly to a low bass sound which rose and fell, then gradually died, to be again repeated.

One of the warriors who was concealing the bones swayed his body, arms, and hands in time to the music and went through all manner of graceful and intricate movements for the purpose of confusing the guessers.

This went on for some time.

Jolena was proud when Spotted Eagle came away with many prizes, the most precious of them all a bracelet made of pink, iridescent shells, which he promptly slipped onto Jolena's right arm.

They were laughing and following the pleasant aroma of food roasting close by over another large, outdoor fire, when Kirk came suddenly into view. Glowering, he came to Jolena and took her by an arm, ushering her away from Spotted Eagle.

Stopping in the shadow of a tepee, Kirk turned Jolena to face him. "Sis, I'm strong enough to travel," he said. "If I have to beg you to go with me, I will."

"Please don't," Jolena said, casting her eyes downward. "My mind is made up, Kirk. I hope you will understand one day why I had to make the choice that I did."

"Your love for Spotted Eagle?" he said, placing a finger to her chin and tipping it up so that their eyes could meet and hold.

"That, and also my love for my people," Jolena said, over Kirk's shoulder seeing Spotted Eagle coming toward them.

"I can understand how you could become infatuated with a handsome warrior," Kirk said, dropping his hands to his sides. "I, too, am infatuated with an Indian. I could easily love Moon Flower—but not if it meant forgetting all of my loyalties to the family who raised me from a baby to adulthood."

"Then love Moon Flower and leave *me* alone," Jolena said, sighing heavily. "I shall never change my mind. *Never.*"

Kirk frowned. "I knew that you wouldn't," he said, giving Spotted Eagle a troubled glance over his shoulder as he came protectively to Jolena's side.

Then he gave Moon Flower a nod, bringing her to *his* side. When she came to him, bashfully smiling, he placed an arm around her waist. "Moon Flower is traveling with me to Saint Louis," he said, his eyes lighting up, his lips quavering into a smile. "She's promised to marry me."

Jolena's heart seemed to stop, and she felt a coldness enter her heart as she gazed into Moon Flower's eyes, stunned at her brother's quick decision.

Jolena knew why Moon Flower might be eager to leave her village—to hide the shame of an unwed pregnancy?

But did Kirk know about the pregnancy?

Jolena knew that he must not know, for he was not the sort to tolerate a wife heavy with another man's child, especially an Indian's.

Nor would he be the sort to raise that child!

Jolena wanted to reach out and tell her brother the truth, but a part of her that resented his attitude toward her heritage would not allow her to warn him of the deceit.

Smiling, she reached a hand to her brother's arm. "I hope you both will be happy," she said.

Chapter Thirty-One

Shivering in the cool breeze of the morning, Jolena stood solemnly by, watching Kirk preparing to leave for Fort Chance. Word had been received that a riverboat would be passing through and would be making a stop at Fort Chance. Kirk had just enough time to get there.

Jolena frowned as she watched Kirk help Moon Flower into her saddle, then swung himself onto a horse that had been assigned him for the journey.

Then her eyes were drawn around and she smiled weakly up at Spotted Eagle. "I'm glad that you are riding with the warriors who are accompanying my brother to Fort Chance," she murmured. "And I understand why you don't want me to go with you. Please hurry back, my love. The nights are getting colder. The blankets will be cold and empty without you at my side."

"It is good that you understand why you must stay behind," he said, lifting her chin with a forefinger, so that her lips were only a breath away from his. "Good-byes might be harder to say if you are again thrown into the life of white people at the fort. It is best not to tempt you."

"Darling, I know it would be futile to argue with you, to tell you that I think you are wrong about that," Jolena said. "So I shan't, and I shall stay with my people and learn more of their ways while I am waiting for you to return to me."

"It should be only one night that I will be gone from you," Spotted Eagle said, ignoring Kirk's glare when he brushed a kiss across Jolena's lips. He then whispered to her. "And if the blankets do not warm you enough, let your mind recall our moments together. Will that not warm you through and through, my woman?"

"I can't do that," Jolena murmured, smiling softly up at him. "It would truly be best if I think of other things while you are gone from me. Recalling our moments together would make me want you too much at a time when you are being denied me."

"Perhaps this separation will be good for us both," Spotted Eagle said, chuckling.

He leaned even closer to be sure that no one else could hear, especially Kirk. "Waiting will enhance the pleasure," he whispered. "When I return, we will make love as though it were the first time."

"My every heartbeat will count the minutes for your return," she whispered back, giving him a soft kiss, then moved away from him and went stiffly to her brother.

"Kirk, I hope there are no hard feelings between us," she said. "And please, *please* do your best to make father understand. He, of all people, should. He is the one who took me from my true people. He had me for many years, as his own. My true father will have me for less, for his years are already too many in number to count many more."

Kirk sat stiffly for a few moments as silence fell like a wall between him and Jolena, then he reached a hand to her cheek.

"Sis, I hold no grudges," he said, his voice drawn. "If it were me, and had I been denied my true people for so long, I am sure I would do the same as you. Please be happy, sis. That's what's important now. That you are happy in your decision to live with the Blackfoot people. You . . . have my blessing."

Jolena knew that he was saying things that he did not feel and was grateful that he could do this for her, placing his true feelings aside to deal with later, after he was away from her.

"Thank you, Kirk," Jolena said, a sob lodging in her throat. She gazed at Moon Flower, her spine stiffening at the thought that this Blackfoot maiden was deceiving Kirk.

But still she could not find it in herself to warn Kirk, for he was a man now and should be capable of making his own decisions without a sister's interference.

Spotted Eagle mounted his horse and guided it next to Kirk's. "White brother, it is time to leave," he said, then turned his eyes to Jolena again. "When the sun rises again and slides upward to the highest point in the sky your man will return to you."

"Please be careful," Jolena said, nervously clasping and unclasping her hands behind her.

Spotted Eagle nodded, then rode on ahead to join the other warriors who were riding with him.

Kirk and Jolena stared at one another a moment, then Kirk nudged his heels into the flanks of his horse and rode away, Moon Flower dutifully at his side on her white mare.

Jolena watched until they became only spots on the horizon. Then she turned around and looked at the activity in the village.

The sun was just rising. Thin columns of smoke were creeping from the smoke holes of the lodges, ascending into the still morning air. Everywhere outside, women were busy carrying water and wood. Some were digging in a bank near the river for red clay, which would be used for paint.

Inside their dwellings the women were preparing meals.

The men were coming out and starting for the river. Some were followed by their children. Some were carrying those too small to walk. When they

381

reached the water's edge, they dropped their blankets and plunged into the cold water.

Jolena knew now that winter and summer, storm or shine, this was their daily custom. The Blackfoot had been taught that this made them tough and healthy and enabled them to endure the bitter cold while hunting on the bare, bleak prairie.

Jolena had already eaten her morning meal with Spotted Eagle before he left and now planned to do many things to help pass her long and lonely day without Spotted Eagle near.

As soon as the women left their dwellings and began their daily chores, Jolena joined them, following their lead so that she could learn the proper way to do everything. Today the women were making foods from dried meat, the thicker parts of the buffalo having already been cut in large, thin sheets and hung in the sun to dry.

The back fat of the buffalo was also dried and would be eaten with the meat as Jolena had eaten her bread and butter when she lived in Saint Louis.

Pemmican was made of the flesh of the buffalo, the meat having been dried in the usual way, and for this use, only lean meat was chosen.

Two large fires had been allowed to burn down to red coals. The women threw the dried sheets of meat on the coals of the fire allowing it to heat through, turning it often to keep it from burning.

After a time, the roasting of this dried meat caused a smoke to rise from the fire in use, which would have given the meat a bitter taste, so the women turned to the other fire and used that until the first one had burned clear again.

After enough of the roasted meat had been thrown on a fleshy piece of hide nearby, it was flailed with sticks, and being very brittle, was easily broken up. This was constantly stirred and pounded until it was all fine.

Meanwhile, the tallow of the buffalo had been melted in a large kettle, and the pemmican bags prepared. These were made of bull's hide and were in two pieces, which when sewn together made a bag which would hold one hundred pounds.

The pounded meat and tallow were put in a trough made of bull's hide, a wooden spade being used to stir the mixture. After it was thoroughly mixed, it was shoveled into one of the sacks, held open, and rammed down and packed tight with a big stick, every effort being made to expel all the air.

When the bag was full and packed as tight as possible, it was sewn up. It was then put on the ground, and the women jumped on it to make it still more tight and solid.

Jolena was shown how a much finer grade of pemmican was made from the choicest parts of the buffalo with marrow fat. To this, dried berries and pounded choke-cherries were added, making a delicious food which was extremely nutritious.

The process of preparing the meats took most of the day. Exhausted, Jolena went to Spotted Eagle's tepee and grabbed a blanket and went back out into the shadows of evening, toward the river. When she got there, she made sure no one else was around, then undressed and dove into the water.

She swam and swam, tiring herself even more, knowing that this was necessary for her to get to sleep, for she was restless over thinking of spending the full night without Spotted Eagle there with her. Although she was with her true people, she was feeling apprehensive about being alone with them.

This was a good test, one that would prove whether or not her decision to stay with the Blackfoot was right.

Jolena paused and treaded water. She held her head back and allowed her long hair to drift into the water behind her as she stared up at the stars that were just beginning to fill the black velvet sky, the moon only a tiny, bent sliver of white overhead.

When the breeze brushed across Jolena's face, she shivered and began swimming back toward shore. Just as she was about to climb out of the water, she stopped and her breath caught in her throat when she discovered someone standing in the shadows watching her.

Jolena slipped down into the water again, except for her head. With a pounding heart she gazed stubbornly at the person in the shadows. "Who's there?" she asked, her voice wary. "Show yourself, whoever you are."

Brown Elk stepped into view. He bent over and picked up the blanket that Jolena had left there for drying herself, then walked on to the embankment, holding the blanket out for her.

"It is I, your father," he said. "When I did not find you in Spotted Eagle's dwelling, I feared you might have been foolish enough to come to the river alone for a bath. And I see I was right. Daughter, do you not know the dangers of such foolish notions as this?"

Jolena sighed with relief, understanding now that she shouldn't have come alone to the river, especially at night. Someone besides her father might have been watching for her to leave the water. "I was too restless by the fire, alone," she murmured. When he held the blanket out farther, so that she could reach it, she took it and stepped quickly out of the water and wrapped herself in it.

"Did you not know that I was just as alone?" Brown Elk said, his voice filled with a sad weariness. "You could have come and filled this old man's heart with your company, instead of the river's."

"I'm sorry," Jolena murmured. "I wasn't thinking clearly, Father. I should have come and spent the evening with you. I shall even now, if you will have me."

She was awash with guilt that she had been thinking only of herself and her own loneliness, when she should have realized how abandoned her true father was feeling. Not only had she left his dwelling to live with Spotted Eagle, Moon Flower had also been quick to leave him after he had so generously opened his heart and arms to her, inviting her to stay with him when her parents had banished her from their lives.

"My dwelling is yours whenever you wish to be a part of it," Brown Elk said. "Especially tonight."

After she was dried enough, Jolena accepted the clothes that her father picked up from the ground. She moved behind a tree and dressed while he waited for her. Then, feeling much better, she went with Brown Elk to his lodge and enjoyed sharing a bowl of soup with him while they laughed and talked.

Then there was a sound outside the tepee. Both turned their eyes as the entrance flap was shoved aside.

Jolena and her father gasped when Moon Flower entered the tepee, her eyes downcast.

Jolena's eyes shifted when Spotted Eagle came in behind Moon Flower. She moved quickly to her feet as Brown Elk shuffled to his. Jolena went to Spotted Eagle and stood at his side, her eyes on Moon Flower as Brown Elk embraced her and welcomed her to his dwelling.

Then Brown Elk stepped away from her and held her hands. "Why do you return?" he asked, his dark eyes seeing much sadness in Moon Flower's as she slowly looked up at him.

"I could not do it," she said, tears streaming down her cheeks. "I loved him too much to deceive him. I . . . told him about the child. He . . . turned his eyes away from me and did not look back. He also banished me from his life."

Jolena was not certain how she felt about Kirk having done this to Moon Flower, but she knew for certain how she felt about Moon Flower—she admired her for her bravery and honesty!

From the beginning, after having become acquainted with Moon Flower, Jolena would never have thought her capable of carrying out such a deceit.

And she had been right!

Tears rushing from her eyes, and knowing how devastated Moon Flower must be feeling, Jolena went to her and drew her into her embrace. "I'm sorry," she whispered as the lovely, slight maiden clung to her, sobbing. "I'm sorry my brother couldn't accept both you *and* the child. I understand how you are feeling, and I want to be your friend."

Spotted Eagle watched the emotional scene with much love in his heart for his woman. He went to her and drew both her and Moon Flower into his arms.

Moon Flower enjoyed the closeness of her special friends for a moment longer, then broke away and went to Brown Elk. She gazed humbly up at him. "You will still have me in your dwelling?" she asked, her voice breaking.

"As long as you wish to be here," Brown Elk said, then drew her into his arms. "My little Blackfoot princess, you and your child will fill my dwelling with much happiness. That will be good for an old man like Brown Elk."

Jolena and Spotted Eagle crept from the tepee. When they got outside, Spotted Eagle swung Jolena around into his arms. He crushed his lips to hers and kissed her passionately, then swept her into his arms and began carrying her toward their tepee.

"Kirk? Did Kirk treat her terribly?" Jolena asked, as she peered up at Spotted Eagle.

"He said nothing to her after she told him," Spotted Eagle said. "He just mounted his horse and rode away. I stayed behind with her, to return her safely home. The other warriors went on with your brother."

Jolena sighed. "Well, at least the truth is out," she murmured. "Had Moon Flower waited, it could have been tragic for them both—and also the child."

Spotted Eagle carried Jolena into their tepee and laid her down on a pallet of furs beside the fire. Hurriedly, they undressed each other. Spotted Eagle knelt down over Jolena and brushed a kiss across each of her breasts, then moved his lips lower.

"Tonight," he said between kisses, "who needs blankets?"

He worshiped her flesh with his lips and tongue, then moved over her and filled her with his thick shaft. He held her hands above her head as he began his strokes within her, his mouth covering her lips with another fiery kiss.

Jolena could feel the passion rising in her. She lifted her legs and locked them around his waist, allowing him to move more deeply into her.

"I love you so," she whispered, as he slid his lips away from her mouth and moved them lower, where he could flick his tongue over her nipples. She strained her breasts upward, sucking in a wild breath of pleasure when he placed his mouth fully over one of them, sucking, licking, biting.

Spotted Eagle began moving his hands over Jolena, finding and caressing her every sensitive place until she was tossing her head back and forth, writhing from the rapture.

Then the explosion of their passion erupted. They clung and rocked and sighed.

Afterwards, they lay together, Jolena's leg draped over Spotted Eagle's thigh.

"Tomorrow you will be shown what is required of the Blackfoot woman before she becomes a wife," Spotted Eagle said, smiling down at her.

Chapter Thirty-Two

Spotted Eagle had eaten his morning meal of cooked sarvis berries without saying a word, making Jolena more anxious than ever. She had a hundred questions to ask about the marriage ceremony, and he had chosen to be uncommunicative. She was so excited that her life was finally turning into something sweet and peaceful, perhaps even *normal*—how could she not want to make sure that she did everything right at the wedding?

Picking at the berries in her wooden bowl, she kept giving Spotted Eagle harried glances but did not disturb him, for he seemed to be lost in deep thought about something.

Then she jumped with alarm when he set his bowl aside and rose to his feet. He began walking toward the door, still without saying anything to her. She wanted to go after him but refrained from doing so.

When he left the tepee, Jolena scampered to her feet, went to the entrance flap and slowly shoved it aside. Scarcely breathing, she watched Spotted Eagle walk through the village and then enter her father's dwelling.

"Why did he go there and not ask me to go with him?" Jolena whispered to herself, hurt that even in this way he was leaving her out this morning.

Her eyes widened when Moon Flower stepped from Jolena's father's tepee and headed toward Spotted Eagle's. When she got inside the tepee, Jolena gave her a warm hug, then took her hand and led her down on soft mats by the fire.

"I know that I should offer you food, but I'm so anxious to ask you about Spotted Eagle's strange behavior that I wish to discuss that with you first," Jolena said in a rush of words.

She moved to her knees and faced Moon Flower who was sitting calmly. In her eyes there was a mischievous, merry glint.

"Well?" Jolena prodded. "Why is Spotted Eagle in my father's tepee? He told me nothing—just left and went directly to my father's dwelling."

"You truly do not know, do you?" Moon Flower said, giggling behind her hand as she gazed into Jolena's anxious eyes. "You do not know the actions taken by a warrior when he wishes a Blackfoot woman's hand in marriage?"

Jolena's heart skipped an anxious beat, and she could feel a flush warm her cheeks. "That . . . is why he went to my father's tepee?" she murmured. "It's about our marriage?"

"Yes," Moon Flower murmured. "Everything today is about your marriage. And since you have no Blackfoot mother, I will take her place."

"You will?" Jolena said, her eyes widening. "You would do this for me?"

"It is not only for you, but also Brown Elk," Moon Flower said softly. "It is my way of saying thank-you for his kindness to Moon Flower—and yours."

Guilt momentarily tugged at Jolena's heart for having doubted Moon Flower's honesty for a short while. But wrapped up in the excitement of the day, she cast these feelings aside and allowed herself to feel wonderful over finally realizing her plans to marry the man she loved. There was no doubt whatsoever in her heart over her decision to stay in the Blackfoot village, to be one of them.

Everything looked so bright.

The future looked so promising.

How could she feel anything but blessed?

Euphoric, she listened raptly as Moon Flower began explaining what must be done to prepare her for her wedding day tomorrow.

"First, Jolena, you must move into your father's lodge," Moon Flower said, softly folding her arms across her breasts.

Jolena blushed, hoping no one, especially her Blackfoot father, saw her as shameful for having spent her nights with Spotted Eagle.

But she knew that Spotted Eagle wouldn't have encouraged it had he thought that it would damage her reputation in the eyes of his people. She had never taken the time to worry about it, for deep in her heart she had known that they would already have been married had there not been so many obstacles in the way.

In her heart, mind, and soul she was already his woman—his *wife.*

The ceremony was necessary only to formalize it.

"I look forward to spending this special time with my father," Jolena finally said.

"While there, you will select the choicest parts of the meat from your father's lodge," Moon Flower said softly. "You will cook these things in the best style, and in the company of Moon Flower you will go to Spotted Eagle's lodge and place the food before him. He will eat it. Then you will take the dishes, and we will return to your father's lodge. Everyone in the village who sees you carrying the food in a covered dish to Spotted Eagle's lodge will know that a marriage is to take place."

"And then what else do I do?" Jolena asked anxiously, thrilling inside to actually be talking about her marriage to Spotted Eagle. That made it so very real! Nothing would stop it now. There was only today, tonight, and then tomorrow it was to happen!

She was so excited, she could hardly sit still any longer. But she knew that she must listen to all of Moon Flower's teachings today. These were perhaps the most important lessons of all as she turned herself over to the Blackfoot way of life.

"If your mother were alive, she would make you a new lodge, complete with new poles," Moon

Flower said. Her voice was filled with compassion as she remembered listening to her own mother tell the tale of Sweet Dove and how she had died giving birth to a child that no one had ever found. It seemed a miracle that here before Moon Flower sat this child who was now a woman.

How wonderful it would have been if Sweet Dove could have lived to see her daughter molded into someone as beautiful and sweet as Jolena, and to see the man she was to marry! No mother could have been more proud. She would have made the cowhide lodge with eager, happy fingers, as her heart sang and her eyes danced.

"And since she is not alive?" Jolena murmured. "Who then makes the lodge for me?"

"Your father appointed one of the women of the village many days ago to make the lodge," Moon Flower said, smiling at Jolena. "It is a handsome one that you will be pleased to erect in the midst of the village for all to see. It will be a lodge your father will be pleased with as his dowry is placed there."

"My father's . . . dowry?" Jolena said, gasping softly. "Whatever might it be?"

"It is not for Moon Flower to say," Moon Flower said, laughing softly.

Spotted Eagle sat opposite the fire from Brown Elk, staring across the flames at his future father-in-law, feeling humble in the presence of such a great and honorable elder as he.

Brown Elk rose and brought his beautifully decorated pipe with its long stem over to Spotted Eagle and handed it to him, to partake of a smoke with him.

Brown Elk waited until Spotted Eagle was blowing smoke from his mouth, then took the pipe back and again sat down before the fire opposite his future *nis-ah*—son-in-law.

"You have come to speak of my daughter?" Brown Elk said, crossing his legs at his ankles and resting the bowl of his pipe on one of his knees.

"That is so," Spotted Eagle said, nodding.

"The time is good for a marriage," Brown Elk said, smiling at Spotted Eagle. "You will make a fine son-in-law. I gladly give my daughter to you, even though I have not had her long myself. I trust you will allow this elder to share his daughter who will soon become your wife? I will be the first to know of the growing of a child within my daughter's womb? I will be second to you to hold my grandchild once it is born?"

Brown Elk's eyes lowered to keep from revealing the sudden sadness that was creeping into them. At this time he couldn't help thinking of his son.

"This old man has known the joy of holding only one infant to his breast in his lifetime," Brown Elk said. "And he is gone from me now, as Jolena was gone from me when she was stolen by people with the white skins."

Brown Elk looked slowly up at Spotted Eagle. "I look forward to holding an infant again next to my heart," he said. "Make babies soon, Spotted Eagle, so this old man can watch the child grow some summers before wandering off to the Sand Hills to join his ancestors."

"There will be sons and daughters soon to fill your arms," Spotted Eagle said, smiling. "My woman—your daughter—will make beautiful daughters and strong, courageous sons. You will be proud, and yes, you will be drawn into their lives and your daughter's and mine as though we were of one heart and soul. My children will be blessed to have such a grandfather as Brown Elk!"

Brown Elk's eyes danced as he leaned closer to Spotted Eagle. "Jolena will soon erect her lodge in the center of the village. There I will place her dowry, for your taking. I hope what I choose for this dowry will be adequate to show my admiration for the man my daughter is to marry!"

"Having your daughter as my wife is dowry enough for this man," Spotted Eagle said, chuckling low. He rose to his feet and went around the fire and embraced Brown Elk as he rose and stood before him.

"It will be good to have two fathers," Spotted Eagle said, stepping back from Brown Elk. "I fear that my true father's summers are lessening much too quickly. He may not see his first grandchild. That saddens me."

"Do not bring such sadness into your heart until it happens and you are forced to accept it," Brown Elk said. "Cherish the time now with him, so that when he passes to the other side you will not be as heart sick over the loss."

"That I will do," Spotted Eagle said, then nodded a silent farewell. He went to the entrance flap and raised it, only to find himself peering down into the eyes of his beloved.

Jolena blushed and lowered her eyes, feeling awkward at this moment because of what was taking place between her and Spotted Eagle. For the first time in her life that she could recall, she was actually feeling bashful! She said nothing, nor did he, and she slipped past him into the tepee, laughing softly as she turned a wondering look at Moon Flower.

"This is such fun," she said, clasping her hands before her. "I suddenly feel more like a child than a woman preparing for marriage. It all seems so secretive. It makes it all seem so—special, somehow."

"It is good to see your eyes shining and to hear the excitement in your voice," Brown Elk said, going to Jolena.

He drew her into his arms and held her to him. "My daughter," he said fondly. "Do you know how good it is to hold you? For so long this was denied me!"

"I, too, enjoy being held by you," Jolena murmured, clinging to him. "You are everything I would ever want in a father."

Brown Elk stepped away from her and knelt down before a trunk that he was slowly uncovering by lifting one blanket and then another away from it. "This father has gifts for you from myself and your mother," he said, his voice drawn. He cast Jolena a glance and nodded for her to join him at the trunk. "*Ok-yi.* Come. See. They are yours to wear on your wedding day."

Her pulse racing, anxious to know what could be in the trunk that could be from her mother as well as her father, Jolena sat down on a thick cushion of pelts beside Brown Elk. Her eyes were glued to the lid of the trunk as her father's trembling fingers began raising it.

Her eyes widened when she saw the beautiful things inside the trunk, laid out so carefully. The light of the fire reflected on leggings adorned with many colorful beads and bells and brass buttons. As her father lifted the garment from the trunk and laid it on Jolena's lap, she saw that it was made of deerskin and was heavily fringed, as well as beautifully decorated.

She gently touched the leggings, sighing as she discovered the softness of the buckskin, but her eyes were elsewhere as her father slowly lifted a beautiful Indian dress from the trunk. It was made of antelope skin and was as white as snow and ornamented with at least three hundred beads made from elk tusks!

This, too, was laid across Jolena's lap for her to gaze upon and to touch, but again her attention was drawn to something else her father was taking from the trunk.

It was a summer blanket made of elk skin, well tanned, without the hair, and with the dew-claws left on.

Brown Elk reached into the trunk one last time and drew out a beautiful pair of black moccasins. They were of deerskin with parfleche soles and worked with porcupine quills.

"These were your mother's on the day of her marriage to your father," Brown Elk said, gently stroking his hand down the full length of Jolena's unbraided hair. "This old man never thought there could be another woman as lovely as your mother . . . not until now. Not until you. You will be as beautiful. And your mother will be watching from her place in the heavens as you become a radiant wife to Spotted Eagle. She will bless this marriage, as I have already."

Jolena was at a loss for words. Tears splashed from her eyes. She felt both happy and sad. The clothes gave her a sense of her mother's nearness, yet they also made it all the more real that Sweet Dove was not there to witness her daughter's happiness!

At this moment, Jolena realized just how cheated she had been by fate. Her mother had been taken from her before she had known the wonders of her touch, her kiss, her blessings—even before Jolena had been able to drink that first drop of milk from her mother's breast!

She turned her eyes from Brown Elk, willing herself to stop crying!

This was a time meant for happy thoughts, not a past that she had never had any control over!

When the tears had dried, she turned a smile to her father. "I love them all," she murmured. "Thank you, father, for allowing me to wear the clothes my mother wore when she became your wife. I wear them with much pride and love."

A soft voice outside the tepee speaking Brown Elk's name made him smile broadly. He rose to his feet and walked toward the entrance. Then he nodded at Moon Flower. "Go to Jolena," he said softly. "Take the clothes from her arms. Her arms must be free to accept the gift One Who Walks With A Limp has made for her. Lay the clothes aside and go with Jolena and assist her in setting up her lodge, for she has no knowledge yet of how this is done."

Brown Elk gave Jolena a glance over his shoulder. "*Ok-yi.* Come, my daughter," he said. "Come and see what One Who Walks With A Limp has brought you."

Moon Flower went to Jolena and carefully took the clothes from her arms, then gave her a quiet smile as Jolena got to her feet and moved toward her father with soft steps.

As the entrance flap was lifted, Jolena saw an elderly lady with waist-length gray hair and wrinkled face, burdened down with a beautiful cowhide decorated with elaborate drawings.

"These are for the daughter of Brown Elk," One Who Walks With A Limp said, as she smiled a toothless smile up at Jolena. "The lodge poles, back rests, and inner lining for the tepee lies where you will build your tepee."

Jolena stepped from the lodge and took the burden from the slight, elderly lady. "Thank you so much for doing this for me in the absence of my mother," she murmured. "It is something I shall never forget."

One Who Walks With A Limp nodded and bowed her head humbly, then slowly lifted it and gazed at Brown Elk as he placed a gentle hand on her shoulder. "It is with much joy that

I made this for your daughter," she murmured. "It was good to be singled out for such an honor. Thank you, Brown Elk. It is as though I was a young girl again, making my own lodge, for my own man. It was good ... feeling young again."

Brown Elk drew the woman into his arms and gave her a generous hug. "You will always be young in your heart, and in my eyes," he said.

When he eased her from his arms, she turned and walked away, limping heavily with each step.

Moon Flower moved quickly to Jolena's side and helped relieve her of some of the burden by taking one end of the cowhide into her own arms. "Let us go and build the tepee so that the dowry can be soon placed there," she said, giving Brown Elk a laughing smile.

Jolena raised an eyebrow, still not knowing exactly what this talk of a dowry was all about. "Yes, let's," she said, laughingly walking away with Moon Flower, clumsily sharing the hide as they half stumbled along across the stamped-down ground of the village.

As he watched Jolena and Moon Flower, Brown Elk smiled and folded his arms across his chest.

Spotted Eagle watched from his tepee as Jolena and Moon Flower stepped into the center of the village and began erecting the lodge.

Then his gaze shifted as he looked over at Brown Elk, wondering what the dowry might amount to, for he wanted to send over to his father-in-law's lodge twice the number of gifts his bride's father would pay his son-in-law.

Chapter Thirty-Three

Jolena had tried to sleep but found it impossible, so she'd spent the night preparing the special meal for Spotted Eagle, with Moon Flower giving her hints in cooking the sorts of meats that Jolena was not familiar with. The morning sun was now splashing its golden light down the smokehole, and Jolena's father's dwelling smelled pleasant with fragrances of the best of foods taken from his food supply, some choice berry pemmican, and the tongue and "boss ribs" of the buffalo, said to be the most desired parts by the Blackfoot warriors.

"I see that my daughter is ready to take her offerings to the man who will soon be her husband," Brown Elk said, as he came to the fire, yawning and stretching. He gave Moon Flower a pleasant smile and nod, then continued talking to Jolena. "Spotted Eagle surely has not ever had such a feast as that which will be placed before him today."

Jolena turned from her preparations and gave her father a bright smile. "I've never been so excited," she said, giving her father a hearty hug. "Will I actually become Spotted Eagle's wife today? It isn't just one of my dreams?"

"If this is a dream, it is a good one, is it not?" Brown Elk said, chuckling as he eased Jolena from his arms. He reached a hand to her brow and smoothed some loose locks of her hair back in place.

"Oh, yes," Jolena said, clasping her hands together behind her. "It is all so wonderful. But it *is* real, and so much better because it is."

"The lodge you prepared for my son-in-law is handsome," Brown Elk said, sitting down on a couch cushioned with soft pelts. "You have placed your wedding attire in it already?"

"Yes, father," Jolena murmured, watching as Moon Flower devotedly ladled Brown Elk a large bowl of buffalo stew. "I am now ready to take the meal to Spotted Eagle. Do you think he will be awake?"

Brown Elk accepted the bowl of stew and a spoon, then gave Jolena an amused smile. "Will he be awake?" he said. "Daughter, I doubt he slept a wink all night."

Jolena nervously brushed her fingers through her hair, then noticed some stains on her skirt that had splashed there while she was cooking. She turned anxiously to Moon Flower. "Perhaps

I'd best take a bath in the river and change clothes first," she said.

"Your bath should be taken just before you change into your wedding attire," Moon Flower softly suggested. "You will then smell fresh and clean like the river for your husband when you go to him later, after you move your tepee beyond the village, close to the outer fringes of the forest, where you can have privacy from prying hearts and listening ears."

"I must move the tepee after having taken so long to erect it?" Jolena asked, her eyebrows raised in puzzlement. "I have even gone many times through the night to add wood to the fire, so that the tepee would be warm and cozy when Spotted Eagle went inside. I wanted everything to be perfect. Why must I change it?"

"Moving into the middle of the circle is considered an honor," Moon Flower explained. "Only important people build the marriage lodge in the center of the village. Next to his father, Spotted Eagle is the most important person in this village. He will one day be chief. You have erected a wonderful lodge for him to show off to his people. And there are other reasons for the lodge which you will discover through the day."

Jolena had felt that her efforts with the marriage tepee had been wasted. But now she understood.

"Your warrior should not be made to wait much longer for the meal his woman has prepared for him," Brown Elk reminded her. "Go to him, Jolena. Accompany her there, Moon Flower.

Fill both your arms with platters of food for this man who will soon be a husband."

Jolena nodded. Her heart hammered inside her chest as she placed her many offerings of food into a basket. After Moon Flower had her own basket filled, Jolena and Moon Flower left the tepee. They stepped out into a glorious morning of cool, soft breezes, a clear, blue sky, and the songs of birds as they began awakening in the forest beyond.

Jolena walked beside Moon Flower with a proudly lifted chin, racing heart, and trembling fingers, feeling many knowing eyes on her. She could hear the hushed buzzing of voices as everyone pushed closer to observe the first stages of the wedding ceremony. Jolena could feel a hot blush rise to her cheeks as more and more people pressed closer, the children giggling.

Doing her best to ignore her audience, Jolena set her eyes on Spotted Eagle's tepee. She felt her heart do a flip-flop when she noticed that the entrance flap was open, held back by a young brave.

Not knowing how long this lad had been forced to stand there holding the buckskin flap open, Jolena hastened her steps.

When she finally arrived at Spotted Eagle's tepee, she smiled a silent thank-you to the handsome young brave, then went on inside, with Moon Flower following close behind her.

Jolena's heart melted when she found Spotted Eagle sitting beside his lodge fire in only a brief breechclout, his legs folded before him, his hands resting on his knees.

When he looked her way and gave her a slow, teasing smile, she almost swayed with the force of the passion between them.

She had to swallow hard and will herself to continue with these chores that came before the actual coming together as man and wife. She had thought of nothing but being with Spotted Eagle through the long hard night while her hands had been preparing the food for him.

She had wanted to slip away and go to his tepee and snuggle up next to him. She had wanted to be held within his powerful arms as he whispered sweet nothings in her ear.

Jolena wrenched her thoughts back to the chore at hand. She followed Moon Flower's lead in placing the food before Spotted Eagle, taking one empty bowl away so that he could eat from another.

He spoke not a word as he enjoyed his meal.

He refrained even from gazing Jolena's way, which unnerved her.

Soon the feast was over. Jolena and Moon Flower left the tepee and rushed back to Brown Elk's dwelling, again watched by everyone of the village.

Jolena and Moon Flower began taking the empty bowls and platters from the basket to wash in a basin of water that was already sitting beside the firepit. As Jolena was doing this, she wondered about her father's sudden silence as he prepared himself to leave.

"Do not question him now about anything," Moon Flower whispered to Jolena as she busied her hands washing the dishes, while Jolena dried them with a thin strip of buckskin. "It is a solemn time for your father and Spotted Eagle. Soon I shall show you why."

Out of the corner of her eye, Jolena watched her father leave the tepee, then she continued drying the dishes until they were stacked and ready to store away.

"I think we can look now," Moon Flower said, taking Jolena by the hand and urging her to come to the entrance flap. "Look toward your marriage lodge. See what your father places there as your dowry."

Moon Flower lifted the flap. Jolena's eyes widened as she watched her father instruct several young braves to lead fifteen horses to her lodge, tying them there on posts that had been hammered into the ground.

"My dowry?" Jolena whispered. "And ... so many?"

"Hurry away from the door now," Moon Flower said, half dragging Jolena back to sit down by the fire, just in time for Jolena's father to enter the lodge again, followed by the same young braves who had placed her father's horses in front of her lodge.

Jolena watched breathlessly as her father gathered up his very own war clothing and arms, a lance, a fine shield, a bow, and arrows in an otter-skin case, his war bonnet, war shirt, and war leggings ornamented with scalps. He then sent his complete war equipment out with the young braves and followed proudly after them.

"We can watch again," Moon Flower said, giggling as she scrambled to her feet. "Come, Jolena. See what is happening!"

Stunned by all of this, Jolena moved to her feet and again went to the entrance flap and watched from it. Her lips parted in a gasp as she watched all of her father's warring gear being set up on tripods in front of her lodge.

"The gift of those things from your father to Spotted Eagle is evidence of the great respect felt by him for his new son-in-law," Moon Flower said, looking softly over at Jolena. "His respect is great, Jolena, for see what he has given? Everything that means so much to your father is now Spotted Eagle's."

Spotted Eagle was watching from his tepee, touched deeply by the gifts of his woman's father. Several young braves were standing before him, awaiting his orders as to the number of gifts that would be given back to Jolena's father. He had already decided that he would give back twice the number of horses that Jolena had brought with her into the marriage.

"Go," Spotted Eagle said. "Take the horses from in front of my woman's lodge, and also the warring gear of her father. Place them in my corral. Then choose thirty of my finest horses and place them in front of my father-in-law's lodge."

The braves scampered away. As soon as Brown Elk and the other young braves had left Jolena's lodge with the gifts that had been left there for

Spotted Eagle, Spotted Eagle left his tepee and walked with a lifted chin and smiling heart toward the lodge of his woman.

When he entered, he found a good fire and soft pelts beside it, but as was the .custom, he took his place at the back of the lodge, awaiting his woman's arrival.

Already he could hear the steady beating of drums in the distance, songs being sung by the women of his village, and the gay voices of children at play, all of which signaled the beginning of a long day of celebration among his people.

Spotted Eagle smiled and folded his arms across his bare chest, savoring every minute of this time—a time for which he had waited a lifetime!

Laughing and giggling, Jolena and Moon Flower ran to the river and found an isolated place for their bath and swim. After they were unclothed, they dove in unison into the river and swam and played and laughed.

Then, in a more somber fashion, Jolena and Moon Flower left the river. Moon Flower dressed quickly, then helped Jolena into her mother's wedding dress, which they had taken from Jolena's lodge before the sun had replaced the moon in the sky. After the dress was hanging beautifully and clinging sensuously to Jolena's curves, Moon Flower prepared Jolena's hair, brushing it, then braiding it and placing daisies above Jolena's ears.

Moon Flower added the final touch. She placed earrings made of shells on each of Jolena's ears, then held Jolena's hands as Jolena stepped back for her friend to see.

"The elk tusks that decorate your dress are worth two good horses," Moon Flower said, giggling.

Then she grew serious. "You are a beautiful bride," Moon Flower murmured, tears filling her eyes at the thought of her own marriage vows that had been denied her not only once, but twice!

"I *feel* beautiful," Jolena said, her pulse racing. "Now what do I do? I'm so excited, Moon Flower, I feel as though I may faint!"

"Go to Spotted Eagle," Moon Flower said softly. "He is waiting for you in your lodge."

"He is there, in my lodge that sits in the circle?" Jolena said, the beats of her heart a great pulsing sound in her ears, her excitement was so intense. "Do you think he approves of the lodge?"

"Who would not approve, if *your* hands were responsible for it," Moon Flower said, drawing Jolena into her soft embrace. "Go. Be happy."

Tears of joy stung the corners of Jolena's eyes. She eased from Moon Flower's embrace and turned and walked with weak knees and throbbing heart toward the village, where her loved one waited to make their union complete. She felt as though she were floating high above herself, looking down on someone else experiencing such blissful happiness!

She smiled heavenward, silently thanking the one who was truly responsible for this special day. "Lord, I shall forever be grateful," she murmured.

Smiling, she knew that this was one custom of her white heritage that she could never leave behind her—her belief in her God was solidly imbedded within herself.

When she came to the edge of the clearing that led into the village, she stopped and stared at the tepee that sat in the center, wondering if Spotted Eagle was as feverishly anxious as she.

Lifting her chin, proud and sure, she moved onward, pushing her way through the throngs of Blackfoot who were already in the midst of a grand celebration.

Chapter Thirty-Four

Jolena hesitated only a moment before stepping inside her lodge—long enough to take a deep, quavering breath—then she lifted the entrance flap.

She had expected to find Spotted Eagle sitting beside the lodge fire. Instead he was sitting in the shadows at the back of the tepee. When he reached a hand out to her, she went to him and knelt down before him.

His eyes devoured her as he ran his gaze over her. Anxiously, she waited for him to say something.

When his gaze moved upward and his eyes locked with hers, she still waited, for he did not speak, only looked.

"Is there something about what I have done in preparation for our marriage that displeases you?" Jolena finally asked. "Darling, please say something. I am at a loss. I have done everything that Moon Flower instructed me to do. Is there . . . more?"

"You have done everything to perfection," Spotted Eagle finally said. He reached a hand to her hair and touched one of her braids, then smoothed his fingers over the daisy at her left ear. "In my eyes you have always been beautiful, but today your loveliness surpasses anything I would have thought possible."

He cupped her chin with one hand. "Today two hearts come together to become one life," he said solemnly. "Today you have become my 'sits beside me' woman. You are my wife."

Jolena sucked in a wild, surprised breath. "We are married?" she murmured. "There are to be no words spoken over us? No vows exchanged?"

"Everything you did today, preparing and bringing me food and erecting your lodge, and *my* payment to your father are the things that sealed our hearts together as man and wife," Spotted Eagle said, placing his hands at her waist, bringing her onto his lap so that her legs straddled him. "There is something more, my wife, to make it truly complete."

Jolena twined her arms around his neck, rapture building within her. "Making love in my lodge?" she murmured.

"Yes, making love in your lodge," Spotted Eagle said, his eyes twinkling into hers. "But not here in the center of the village for everyone to witness."

"Oh, yes, I remember now," Jolena said, sighing heavily. "I must take the tepee apart and set it up away from the village." Her lips curved into a pout. "That will take so long, Spotted Eagle. I am not skilled enough at building lodges to remember which pole goes where or how to remove the covering and replace it again as it should be."

"It is not usually the place of the husband to assist the wife with the lodge on the day of the marriage, but I am sure this time it will not look all that unusual should I help you. Our people know you are new to our customs," Spotted Eagle said.

He drew Jolena's lips to his and gave her a passionately hot kiss, then lifted her from his lap and drew her to her feet beside him.

"Let us move the lodge elsewhere quickly," he said huskily. "Then we shall seal our bond of marriage. We shall make love, my wife, as our people celebrate and await our return. There will be many gifts then from the women of our village."

He gave her a slow smile. "They are always most generous on a special wedding day," he said softly.

Spotted Eagle stepped away from her and snuffed the flames of the fire in the firepit by smothering them with blankets.

He then held out a hand for Jolena.

She took his hand and walked outside with him. They were received with much shouting, chanting, and singing.

Jolena smiled a thank-you to those who were crowded around her, touching her, brushing her with quick kisses, and hugging her.

Then she turned away from them and helped dismantle the lodge.

Soon she and Spotted Eagle were carrying the lodge and its poles through the village.

Jolena was surprised when no one followed, and the gaiety was left behind them. When they came to the outer fringes of the village and were standing in the cool shadows of the forest, Spotted Eagle took over most of the chores of rebuilding the tepee. Once it was in place, and he had blankets thrown across the ground inside, he grabbed Jolena up into his arms and carried her into their wedding temple.

Clinging to his neck, Jolena lifted her lips to his. As he kissed her, one of his hands began creeping up the inside of the skirt of her dress and was soon caressing her where she was already wet and hot for her new husband.

She sighed against his lips as he thrust a finger inside her and touched that part of her that was the most sensitive.

She closed her eyes and allowed euphoria to claim her as Spotted Eagle laid her on the blankets and quickly undressed her, his lips and fingers soon arousing her to heights of pleasure that seemed to know no bounds!

Then he stepped away from her, and she opened her eyes. She still felt drugged and weak from his foreplay.

She discovered him standing over her, nude, looking like a copper god. When Jolena's eyes moved to that part of him that was ready for

415

lovemaking, she reached a hand to his manhood and wove her fingers around it.

She watched his eyes close and his lips part in a groan as she began moving her hand on him. She moved to her knees before him and flicked her tongue against the glistening tip of his hardness, drawing a guttural groan of pleasure from deep inside him. His body stiffened.

Placing his hands at the back of Jolena's head, Spotted Eagle urged her lips closer, and when she drew him into the warm cocoon of her mouth, she heard him suck in a wild gasp of pleasure.

She pleasured him like this for a moment, then Spotted Eagle drew himself away from her and placed his hands to her shoulders, easing her down on her back on the blankets.

His eyes dark and passion-filled, he leaned over her and showed her exactly how wonderful a mouth, tongue, and lips could feel as he found her every secret, sensitive spot. He pleasured her until she was thrashing her head from side to side, emitting soft gasps. She felt as though she were swimming through a great, warm void, her every nerve ending tingling and thrilling from the rapture.

Just as she felt as though she might go over that edge into total ecstasy, Spotted Eagle moved over her and thrust his shaft within her.

Framing her face between his hands, he gave her a kiss that was all-consuming.

As his thrusts became more insistent inside her, Jolena lifted her legs around him so that he could fill her more deeply, more completely.

And then his lips lowered so that he could lick and his teeth could nip and tug at her nipples.

Jolena gasped softly as his teeth pulled a nipple between them, his tongue moving in circles around it as it lay captured between his teeth.

When he moved his lips to the hollow of her throat and licked her skin, as though she were something wonderfully delectable and sweet to eat, she threw her head back and closed her eyes, then scarcely breathed when once again his lips and tongue made their way down her body, stopping where he had only moments ago been so magnificently filling her.

Jolena breathed shallowly as she waited for the glorious feelings to overcome her again. She shook and trembled when his tongue touched the tip of her woman's desire, then felt his teeth nipping at it. The pleasure was so intense that it momentarily drew her breath away.

She sighed heavily when he moved over her again and filled her with his throbbing hardness.

Spotted Eagle wrapped his arms around her and cradled her close as he began his rhythmic strokes again, this time moving much more quickly—desperate, it seemed to reach that final plateau that would momentarily make him mindless.

Jolena kissed his shoulder, then his ear, then his lips as she felt the pleasure rising, then rushing through her like wildfire as his body trembled into hers, spurting his seed deeply into the warm depths of her desire. . . .

They then clung to one another, blissfully happy.

"There is one more thing that would make my happiness complete," Spotted Eagle suddenly said, moving to his knees and straddling Jolena as she lay on her back, gazing lovingly up at him.

"What is it?" she murmured, reaching a hand to his chest and stroking it. "My beautiful Blackfoot husband, don't you know that your every wish is my command?"

"Your name," Spotted Eagle said, his voice guarded. "You are Blackfoot. Your name should be Blackfoot. Would you allow this husband to give his wife a Blackfoot name?"

Jolena's smile faded, and her heart seemed to skip a beat. She felt that if she lost the only name she had ever known, it would be like parting with her identity!

Yet, she saw her husband's reasoning and knew that to make him totally happy, she must abide by his wishes, even this one.

"And what would you have me called?" she said, reaching her hand to his cheek.

"When you walk, you are as graceful as a fawn," Spotted Eagle said. "The name Fawn would fit you best. Do you like it?"

Jolena's eyes brightened. She smiled up at him. "I think it's lovely," she murmured. "Yes, I like it. Fawn. I shall only answer to Fawn from now on."

"I will tell our people," Spotted Eagle said, taking her hand and kissing its palm.

Then he moved to his feet. "Let us get dressed and go to our people," he said, offering Jolena a hand. "Without us, the new bride and groom, there is no true celebration."

Jolena hurried into her clothes, and Spotted Eagle pulled his breechclout on and stepped into his black moccasins. Then he went to Jolena and rebraided her hair which had come loose during their lovemaking.

"It is now time to go," he said, taking her hand. He looked slowly around him at the beautiful lodge. "Take a last look. This will be gone by sunrise tomorrow. It has served its purpose."

Jolena felt a twinge of sadness as she gazed around the lodge, then smiled softly as she looked down at the mussed-up blankets, still thrilling inside from the lasting effects of Spotted Eagle's lovemaking.

Then she turned and left the lodge with her beloved.

Soon they were catapulted into the midst of the celebration. As the drums vibrated and spoke to the spirits, the warriors and wives chanted and danced. The young braves with their brilliant raiment, grace and agility, were dancing the ancient feather dance, not for the purpose of impressing the other braves, but to impress the young girls maturing into womanhood whom they would have, if only in their midnight dreams.

Chief Gray Bear, leaning heavily on his staff, met Jolena and Spotted Eagle's advance into the crowd. He stepped before them and gave Jolena a warm hug, then gave Spotted Eagle a solid embrace. "*No-ko-i*, my son, you have given this father a beautiful daughter-in-law," he whispered into Spotted Eagle's ear. "You make this old man wish he were young again."

Spotted Eagle gave his father several fond pats on the back, chuckling, then stepped away from him when Brown Elk came up behind Spotted Eagle's father, smiling broadly from Jolena to Spotted Eagle.

Brown Elk then stepped between them, putting an arm around their waists as he gazed from one to the other. "My daughter, Spotted Eagle is a brave warrior, a man of good character," he said. "*Kyi!* Spotted Eagle is sober-minded, steadfast, and trustworthy. I know Spotted Eagle will make a good husband."

Spotted Eagle stepped away from Brown Elk. He drew Jolena to his side and placed an arm around her waist. "The words of both my fathers today warm this warrior's heart," he said. "This warrior will try to live up to all expectations as a husband to this wonderful woman at my side."

Then remembering that everyone needed to be told about Jolena's name change, he walked her to the center of the village, where her lodge had stood for only a short while. Spotted Eagle raised a hand in the air, momentarily giving pause to the celebration.

"Here stands a happy man!" he shouted.

He gave Jolena a soft smile. "Here stands a happy woman," he said softly, but with much feeling.

Then he gazed slowly around him at his rapt audience. "My wife not only gains a husband today, but also a new name!" he said, his voice echoing across the land, through the forest, and into the hills and mountains. "She is now called Fawn!"

There was a moment more of silence, then the drums were beating again and everyone was chanting, the chants soon turning into songs as the women, most dressed in gala dresses embroidered with ribbon work, began bringing gifts to Jolena and Spotted Eagle, laying them at their feet. Many of the presents were dried meats, pemmican and berries, and items of clothes such as black moccasins, handsome headbands, and beautiful necklaces and bracelets.

Moon Flower stood in line, patiently waiting, and then she stepped in front of Jolena and held her gift out to her, instead of laying it on the ground.

"Fawn, this gift I give you today was made by my grandmother's hands," Moon Flower said softly. "It is with much love for you that I hand this special gift over to you for your wedding present."

Jolena was touched deeply by the generosity of this young woman who had recently lost so much, yet still found giving so easy. "It is so lovely," she murmured, as she stared down at what was either a blanket or rug. "Are you certain that you wish to part with it?"

"It would please Moon Flower very much," Moon Flower murmured. "It is the best that Moon Flower has to give."

Jolena reached her arms out and allowed Moon Flower to drape the lovely garment over them.

And as though Moon Flower had read Jolena's thoughts, she explained the meaning of the gift to her.

"This is a prayer rug," Moon Flower murmured, knowing the many hours it had to have taken her grandmother to make the rug from a deerskin. She had first tanned the skin and then softened it using the brains taken from the skull of the animal. She had then placed her designs and symbols on it, some with paints, others with shells and beadwork.

"See how it is so intricately ornamented with symbols and prayer thoughts adorning the skin in ceremonial colors?" Moon Flower said, stretching the rug out so that it could be more easily admired. "See the white clouds and white flowers, the sun god and the curve of the moon? Above it all zigzag lines run through the blue of the sky to denote the lightning by which the children above sent their decrees to the earth children who roam the plains. It is for you to use, my friend, as you send your daily prayers to the sun, moon, and stars."

Tears flowed down Jolena's cheeks. "Thank you," she said, gathering the rug across her one arm so that it gave her room to hug Moon Flower. "I shall cherish this rug, forever and ever."

Moon Flower returned the hug, then gestured with a hand toward the feast that had been prepared for the celebration. "I know that you did not sleep last night, nor did you eat today," she said in a motherly tone. "It is time now to sit down and eat your fill."

Laughing softly, Jolena nodded. "Yes, mother," she teased.

Moon Flower took the prayer rug. "I will take this to Spotted Eagle's lodge which is now also yours, for safe-keeping," she said, then walked in a skipping fashion away from Jolena.

"She seems so happy," Jolena said, gazing up at Spotted Eagle as they sat down on a blanket. Their fathers sat together nearby, chatting and already eating.

"I know her well," Spotted Eagle said, as One Who Walks With A Limp served Jolena, then Spotted Eagle, a bowl of steaming greens, little corncakes dried in oil from sunflower seeds, and piles of meat cooked in various ways.

Spotted Eagle nodded a thank-you to the elderly woman, then continued speaking with Jolena. "Yes, I know Moon Flower well and she may appear happy, but in her eyes I see much sadness," he said, nodding his head.

"Well, I must find a way to remedy that," Jolena said, glancing over her shoulder as Moon Flower came walking back toward them. "Somehow."

Her eyes brightened when she saw Double Runner step from the crowd and offer Moon Flower a tray of food. When Moon Flower smiled up at him and accepted the tray and sat down with him so that they could eat together, Jolena concluded that she did not have to worry too long about this beautiful, slight woman. Even though she was pregnant, what man—besides her brother Kirk, who could not see past his prejudices—could not see the worth of a woman such as Moon Flower?

Jolena leaned close to Spotted Eagle. "I think we have nothing to worry about," she whispered. "Moon Flower is too lovely not to have a father for her child well before it is born."

Then Jolena laughed softly. "I will be sure to have a dream that will make that prediction come true," she said, then began eating the meat with her fingers, contented through and through.

When the time came for games to be played among the warriors, Double Runner came to Spotted Eagle, his eyes gleaming mischievously.

"My friend, you have won the challenge of finding a woman of your desire, but can you today win the challenge of the *it-se-wah*?" Double Runner taunted. "Or is your mind only on one thing? *Hai-yah! Ok-yi*—come! Join the game!"

Spotted Eagle gave Jolena a wavering glance. When she nodded and smiled, giving her silent approval, he jumped to his feet and followed Double Runner to a level, smooth piece of ground that had been selected for the game. At each end a log and two bows and quivers of arrows had been placed.

Jolena stood among the crowd of Blackfoot who were going to watch the warriors gambling with a small wheel called the *it-se-wah*. It was about four inches in diameter and had five spokes, on which were strung different colored beads made of bone.

Spotted Eagle and Double Runner took their places at each end of the course. Jolena looked anxiously around her as the men who were not playing began to bet on the side, some choosing Spotted Eagle as the winner, others choosing Double Runner.

When the game started, Jolena cheered Spotted Eagle on as she watched, wide-eyed, to see how this game was played. The wheel was rolled along the course, and Spotted Eagle and Double Runner aimed their arrows at it. Points were counted accordingly as the arrows passed between the spokes, or when the wheel, stopped by the log at the other end, came in contact with the arrow. The position and nearness of the different beads to the arrow represented a certain number of points. The player who first scored ten points won. Jolena could tell that it was a very difficult game and that a player had to be very skillful to win it.

Spotted Eagle was the victor. Double Runner embraced him, laughing and sweating. "You have won it all today, my friend," he said, his eyes dancing. "You have much to celebrate tonight in your lodge."

Jolena blushed, understanding his meaning and anxious to be a part of her husband's victory!

Chapter Thirty-Five

Five Years Later

It had been a long and tiring day for Jolena. She had gone with the other women of the village to dig up a good supply of camas root while it was still in its blooming stage. A large pit had been dug in which a hot fire was built, and the women had baked the camas for hours.

Now the sun had set and a cool spring breeze was blowing through the camp. A roaring fire was burning in the firepit as Jolena sat beside her father inside Spotted Eagle's lodge. They had just eaten a delightful meal of camas, the fresh-roasted roots tasting like a roasted chestnut, with a little sweet potato flavor.

Jolena gazed proudly over the fire at Spotted Eagle as he was telling their son, Yellow Eagle, the different ways to count *coups*.

Although only four, Yellow Eagle was an apt student of Blackfoot lore and customs, already able to ride a horse and shoot the small bow and arrow that his father had made for him.

Yellow Eagle was just like his father in features, manner, and habits. And this made Jolena very proud and happy.

The only thing missing from their lives now was Spotted Eagle's father. He had passed to the other side, over the mountains into the ghost land, the Sand Hills. On the day of his burial rites, Spotted Eagle had stood before his people and had spoken to them of being their chief.

The people of his village had cheered him on, looking to him as a leader who would keep them in peace, for Spotted Eagle took pride in the fact that from his earliest days never had he fought the white man.

Now Spotted Eagle was beginning to prepare his own son for the role of chief. "Long ago, my son, when I was a small child of three, my father sat me down beside him, as you are sitting with me now, and taught me many things," Spotted Eagle said.

Spotted Eagle stopped in mid-sentence and eased Yellow Eagle from his lap when the sound of horses approaching outside broke the silence of the moon-splashed village.

"Who can that be?" Jolena said, scrambling to her feet.

She joined Spotted Eagle at the entranceway and stood aside as he lifted the buckskin flap and peered outside. Then he stepped from the tepee, Jolena following him.

She slipped her arm through Spotted Eagle's as they awaited the arrival of those who were approaching. There were ten horsemen, flanked on each side by Spotted Eagle's sentries, who kept a constant vigil surrounding the village, to keep enemies from attacking.

The moon was bright, and as the horsemen grew closer, Jolena recognized more than one of them as white people, not only by their attire, but by the beards that some of them wore.

"It has been many moons since white people came into our village, especially without an invitation to do so," Spotted Eagle said. "I do not wish to share a smoke with any of them. Too many are taking land that does not belong to them! If ever I make war, it will be against them!"

"Warring is not the way," Jolena murmured. "I hope that you will not become as the Sioux, Sitting Bull, who is seeking confrontation with the white soldiers. I hope that you would still follow your own heart, darling, by never seeing war as the only way to find justice for our people."

Spotted Eagle gazed down at her. "It is always good to hear you say 'our people'," he said, smiling. "Fawn, for so long you were not a part of us." He paused, then said, "And do not worry about warring. I differ from Sitting Bull. It is still my intent never to see the blood of our warriors spilled across the land. If there is a peaceful means to settle disputes between our people and the whites, I shall always find it."

"And what of the Cree, your archenemy?" Jolena dared to ask, glad that while she had been married to Spotted Eagle the Cree had kept their distance.

Spotted Eagle's eyes lit with fire at the mention of the Cree, and his jaw tightened. He chose not to respond.

Jolena turned her eyes toward the approaching horsemen again. When she recognized the lead rider, she grew cold inside and swayed from dizziness.

Kirk!

It was Kirk!

She had not seen or heard from him since his departure those five long years ago. Even when she had sent a message from Fort Chance to her father and brother, she had been ignored.

A feeling of foreboding swept over Jolena at the sight of her brother.

She had missed him, but she did not want him to complicate her life again with talk of life back in Saint Louis and the friends and family she had turned her back on.

If he spoke of that life again, she would absolutely refuse to listen. She never could have been as happy anywhere as she had been these past years in the village of her true people, married to her beloved Spotted Eagle.

When Yellow Eagle came in a rush from the tepee and clung to the skirt of her buckskin dress, Jolena's father followed him to stand at Spotted Eagle's right side. Jolena squared her shoulders. Nothing would take them away from her.

But she could not deny her anxiety as Kirk swung himself out of his saddle and walked toward her. She had loved him for so long, long before she had ever thought it possible to live with her true people. She could not deny the claim he had on her.

"Kirk?" Jolena murmured, then ran to him and flung herself into his arms and hugged him. "Oh, Kirk, why have you ignored my messages? Why? And what of father? How is he?"

"Father is the reason I have come," Kirk said, easing her from his arms. "Jolena, he lasted until only a few months ago. Then . . . then he just went to sleep. He died without pain."

Jolena's heart seemed to stop beating for a moment. In her mind's eye she saw her white father as she had loved and known him as a child. She had shared her secrets with him. She had laughed and joked with him. Those things she *had* missed these past five years.

"Kirk, did he die hating me?" she asked, tears streaming down her cheeks.

"No, sis," Kirk said softly. "He knew from the moment he took you from your mother that you would one day leave him. It hurt, but he accepted it. These past years he was happy, writing his journals, and enjoying your contributions to his butterfly collection."

"*My* contributions?" Jolena said, her voice drawn.

"Yes, sis," Kirk said, smiling down at her. "After I reached Fort Chance, I led a detachment of soldiers back to the site of the accident. While they were burying the dead, I found several of your journals, as well as the butterfly collection that you had begun. There were enough cards left unharmed to give our father much pleasure."

He nodded toward his horse. "Sis, father finally wrote a book," he said. "It's about butterflies—and his life. I've brought you a copy."

Jolena's pulse raced as she waited for Kirk to go to his horse and lift the book from his saddlebag. She took the book and held it tenderly within her hands as she gazed down at it. Seeing her father's name on the cover made her very proud.

"Thank you, Kirk," Jolena murmured, hugging the book to her chest. "You went to a lot of trouble bringing it to me. I shall always cherish it."

Kirk looked around at the people who were coming from their dwellings to see who the late night visitor was. "Sis, I've come for more reasons than I've confessed," he admitted, his gaze moving from face to face, searching for one in particular.

"And that is?" Jolena asked, seeing that he was studying everyone and suddenly guessing why. She glanced over at Moon Flower's tepee, then heard his gasp as his former love walked slowly toward him, Double Runner at her side, one child in his arms and another in Moon Flower's.

Kirk paled and quickly looked away from Moon Flower. "I should have known that she would be married," he said, raking his fingers through his hair. "I should've come sooner."

"If you loved her, you shouldn't ever have let her

go," Jolena said, remembering the day that Moon Flower had returned to the village, heartbroken. "Double Runner is a good husband. Moon Flower loves him very much. Their children are beautiful, are they not?"

Kirk glanced again Moon Flower's way, their eyes momentarily locking. Then he shifted his gaze to the children. "They are lovely children," he murmured, bowing his head.

"Even Two Ridges' son," Jolena said stiffly. "He plays with my son often."

Kirk looked down at the child at Jolena's side. "Your son?" he said, his eyes wavering when he saw the likeness of the child to Spotted Eagle.

"He's a handsome boy," Kirk forced himself to say, his resentment toward Spotted Eagle no less today than five years before. He still thought that had it not been for Spotted Eagle, Jolena would not have felt such a strong need to stay with the Blackfoot.

"His name is Yellow Eagle," Jolena said, pushing her son toward Kirk. "Yellow Eagle, This is your Uncle Kirk."

Yellow Eagle stared up at Kirk for a moment, then smiled. "I already know you," he said. "My mother has talked of you often."

Kirk's eyes lit up. "She has?" he said, then suddenly swept Yellow Eagle into his arms.

Yellow Eagle took to Kirk quickly. He swung an arm around his neck. "How long are you staying?" he said, his eyes wide as he gazed with sudden affection at his only uncle. "We can ride horses together. Would you like that?"

"I would like that very much," Kirk said, giving Jolena a quick smile.

Then his smile faded. "But I won't be here long," he said, a tinge of sadness in his voice. "I'm with some lepidopterists who have come to find that elusive butterfly. This time I damn well plan to find it."

"Elusive?" Yellow Eagle said, raising an eyebrow.

"The butterfly called the *euphaedra*," Kirk said, giving Jolena a knowing look.

"I have seen it often," Yellow Eagle said innocently, shrugging his shoulders. "Mother has also seen it. We have watched it flutter among the wild flowers of our country. It is beautiful with its turquoise, black and orange colors. You want to see it, also?"

Jolena watched Kirk's expression, knowing that he must be astounded that she had not caught the butterfly. And she was not going to allow anyone to catch it, even if it caused another family feud with her brother!

"Yes, it's been sighted often," she murmured. "But it's gone again, Kirk. You may as well tell your friends they have come for naught."

She looked anxiously at Yellow Eagle, who was giving her a puzzled stare. She hoped that he wouldn't blurt out the truth, that the butterflies were just now beginning to crawl from their cocoons in the forest.

"Sis, do you mean that it has migrated back to South America?" Kirk said, sighing heavily. "Damn."

"Exactly," Jolena said, her eyes innocently wide.

"Well, then, I guess we'll head back for Fort Chance tomorrow," Kirk said. "At least it's given us a chance to catch other species of butterflies."

"Yes, at least," Jolena said, clutching her father's book to her bosom.

"Can you make room for one more person in your tepee tonight, Sis?" Kirk said softly.

"We have plenty of blankets," Spotted Eagle said, answering for Jolena. He placed a hand on Kirk's shoulder. "You are welcome, white brother. Always welcome."

Kirk's eyes wavered as he looked at Spotted Eagle, feeling guilty for still resenting him, yet knowing that he would never feel any different.

"*Ok-yi.* Come," Spotted Eagle said, motioning with a wave of a hand toward the entrance flap that Jolena was raising. "We will share a smoke and food tonight. Tomorrow my warriors will see you safely back to Fort Chance."

Jolena cast a smile of thanks at her husband. He smiled back knowingly.

Chapter Thirty-Six

Having gone to a high butte with Spotted Eagle to watch Kirk until he was lost from sight, Jolena shielded her eyes from the bright rays of the sun as she peered into the distance. Her brother was still in view, moving steadily onward through a meadow dotted with wild flowers of varying colors and shapes. The forest was just beyond.

Spotted Eagle stood at Jolena's side. She gave him a warm smile as he slipped his arm around her waist, then once again she gazed ahead, disappointed when Kirk rode into the shadows of the forest and disappeared.

"I wish that he could have stayed longer," Jolena murmured, leaning into Spotted Eagle's embrace.

"Your brother was here long enough for your husband and brother to make peace," Spotted Eagle said, turning her to face him. "That is the important thing."

"Yes it is," Jolena said, reaching a hand to Spotted Eagle's cheek, reveling anew in his handsomeness. "And was he not taken with his nephew? Yellow Eagle most certainly liked his uncle. Why, Spotted Eagle, he even cried when Kirk rode away. Hardly ever does Yellow Eagle allow anyone to see him cry. He thinks it is something only girls do."

Spotted Eagle chuckled and put his hands on either side of her face, framing it with them. He drew her lips close. "My wife, is not life good to us now?" he said as he brushed a soft kiss across her lips. "Are you as happy as this husband who holds you in his arms?"

"Yes," Jolena whispered, feeling glad that catching the elusive butterfly was no longer important to her.

There were many more important things in her life now—her husband, her son, and her beloved Blackfoot father!

Jolena eased her lips from Spotted Eagle's. "Let's go home," she murmured, wanting to be there to bask in these things that made her happier than she had ever been in her life.

Arm in arm, they made their way down the steep hillside, then walked toward their village. Jolena smiled to herself. She had not yet told Spotted Eagle the most wondrous of news— that she thought she might be with child again.

She had already dreamed that it would be a girl child.

Giving Spotted Eagle a half glance, she gently placed a hand over her tummy, envisioning a daughter for her to share things that sons would not share with their mothers!

"Spotted Eagle, I have something to tell you," Jolena said, thinking this was a perfect time to tell her husband of their second child.

Spotted Eagle smiled down at her. "I too have had a special dream," he said, his eyes twinkling into hers. "And, Fawn, it *will* be a girl child."

Jolena gazed up at him in wonder, then laughed happily as he swung her up into his arms and carried her the rest of the way to the village.

Behind them, on a tree limb, the dreaded *nymphalid*, the butterfly that portended death, flew out of its pupa, dropping its red liquid that resembled blood from the air. The *nymphalid* fluttered about, trying its new wings.

Then it flew away, high above the hills, away from the Blackfoot village.

Dear Reader:

I hope you have enjoyed reading *Savage Illusion*. To continue my "Savage Series," in which it is my endeavor to write about every major Indian tribe in America, my next book will be *Savage Embers*, written about the Arapaho Indians. This book will be filled with much excitement, adventure, romance and suspense! I hope you will buy *Savage Embers* and enjoy it! It should be released six months from the release date of *Savage Illusion*.

I love to hear from my readers. I respond, personally, to every letter. For my newsletter, please send a legal-size, self-addressed, stamped envelope.

Warmly,
CASSIE EDWARDS
R#3 Box 60
Mattoon, IL 61938

SAVAGE SPIRIT

CASSIE EDWARDS

**Winner of the *Romantic Times*
Lifetime Achievement Award for Best Indian Series!**

Life in the Arizona Territory has prepared Alicia Cline to expect the unexpected. Brash and reckless, she dares to take on renegades and bandidos. But the warm caresses and soft words of an Apache chieftain threaten her vulnerable heart more than any burning lance.

Chief Cloud Eagle has tamed the wild beasts of his land, yet one glimpse of Alicia makes him a slave to desire. Her snow-white skin makes him tremble with longing; her flame-red hair sets his senses ablaze. Cloud Eagle wants nothing more than to lie with her in his tepee, nothing less than to lose himself in her unending beauty. But to claim Alicia, the mighty warrior will first have to capture her bold savage spirit.

_3639-8 $4.99 US/$5.99 CAN

Dorchester Publishing Co., Inc.
65 Commerce Road
Stamford, CT 06902

LEIGH GREENWOOD'S

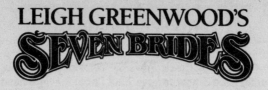

SEVEN BRIDES

"Leigh Greenwood is a dynamo of a storyteller."
—Los Angeles Times

Laurel. Although Hen Randolph is the perfect choice for a sheriff in the Arizona Territory, he is no one's idea of a model husband—especially not Laurel Blackthorne's. Only when Hen's pistol is snug in its holster will Laurel reward the virile gunman with the rapture of her love's sweet splendor—and take her place as the newest bride to tame a Randolph's heart.
_3744-0 $5.99 US/$6.99 CAN

Daisy. Attacked, wounded, and left for dead, Daisy is horrified to wake up in mountain man Tyler Randolph's cabin. Then a blizzard traps them together, and she is convinced that the mountain man is a fourteen-carat cad—until his unpolished charm claims her love. Before long, Daisy is determined to do some digging of her own to unearth the treasures hidden in Tyler's heart.
_3833-1 $5.99 US/$7.99 CAN

FROST FLOWER

SONYA BIRMINGHAM

Out in the wilds of Red Oak Hollow, pretty Misty Malone has come across plenty of critters, but none surprises her more than a knocked-out, buck-naked stranger. Taught by her granny to cure ills with herbs, Misty knows a passel of cures that will heal the unknown man, yet does she dare give him the most potent remedy of all—her sweet Ozark love?

After being robbed, stripped, and left for dead, Adam Davenport awakes to a vision in buckskins who makes his heart race like white lightning. But since the Malones and the Davenports have been feuding longer than a coon's age, the St. Louis doctor's only chance to win Misty is to hide his real name—and pray that a dash of mountain magic and a heap of good loving will hold the rustic beauty down when she finds out the truth.

_3775-0 $4.99 US/$5.99 CAN

An Angel's Touch
Where angels go, love is sure to follow.

Don't miss these unforgettable romances that combine the magic of angels and the joy of love.

Daemon's Angel by Sherrilyn Kenyon. Cast to the mortal realm by an evil sorceress, Arina has more than her share of problems. She is trapped in a temptress's body and doomed to lose any man she desires. Yet even as Arina yearns for the safety of the pearly gates, she finds paradise in the arms of a Norman mercenary. But to savor the joys of life with Daemon, she will have to battle demons and risk her very soul for love.

_52026-5 $4.99 US/$5.99 CAN

Forever Angels by Trana Mae Simmons. Thoroughly modern Tess Foster has everything, but when her boyfriend demands she sign a prenuptial agreement Tess thinks she's lost her happiness forever. Then her guardian angel sneezes and sends the woman of the nineties back to the 1890s—and into the arms of an unbelievably handsome cowboy. But before she will surrender to a marriage made in heaven, Tess has to make sure that her guardian angel won't sneeze again—and ruin her second chance at love.

_52021-4 $4.99 US/$5.99 CAN

Dorchester Publishing Co., Inc.
65 Commerce Road
Stamford, CT 06902

Please add $1.75 for shipping and handling for the first book and $.50 for each book thereafter. NY, NYC, PA and CT residents, please add appropriate sales tax. No cash, stamps, or C.O.D.s All orders shipped within 6 weeks via postal service book rate. Canadian orders require $2.00 extra postage and must be paid in U.S. dollars through a U.S. banking facility.

Name_____
Address_____
City _____ State _____ Zip _____
I have enclosed $_____in payment for the checked book(s).
Payment <u>must</u> accompany all orders.☐ Please send a free catalog.

An Angel's Touch

Where angels go,
love is sure to follow.

Time Heals by Susan Collier. Tired of her nagging relatives, Maeve Fredrickson asks for the impossible: to be a thousand miles and a hundred years away from them. Then a heavenly being grants her wish, and she awakens in frontier Montana. Saved from the wilderness by a handsome widower, Maeve loses her heart to her rescuer—and her temper over the antics of his three less-than-angelic children. As her angel prods her to fight for Seth, Maeve can only pray for the strength to claim a love made in paradise.

_52030-3 $4.99 US/$5.99 CAN

Longer Than Forever by Bronwyn Wolfe. Patrick is in trouble, alone in turn-of-the-century Chicago, and unjustly jailed with little hope for survival. Then the honey-haired beauty comes to him, as if she has heard his prayers. Lauren has all but given up on finding true love when she feels the green-eyed stranger's call—summoning her across boundaries of time and space to join him in a struggle against all odds; uniting them in a love that will last longer than forever.

_52042-7 $5.99 US/$7.99 CAN

Dorchester Publishing Co., Inc.
65 Commerce Road
Stamford, CT 06902